The Pilgrim Prince

Books by Gladys H. Barr

THE PILGRIM PRINCE

THE MASTER OF GENEVA

MONK IN ARMOUR

CROSS, SWORD AND ARROW

For Children

THE TINKER'S ARMOR

The PILGRIM PRINCE

A NOVEL BASED ON THE LIFE OF

John Bunyan

by Gladys H. Barr

HOLT, RINEHART AND WINSTON

NEW YORK   CHICAGO

SAN FRANCISCO

Designer: Ernst Reichl

80814-0213

Printed in the United States of America

To Hattie D. McGavock

with affection

Acknowledgment

The author acknowledges with deep gratitude the kindness and assistance of Cyril Hargreaves, Curator of the Bunyan Museum and Librarian for the Borough of Bedford, England, considered by many the greatest living authority on Bunyan. She further expresses her appreciation to the Chief Librarian of the British Museum and his staff for their courtesy while she was doing the research for this novel. And to her husband, Thomas Calhoun Barr, she owes a debt for all the information he discovered about Cromwell's Army, and the Civil War.

G.B.

Nashville, Tennessee

The Pilgrim Prince

"They said, moreover, that he had made many pilgrims princes, though by nature they were beggars born, and their original had been the dunghill."

The Pilgrim's Progress, Part 1
J OHN B UNYAN

I A FAINT breeze fingered the green leaves on the tall elms as ten-year-old John Bunyan bumped along the potholed road in a homemade cart. Some cows meandered slowly to an unpainted barn where the hiss of geese greeted them. Twilight was settling over the peaceful town of Bedford, and the evening sun cast long shadows across the path. When the bony brown horse reached the Great Bridge over the River of Ouse, some ducks rose from the reeds along the curved shore, wedging on their way. Beside John, his father, Thomas Bunyan, sat in scowling silence, his sunburned face thoughtful and his blue eyes fierce above his shaggy red beard.

John knew what was troubling him. When they had stopped at Ridgemont that morning to repair some pots and kettles, three soldiers, traveling north toward the Tweed to fight for King Charles, had told Papa that many of the common people of England were refusing aid to the King in his attempt to subdue the rebellious Scots. Charles was furious because the Puritans and Independents favored the cause of the rebels who were stubbornly Calvinistic in their religious beliefs.

"Which side are ye on?" Papa had roared with his mighty voice.

"We fight for the King, but only because we are paid. Our hearts are not in it," one of the men had said.

Papa had bellowed with his customary heat, "The Scots be traitors. I wish I could slit some Scotch noses!"

The soldier had winked at his companions, and John's heart had

11

dipped. He hated to have people laugh at Papa, who really loved the King.

"Ye can muster in today if ye truly have a mind. Ye would terrify the Scots!" said one dragoon, and all three of them guffawed.

Papa's eyes had shifted about as he cleared his throat and said brusquely, "I wish I could go. That I do. But ye see I am a family man with a wife and three young uns. If I could just save a little money——"

One of the three had interrupted him. "We know. But remember that the Scots were forced to take up arms to preserve their liberty. If we don't watch out, we may lose ours."

Papa had put up a stout verbal battle, but he had been outnumbered and had lost the argument. Now he glowered.

"Rotten thing," he muttered. "Englishmen talking treason. Soldiers in the King's Army siding with traitors. A pretty day for England."

The King's side, which Papa always took, was not popular in that year of 1639, in a shire where even the humblest man believed that no king had any right to rule without Parliament, which was what King Charles had been doing for eleven years. A lot of discord had been caused when he had levied a ship tax. The people complained that two important documents, the Magna Carta and the Petition of Right, forbade taxation not approved by their representatives in Parliament.

Many men in the wealthier classes were opposing the King, too. In 1637, a prominent man, John Hampden, had been indicted for refusing to pay the tax. His trial, which had lasted twelve days, had thrown all England into confusion. But sentence had been pronounced against him, and he was still in jail. A cousin of Hampden's, Oliver Cromwell, who lived in Cambridgeshire, was quietly carrying on the fight, urging the people to resist tyranny.

Grandfather Bunyan, although he could neither read nor write, was on the same side as Hampden and Cromwell. Each Sunday after church he joined the people gathered in small groups in the churchyard of the Elstow Parish Church. John had listened to them often and had learned that the hated tax had been devised by Attorney-General Noy, whom the indignant citizens called "Monster to the King." They disliked William Laud, the Archbishop of Canterbury, too, and whispered that he was influencing the King to compel his subjects to worship in the Protestant Church of England.

Everyone said that from the earliest times the people had met to make important decisions. An assembly called the Folk-Moot had been the forerunner of Parliament. When these Anglo-Saxon tribal meetings had been held, the freeholders had had the right to vote. The Witena-Gemot, or Meeting of the Wise Men, had been summoned by the King. His opinion had been respected, but new laws had never been imposed without the consent of the people. During the reign of Henry III trouble had arisen in the form of a struggle for power between the King and the barons. But by the time of Edward I the principle had been firmly established that there were to be no taxes without the people's consent. So what Charles I was doing was contrary to the established procedure in England.

John had heard a lot of talk, too, about the religious Reformation that had turned England upside down during the last century. Queen Elizabeth had, with an iron hand molded the Church of England into a strong power. There were, however, those who talked so much about "purity of worship" that they were called "Puritans." Others, desiring simplicity of worship, sided with the Puritans and worked for a separation of church and state. There were those, too, who longed for a return to the Church of Rome; included in this group was Queen Henrietta Maria, the wife King Charles adored. Although he permitted her and her court to have a chapel and some priests, he refused to tolerate Catholicism anywhere else. Puritans, Catholics, and Independents were cruelly persecuted. The rumor was that many people had built hiding holes for their priests in the eaves and walls of fine manor houses. Many Puritans had fled from England to save their lives, and a group dubbed "Pilgrim Fathers" had sailed for America in 1620 to found a colony where they could worship God as they chose.

As for John Bunyan, he attended the services in the parish

church because his mother made him, but he often wished that he did not have to go to any church. Papa did as he pleased, often staying at home to climb trees, which was his favorite sport. To John all churches were dark and gloomy with frightening gargoyles at the corners of the roof and loud-mouthed men in the high pulpits.

The iron-studded gates before the Swan Inn stood open, and Papa guided the horse into the innyard where other horses champed and moved restlessly. Papa threw John the reins, nodded toward the nearest swan's-head post, leaped down, and said, as he always did before he disappeared into the tavern, "Rest yourself, John. I need a good draught. I'm weary."

As John watched him lumber through the deep doorway, a feeling of unease spread through him. Papa was in a fighting mood; he might start a brawl. When Papa went home with blackened eyes and a bloody nose, Mama was upset. And Mama was like the light and warmth the candle gave; John never wanted her to be unhappy. Then, too, John was hungry; he wished Papa would go on home.

After tying the horse to the iron post, John got the wooden bucket out of the cart and carried it to the round well in the center of the yard, where he drew some water for the thirsty animal.

The black sign with the white swan painted on it was swinging gently above the doorway as John entered and sat down on a high-backed settle at one side of the wide hearth. A woman who appeared to be about the age of his mother was turning a spit above the fire. She wore a blue gown and a frilled mob cap. Her black eyes were bright, her cheeks rosy, and she was humming a gay tune.

John, hungrily sniffing the delicious smell of roasting beef and baking bread, was aware that the last ray of sun no longer shone through the deep, narrow windows. In the shadows against the dark oak paneling he could imagine a knight in bright armor, a lion with glaring ruby eyes, or a dragon snorting flames. Suddenly he sat up very straight. There *were* bright eyes in the corner.

14

They began to move and out of the shadows leaped a wolfhound. John cringed as the beast sped toward him, teeth bared. But it merely leaped up on the settle and began to lick his face.

The woman at the spit laughed. "John Knox just looks mean, lad. He's not. He shows his teeth like that when he's happy. But he frightens everyone and the innkeeper is going to have to get rid of him."

John's mouth watered as he watched her pull a piece of skin and meat off the round of beef. "Here," she said, "give this to Knox and he will worship ye."

He likes me too much now, John thought helplessly. Before he could offer the meat to the dog, the animal grabbed at it and gobbled it. Then he draped himself heavily across John's lap and sighed contentedly.

The woman opened the oven, took out the pan of loaves and broke a piece off one of them. John, watching her, licked his lips. As she tore off a huge hunk of beef, placed it on the bread, and lifted it toward her wide-open mouth, she glanced his way. Impulsively she handed him the meat-stuffed bread.

"Ye wouldn't be a boy if ye weren't hungry," she said, and her big mouth spread in a smile like that of a clown at a fair. "Here. I can wait until the guests are fed."

John took her offering with one hand, holding John Knox down with the other. He was very grateful and he wanted to tell the woman so, but he didn't know a lot of fine words.

All he said was, "Thank ye, ma'am."

She didn't answer him. She had gone back to turning the meat, and soon she began to hum and then to sing in a low voice:

> A maid needs a man-a-courtin';
> A good man, if sech there be.
> A bad man's better'n no man,
> But a fair man I wish he'd be. . . .

I hope she finds a fair man, John thought. She's not pretty like Mama, and she has a too-loud voice, but she's generous.

15

"Why is the dog named John Knox?" he asked, remembering vaguely that somebody had said the Scots preferred a worship service drawn up by a preacher by that name instead of the Liturgy the King wanted them to use.

The woman laughed. "The hound has a long, solemn face like the reformer, and he's just as determined to have his own way. When th' hostler's wife saw him, she screamed, 'John Knox come back from the dead!' And ever since we've called him that."

"She didn't really think it was John Knox?"

"To tell ye th' truth, she had crooked stockings at the moment. But the name stuck."

John knew it was customary in the shire whenever anybody had had too much strong water to say they had "crooked stockings" because they staggered and stumbled. But he liked the name and it seemed to suit the dog, who now sat beside him on the settle staring about with dignity.

Grandfather had explained how rioting had been brought about in Scotland by the King's command that the Scots use the service based on the Book of Common prayer which was used in the Elstow Parish Church. Two years before a woman named Janie Geddes had flung her cutty stool at the heads of the Dean of Edinburgh and a bishop who was conducting services in obedience to the King. When King Charles had refused to withdraw his orders about the prayer book, the Scots, assembled around a flat tombstone in Greyfriar's Churchyard in Edinburgh, had drawn up a National Covenant. They had forced the King to withdraw his Liturgy, allow a free Parliament and a free assembly in Scotland. But when the General Assembly had convened, the Marquis of Hamilton who was the King's Commissioner had ordered it to adjourn. The Scots had continued to meet, voting to establish Presbyterianism and to abolish the Church of England.

That was why the dragoons were going north. Almost everyone in Bedford and nearby Elstow, where John lived, echoed the sentiments of John Hampden and Oliver Cromwell. They hoped the rebellion in Scotland would force the King to assemble a Parliament.

16

Stroking John Knox's smooth coat, John leaned his head back against the settle, closed his eyes for a moment, and dozed.

A commotion in the tap tavern aroused him. He shoved John Knox to the floor, jumped up, and ran to see what was happening. A group of men circled Papa and a stranger, who towered a head above him. The stranger was dressed like a merchant in a soft hat and gray clothes. He was tall, and his head was massive, his arms long. His brown hair curled to his broad shoulders. He had a healthy tan, a strong nose and mouth, and honest hazel eyes.

Papa gave the man a defiant look, compressed his lips for an instant, and lifted a flagon: "To King Charles of England. May all his enemies lose their heads."

There was a silence. Not a man lifted his flagon. There was a dangerous gleam in Papa's blue eyes.

"Drink, ye traitors!" he roared, his face coloring in anger. "Drink to your King!"

The woman shoved through the crowd to John's side. "By th' saints!" she cried. "Th' chandler from London will kill th' fool tinker!"

John grabbed her sleeve. "Help me! Th' tinker's my father."

"There's naught I can do. Th' chandler is John Okey, a Parliament man. He'll tear your father apart if he has a mind to."

John left her side and ran forward, thrusting his small body between the two men. He yanked on Papa's leather doublet. "It's time to go home, Papa. Come quickly."

With an oath Thomas Bunyan shook himself free. "Go back to the cart, John. This be a man's affair."

John looked up at the chandler. "Sir, please make my father come home. Mama's waiting."

"I am not keeping him here, lad. I have just been telling your father that the King errs in claiming *he* is England."

"That's a lie," Papa roared, his face livid.

He set his flagon on the oaken table beside him, and lunged at the chandler, swinging his fist.

John leaped back as the blow sent John Okey reeling. With an effort he kept his footing, and the two men faced each other: the chandler burly and vigorous; Papa big, but awkward.

The hangers-on moved back, but before Papa could strike the chandler again, John Okey deftly lifted a heavy candlestick from a nearby table and crashed it across Papa's temples. Papa's eyebrows flew up in surprise. He slumped to the floor in a limp mass beside the black oaken table. The woman brought a cloth to dress his wound, and as she finished, Papa opened his eyes and focused them slowly on John Okey.

The chandler took a step forward. "You forced me t' do that, Bunyan," he said in a blaring voice.

"What if the King beats the Scots? What then?" a yeoman in the crowd asked.

John Okey's strong face lengthened. "That would be an evil day for England. The road to liberty must not close!"

"Are the King's generals capable?" another farmer asked.

"That they are," Okey answered. "The commander in chief of his army, the Earl of Arundel, is a leader of ability. His lieutenant general, the Earl of Essex, has proven himself many times." He added, "The commander of the fleet, the Earl of Holland himself, is sailing north to the Firth of Forth."

While the hangers-on continued to ask questions, Papa, with some effort, stood up and started meekly toward the door, motioning John to follow. By the time they had climbed onto the cart seat, Papa's rage had spent itself.

As the wagon rattled back over the Great Bridge, Papa was thinking out loud: "The King says a subject and a king are clear different things. He commands the people to trust him as to what is God's Truth and to stop searching for it. We should obey him."

Ye don't attend worship, John thought. Ye do a lot of talking, but the King demands all subjects to worship in the Church of England. How often do ye go? But John didn't remind Papa of that. Papa had been beaten twice in one day, and John was sorry for him, so he held his peace.

The cart had crossed the Great Bridge and was turning into

the Elstow Road when there was a fierce barking behind them. John looked back and saw John Knox leaping after them, his teeth bared. The big dog overtook the cart, jumped up on it, and grinned as if to say, "Ye can't leave me behind."

Papa grabbed the whip to knock him off. "Go home!" he said roughly, shaking the whip. "Go back."

But John gripped his hand. "No, Papa! When John Knox bares his teeth, he's happy."

John Knox continued to grin his silly grin.

"The tavern maid says the innkeeper wants to find another home for him. Papa, please may we keep him?"

"That monster! He would eat more than a horse!"

"I will hunt food for him. He's a valuable dog. We could never buy such a fine one. All the neighbors would envy us."

Papa cocked his head, eying John Knox. "Well—we'll ask your mother. If she agrees, I'll stop and see the innkeeper tomorrow to be sure it's all right."

John Knox leaped off the cart as it stopped beside the cottage and ran around in circles, leaping and barking.

"See, Papa. He knows he's home."

Mama agreed that the dog could stay if John provided his food, and taught him not to chase chickens or cats.

"Watch out for queens!" Papa snorted. "He'll have their heads."

John didn't know why Mama laughed so hard, until she explained that preacher John Knox had written a bold book against queens and had been responsible for stirring up the people against Mary, Queen of Scots. His great plea in his day had been for freedom of conscience, too.

The innkeeper was glad to get rid of the dog, and whenever any Presbyterian expressed his disapproval of naming a dog after a brave man like John Knox, John pointed out that it was an honor when a boy loved a dog as much as he did.

The weeks that followed were filled with excitement as the people of Elstow and Bedford waited for news from the Scottish border. There was great rejoicing in June when two peddlers arrived from the North with the tidings that the Scots had marched to the border with twenty thousand troops. The size of the Scots' Army had frightened the King and he had agreed to their demands.

Everywhere citizens gathered, the question was asked: "Is the trouble really over?" Travelers from London kept saying that Thomas Wentworth, the King's Lord Deputy for Ireland, was urging the King to beat the Scots into submission. But he couldn't do it because he lacked money and couldn't raise any without calling a Parliament.

Grandpa Bunyan came over for supper one October afternoon when his second wife, Anne (who was not John's grandmother), had gone to Ely for a few days.

"How is the tinkering business, John?" he greeted in his warm voice.

"Fine," John answered, "just fine, Grandpa. We are honest tinkers who make no more holes than we find."

Grandpa guffawed, deepening the dent in his chin, and crinkling the corners of his clear eyes, which were as blue as cornflowers.

John looked up at the tall, stalwart old man. I really want to be like Grandpa when I grow up, he thought.

Sometimes his mother laughingly told her friends, "When John was four, he used to say he wanted to be a grandpa when he grew up." In another month he would be twelve, and he still wanted to be a grandpa. "Lord Jesus, take me back to Grandpa's house," had been his small boy's prayer, for in his grandfather's company he found contentment.

When supper was ready, everyone sat down to eat the browned deer meat, and drink the cat larrup which was the water pork and potatoes had been cooked in. John speared a chunk of meat with the point of his knife and began eating it on a piece of bread.

But Mama lifted a restraining hand. "Just a minute. We are

not that hungry. We'll bow our heads while Grandpa asks the Lord's blessing."

No mention of the fighting was made by anybody until the meal was almost over. Then Grandpa cocked a bushy white eyebrow and looked at Papa.

"Did ye get any news of the Scots this day, Thomas?"

Papa shook his head and went on noisily gulping cat larrup. When he wasn't looking, Grandpa winked at John.

"Well, I have news for ye, Thomas, an' I've never been one t' keep news t' myself."

"No, Grandpa. Ye tell everything ye know," John's young sister Margaret agreed innocently.

Everyone laughed, except Papa, who grunted.

"There's a terrible stir in London over what the Puritan soldiers have been up to," Grandpa confided with delight. "When they marched north to help the Scots fight the King, they entered Anglican churches all along the route; they removed altars from the east walls and buried the communion rails old Laud has been making such a fuss about."

Papa shoved back from the table in disgust. "Ye should know all about troublemakers, Father. Once ye were cited by authorities of the parish church for defying them."

"That were twenty-three years ago, Thomas. Ye know that. And they are skunks."

"There is no need for Archbishop Laud to interfere in our churches." Mama's voice was firm, her oval chin set. "The Bible says a Christian renders unto Caesar, the king, that which is his, and unto 'God the things that belong to God,' " Mama rose and went to the long shelf above the hearth and lifted down the Bible. "It is time to render our hearts to Him in worship."

While Mama was reading the Sermon on the Mount, John's mind wandered. The next day would be Sunday, and just as soon as Vicar Kellie finished reading the sleepy liturgies, John would go to the Village Green to play cat or football with Harry Rodant, a goose farmer's son; Tom Sorrow, a game warden's son; Froggy Foster, the nephew of Royalist William Foster, who influenced Papa; and Melbourne Mooney, said to be a papist in secret with the rest of his family. John liked Mel best of all.

When Mama closed the big Bible, John knelt with the others. Margaret pinched him and he snickered out loud, but Mama pretended she did not hear him. As soon as she said, "Amen," Papa got up and strode out. In a few minutes there came the sound of his mighty anvil iron striking metal in the lean-to behind the cottage.

While Mama and Margaret put away the supper things, John sat near Grandpa on Grandmother Bentley's joined stool. John Knox stretched out in front of the embers beyond the brick hearth, and John leaned over to stroke his warm coat. Mama was humming a psalm, and the problems of England seemed unreal and far away; he felt secure and at peace.

But that night he had a terrifying dream. Devils and wicked spirits moved in the corners of his room. "Beware of Hell fire." "Beware." "Repent. Repent!" they moaned. Their faces were horrible like the faces on the baptismal font at the Abbey Church, and he woke up screaming. I wish I were a Devil, so that I could torment others, he thought. I would start with Archbishop Laud.

When John came downstairs, Mama was moving the handle of the sugar cutter up and down to slice the sugar loaf. Oatmeal was bubbling in a big black pot, and Margaret was stirring it.

"Did you wash behind your ears, John?" Mama demanded. "Last Sunday you forgot."

"I'll have to go to the creek for some water. My pitcher is empty."

By the time John got back, the family was seated.

As soon as God had been thanked, Papa made an announcement. "Margaret," he said, looking directly at Mama, "I've been thinking. I won't have John raised ignorant of what a king is. He should learn to read and write well, so that he can read about such things. He is going to the Grammar School at Bedford."

Mama's eyebrows lifted, and her sensitive face clouded. "I've

22

already taught him to read a little. You know, Thomas, that Master Vierney is a cruel man. He beats any boy who thinks for himself. We've raised John to be independent. He knows what your father and others think about the ship tax and the rebellion of the Scots. Is it fair to send him to a schoolmaster who teaches it's a crime for a boy to use his mind?"

"Ye don't want him t' learn t' read like ye do? Ye want our John t' be ignorant like me?"

Mama shook her head. "Now, Thomas, be honest. That's not the reason ye are so set on sending John to the Grammar School. Ye want to make a King's man out of him."

"I'll never be a King's man, Papa. I'm on Grandpa's side," John said quickly, squaring his shoulders. "Who wants to be a slave, even to a king?"

Papa pounded the table with his huge fist, and the dishes clattered. "That settles it, John. Ye're going to school in Bedford."

John could hardly believe it. School! He would learn to read well. His mother was busy, but she had found time to teach him the alphabet and to pick out simple words, and sometimes read to him, Margaret, and Willie. What fun it would be, to enjoy whenever he chose tales about giants, magicians, witches, and dragons.

A week later John walked the bridle path to Bedford with his friend, Harry, who had been attending the Grammar School for a year.

"Master Vierney uses a stick as big as my father's thumb," Harry told him. "When he beats a boy until th' blood comes, he's so happy he hops."

John determined not to let the schoolmaster know he was not a King's man, but he was so excited about going to school that he forgot to be afraid. The willow trees along the path waved as he passed through Medbury, walking toward the ancient hospital of St. John. A chorus of birds seemed to sing just to him. He followed Harry to the building where school was held, squared his shoulders, and went in.

A dozen students lined the rough board table. At one end stood a tall, raw-boned man with a sharp face and a long nose like a weasel's. As the door creaked shut behind John, the schoolmaster turned and stared at him with glittering black eyes. "What's your name, boy?" he demanded.

John took off his rabbitskin cap. He swallowed. "John Bunyan, sir."

"The son of the tinker. Your father spoke to me. You are also the grandson of the petty trader near Harrowden. H-m-m-m-m."

The lump in John's throat was choking him, but he nodded.

Master Vierney moved toward him, shaking his stick, and John felt like an eel on a spit above the hearth. He wished he was back at Elstow.

"There is one thing every pupil of the Grammar School must learn," the schoolmaster thundered. "That is that we tolerate no traitors here. We demand loyalty to the King!"

"What does a traitor do?" John asked, because he felt he had to say something.

"He questions the authority of his King. Traitors like John Okey and Oliver Cromwell ride up and down the highways, calling on the people to vote for Puritans as Parliamentary burgesses. They criticize patriots like Dr. Giles Thorne, the God-fearing rector of St. Mary's and St. Cuthbert's, for holding confession and insisting that Christians use the Prayer Book, and come to the altar rails for Communion." The schoolmaster turned and addressed the other boys. "Confession to a priest is as old as religion and even as God Himself. The enemies of the Church of England are the enemies of the King!" His eyes turned back to John. "You understand?"

"Yes, sir," John managed in a small voice.

There was a maniacal glare in Master Vierney's eyes now like a lot of little candles. John shivered, but he continued to stand at attention before the towering teacher and his stick.

"Do you know what happened to absentees from church in the days of Queen Elizabeth?"

"No, sir."

"At first they were fined a shilling. Later a law was passed pro-

24

viding for their imprisonment. That law is still on the statute books! Don't forget that!"

"No, sir, but——"

"But what, John Bunyan?"

"Does a boy have to think what the King tells him to think?"

"Yes. Unless he wants such a whipping that he will have to limp to school."

"Yes, sir." John's voice was a whisper.

The schoolmaster stood for a long moment glaring down at him, his pale lips set in a downward curve.

"You may state now, John Bunyan, whether or not your grandfather has imbued you with his beliefs. It is well known that he favors the treasonous ideas of men like Sir John Burgoyne of Sutton, Oliver Cromwell, John Hampden, and John Okey, who are all dissidents."

John felt the hair on the back of his neck prickle. He didn't know what dissidents were, but he supposed they were trouble-makers. The other boys were looking at him. The teacher's back was to Harry, who sat with his tongue sticking out, his face with its coarse features as spotted as a speckled hen. There was no help there. But two faces in the room had sympathy written on them. And suddenly John no longer felt alone. One of the boys, Tad Bradshaw, was narrow-chested with melting blue eyes set in a thin face. The other was his playmate, Mel, a large round-faced boy with warm brown eyes. Some of the students wore clothes of fine cloth, and leather shoes, while others wore homespun and hobnailed boots or leather slippers. John longed to cry out that every Englishman had certain rights, that his grandfather was loyal, that he loved England, and wanted only what was best for the realm. But he trembled and stood in silence and defeat, his eyes on the big, black stick.

"Well?" Master Vierney roared.

"I want to be loyal to the King," he managed. "Ye know how my father feels."

"Then see that you are loyal, John Bunyan. And stop saying 'ye' like every country bumpkin!"

As John took the vacant seat next to Harry, he felt miserable. He had lied. He had not defended the good name of his grandfather; he was a coward.

Master Vierney handed him a horn book with some letters and words, mounted on wood covered with thin horn. "Study your alphabet," he said in a surly voice. "Boys have to work hard if they want to stay in this school."

The schoolmaster's cruelty to Tad and Mel, the only two boys who stood up with courage against his bigotry, made John cringe inwardly. Day after day he rebuked them, whipping them for the least transgression. Tad, only ten, was the son of John Bradshaw, the Vicar of St. John's, who was said to think for himself. Mel, aged twelve and large for his years, was one of ten children of a butcher, John Mooney. Gossip ran that the Mooneys harbored priests. Master Vierney had a habit of paring his dirty finger nails with a sharp knife and once he hurled it, point first, at Mel's arm and the blood gushed through his homespun sleeve. On the slightest provocation, or with none at all, Master Vierney beat the two boys in such sadistic fashion that John had to look away.

John noticed that the sons of the influential patrons like Froggy Foster, whose family had the King's ear, were privileged. Froggy was always whispering tales to Master Vierney, and John was sure he was making trouble for Tad and Mel.

One October day a scene took place that haunted John for weeks. The schoolmaster cocked his head, focused his narrowed eyes on Tad, and moved toward him like a hound stalking a hare.

"Should a vicar take the communion out to the people when the Archbishop of Canterbury says the people must come up to the altar rail?" he thundered.

Tad's big melting eyes met the glinting ones of the teacher. His thin face drew long in sudden resolution, and he lifted his chin. "If you're thinking about my father, you may ask him about that," he said in a frightened voice. "He is a vicar and should know about such things."

"You do not think the King is head of the Church of England?" Master Vierney thundered. "Is your King to be obeyed or not?"

There was a long silence while the boys moved uncomfortably on the hard benches, and shuffled their feet. Somebody coughed nervously. Then quietly Mel Mooney slid off his stool. His cherubic pink face paled as he moved between the schoolmaster and Tad.

"Please, sir," he said, "how a boy worships God is something he must decide. No man can command a soul."

"That's what the treasonous Scots say!" the schoolmaster roared, his face purple with rage. "The fate of England hangs in the balance. The King has a hard enough time with scoundrels like John Pym and John Okey fighting him. And you have the audacity to stand there and tell me the King has no right to direct his Church!"

The small voice of Tad sounded: "God's Church, sir!"

Master Vierney stood very still for a moment, his eyes full of hatred and fury. Then with a swift movement he reached out and pulled Tad off the stool. Tad looked like a desperate, hunted animal as Master Vierney's huge hand ripped the shirt from his back, and the big stick came down on his bare flesh. The blows were loud and terrible in the high-ceilinged room. Tad cried out, and each cry was like the stabbing of a dagger into John's heart. He put his hands over his ears and turned away, shutting his eyes. When he opened them, Tad was lying senseless on the floor with ugly red welts all over his back. Mel ran to him, turned him over, and as soon as consciousness returned helped him gently to his seat.

I wish I could break Master Vierney's head against the stone wall, John thought, gritting his teeth. But he sat and did nothing while the schoolmaster's harsh voice softened in a pious prayer, asking God to forgive the wickedness of boys.

"Somebody ought to write the King and tell him that Master Vierney brutally beats his students," John protested to Mel as they left school that afternoon.

"Everybody knows that he is the King's spy in the shire," Mel said. "There is little freedom in England."

"Is it true that your family is Catholic?"

Mel frowned. "We are Christians and prefer that church," he said.

"I have heard that Queen Henrietta Maria worships as she prefers. Why can't everybody?"

"The King rules absolutely in Church and State."

One afternoon the middle of April, William Foster, the lawyer whose Royalist sympathies Papa shared, stopped at the forge to say he had just come from London where he had seen King Charles, wearing his royal diadem, ride through the streets to proclaim that Parliament was in session.

The rest of that spring and all summer the county, or shire, was in an uproar as John Pym presented the grievances of the people before the House of Commons, which passed a resolution asking the King for redress before voting him financial aid for his war. The House of Lords debated whose wishes should have precedence, the King's or the people's, and then voted in favor of the King. Charles demanded that the House of Commons give him eight hundred and forty thousand pounds, but they refused, and on May 5 he dissolved Parliament. Shortly after that Thomas Wentworth, the Lord Deputy of Ireland, held in Dublin an Irish Parliament which granted subsidies to the King and raised over eight thousand troops.

That summer Papa had several tavern brawls and came home with his eyes blacked. Mama remonstrated that it was foolish to go about looking for trouble, but Papa just shook his head. "A man with any red blood in him has to stand up for his King," he said testily.

One Sunday afternoon, when John was playing football with Harry on the Village Green opposite the church, Froggy Foster came hopping up, his eyes bulging. "The people of Bedfordshire are preparing a petition to send to the House of Lords," he announced, "but the King's spies will ready the Parliament. We'll show Mr. Pym, Mr. Hampden, and Mr. Cromwell who rules England."

Harry shrugged. "Whoever wins, I'm on the winning side."

As John walked home later that afternoon, he imagined the King's spies peering from behind the big elms. He thought about Harry to whom principles didn't matter; he had no character. But am I not just as bad, John asked himself, for remaining silent in the Grammar School instead of going to Tad's defense as Mel did?

When he reached home, his mother was browning an eel pie on the salamander, a circular piece of iron fastened to a long handle. There was a platter of oatmeal cakes on the table, and apples were bubbling in the pot above the embers. He changed into an old shirt and breeches and ran out to do the chores.

While he was shoveling manure from the horse's stall and spreading it on the cornfield, the morkin, or scarecrow, waved a stuffed arm in the wind.

John paused to chat: "Good evening, Sir Morkin. What should I do to help Tad and Mel? They are beaten all the time. But what can I do?"

The morkin just looked down in silence.

"I know. Ye—you're afraid to tell me you're not a King's man. They'll hang us at the crossroads if they find out we want to think."

John imagined that the morkin winked one painted eye. He bade his silent friend good-bye and ran back to the barn where he milked the brown and white cow. He arrived at the cottage door with a pail full of rich, warm milk, just as his mother was placing the browned pie on the table.

As he washed his hands, he glanced up at his reflection in the copper mirror which hung above the iron basin. I look like a morkin, myself, he thought. The wind had blown his long reddish hair into tangled curls around his sturdy shoulders, his cheeks were red, his eyes large and deep blue. There was mud in the cleft of his chin, and on the end of his impudent nose. I look older than twelve, he thought. If war comes to England, I can fight. I might even be sent to London. Then I would see London Bridge, the White Tower, and the Tower of London!

During supper he listened while Mama told Papa how William Walker, the Commissary of the Court at Bedford, was trying to ingratiate himself with Archbishop Laud by persecuting John Bradshaw, Tad's father. Another vicar had been suspended for criticizing the government in a sermon. Every day excessive assessments were made against the clergy, and they were threatened with removal from their living if they failed to obey the Archbishop.

"That is fine," Papa said enthusiastically. "Why don't they obey?"

John remembered with a pang the way the schoolmaster treated Tad and Mel. He wanted to confess to his mother that he was a coward. But he couldn't tell his father how he felt about people being free. Papa was so unreasonable these days and John knew what he would say—that Tad and Mel were traitors. He bit his lip and sat in silence.

After supper Papa sat down in the only armchair, laid his head back, and was soon asleep. John Knox, having finished a long piece of dried deer meat, wanted to play. Margaret stood at one side of the family room and threw a ball, which the big dog tried to catch. Papa snored through all the confusion until the ball hit him on the nose. With a roar he stood up and shouted, "Begone, ye rascals."

John obeyed and went upstairs to bed, but he slept fitfully and dreamed a dream that left him shaking. He saw a scaffold bleak against the sky. The Devil was leading a man toward it, while on either side of them, soldiers in scarlet coats stood beating great drums in a slow, sad dirge. The man wore a wide hat with a long feather on it, a black velvet doublet over a white silk shirt, and breeches of gray brocade. His leather boots had turned-down cuffs below the knees. He held his head high while the drums rolled on. John ran after them to see the man's face. To his horror it was the face of Charles I with its black penetrating eyes and slim beard, and sadness like the sadness of Golgotha was written upon it.

The dream was still haunting him the next morning. It was Saturday and Papa left for Ampthill at dawn. As soon as John finished his morning chores, he began to think about fishing. There was a pond on the estate of Sir Thomas Hillersdon beside the Abbey Church. The common people of the parish were never permitted inside the shady park that surrounded the pond. But Tom Sorrow, the game warden's son, told tales of fish two and three feet long that fought like whales and had teeth like sharp knives. "But don't ye ever come a-sneakin'," Tom had said, his thin face drawn up in a frown. "Nobody can fish in that pond without endin' up in th' stocks. Nobody."

I think I'll go to the pond, John decided. But I won't take Margaret today. She would cry if they fastened her in the stocks. He smiled to himself as he put some hunks of bread and a small jar of honey in a basket: honey balls caught more fish than worms. He took his fishing pole from the corner of the cow stall and slipped quietly toward the footpath that led to the Abbey Church.

When he reached the wicket-gate leading into the churchyard, he paused. There was something mysterious about the gate. For an instant he wondered if the Heaven that Vicar Kellie preached about could have a gate like that, and if he would ever see it.

2

THE land John's father owned at Bunyan's End was on the edge of the small hamlet of Harrowden in the east part of Elstow Parish. Here a Saxon Church, dedicated to St. Mary and St. Helena, had flourished until the time of Henry VIII. He dissolved it and pensioned the Abbess and the nuns. A grant of the grounds was made by Queen Mary to Sir Humphrey Radcliff, whose widow lived there until the end of the sixteenth century. Her son, Sir Edward, sold the property to Sir Thomas Hillersdon, who built a fine stone mansion on it.

From the corner of the field where the Bunyan cottage stood, wide meadows stretched toward Elstow Village. A thatched roof hung so low over the latticed windows that a tall man like Grandpa could reach up and touch it, but two chimneys made the little house appear higher than it was. The cottage was full of laughter and living with Mama at the heart of it.

There were many nearby places to fish and John knew he did not have to trespass on the Hillersdon estate. Fish were plentiful in the stream, the brook, and the river. But he had thought about the pond until fishing there had become an obsession. He dreamed of big, plump fish, and struggled to land them in his dreams. Above all, he wanted to show the other village boys that he dared do something they would be afraid to do. He had to maintain his reputation as the worst boy in the parish.

This chill October morning, as he trudged along barefoot toward the stone mansion, he noticed the grotesque heads on the pedestals of its upper story, and shivered. They reminded him of the horrible little figure with leaves growing out of its ears that sat on the corbel of the Abbey Church. There was a legend that, in the thirteenth century, a man, creeping toward the altar to steal the offering box, had been turned into this thing of stone as a horrible example to others who lied, swore, and stole.

John moved stealthily through the wide gates and ran quickly along under the elms. The sun quivered through the trees as he neared the fish pond. Some wild marsh hens, feeding in the tall grass, flew up as he thudded past. What if Tom Sorrow's father catches me and calls the constable? he thought.

Out of breath from running, he flung himself down on his belly at the edge of the dark pond, gulping the chill air like a fish flung up on the bank. There was the smell of dank vegetation, and wind-blown willows looked down at their stark reflections in the water. There were fish in that water, fish two and three feet long!

John sat up; opened his basket, took out a piece of bread and the jar of honey. He dipped a small portion of bread in the honey and rolled it between his fingers until it was a round, smooth ball. When he had tied the ball to the hook, he stood up and threw the line out as far as he could. Then he washed his hands in the pond and sat back to wait for a foolish fish to take the bait.

Against the blue sky a black rook circled, flapping its wings. John began to sing quietly:

> "Fly up, bird. Fly high.
> For I'll pick up my clappers
> An' knock ye down back'ards.
> Fly away, bird. Away!"

He had the sudden feeling that somebody was watching him and looked about uneasily, expecting to see Warden Sorrow standing with pointed musket. A man, seated perhaps thirty yards away on a curve of the pond, was scrutinizing John intently.

The man wore old homespun clothes and a hat with hooks stuck in it. In one large hand he held a fishing pole. His face was an arresting one with a wart over one of its keen blue eyes, and another on the chin. The nose was big with full nostrils, and a pipe hung from the determined mouth. John had seen that face before. . . . The hair on the back of his neck prickled. Merciful God! The man was Oliver Cromwell, the famous farmer from Ely who opposed the King.

"What is it, lad?" The voice was deep and kind. "Is something wrong?"

"Mr. Cromwell, sir," John managed with a gulp.

"Then we have met before? Let me see——"

"No, sir. We've never met before, but I saw you once on the Village Green in Elstow when you were talking to the people about liberty. My grandfather was one of them."

"Are you young Tom Sorrow, the warden's boy?"

John shook his head. "No, sir, I'm John Bunyan. My father's a tinker. I——"

Before he could say any more, there was the heavy tread of feet on the hard ground and Warden Sorrow crashed through the bushes behind Mr. Cromwell. He looked about quickly, lifted his musket, and pointed it right at John's heart.

"A ragamuffin trespasser, is it? I'm sorry, Mr. Cromwell. That I be, t' have this—this tinker's boy sneakin' in and botherin' ye, when ye said ye wanted t' be alone."

Mr. Cromwell's arched brows lifted. For an instant his eyes bored into John. The next minute his big mouth broadened in a smile.

"Trespasser, Warden Sorrow? This lad's no trespasser. John Bunyan's my friend. He's going to fish with me. Put that weapon down, Sorrow. Have you lost your senses?"

The warden looked incredulous, but something flashed in Mr. Cromwell's blue eyes, and the musket was lowered abruptly.

"Guess if ye say so," Sorrow mumbled. "Sir Thomas has a rule that no local boys be allowed to fish in th' ponds. He'd be overrun with ragamuffins otherwise, but if he servins ye—"

34

"He is not serving me, Sorrow." Mr. Cromwell's voice was sharp. "He is my friend. You may go now. And tell Sir Thomas I will be a little late for dinner. My friend and I have fish to catch."

Warden Sorrow went off muttering to himself, and Mr. Cromwell chuckled. "Sorrow complains about taxation without the consent of the people, but he tries to act like a king in his little domain. People. People." Mr. Cromwell shook his head sadly.

John got up and walked along the edge of the pond trailing his fishing line. The mud squelched and gripped his bare toes and the eel grass scratched his ankles. When he reached the place where Mr. Cromwell was, he sat beside him.

"Why did you do that, sir? You don't even know me."

"I like what I see."

"I am the ringleader of everything bad that the village boys do. We rob orchards and ring the church bells. And I *am* a trespasser. I can catch fish in Cardington Brook, in the stream, or in the River of Ouse. But I had to sneak in here so that I could tell the others boys about it and watch their eyes pop!"

"Long ago I was an orchard robber," the great Cromwell said. "I smuggled other boys into the grounds of Hitchinbrook, my grandfather's estate, where we fished out his private stock."

"Did your grandfather beat you?"

"No. He was a kind, gentle man. He was called the Golden Knight because he was so generous and gave away so much money to others."

"He was a real knight?"

Mr. Cromwell nodded. "Knighthood in the day of Queen Elizabeth was a great honor. From the time my Uncle Oliver inherited Hitchinbrook it was never as significant. King James created over two hundred knights in the first six months of his reign, and always for the presents they would give him, so the honor was belittled."

"The Golden Knight," John said musingly. "And he was your grandfather!"

"That title was symbolic, too, John. You see not even fire will

35

destroy gold. It is an invincible metal. The fire may melt it, but the gold remains."

John sighed. "I wish I were a brave knight."

"Most boys do, John. Never lose your dreams. I did a lot of things when I was a boy that I'm not proud of. I'll tell you a terrible secret. I once punched the King in the nose. He lost a lot of blood. It was at Hitchinbrook and my uncle was furious. But we were very young, only four."

Farmer Cromwell laughed heartily at the recollection.

"You punched King Charles in the nose?" John was incredulous.

"Yes, but I am not proud of it. It seems I began life doing all the wrong things."

"But now all the common people look to you for help. I bet you will punch the King again."

"Heaven forbid! He's my own flesh and blood—an eighth or ninth cousin, so my mother brags."

"There's one man I would like to punch in the nose—my schoolmaster Vierney."

Mr. Cromwell looked sharply at John. "You attend the grammar school at Bedford?"

John nodded. "Master Vierney whips any boy who thinks for himself. He teaches that it is treason to disobey the King. He beats the only boys who dare stand up to him; I sit and do nothing."

"Men like my cousin John Hampden, John Pym, John Okey, and myself fight the political schemes of ambitious men like Laud, Wentworth, and the King himself. But we do not fight England or the Church of England."

The next two hours were hours John knew he would never forget. The sun shone brightly, warming the air, and the wind blew through the willows. Wild ducks winged above the dark water. A black swan glided past like a majestic ship. There were rooks in the sky and smaller birds in flight. The coo of the cuckoo blended with the warble of a bluebird. A squirrel came close to stare at them with curious beady eyes. Chipmunks scuttled about, rustling the fallen leaves. John showed his new friend how to make honey balls, and darting eager fish, one after another, took the bait. Mr. Cromwell put them on a forked stick until there were eleven large ones and many smaller.

John was about to bring in his line when there was a sudden jerk. He leaped to his feet, and waded out. Something big was on the end of that line, struggling, pulling.

"Be careful, John. Not too suddenly. Give him a little play. Then pull in slowly."

John took another step. And suddenly the cold, black water was closing over his head. He came up and heard Mr. Cromwell shouting above him; then he was sinking once again into the blackness. . . .

When he opened his eyes, he was lying on the muddy bank. His chest hurt and Mr. Cromwell was moving his arms about.

"The good Lord wants us to be fishers of men," Mr. Cromwell said. "Maybe He'll be satisfied, for I've fished a foolish boy."

John sat up. He couldn't talk very well, because his throat smarted and he was shivering, but he managed, "Thank you—for—saving me."

"Get on home now, John. Get into some dry clothes. Take the fish to your mother with my compliments. After I have dinner with Sir Thomas, I'll be on my way to London."

"Take—care—of yourself, too, sir. Thank you—for the fish."

"I have something to thank you for, John. When life is too complex, I like to get off alone and fish, but I needed a boy's companionship this morning to bring me back to verities."

"What are 'verities'?"

"Those values which are as real and indestructible as gold."

They walked slowly toward the carriage drive.

"I can't wait to tell my grandfather I met you," John said, as Mr. Cromwell smiled farewell.

John ran all the way home and held the string of fish behind him as he went inside. His family was at the table eating soup, and his mother got up to ladle some out for him.

"Look what I've brought you," he shouted, holding up the fish.

Mama's pretty mouth dropped open, and Margaret and Willie squealed. The sight of the catch set Papa's eyebrows lifting.

"Those will make many kettles of fish stew," he said. "Where did ye hook them?"

"I didn't take them all. A friend helped me." He wanted Papa to ask him who the friend was.

"And who is this great fisherman? And where did ye fish?"

"On the estate of Sir Thomas Hillersdon. My friend was Oliver Cromwell."

Mama put the bowl of soup on the wooden table, and placed her hands on her hips. "So now ye imagine ye're fishing with Mr. Cromwell. Ye caught those fish in the river. And nobody was with ye!"

"I caught them in the private pond and Mr. Cromwell was with me."

"Are you sure it wasn't King Charles or Cardinal Richelieu?" Papa said with a grimace. "Or maybe it was Thomas Wentworth, Lord Deputy of Ireland!"

They don't believe me, John thought, but Grandpa will know I'm telling the truth! He hurriedly gulped his soup, then climbed up the stairs, replaced his damp clothes, with dry ones, and started for his grandfather's cottage.

Late the next month the news blasted Elstow that Thomas Wentworth, now the Earl of Strafford, had been imprisoned and charged with high treason. The Secretary of State, Windebank, had fled to France. Archbishop Laud and the Lord Keeper Finch, two others high in influence with the King, were also in trouble. The Archbishop had been locked in the Tower of London and Finch had fled to the continent.

All winter and spring travelers from London brought startling news: Parliament declared the ship tax illegal. John Hampden was released from prison. A new law was passed providing that no subject would be taxed without the levy of Parliament. A Committee on Church Reform was appointed. Parliament passed another law providing that bishops could no longer sit in the House of Lords. Still another made certain that Parliament would never have to depend on the King to summon it. Some of the King's own army men plotted against him.

In May, with the King's consent, the Earl of Strafford, Thomas Wentworth, was beheaded. The bells in Elstow Church were rung wildly and John helped ring them. People danced on the green, shouting: "His head is off." "Strafford is dead."

Some said happily, "The King will no longer be under his evil influence. The scoundrel will do us no more harm!" But there were others who mourned his death, and Papa was one of them.

"The Earl of Strafford was a hero!" Papa declared. "He gave his life to help the King!"

William Foster said everywhere, "Because Strafford loved his sovereign, he was murdered by those who hate the crown."

One afternoon early in June, while waiting for Papa at the Swan Inn, John heard Mr. Okey telling the hangers-on that he had actually seen Strafford's head roll.

"He was a brave man!" Papa shouted. "No one can say he died like a coward."

To John's surprise John Okey agreed. "You're right; he died bravely, Bunyan. He was a great man. I only wish the Parliament had had him on its side."

"Will the King accede to Parliament's demands now?" asked Anthony Harrington, who had often befriended Vicar Bradshaw.

John Okey shook his head. "All London is in an uproar. Anything can happen. The House of Commons has sworn to protect political liberty and the freedom of religion."

"What has the King to say to that?" a stranger demanded.

"He still insists a king has the divine right to rule as he chooses, and he chooses to order everyone, except the Queen and her court, to worship in the state church."

"Why do Christians have to hate each other?" John Mooney,

Mel's father, asked sorrowfully. "The Queen is a Catholic, yet there are those who begrudge all Catholics their God-given rights!"

"Why can't ye and all th' other papists worship in England's Church? Ye're an Englishman, or are ye?" Papa looked truculent.

"I thought the Church belonged to God," the butcher said blandly.

It was late summer before word reached Bedford that the King's unjust courts, the Star Chamber and the Court of High Commission, had been abolished.

"What can the King do now?" everybody asked.

"He will woo the Scots," Vicar Kellie told his church wardens. "It is expected he will try to set the Presbyterians against the powerful Puritans."

Out of a dusky depth of slumber John awoke slowly into consciousness. The breath of a spring morning blew through his dormer window and the meadow was awake. He could hear the lambs bleating, the rooks cawing, and Noise-Ding, the red rooster, crowing.

He sat up suddenly. This was no ordinary day. It was May 17, 1642, and he was to be allowed to go to Lynn on the big river boat with his father on the annual metal-buying trip.

His little brother Willie still slept beside him in the trundle bed. John's heart swelled with warmth as he looked at the golden brown curls, the freckled face, and ball-like nose. He didn't want to waken Willie, so he tiptoed about pulling on his russets.

Downstairs the smell of oat cakes filled the room. Mama, dressed in a blue gown and housewife's white cap, was leaning over the hearth, turning salted hog meat and cakes on the big black skillet.

At one end of the unpainted plank table sat his father, and John slid into his place beside him. Mama hurried to ply them with meat and cakes. Before she sat down, she gave her son an affectionate pat on the shoulder.

"Eat up, John. With a long trip ahead of ye, it is well to be filled."

He smiled his thanks.

In a few minutes Margaret came down the narrow stairs and took her place across from him. Slim as the river reeds and only two years younger than he, she was his companion on many adventures: wandering through the meadows, wading in Cardington Brook, listening to the song of the birds, milking the brown and white cow, hearing the hoot owl's question: "Who-o-o-o?"

"I'm glad ye're going to have the trip," Margaret told him, her brown eyes sparkling. "Remember everything, so that you can tell me when ye get back."

John stood at the rail as the big boat moved over the glassy river. At Great Barford, John Holden, another tinker who sometimes visited the Bunyans, got on board.

"Have ye heard, Thomas, that there may be a war between the King and Parliament?" he asked, his green eyes wide.

Papa began to scowl. "Surely the Parliament would never dare fight the King! The scoundrels managed to murder Stafford, the King's best friend. Wasn't that enough?"

Some other men standing nearby joined in the discussion.

"The Queen has sailed for Dover with the crown jewels to exchange them for munitions," one farmer said. "The two Houses of Parliament are united now in their stand against the King. War seems inevitable."

"The Cavaliers have deserted King Charles; he is alone. He told the Parliament that, if he granted all their demands, he would be no more than a phantom of a king," another man said.

"This way he's likely to be a dead king," John Holden said. "Why can't he agree?"

For the rest of the trip nobody talked about anything but the impending war. And Papa's mood was bad. Despite all that, John enjoyed seeing the towns and watching strange people. He kept wondering if Papa would be mustered in, and what kind of soldier he would make. Of course Papa would fight for the King, he thought. If I were old enough to fight, I would be on the side of Parliament. But he didn't tell Papa that!

The Saturday after his return from Lynn, John started for a favorite spot on the River of Ouse in Bedford. Papa had gone to Ampthill Heights to mend a roof. John had finished his chores and was free to fish. He wished that he could fish with Oliver Cromwell again, but news from London reported that he was in the midst of the revolution. John had never forgotten the big farmer with the gentle heart. He was sure Mr. Cromwell was like his grandfather, the Golden Knight.

As John walked through the weeds and bushes below the ruins of the castle behind the Swan Inn, he came upon the schoolmaster lying upon the partially disrobed body of Theny Talbot, the daughter of Widow Talbot who sewed for a living. The sight made his spine tingle. The girl's lewdness had never been whispered about in the town.

John, his heart thumping rapidly, slipped back the way he had come through the weeds and bushes hoping Master Vierney had not seen him. John paused on the Great Bridge, staring down at the fast-moving water. He had always liked Theny, a plump girl with a round, happy face, but he knew he should tell somebody what he had seen. At length he decided to go to the Vicar Giles Thorne. The schoolmaster was one of his parishioners.

When he reached St. Mary's, he asked the serving woman who greeted him if he could speak to the vicar.

"He is a very busy man," she said sternly. "What would ye be wanting?"

"I can only tell the vicar."

"Wait here. I will ask him if he will see ye."

It was a few minutes before she returned. "The vicar will give ye a minute," she said grudgingly. "He is trying to write a sermon."

Vicar Giles Thorne sat in his paneled study behind a large polished desk piled with papers and books. He looked like a flabby spider.

"Well, what is it?" He belched unconcernedly.

"Somebody should do something. There's a girl . . . she's very young . . . and there's an evil man . . . I thought . . ."

"Yes. Yes. Hurry on. I have no time to waste."

"First promise ye—you will not tell anyone who told you."

A look of annoyance crossed the vicar's pasty face. "All right. Tell me who you are, and get to the point."

"It's Master Vierney, sir. He's lying with Theny Talbot in the bushes. I saw him, sir. I'm John Bunyan of Elstow."

The vicar's pale eyes narrowed. "You're not your brother's keeper. If I were you, I wouldn't mention this to anyone."

"But she's only fourteen, not much older than my sister. Master Vierney destroys everyone."

Giles Thorne frowned. "I take it you don't like the schoolmaster."

"No, sir. I hate him."

"Then you made up this lie?"

"I didn't, sir. It's th' truth. You can go and see for yourself. I thought——"

The vicar looked down his fat nose and shook his head. "We have to be careful. Master Vierney is a very influential man. He has the King's ear. My advice to you, young sir, is to obey your schoolmaster at all times, and to forget what you have seen."

"Yes, sir." John turned toward the door. "But you will speak to him?"

"I will speak to him."

"And you will never tell who told you?"

"I gave you my word."

But John felt uneasy as he returned to the river to find another spot to fish. The vicar had revealed plainly that he was more afraid of Master Vierney's influence in London than of what might happen to Theny. But surely he would keep his promise. A man of God should be trusted.

John was still uneasy when he entered the schoolroom on Monday morning. Although it was early, Master Vierney had arrived. Tad came in right after John, and as soon as Master Vierney saw him, he began to swish the big stick.

"Come here, Tad," he said in an ominous voice. "It's time to show you what punishment I give a boy who runs to the vicar with tales!"

Tad's small, pointed face took on a frightened look. "I don't know what you mean, sir," he said in a small voice.

"Come here." Master Vierney sounded like an angry man calling his dog.

Slowly, haltingly, Tad moved forward.

He's going to beat Tad for what I did, John thought in distress. But if I confess, he'll beat me. He trembled as he watched the furious man rip the shirt from Tad's back, clutch the yellow hair, and begin to rain mighty blows on the boy's bare flesh. Tad's sobbing cry made John cringe; each smack was like a knife in his heart. After a dozen strokes, Tad fell senseless to the stone floor. The schoolmaster jerked him up by one arm.

"He's ill, sir," Mel Mooney said, coming forward. "He fell."

"Attend to your own business," Master Vierney ordered sharply. "I will ask your opinion if I need it."

Mel did not budge, and John leaped up and stood beside him, shrieking, "He has been beaten too much already!"

Purpling with rage, Master Vierney lifted his stick again. Before it could strike Tad another blow John grabbed it, broke it in two, and threw it to the floor. In that moment his courage could have slayed dragons.

The other boys stood in stunned silence. John Cecil, who had inherited the castle estate from his uncle, let out a whoop. "Good for you, Bunyan!"

"I've been wanting to do that for a long time," Mel said, admiration on his round pink face, "but I didn't have the nerve."

"Something made me do it," John said quietly. "I had to."

Master Vierney shook his fist and began to bellow. John gathered up his doublet, slate, inkpot, horn book, and quill. Without another word he made a hasty exit through the arched doorway. His schooldays were at an end. Master Vierney would never let him return. It was time, anyway, that he learned more about his trade. A feeling of exultation filled him. And somehow, for the first time in months, he was at peace.

After that John helped his father in the forge. He rode with Papa and gave the tinker's cry: "Have ye any kettles and pots to mend?" He felt better inside than he had in a long time. His father did not taunt him because he had had to leave school. Even Papa realized at last that the schoolmaster was brutal and of low character. Somehow the terrible memories of John's schooldays diminished. And he kept reminding himself that he had shown the boys that Master Vierney and his cause were not invincible. He never regretted what he had done.

On a morning in late June, John climbed onto the wooden seat of the cart, and Papa gathered up the reins of the deerskin harness. Margaret fluttered her fingers in farewell; Mama waved energetically; and the wagon rocked out to the highroad. Papa had been summoned to Woburn Abbey to repair a spout on the roof, and it was a long ride. They would have to spend the night in the stables there and return the following day.

The road led through a long avenue of elms. The hedges were alive with birds, butterflies, insects voicing their joy. Newborn lambs frolicked in the meadows, and colts frisked about. The rich, dark earth was green with growing crops. Narcissi, forget-me-nots, and lavender were in bloom. Swans glided on the river, mirroring their reflections between those of the willow trees on the glassy surface.

Suddenly the road filled with men, riding in pairs and shouting as they galloped by. When Anthony Harrington came along, Papa drew rein to ask him what was happening.

"Haven't you heard, Thomas? Our Bedfordshire men in the House of Commons have appealed to the people in what they call the Grand Remonstrance. They are making an effort to let the King save face by relieving him of all the blame for our grievances and putting it on the politicians who advised him. The plan might avert a civil war. We ride to London to let King Charles know that we are backing the Commons."

Papa shook his head. "Why don't ye leave the King be?"

"Don't you understand? This is to give him a chance. The Grand Remonstrance states that he had been abused by evil counselors."

Papa looked doubtful. "Do ye expect the trouble to cease?"

"There is some hope," Mr. Harrington said, putting spurs to his gray horse and galloping away.

The next night, after John returned from Woburn Abbey, he went over to Grandpa's to tell him about two huge lions he had seen at Woburn, guarding the entrance to the estate. And then he told him about the Grand Remonstrance.

"There is terrible news from Ireland, John," Grandpa said excitedly. "In an uprising there hundreds of Protestants have been slaughtered. The rebels declared they were Confederated Catholics. That may be, but Puritans and Catholics are blamed for everything these days. Anyway, 'tis said women were attacked, men hacked to pieces, and children beheaded. 'Twas the awfulest rebellion, a terrible slaughter!"

"I wish I were a man!"

"Ye would fight for th' Parliamentary cause?"

John nodded. "But I hope the King listens to the people!"

The King did not listen. That August he raised his standard at Nottingham with the motto: Give Caesar his due! A civil war had begun.

Before the end of the month Grandpa died! His wife sent for Papa late one night and John went to Grandpa's cottage with him. Grandpa was lying on his back looking like a marble statue, his eyes closed forever.

A book bound with soft leather lay on the stool beside him. John read its title: *The Seven Champions of Christendom*.

"Your birthday gift, John," Grandpa's wife said. "Your grandfather walked all the way to Bedford today to get it. He wasn't feeling well, and it was too much for him."

46

Swallowing hard to keep back the tears, John lifted the book reverently in trembling fingers. Grandpa had given him so many things, unseen gifts a boy couldn't hold in his hands. In that instant he vowed to try to be a better boy, to stop robbing orchards, tying rocks to the tail of Dame Whale's motley cat, telling lies, playing mean jokes on people he didn't like, and using the bad words Papa used which took God's name in vain.

Papa let out an oath and rushed from the room. He ordered John to go home and John obeyed. Papa did not come in until after midnight, and John knew by the way he stumbled through the family room that he had "crooked stockings."

The grave was dug in the little churchyard where Grandpa had talked to others about England and liberty. As the plain box coffin was lowered into the black earth, John said a silent prayer, "O God, help me to be like Grandpa."

Before Christmas, travelers on their way from Scotland to London brought news that the King had not commissioned the Irish rebels to kill Puritans and Independents, as rumored. A group of bigots had wrought the havoc.

The King, it was learned had returned from Scotland where prominent Scots had accused him of treason. In Parliament, under Edward Hyde's leadership, a Royalist Party had been organized. Two other Royalists, Lucius Cary (Lord Falkland) and Sir Edmund Verney, were aiding Hyde. Everywhere Cavaliers, or gentlemen, were coming to the King's defense, and the Grand Remonstrance had been adopted by a majority of eleven. But organizations had also been formed in every shire to help the Parliament.

In January, the King appeared through his attorney at the bar of the House of Lords, accusing John Hampden, John Pym, and three other members of the House of Commons of high treason. The outcome of it was that the King returned to Parliament the next day, accompanied by a group of Cavaliers in long tunics, fine breeches, polished shoes, gaily colored stockings, and broad hats with plumes over their wigs. Prince Rupert, the King's nephew was there, too, resplendent in a gold-colored suit and a white hat with a gold plume.

The five accused men were not in their seats. Other members of the House received the King and his company politely, but the Sheriff ignored the writ of arrest as well as the King's Proclamation that the five were traitors.

When the King heard that the accused men were returning to Westminster, he fled with his Cavaliers. The Earl of Newcastle was sent north to recruit men for the King's Army. The King, himself, went to Hampton Court and then to Windsor. And all London turned out to see the accused members of Parliament, guarded by the soldiers of Southwark and London, march triumphantly along the riverbank to the House of Commons.

One afternoon the same spring, when John was helping his father in the forge, John Okey appeared in the doorway. Papa looked up, frowned and dropped his heavy anvil iron to the dirt floor.

"Some men rally to the Stuart colors while others fight for Parliament," the chandler said directly. "Now that it is liberty against tyranny, Tom Bunyan, perhaps you have reconsidered. Parliament needs fighting men."

Papa stooped to lift the anvil iron and prop it against the wall. Then he placed his hands on his hips and spat on the earth in front of John Okey.

"That's what I give for your traitor's army! If the King needs swords, I will forge them for him."

"Perhaps you will change your mind when I tell you that the whole shire with a few exceptions is behind Parliament. Gibbets are being built for any who aid the Royalists."

Papa paled visibly and scratched his head with nervous fingers. "Well, now, Okey, if that's the way it is, I'll ponder a mite. Perhaps I am being hasty."

"Parliament needs your help."

"I couldn't make any blades to fight the King."

John Okey's hazel eyes flashed. "I will give Mr. Hampden,

48

Mr. Pym, and Mr. Cromwell your message. I have delivered mine."

After John Okey rode away, Mama came out to the lean-to. "Mr. Okey rode off as if he were angry. What did he want?"

Papa told her. "I am still a King's man," he said stubbornly.

The rest of the afternoon he worked in silence, frowning and smiting the metal with mighty blows as if that eased the storm within him.

I wish I were old enough to fight for Parliament, John thought. Sir Samuel Luke was conscripting men from sixteen to sixty, but John would be only fourteen next November.

After that he often dreamed that he was fighting for liberty for England beside Oliver Cromwell, John Okey, and John Pym. In imagination he wrestled with Prince Rupert, the King's nephew. And all about John, men and boys vowed to give their lives, if the need arose, for the Parliamentary cause.

That August of 1642, John's idol, who was now a captain, seized the magazines in the Castle of Cambridge. Everyone was praising Captain Cromwell, and as the strong feeling against the Crown increased, Papa grew more careful about expressing his Royalist sympathies.

In March of 1643, almost the time of the new year, according to the Old Style Calendar then in use, John and his father were riding through Stevington, a village four and a half miles north-west of Bedford. They saw a group of people gathered at the stone cross near the well of the Holy Sepulchre, talking and gesticulating. Papa drew rein and asked what had happened.

"Smallpox is spreading through the Midlands," an old crone told him in fright. "Captain Cromwell's son has just died of it at Newport."

Smallpox! I hope it does not come to Elstow, John thought.

All spring the rumors said that it was here or there, in this village or that. John worried about it so much that one September night he dreamed his mother had it. He could see her body covered with pockmarks and he cried out, waking the whole family. The dream had been so real that he could not get back to sleep.

Still awake when Noise-Ding crowed in the early dawn, he rose, put on his doublet and breeches and went out to the stable to clean the stalls and milk the cow.

By the time he had finished, the sun was up. As he started back to the cottage, he saw Harry Rodant riding along the path. Harry drew his black horse to a sudden halt and waved.

"I mustered in yesterday, John. Now I know which side will win; I joined that side. This is good-bye."

"You joined the side you think is going to win?"

Harry grinned and nodded. "Who wants to be a loser?"

"Which side will win, Harry?"

"The Roundheads. Cromwell—he's a Colonel now—has the soldiers praying and singing hymns until they think they are invincible. They'll win!"

"Gossip says the Roundheads are men of low character, tapsters, apprentices, adventurers."

Harry shook his head. "Now Colonel Cromwell is calling for godly men. Each one is given a Soldiers' Pocket Testament and a Catechism. Church attendance is compulsory. He declares that the Parliamentary Army fights for God and England."

John looked at Harry for a long moment. "Then how did you get in, Harry? You're as ungodly a scoundrel as I. I keep thinkin' you should mend your ways, turn about, and reform. I am trying. What will be your end, Harry, if you go on swearing, lying, stealing, wenching, and drinking strong waters?"

Harry cocked his head. His black eyes glistened. "What would the Devil do if it were not for such as I?" he said glibly.

"If I were Sir Thomas Fairfax, I would hate to have you in my army. You'd sell the Roundheads for a tankard of ale."

Harry threw back his tousled head and laughed uproariously. "That I would, John. That I would."

"If King Charles wins, John Okey says the people won't have any freedom at all."

"If he loses, he'll be a better king."

"I wish I could fight. I wish I were sixteen."

50

"You will be in about a year."

"A year is a long time."

Harry looked him up and down. "You might lie about your age. You'd be gone before your Pa found out. He'd be too busy cussin' us Roundheads to come to the Newport garrison to fetch you home."

John shook his head.

"Then what do you say to a last stunt?" Harry urged. "How about coming and ringing the bells of the church? It's very early, and the people will think the Cavaliers are coming. They'll run out of their houses. There'll be a lot of excitement. Everybody will be mad."

"All right. Let's go."

The bells rang out powerfully, shaking the tower and John was filled with sudden jubilation. A thrill of awe spread through him as the rumbling music sent shivers along his spine. The rope slid upward. John tugged it down, rising on tiptoe with its next upward pull. Harry took his turn. Up and down. Up and down. The bells pealed over the hamlet.

John had a moment of panic. What if the beam gave way and the heavy bell fell on us and killed us? he thought. The Devil would get Harry. Would he get me?

Harry tugged on his doublet. "Come away, John. Hurry before the people get here. This is our last prank until the war's over."

Sweating from exertion, John ran across the meadow behind Harry. He looked back and saw people dashing across the field and along the road to the church. The bells had alarmed the whole countryside.

"They may suspect us," Harry said with a grin, "but I'm leaving. They can't question me. You'd better run off like I said."

Again John shook his head. Mama would cry, he thought. Mama was all light and kindness. She moved quickly about the tiny cottage cooking, spinning, sewing, and scrubbing, making everyone comfortable. If he mustered in now, it would break her heart. When he was sixteen, perhaps she would try not to

51

grieve. He sighed. A year was a very long time when a boy wanted to fight for England.

As he waved good-bye to Harry, a feeling of sadness came over him. It wasn't because he would miss Harry, but he knew in that instant that an era in his life had ended. What lay ahead nobody knew.

3 A WREATH of mist floated over Elstow and Cardington Brook meandered through the browning meadow, as John left the cottage that October Sunday before the rest of the family were up. He couldn't bear the thought of sitting in the gloomy church on such a beautiful morning while the birds sang outside, the wind blew softly, and the whole countryside was alive with moving creatures. John Knox trotted happily behind John, as he idled through the Ellensbury woods where the floor was filagreed with the dappled sun. Mama would go to church on time, even if she had to go without him. He continued to dally.

The thought came to him that Christopher Hall, the Vicar of the Elstow Parish Church, did not pray publicly for the King or preach against Parliament as Giles Thorne had done. The summer before, the Vicar Thorne had been arrested for a pulpit attack on Parliament. John, who disliked sitting in the dark sanctuary while Vicar Hall preached with uplifted finger, sometimes let his imagination carry him to the Parliamentary garrison where Harry was. He saw himself guarding Colonel Cromwell or being sent on a dangerous mission by Sir Samuel Luke.

Some said the tide of war was turning. For a long time it had looked as if Lord Essex and his Parliamentary forces would be defeated. The Royalist headquarters at Oxford were fortified strongly, and the Parliamentary Army had not been able to cap-

53

ture the men stationed there. The previous February the troops of Essex had had to retreat to the manufacturing towns where the Puritans were in the majority. But the leaders of Parliament refused to admit defeat, demanding that the King return to fortified London and acknowledge their constitutional authority. In the West the Celtic Chieftains were winning. Colonel John Hampden had been injured in June by the forces of Prince Rupert, and he had died six days later. With the surrender of Bristol to the Prince, the King's Army controlled the West.

It was common knowledge that King Charles was seeking aid from the Confederated Catholics of Ireland, and that he was negotiating with the Scots to force a Presbyterian form of religion on England in return for their military support. The war may be over before I'm old enough to be mustered in, John thought as he kicked at some big toadstools.

A white-tailed rabbit bobbed across the path. He tried to talk to it, but it ran, with John Knox barking and leaping after it. John quieted the dog and pursued the rabbit through the bushes, but it had disappeared.

"Look what you did!" John scolded, shaking his finger. "The rabbit and I might have had a conversation."

John Knox just grinned, his long tongue hanging out. He didn't even have the grace to drop his eyes.

John sat on some green moss to rest. When he had caught his breath, he stood up and hopped on one leg, and began to crow like a rooster: *Cock-a-doodle-do! Cock-a-doodle-do. Cock-a——*

Suddenly the dog growled, and dashed toward a clump of bushes on the edge of the woods where he began to sniff and then to bark viciously. That silly rabbit, John thought. He doesn't know what a good hunter John Knox is. Reluctantly John scrambled to his feet, and ran to the bushes, parting the branches. A terrible sight chilled his spine. Deep-ringed eyes stared up at him, but they were not a rabbit's eyes. A man with a bald, shiny skull lay on his back, sweat pouring over his jutting cheekbones. The eyes looked very scared in the flushed face, so that his expression was like that of a frightened beast. His clothes were ragged, and a musket lay beside him.

"Are you hurt?" John asked.

"Ill. . . . Please—help me."

John stood motionless, his body tensed. The stranger had not said which army he fought for, and without a uniform John could not tell. He might be one of the King's spies.

The soldier read his thoughts. "I'm a Royalist," he said. "I am a tobacco pipemaker from Bristol. My brother, John Lane, is a captain in the Royalist forces. We disagreed. I protested the King's alliance with the Confederated Catholics. A number of us left the King's Army, and started for London to work with Parliament for constitutional government. The Lords talk of peace at any price!"

Is he lying? John wondered.

"Are there any King's men in the vicinity?" he asked, thinking that if the man was what he purported to be, he would know.

"Some of Sir Lewis Dyve's cavalry are coming to meet Prince Rupert, who is leading an attack on Bedford."

John's heart began to pound. "I must warn the people."

"You will come right back?"

"Yes."

John took a short cut and ran as fast as he could, John Knox leaping excitedly after him. Aiding a Royalist is a hanging offense, he thought, but he is sick. When John reached the crossroads where one path led to Ampthill, the other to Bedford, he froze in his tracks. A tar-blackened body hung on a gibbet, dancing in the wind with a vulture sitting on top of its head. The corpse wore the red sash of the King's Army, and where eyes had been there were holes picked by the hungry birds.

The hair on the back of John's neck stood up and he felt sick all over. That man in the woods was a deserter. Prince Rupert would deal harshly with any who aided one. John's steps slowed because his legs were shaking so that he could hardly move.

He heard the sound of swift hoofbeats and saw a troop of the King's Cavalry, wearing the broad hats with the sweeping plumes, and wide oranges sashes around their scarlet coats, galloping behind him. They rode at breakneck speed toward the Corn Market Square, the Swan Inn, and the heart of town. He was too late!

Soon soldiers covered the streets and squares, and citizens were running in all directions. John Knox barked with the other dogs. Horses neighed, women screamed, and men shouted. Royalist soldiers ran in and out of the shops on either side of the High Street carrying barrels and baskets, as they plundered the town. All John could do was turn around and get out of there.

But where was John Knox? He couldn't leave without him. One of the Royalists might be cruel to him, and he couldn't stand that. John wandered in and out of the shops the soldiers were ransacking, calling, "John Knox! John Knox!"

A rough hand grabbed John's shoulder, and spun him around. He looked up into the dark, handsome face of a Cavalier who wore a black helmet with a white plume, and black armor, which extended from his neck to his knees. The black eyes glittered and he spoke sharply.

"Are you daft, boy? The Presbyterian has been dead since fifteen seventy-two!"

"John Knox is my dog. I can't find him."

"Why are you so frightened?"

John threw his shoulders back. "Hereabouts we don't trust Royalists. One of them might steal him."

Instead of showing anger, the young man laughed wildly. "There might be a thief, or two, amongst the Roundheads, too. But I can understand your anxiety for your dog. You see I like dogs, too."

An officer in blue rode up, touched his hat, and addressed the handsome Royalist.

"Your Highness, we have confiscated enough food to last five days. Are your orders to continue to Ampthill?"

John stared like a half-witted yokel, his mouth hanging open. The man in black armor must be Prince Rupert, the King's nephew. Everyone talked about what a great solider he was. Now John could tell the other boys he had talked to him!

But in that instant his heart seemed to stand still. Down the street rolled a cart filled with stolen food, and John Knox was darting into its path. The hoofs of the galloping horses struck him and he collapsed in a heap.

With a cry John raced toward the limp body. The dog lay very still, his eyes closed. John dropped to the hard-packed earth, and called his name over and over. John Knox did not move. The dirty Royalists have murdered him, John thought wildly. He's dead!

The Prince came over and stooped down, too. He felt the dog's body then straightened up, and smiled. "He's just stunned. He'll be all right," he said kindly.

But the minutes until John Knox opened his big brown eyes seemed an eternity to John. Tears of relief ran down his cheeks as he smiled his gratitude to the Prince.

"For a Royalist, you're not so bad," he whispered. "You do like dogs!"

The Prince nodded. "I'm glad he's all right," he said brusquely before he strode off to shout orders to the waiting troops.

As soon as John Knox was able to get to his feet, John started for Elstow, the dog limping behind him. He found his mother on the Village Green talking to a group of villagers. They asked excitedly about the raid on Bedford, and he told them that Prince Rupert himself was in charge of the plundering, and that John Knox had almost been killed by one of their carts.

Mama put her arms around John and hugged him, telling him how glad she was John Knox had been spared. "But those thieving Royalists are taking the bread out of the mouths of Bedford citizens!" she said in fury.

John told her quickly about the sick soldier in the Ellensbury woods, who had said he was a deserter from the King's Army.

"What's the matter with him?"

"His face is red, and he's sweating. He's sick all right."

"Then we must bring him here."

"Papa won't like it!"

"Leave your father to me. Fetch the man."

"He can't walk. He might even have the plague. His companions must have left him to die."

"Fetch him. Take the cart. I will get a bed ready."

"Where are ye going, John?" Papa called from the forge when he saw John harnessing the horse.

"There's a sick man in the woods. Mama wants me to bring him home."

"Wait a minute, John. . . . Margaret. Margaret! Haven't ye enough to do without takin' on the burden of a sick stranger?"

"Somebody has to succor him, Thomas. Ye leave the nursing of strangers to me."

With a grunt Papa turned and went into the cottage, and John mounted the seat of the cart and started off. When he reached the spot where the man lay, he tied the horse to a tree, and ran over to the bushes and peered down.

"I'm back," he said.

The man didn't answer. His eyes were closed and they remained closed even when John took his feet and dragged him out into the clearing. But he was breathing; he wasn't dead, so John ran all the way back to get his father to come and help hoist the man into the cart. Papa grumbled, but he got up from the table, mopped his brow, and followed with long strides. When they reached the unconscious man, Papa's sinewy arms lifted him as if he were a baby and laid him in the cart.

Within a week William Lane was on his feet. Mama knew how to care for a sick man. Dr. Bannister had come and said that he might have been in the last stage of the plague. He couldn't be sure. There was a red ugly sore on his loins. Papa had sworn when he heard that, but Mama calmly began to scrub. There were an old doublet and some worn breeches of Grandpa's in the house, and she gave them to the tobacco pipemaker. They were better than the rags he had been wearing. Mama burned them.

The day Mr. Lane left for London, he took out a purse and gave Mama twenty shillings, although she protested that there was no charge.

"This money is not payment," he said, "simply a gift. There are some things money cannot buy, such as your kindness and friendship."

Mama curtsied and told him to come back if ever he returned to Bedfordshire.

"I would like to come back to live here," he said warmly. "This is the finest country in England!"

After that John was more interested than ever in what happened in the war. Whenever he had any spare time, he went to the Swan Inn and hung around listening to the news. He learned of the death of Cardinal Richelieu, the dictator of Europe, whose aid had meant a great deal to the Parliamentary forces. And in Parliament Royalist opposition was at an end. John wondered if that had been due to the efforts of William Lane and others who had thrown their support to Parliament. That fall the Scots signed an agreement to give military aid to the Parliamentary forces in exchange for their promise to extirpate popery, schism, superstition, and to declare that God's Church in the three kingdoms was one—Presbyterian! And in December of 1643, to the consternation of all Parliament sympathizers, John Pym died, but others continued to carry out the plans he had made.

The fighting continued. The Parliamentary or Roundhead Army had fifty thousand men divided into three armies. Lord Essex waited near Oxford with one army. In the West, Captain Waller was trying to prevent Prince Maurice, the brother of Prince Rupert from further conquests. The men from Bedfordshire and its neighboring countries were part of a fourteen-thousand-man army under Lord Manchester and Oliver Cromwell. By midwinter, Alexander Leslie had come down from the North and Royalist troops rushed to halt his advance. Lord Fairfax attacked some Irish troops who landed at Chester, destroying them. Prince Rupert had been sent to Wales to raise more troops; King Charles was now surrounded by Roundheads.

Spring of 1644 came like a bright wave flowing over Bedfordshire. John wandered in the sunshine, enjoying the sheen of green and gold over the meadows, the hills, the gardens, and orchards. The blue sky curved above him and there was the shining Ouse with the swans gliding on it. There were new leaves rustling, squirrels with curious eyes, the silence broken by the cawing of the rooks and the happy song of robins. The apple and cherry trees at the four corners of the meadow burst into blossom. The brook seemed to chuckle on its way as the trout came out of the shade, but the big ones always seemed to escape John's hook, and there were many times when he longed for his fishing companion of Hillersdon Park.

How joyous it was to come home after his wandering tired but happy, to be met by his mother's cheery welcome where the path turned into their cottage. There were always the delicious odors from the hearth, and supper was a gay occasion when everyone laughed and talked until all had eaten their fill.

John worked six or seven hours each day with his father in the forge, learning the tinkering trade. With Goliath, a favorite cat, sitting on his shoulder and John Knox lying in the doorway, he hammered and soldered. There was music in the hammer, and John often beat time as he worked. He took pride in his trade and believed that whatever a man does should be done well.

After the evening chores were finished and supper was over, John read to Margaret and Willie from the book Grandpa had bought him, *The Seven Champions of Christendom.* There was one story he read over and over, the one about St. George, a brave knight who fought a dragon. Sometimes they made a game of it; John put a cook pot on his head upside down, pretending it was the shining helmet of the knight. A black poker became a glittering sword. Or Willie and John would swoop at Margaret, hissing like dragons, while she, wide-eyed with pretended terror, backed against the wall. At other times Margaret gathered elm leaves, which were the miracle leaves of the story, and healed "St. George's" wounds. On rainy evenings the cottage roared with noise, but Mama never complained. Sometimes she joined in, too, hissing, or crying aloud when the dragon roared. At last, heads nodding, they would creep slowly up the narrow stairs to bed. And sleep was sound.

Early in June of 1644, as John came in from the forge one evening, his mother handed him a letter from Harry, at Newport. John ripped it open and read it out loud to Mama. Harry said that clothes and supplies were so scarce that he had to share a pair of breeches with another soldier, one staying in bed while the other was up. But a new army was emerging which believed itself invincible. "Old Oliver tells us every day that we're fighting God's battle, until we all believe it. When I hear Sir Samuel talking about God as if he were in the room with us, I almost believe in Him. I chose the winning side. I'm certain of that now!"

As John folded the letter, he noticed that Mama was not moving with her usual energy. She was warming a brick which she used to heat the beds, though it was a warm day!

"Don't you feel well, Mama?"

"No. There's eel pie in the oven, and I've cooked a pot of greens. Now I have to lie down."

He followed her into the bedchamber and watched her put the wrapped brick in the bed before she lay down. His heart shriveled as he stared at her. Her brown eyes looked very dark in her white face, and she was sweating. Suddenly she sat up, leaned over the side of the bed and vomited onto the floor, then fell back against the pillow too exhausted to speak.

Margaret, coming in from the hen house with a bowl of eggs, said, "Mama has been feeling poorly all day, but she kept saying she would be all right."

Margaret put the eggs on the table and went to Mama, pulled the dress back from her shoulders, and peered at her skin. Then she threw a quilt over her, and felt her brow.

"Don't worry about me, children," Mama said in a faraway voice. "I just want to lie here a little while." She closed her eyes.

For a few minutes they waited, but she did not speak again, and they tiptoed quietly from the room.

"What should we do, John? Papa's gone to the inn," Margaret

whispered, her eyes wide. "She doesn't have any spots, but *what if she has the plague?*"

John felt sick with horror. "Where would Mama get that?"

"Dunno. It's everywhere—in the earth, in the air ye breathe, just everywhere."

Mama doesn't have the plague, John thought fiercely. She has been working too hard picking peas and crocking blackberry jam. By the time Papa comes home she'll be fine.

There was a sudden scream from the bedchamber and Margaret ran in with John streaking after her. Mama's eyes were open now and she was groaning, her face contorted with pain. She threw back the quilt and grabbed at her groin.

"Is that where you hurt, Mama?"

Mama rolled her eyes. "Yes. . . . My legs ache, too. My back hurts. . . . My head is pounding. And I'm so cold. Perhaps I have the ague."

"You have the ague," John repeated, knowing it was not the ague. "I'm going for Dr. Bannister. Margaret will stay with you."

Mama did not protest. Her body shook and she fell back against the white-ruffled pillow muttering some indistinguishable words.

John, rushing from the room toward the front door, collided with his father staggering in.

"Where are we going, John?" Papa demanded in a thick voice.

"Mama's awful sick. I am going to fetch the doctor."

Papa blinked, and then fell forward on his face. John did not stop to help him up, but rushed out along the narrow path, across the meadow, over the stile to the Bedford Road.

When he reached the doctor's house, he pounded frantically on the wooden door. The doctor himself appeared holding a vial in one hand.

"Come quickly. I think Mama has the plague!"

Dr. Bannister was startled. "Surely not, John. There are no cases that I know of."

"Maybe I'm wrong, sir, but she's awful sick."

The doctor peered through his spectacles. "What are her complaints?"

62

John enumerated them quickly: the pain in her head, loins, and legs; the nausea and the sweating.

"I'll come at once," the doctor said.

He was a tall, distinguished-looking man in his forties, whose presence in any sick room brought comfort and healing. Dedicated to his work, he served selflessly and wisely.

John waited while he got his bag and saddled his horse. He told John to hoist himself up behind him, and they were soon riding toward Bunyan's End.

Margaret met them at the door, her small pointed face grave. She told them that Mama was unconscious now, moving from side to side and moaning.

Dr. Bannister pulled back the quilt to examine her. "The plague!" he muttered. "It is the plague!"

Margaret began to cry. "Will she get well?" she asked.

"You cannot tell about the plague. Fetch a basin of warm water and some clean strips."

When Margaret brought the basin, the doctor washed his hands and lifted a candle to look closely at Mama, his face very grave.

"Dame Bunyan, can you hear me?" he asked, but there was no response.

The room smelled bad, for the mullioned window was closed. Margaret had been afraid to let in the night air. Dr. Bannister went to it, thrust it open, and let in the clean, fresh air.

Mama began to retch again, and Margaret ran to her with the basin.

When Mama was quiet once more, Margaret poured the contents of the basin into the slop pail and carried it out.

"Water . . . water," Mama moaned, and John hurried to fetch it.

Dr. Bannister poured her some and she drank it, and called for more.

"Thomas," she whispered a few minutes later.

John found Papa lying in the corner by the hearth, not moving or making a sound. When John shook him, he rolled over and grunted like a pig.

"Papa, wake up. Mama is very sick. She has the plague."

He sat up straight. "What that ye say, John? I thought ye said Mama had the plague."

"I did, Papa. Dr. Bannister is with her."

Papa leaped up as if a hornet had stung him, brushed his long hair out of his eyes and rushed into the bedroom, demanding, "Will she live? Will she live?"

"She has a chance. See that." Dr. Bannister pointed to a lump the size of an apple in Mama's groin, red and glistening in the candlelight. "More patients die when there is no boil, or bubo. But the disease is mysterious, unpredictable. We know little about it, except that the pus from these bubos spreads when they break. Hands must be washed immediately after anyone touches a person who has the plague."

"Will we all catch it?" Margaret asked, coming back into the room.

"Perhaps not. My advice is to take young William to a friend's. Keep him away from her."

Papa went out and paced up and down in the meadow.

The doctor asked for bread crumbs, mustard, vinegar, and a clean cloth to make a poultice which he tied over the bubo.

"Can you children care for her?" he asked. "I can tell you what to do. I'm afraid there is nobody else."

"We can do whatever you say," Margaret told him.

"Then feed her some onion posset made with milk and oats. It is important that the boil should break. Place a jar filled with hot water against it. Use all the blankets and quilts you have. Warm as the weather is, build a fire. She needs to sweat. Before I leave I will give her an emetic." He fumbled in his leather bag.

"Can ye make the posset, John, while I heat the water and the stone bottle?" Margaret asked.

John had never made posset before, but after heating some milk, he added oats, spices, and chopped onion as he had seen his mother do. Then he poured in some apple wine to curdle it. He got the posset pot off the shelf above the hearth. One of its two spouts was bent, but he poured the brew into it. The pewter was so hot that he needed a piece of homespun to hold it.

They went back to the bedchamber and Margaret laid the stone bottle on top of the poultice and pulled the quilts over it and up around Mama's neck. John noticed that there were deep circles around Margaret's eyes, and she moved slowly. He realized that dawn was beginning to creep through the window. They had been up all night. She saw him looking at her and smiled wanly.

"Give me the posset, John. How good it smells. As soon as I feed Mama, I'll fix you some oats."

Mama struggled, but firmly Margaret placed the lower spout to her lips. "You've got to drink this, Mama. You need it."

It took a long time to force the posset into Mama's mouth. She was increasingly restless, tossing about from one side of the bed to the other.

"Watch her, John, while I cook breakfast," Margaret said at last.

Fear was still there in the shadowy dawn, in the shadows of John's mind. His body was sweating with it. He moved a stool against the wall beside the bed, so that he could lean his head against the wall. He felt as if he could not hold it up. His eyes were heavy, and his head nodded. With the wall to support him, he fell asleep.

He was awakened by a loud hammering on the door and ran to open it. A constable stood there with a hammer in his hand, pointing a long finger at the red-painted sign he had just nailed up. "Lord, have mercy upon us," it read. It was the notice the authorities used to warn others of the presence of the dreaded plague.

As John went back to the bedchamber, he was conscious of somebody screaming.

Papa stood at the foot of Mama's bed, staring at her with wild, dilated eyes. "God in Heaven!" he moaned. "God in Heaven!" Then he began to scream again, a wild, spine-chilling sound.

Margaret ran in and bent over Mama, listening for a heartbeat, feeling for Mama's pulse.

She started back, quivering. "Oh, Papa, she is gone!"

A sudden anguish seized John, stabbing like the blade of a plunging knife. Papa let out a stream of blasphemies. "I'm not fit to breathe. I slept all night and didn't help her. Oh, Margaret, my darling, I never was what ye hoped. I wish th' Lord had struck me in your stead. God, forgive me. Forgive my wicked ways."

The bell of the Elstow Abbey Church began to toll just then in long melodious peals. Somewhere a dog howled in angry protest, and John Knox gave an answering bark. It was Sunday morning; the people of the parish would be going to church—all except one —Mama. On Tuesday she would be carried to the churchyard in an unpainted box. The bell would toll again in mournful tones, and John felt as if he couldn't stand it.

Papa's wide shoulders were heaving as, without another word, he turned and stumbled out. Margaret began to cry softly and John put his arm around her.

"We'll have to take care of Papa and Willie now," she said in a choked voice. "Oh, John, I'm so glad we have each other!"

They stood in silence for a few minutes, holding hands and staring at the still form on the bed. . . .

"Mama's gone to heaven," Margaret explained, when Willie was brought back from the neighbor's house. But Willie, who was only seven, couldn't understand. Margaret tried again. "She is with God."

"I want to go, too," Willie insisted.

"But we need you here."

"I want to be where Mama is."

"We all wish we could be with her, but we can't."

"Margaret, please let me go and live with God, too."

How can you explain death to a seven-year-old boy? John asked himself silently. What happens to a person who dies? Mama had been good. Surely she was in the Holy City she had talked about. But what will happen to people like me and Harry? Will we be shut out of the Holy City? Will we burn forever? That is what the vicar had said one morning, that a hot fire awaited the wicked. *What if I caught the plague and died now?*

66

4   THE FACT of his mother's death continued to appall John. With desperate sadness he moved about the silent cottage. He vowed to improve his ways; he tried to be kinder and more thoughtful of others. He helped Margaret, and late each afternoon after he left the forge, he took Willie to Cardington Brook where they fished until sundown.

Margaret, who had set immediately about her new tasks, stayed at home washing the clothes in the stream, sweeping the house, cooking, making butter and pot cheese. At times she looked very tired, but each day she grew more adept at a woman's work.

Papa hammered and soldered all day at his forge, smiting the metal with his mighty anvil iron, as if each stroke eased the pain within him. Every evening after supper he went across the meadow toward the stile and the villages beyond. Sometimes John, still awake when his father came home, heard him muttering to himself as he did when he had crooked stockings. In the morning he looked sloomy, as the villagers said when describing a man who had been drunk. Papa couldn't have spit six pence a yard.

One June morning when Thomas Bunyan was in that state, John arose early and took his fishing pole to the brook to catch some fish for breakfast. The mist hung over the meadow, floating around him like a gray ghost until it took shape and g-r-r-r-d at him. Just as he caught a fish, the sweetness of the bells of Elstow Church filled the air and he realized it was Sunday morning.

When at length he returned to the cottage, Margaret was walking aimlessly about the family room. When he held up the fish, she smiled wanly.

"Clean it, John. I'll cook it."

He had expected her to be pleased, but that was all she said.

As she lifted the big black skillet from the hook above the hearth, he heard her moan. She straightened up, drew her brows together in a frown and bit her lip.

"John," she whispered faintly. "I feel so tired, I must lie down. You'll have to fry the fish yourself."

She turned toward the bedroom where Mama had died, dragging her feet and moving unsteadily. A cold chill went over John. She's sick, he thought. *What if she has the plague?* He followed her, and saw that she did not wait to draw back the covers, but fell on top of them. He watched her anxiously.

"I'm sorry, John. Can ye manage?"

"Of course. I can finish breakfast, and wash the plates. You've been working too hard."

"It's just that I didn't sleep well last night. Now I can hardly keep my eyes open."

Relief swept John. Then it wasn't the plague.

"I'll bring you some fish, Margaret."

When he fried it and brought it to her, she sat up, but he saw that she was trembling. She ate a little and then handed him the plate.

"I'm not very hungry, John. Thank ye."

He set the dish on the table near the bed. "I'll leave this here in case you change your mind."

"Take it away, please. I'm sick at my stomach. I can't look at food."

He lifted the dish and bent over to kiss her brow. She shrank back. "No, John. Don't." She turned her face away.

In that instant he knew. Margaret had the plague, too!

"I'm going to get the doctor, Margaret."

Margaret felt as if she were in one of John's nightmares. A slow pain spread through her back and down her legs. She began to shudder and nausea overwhelmed her. Sweat soaked her sheets and pillow. She closed her eyes, but the pain beat on.

What if I die? she thought. What will happen to Papa, John, and Willie? But I won't die. I can't. They need me. She fell into a kind of stupor.

When she opened her eyes, Dr. Bannister was standing at her bedside. John stood behind him, his blue eyes filled with worry. John will miss me more than the others, she thought.

She leaned over the side of the bed and began to retch. John mopped up the floor, his face very solemn.

How thirsty she was! She asked for water and John brought her some. It was cool, but she couldn't drink much because her tongue filled her mouth.

"John must not catch it!" She clutched Dr. Bannister's sleeve. "Send him away."

The plague is sent by evil spirits to despair the soul, she thought. She wasn't afraid, but she didn't want to die. There was no doubt in her mind that she would go to the Holy City and be with Mama. The plague was a strange evil ailment. She must not feel defeated, helpless, like a trapped animal. People said the plague was the work of evil spirits, demons, and witches. But God was mightier. She began to retch again and John held the basin for her until she sank back on the soggy pillow. She was very warm. Blackness surrounded her.

"Give her as much water as she will take," the doctor said. "Keep her warm. The more she sweats the sooner the poison will leave her. That's all we can do, John. And I must warn you that you may catch it."

"I know, but I want to take care of her. She will get well?"

Dr. Bannister looked at him. John Bunyan was the most rollicking, all-boy youth in the parish. He liked his fun and he liked it rough. But now he was just a frightened, grieving brother whose sister had the dreaded plague.

"Only by the Grace of God, John. She has as hard a case as I have seen. All I can do is give her an emetic."

"Shall I make her some sack posset?"

"Yes. And broth. And I would send Willie to a neighbor's.

Wash your hands each time you touch Margaret or any of her garments."

When Dr. Bannister left, John could not hold back the tears.

Margaret continued to fight for her life as he moved on tiptoe around the sick room. He filled the stone bottle with boiling water, and wrapped it in some homespun, as he had seen her do when Mama was sick, and placed it at her feet. He left her to make some posset and when he returned, he found her in a coma. He forced some of the warm mixture between her lips, then went back to make a mustard-and-vinegar poultice for her boil.

By this time she was sweating so profusely that the water ran down her face onto her neck. He fetched some warm water and a cloth and wiped it off. But in a few minutes she was covered again with beads of sweat. Then she vomited up the posset.

As he held the basin beneath her chin, Papa strode into the room. "Ye've done your share, John. Ye must be exhausted. Word has got about that we have the plague again. Nobody'll come near the forge. I have no work. Go to bed. I'll sit with her."

John shook his head. "I know what to do, Papa. She's quieter now. If I catch it, I will live. I'm strong."

"The strong die as quick as the frail," Papa said in a funereal voice. "If Margaret dies, too, I don't care if I get it. A man's wife—now his little girl." He pointed furiously. "Look at her. Dying. And nobody can do anything."

"I'm doing what I can, Papa. I'm doing what the doctor said to do."

Papa left and all that long day and into the night John stayed with his sister. Twice she sat up and screamed in pain, and watching her suffer was agony.

It was morning before Papa came home. He was sober, but his hair was matted and his clothes were rumpled and dirty. John did not ask him where he had been.

"Don't you think she looks more peaceful, Papa?"

Papa came closer. He shook his head. "She's goin' t' die."

"She's not, Papa. She's not!"

"Let's not fool ourselves, John. It'll be that much harder."

70

Papa reached down and pulled out the trundle bed. "If ye won't leave, lie down."

John lay down and in a few minutes he was asleep.

When he woke up, it was twilight, and he realized he had slept for hours. His head ached painfully, but he sat up and looked toward Margaret's bed.

Dr. Bannister was there, leaning over her, and Papa stood behind him. The doctor took a lancet and broke the huge bubo on her groin. A yellow pus flooded out. Margaret was a strange color now. John thought with despair: She's going.

"You have taken fine care of her, John," Dr. Bannister said in his brusque way.

"You think she will live?" John's face showed eager hope.

"Perhaps. Nobody can say. It is good when the boil bursts." Dr. Bannister wiped at the pus, and when he had finished, he pointed to the slop pail filled with cloths dark-stained with blood and yellow with pus. "Burn these outside. Clean the table with scalding water. I need some boiling water now to wash."

Margaret must not die, John thought fiercely as he waited for the water to boil. "God, don't let her die! If ye save her, I promise I'll stop lying, swearing, stealing, and ringing the church bells."

Papa walked to the road with Dr. Bannister while John refilled the stone bottle. He heated the posset again and forced some between Margaret's hot lips. Then he cleaned the room as the doctor had ordered, and burned the filthy cloths.

He went back to look at her again, but her color had not improved. Her skin was still very damp, and her breathing was irregular. As he watched, she began to make a strange, gasping sound and her body twitched. Then suddenly there was a gurgling rattle like the warning of a deadly snake. The frightening sound was coming from Margaret's throat. John's heart began to pound in terror.

Then the room was quiet. Frantically he felt Margaret's wrist as he had seen the doctor do. There was no pulse. He sank to the floor dazed and sick. Oaths flooded from his lips. God had not answered his prayer. God had let Margaret die!

In the bleak days that followed the second burial, John worked in the forge and in the cottage.

"Wish we had a woman," Papa said one morning.

"We're managing, Papa."

Papa shook his head and his blue eyes dulled. "Take these oats. Need salt. Taste terrible. It's not easy for men to get along."

He has never before talked as if I were a man, John thought proudly. I am almost sixteen and I am learning to cook. But what if he takes another wife sometime? Papa had been married before he had married Mama and his first wife had died. Would there be a third? Surely not for a year or two because that wouldn't be respectful to Mama. But in time? . . . John couldn't stand the thought of another woman in Mama's place. His world had shattered about him. His heart continued to hunger for a well-remembered presence.

Lonely now, he sometimes lay on a soft knoll beside Cardington Brook and read again about St. George and the dragon. Only here he found escape as he buried himself in the flesh of the knight, wielding his sword to rescue the fair Sabra, and seizing the ugly beast to save the poor peasants.

At other times he dreamed of the garrison at Newport Pagnell and the life of a soldier. How proud Grandpa would have been if he could have lived to see his grandson a soldier of the Parliamentary Army. Under an ordinance passed a year ago, Sir Samuel Luke, the Governor of the garrison, had been authorized to impress men for that army.

One night John dreamed that Grandpa, dressed in a full white robe, stood at the foot of his bed. Wings spread wide from his back, and in one hand he held a shining light that surrounded him with a radiant glow.

"Come, John, follow me," said the dear, familiar voice.

Obediently John rose and walked behind Grandpa across the meadow, over the stile, and along the path to the wicket-gate leading into the churchyard.

"I came to show ye, John, that I'm alive, that death is only an illusion."

"What's an illusion, Grandpa?"

"Something that isn't."

"But you are an angel. Is it fun?"

"Fun, John? It's glorious. Nobody can imagine the joys waiting for one who crosses the river that has no bridge."

"The 'river that has no bridge.' But I can't swim."

"Don't worry about that. You can get through the dark waters."

John shook his head. "I would be terribly frightened."

"Watch me."

To John's consternation, Grandpa ran up the timeworn stones of the isolated tower as if they were a level path. At the top he balanced himself on the edge of the parapet while John held his breath. Suddenly Grandpa spread his wings and floated down to the ground beside John.

"I can run and not grow weary, walk and not faint," he said happily.

Then he spread his wings again and flew off, the light in his hand growing smaller and smaller until it was a star blinking down from the velvet sky.

John opened his eyes and the dawn was coming through the dormer window. In a few minutes the sun was streaming in on Willie in his trundle bed. But Grandpa's presence lingered. He had been there; John was sure of it. And he had flown away to be a star in the Celestial City beside Mama and Margaret who were shining ones, too.

The bells of the Abbey Church were tolling as John went downstairs.

"Get ready for church," Papa ordered as soon as breakfast was over.

John dressed in his russet suit, white stockings, and boots, and helped Willie fasten his shoes. Then they walked in single file behind Papa across the meadow to the Abbey Church.

Attendance at church was a duty Papa dared not evade now with the fear of the plague inside him, and the terror of the Parliamentary or Roundhead troops constantly before him. To Papa the words "Catholic" and "Puritan" expressed the supreme evil. Going to church had suddenly become a virtue, and a challenge to his enemies. John was not enthusiastic; he still hated to go. He preferred the sports on the Village Green, wrestling, leaping, playing cat, shooting arrows, and dancing.

When they reached the church, people were standing in the yard discussing a great Parliamentary victory. Oliver Cromwell's name was on everyone's lips. His brigade had joined Major General Leslie's Scots and routed Prince Rupert's Royalist cavalry at a place called Marston Moor near York. "God is with us," had been the battle cry of the Roundheads. The Royalists had shouted, "For God and King." Lieutenant General Cromwell had stood in a cornfield reading the Scriptures until every soldier understood that he was invincible as he fought God's battle. The assault had been so fierce that Rupert had fled into Lancashire, and York had surrendered. And after the battle the Roundheads had sung a hymn of triumph!

"Odd's skunks!" Papa snorted. "I'll wager the Irish will help King Charles win the next battle."

"Ye cannot beat religious men," Anthony Harrington said happily.

"Odd's skunks!" Papa said again, and spit on the grass.

He was still scowling as they entered the dark, cold church.

During the service Papa moved noisily on the hard bench, and after a while he fell asleep and snored so loudly that the vicar paused in the middle of his sermon. John's heart sank as every eye turned in their direction. He prodded Papa with the Prayer Book, and made himself as small as possible. Papa opened his eyes and his great cave of a mouth and bellowed, "Be gone, ye rascals!" as he had always done at home when the children woke him with their noisy games.

People tittered and John felt his cheeks flush as he hung his head and looked at the floor. But Papa just wiped the sweat from his brow with the sleeve of his shirt and closed his eyes again.

During the rest of the sermon John sat staring at the four

crouching figures on the corners of the Baptismal font. Their ugly faces had always frightened him. "Those are the four vices which Baptism casts out," Mama had told him many years ago, "greed, lust, selfishness, and jealousy." His thoughts roved hither and thither, so that he did not hear one word Christopher Hall was saying. At last the hourglass, which was used to time the sermon, ran out. The long service was concluded. John and Willie were free to join their friends on the Green. Papa waved his big hand to them and started for the Swan Inn at Bedford. All afternoon John's mind kept returning to Papa. The fury of his sprees since Mama's death was something to worry about.

A game of cat with Froggy Foster took a long time. John had never liked Froggy and he liked him less now that his uncle, William Foster, was on the King's side. He was glad when it was time to go home for supper.

As he and Willie started back to the empty cottage, a few clouds sailed the summer sky and the warm, soft wind sang. They paused to watch a male rook feeding a female while she sat on her nest. They strolled on. The leaf-green branches moved happily on both sides of the path. For the first time since Mama and Margaret had left him, John felt a surge of happiness.

At the sudden sound of hoofbeats on the hard-packed ground, John grabbed Willie's hand and pulled him to the side of the road. Colonel Okey, brown hair fluffed around his wide shoulders, and his hazel eyes twinkling under jutting brown eyebrows, galloped toward them on a long-legged horse.

"The young tinker!" he shouted, as he pulled his horse to a halt. "I am on my way to see your father."

Cold fear surged through John. He remembered Colonel Okey's warning to Papa not to oppose the Roundhead Army. Has somebody informed on Papa, telling the Parliamentarians what Papa had said that morning before church? Had Colonel Okey come to hang him?

The Colonel saw his fright. "I want him to forge some short swords for a troop of horse commanded by Lord Brook. As a quartermaster I attend to such things. He will be well paid, for he is a competent workman. Colonel Cromwell will see that the metal is delivered. Until the work is done, your father's forge will be guarded."

"You'll probably find him in the tavern at the Swan Inn in Bedford."

"Then I shall go there at once."

"Shall I water your horse?"

"Fine. Yes. He needs it."

The colonel dismounted, and John helped him to take the bridle off. Willie went inside the cottage, while John led the horse to the stream and Colonel Okey strode after him.

"How is your gracious mother?" the Roundhead asked.

John bit his lip. Then he told him about the plague and that both Margaret and Mama had died.

When they reached the cottage, John invited him in for some bread and cheese and he accepted with thanks. John apologized for the unwashed pewter plates as he cut the bread. While they munched on the food, Colonel Okey was talkative.

"There is so much trouble in the world, John," he said reflectively, almost as if he were talking to himself. "But there's hope when men stand for what they believe is right. Freedom to do that is as necessary as eating."

"Yes, sir," John said to be polite.

"Have you ever heard of Bishop Thirleby, John?"

John shook his head. He wasn't particularly interested.

"People still talk about him, although he died in Queen Elizabeth's reign. Colonel Cromwell's grandfather knew him well. He had been Bishop of Westminster, Norwich, and Ely. The Queen had him imprisoned in the Tower of London, because he opposed her position as head of the Church of England, though all he asked was freedom of conscience. He had taken his vows in the Catholic Church and he remained a Roman Catholic until he died. But he was filled with a spirit of love and never sought vengeance against the Protestants."

"Was he beheaded?"

"No, although he endangered his life by refusing to have a

part in or approve the burning of the Protestant martyrs, Ridley and Latimer. He always said he was trying to live like a pilgrim. He asked to be buried in a pilgrim's dress when he died, because he estimated himself to be a pilgrim on this earth."

"A pilgrim!" John mused aloud. "Everybody's a pilgrim. There were the Pilgrim Fathers who weren't Pilgrims at all, my grandpa used to say. Then there are the Puritans, people who don't like to be dubbed 'pilgrims.' The Pilgrim Fathers separated from the Church of England and went to America, didn't they? And a lot of Puritans went to Holland. Some founded villages in England. But where was Bishop Thirleby going?"

"Why to Heaven. That's where."

"But won't the other pilgrims go there, too?"

"Some of them. Bishop Thirleby had a different idea of the pilgrim, not as one who runs away to another place, but as one who stays where he is and journeys through life as a Christian."

"Was he really a Christian?"

"Yes, he was. He was so lovable that even the clergymen of the Reformed faith loved him, and buried him in a crypt in the old Chapel of Lambeth where a reformer named John Wycliffe underwent an examination before some angry bishops of his day."

"Did Bishop Thirleby love the vicars?"

"Yes. While he spoke like a good Catholic, refusing to forsake his vows, he was filled with love for the reformers."

"I wish I could go to London."

"You will, John, and when you do, go to Lambeth, and look at the painting in the chapel's southeast window. You will see a man walking with a pack on his back, a staff in his hand, and a dog following him. That figure depicts Bishop Thirleby. It depicts me, John. It depicts you. And all pilgrims who take the stony path that leads to the Holy City.

"Bishop Thirleby asked to be buried in a pilgrim's clothes, and he was. They wrapped a pilgrim's traveling cloak about him, placed a staff at his side, and the slouched hat of a pilgrim under his arm. He wanted others to hear about it, and know that they are pilgrims in the world, too, seeking the road to the Holy City.

"Never forget Bishop Thirleby, son. Start living like a Christian. Then one day you will make a good soldier."

The next night, after Willie had gone to sleep, John sat brooding in the still family room. He was lonely. Papa had left after supper to work on the swords Colonel Okey had ordered. He was doing so unwillingly, and all afternoon he had been in an ugly mood.

A draft of cool air blew in, bringing with it the sweet smell of newly cut hay. The shutters creaked. Then there came the sudden pelting of rain, and John Knox jumped up, growling. As John got up to close the window, he heard voices, the sound of footsteps on the path, and laughter.

A moment later the door was thrust open, and John stared in disbelief as a woman came in, followed by Papa. The woman from the Swan Inn at Bedford. Rain dripped from her pink-cheeked face, and her eyes sparkled. The two paused when they saw John, and exchanged glances. Papa looked awkwardly at the stone-flagged floor.

"Ye're still up, John. I thought ye'd be in bed."

"Hello, John," the woman said in her too-loud voice. "Hello!"

Papa cleared his throat. "John, Anne and I were married this evening. She's your new ma."

John stiffened as if a whip had flayed him. Mama had been dead only two months and Papa was bringing this—this inn woman home to take her place. In God's name, how could he do such a thing? A sob rose in John's throat and choked him.

Anne came over and placed a hand on his shoulder. "Don't fret, John," she said, in a tone softer than her usual one. "Your pa loved your ma, but he was very lonely. I'll try to be good to ye, John. I can cook and weave and sew. It won't be so bad. Ye'll see!"

John stood still, his thoughts whirling. The thought came that Papa and Willie didn't need him any more. He could do as he pleased now. He liked Anne; he had always liked her. But Papa's hasty marriage was disrespectful to Mama.

He tore his thoughts from Mama and gave attention to Papa's

bride. He remembered the song she had sung the day he had first met her:

> A maid needs a man a-courtin';
> A good man, if such there be.
> A bad man's better'n no man,
> But a fair man I wish he'd be. . . .

Papa was a fair man. When he didn't have crooked stockings, he was good company. And he wasn't lazy; he would provide her wants. He wouldn't go on as many sprees now. But John wished Papa had waited. The neighbors would think he cared nothing for Mama. The haste was indecent. And John couldn't forgive him.

"I hope you'll be happy," he told them slowly, "but you could have waited, Papa."

With a look of contempt in his father's direction, John marched out of the room and up the stairs. In his bedroom he threw open the leaded window and drew up a stool to sit staring at the stars. I'm not rooted here like one of the great elms, he thought. Papa and Willie don't need me any more, and I have a notion of leaving.

5 THE SUN came out and quickened the November dawn, lighting the casual beauty of the barren trees and brown fields, spreading quickly to the white, low swell of the chalk hills as John began the twelve-mile march to Newport Pagnell with the other recruits. When he had signed up, he had lied about his age; he wouldn't be sixteen until the end of the month. He had left a note for Anne, asking her to take good care of Papa, Willie, and John Knox, and had slipped out of the cottage while it was still dark to join his fellow soldiers leaving from Bedford Market Place.

John had lied about something else. The recruiting officer had asked, "Are you a young man with religious convictions?"

John remembered that Colonel Cromwell wanted men like that. "Yes," he had answered piously, "I read my Bible, pray, and do good."

"Then ye can read?" John nodded and the officer had handed him two small volumes, *The Soldier's Pocket Bible* and *The Soldier's Catechism*. "Read them well," he had admonished.

As John marched long the curving road, the sun warmed the air. Black and white cows, standing in front of a stone barn, chewed unconcernedly. The road wound right, then left, right and left again past old stone walls enclosing brown fields dotted with sheep. When he reached the Abbey of Turvey, John thought of the Tinker of Turvey, who sometimes visited Papa. His heart sank a little at the realization that he was leaving work he had liked. He was, in fact, leaving everything he had ever known, going far away where he could forget the pain Papa's marriage had caused him.

When the men and boys reached Buckinghamshire, their steps lagged a little. The great round trunks of the elms were of gigantic size here, and fragrance wafted from a cluster of pines near a cemetery. At an old stone farmhouse near Olney, the captain called a halt.

John sat on the moss-spotted stone wall, swinging his legs. His feet hurt and his head ached. He wished he were home in bed, but Harry was stationed at Newport and it would be fun gossiping with him. A playful young recruit came up behind him and shoved him to the ground. As John let out a string of oaths and swung at the recruit, the balding captain approached and shouted a command to stand at attention. John noticed that he was glaring, his face as tart as a crab apple.

"Any soldier in this army who uses profanity will be punished!" he shouted. "What's your name?"

John told him.

"You are fined two shillings, Bunyan. If this happens again, you will ride the wooden horse!"

Two shillings. Just for swearing. Why, swearing was as natural to John as breathing! He was accustomed to Papa's outbursts, and to hearing men curse in the taverns Papa frequented, as well as on the streets or squares of neighboring towns and villages. The army might as well forbid a man to open his mouth.

"Aye, sir," he mumbled, because Captain Bladwell's eyes were blazing.

The captain addressed the men within earshot. "There will be no hard drinking, no swearing, no plundering, and no violence to women after victory. This troop will go into battle sober of mind, praying, and singing the Songs of David!"

His voice had such a ring of displeasure that some of the recruits cringed. A few said, "Aye, sir." The rest remained silent.

"This is God's army," the captain continued, "and you are God's men."

Something in John rebelled. He had a quick vision of himself being told what to think, how to pray, what to read, and what to say. *Was this the freedom men were fighting for?*

He clenched his hands tightly and blurted, "Not me! I will follow your orders in battle, sir, and at the garrison. But not even my captain's going to tell me what to think. Remember the Magna Carta!" His voice blared like a trumpet.

Actually he wasn't sure exactly what the Magna Carta said. He didn't know what it meant, except that it guaranted freedom and made common men a lot more important than King Charles thought they were.

For a moment Captain Bladwell's rough-hewn face was a mask of incredulity. The next instant it looked appropriately stern and an expression of anger tightened it.

"We shall see about that," he said shortly. "In addition to the two-shilling fine, which will come out of your first pay, you will ride the wooden horse!"

Conquering a momentary feeling of panic, John managed to speak in a clear voice. "I know Lieutenant Colonel Cromwell, sir, and he would not approve of any officer who attempts to control a man's thoughts!"

Some of the other men applauded. The captain whirled on them. "There will be discipline in this troop. I promise you all that!" His black eyes glittered as they turned back to John. "You have the right of appeal to Sir Samuel Luke, the Governor of the garrison, who sits on Friday mornings to hear complaints. Otherwise your punishment will be meted out at sundown tomorrow."

Mercifully at that moment an argument broke out between two recruits on the opposite side of the road. Captain Bladwell strode off to rebuke them.

A bearded youth standing nearby introduced himself to John as John White. "A captain who bears a grudge against a soldier can make his life miserable," he said. "Why did ye talk back to him?"

John didn't know why.

As they marched on, his pack seemed to grow heavier and

82

heavier. The soles of his feet began to burn in his round-toed boots, and his lips felt parched. The sun was sinking as the column rounded the last curve where the Ouse and the Louvat rivers met. John's sense of excitement returned. He marched up Sherrington Hill with renewed strength, and gazed across a swampy plain toward the town.

Situated halfway between Nottingham and London, Newport was a thriving center. To the left sprawled Tickford Abbey, a monastery for Cluniac monks until the last century when the Act for the Dissolution of Monasteries had emptied it. It was known that the Parliamentary sympathizers outnumbered the Royalists in Newport. As the men marched across the three-arched bridge which spanned the Ouse and past St. John's Church with its tall weathervane, John was reminded of St. Cuthbert's, and homesickness for Bedford and Elstow struck him.

As they passed into the town, he noted that the houses along the High Street had been built close to each other. Here, too, there was an inn with the picture of a swan like the sign on Bedford's Swan Inn, and again he felt a momentary nostalgia. The life for Bedford was centered in the Swan Inn and, except for Papa's brawls, John's memories of it were happy ones.

With eight hundred soldiers in the garrison, Governor Luke found it necessary to maintain strict discipline. He listened to the men's appeals and complaints and displayed fairness in the decisions he rendered.

A clean-shaven man with good features, which included deep-set brown eyes, the Governor sat on a bench in his headquarters at the Saracen's Head and gave John a shrewd, appraising look. There was no rigidity about his back that suggested stubbornness, but there was an air of independence that suggested individuality. The Governor's secretary, Samuel Butler, sat at his right reading and making notes on some ivory parchment. His big, comic mouth seemed to turn down as his blob of a nose moved up.

"Now," Sir Samuel said, "what is your reason, young man, for appealing your captain's sentence?"

John answered with his customary glibness, in spite of the breathlessness within him, stating that he thought a soldier should be free to decide whether he wanted to use profanity or not!

Sir Samuel was quiet for a long moment, frowning. At length he spoke: "Bunyan, you are very young to be defending the taking of the Lord's name in vain."

"Then the Parliamentary Army is not fighting for freedom of thought?"

"That is one end we're fighting for. In this garrison we allow different views within certain limits of belief, but we have to take into consideration the morale of the entire army. For that reason we have a rule that there is to be no profanity. My decision is that your captain's recommendations for punishment are to be carried out."

A gesture of dismissal brought the audience to an end.

At sundown the entire garrison was summoned to witness the discipline meted out to a rebellious recruit. Drums rolled as John climbed up on two boards which had been nailed to four wooden legs. At a signal from Captain Bladwell two muskets, which had been tied together, were fastened to each of John's limbs. His hands were bound behind his back and a placard was fastened around his neck with the word BLASPHEMER lettered on it in red paint. The captain read his punishment, stating that he had been heard using profanity and was being dealt with accordingly. John had the impression that he was not enjoying what he had to do. The beardless boys all about John stared solemnly as the captain concluded with the warning that upon a third breech of this rule a soldier would have his tongue cleft! The captain dismissed the group and the men wandered off. Only Harry lingered.

"John," he whispered when they were alone, "I know a couple of wantons who live down by the river." He winked and a lewd grin came over his coarse features. "Time you became a man."

"I want none of them," John said shortly. "And you can go away and let me be!"

"I've always suspected you weren't very bright, John. All right.

I'll leave you. Pretty soon your muscles will pain so that ye'll wish ye had some exciting memories to help you forget!"

With a curse Harry turned on his heel and strode off.

John's temper flared. Even before Harry had left Elstow, he had allowed full rein to the lust that flowed in his blood. John had seen him sneaking into the Ellensbury woods with Theny Talbot, who was notorious in Bedford and the surrounding countryside. She drank strong waters and poked food into her mouth all day until she was a blowsy slattern. Harry beheld each girl he saw with a mental smacking of his lips, as if she were a little lamb waiting to be gobbled. He bragged of his conquests and the other youths had to listen. At such times John remembered that there were women like Mama and Margaret, and he hated Harry.

He was soon in agony as the heavy muskets stretched his muscles. He tried to think of happy things such as the hours he had spent wandering the woods and fields with Margaret, fishing, hunting, and exploring.

The hour wore on, and then another, until the pain made him moan. How can I avoid profanity when I've heard it all my life? But I'll try. It isn't worth this punishment, he thought wearily, just before he fainted.

No soldier could be out after nine at night, for the curfew was strictly enforced. John, billeted with Harry, since they were both from Elstow, had a double problem. Breeches continued to be scarce and they shared one pair. One had to be in bed while the other was up. More were expected, but John's had been taken away to give to two other men.

John piously offered to stay at home on Thursday nights when church attendance was compulsory, so that on Friday nights he could wear the breeches and stroll along the High Street at dusk. He dreaded the time when the new clothing arrived, because he hated the long sermons preached to the troops. It was bad enough to have to attend one of the Sunday Services, and he knew that, once he was supplied with a uniform, he would have to be present on Thursday night, too.

One night he started for a gambling hole, where the dicebox rattled. As he passed Cowley's Book Shop, he noticed in the window a beautiful copy of *St. George and the Dragon,* opened to a picture of St. George facing the beast. The knight wore a red tunic and his dark hair curled over shining armor which covered only the front of his body, so that he had to fight facing his antagonist.

There was a light burning within the shop, and a man with wispy gray hair hanging below his shoulders sat at a small table at the back of the square room. As John opened the door, the man lifted watery blue eyes and peered at him through narrow spectacles.

"*St. George and the Dragon* is my favorite book," John said apologetically. "May I look at the copy in the window?"

The little man smiled. "Yes, indeed. It does me good to find a young man who appreciates books. My name is Matthias Cowley and I own this shop."

He rose and walked to the window, took the volume out and handed it to John. "Have a chair. Stay and read as long as you like. There are other books on the shelves."

John thanked him, and was soon lost once more in his hero's battles. The print was large and easy to read. There were several pictures, all in color. John thought he had never seen such a lovely book.

"Wouldn't you like to look at some other books while you're here?" Mr. Cowley invited.

Two hours passed, as John fondly handled the beautiful leather bindings, and read portions of the books that interested him most. He forgot about the curfew until suddenly the sound of the watchman's voice brought him to reality: "Nine o'clock and all is well except for those who be not in their beds. Lock your doors and put out the cat. See that you do not neglect that."

John leaped up, replaced the book he had been reading, said a hasty good night, and ran out of the door into the High Street. He arrived at the barracks just after the guard had locked the iron-studded gate. He pounded on the wood until the gate swung

86

open, and he was allowed to enter. He knew that he would be summoned before Captain Bladwell in the morning and that punishment would be meted out. In spite of that he dreamed all night about the beautiful books.

A week later when he returned to the book shop, Mr. Cowley looked up from his table, smiling.

"I thought you were a young man who would be back," he said.

John had been reading for over an hour when he heard the door open. Two girls about twelve and fourteen came in, followed by a pretty round-eyed child of perhaps four or five. It was the sight of the older girl that caused John's heart to hammer. Slender and of medium height, the hood of her cloak was thrown back revealing yellow hair flowing about her shoulders. Her cheeks were pink from the cold as she glanced up at him with blue eyes framed in long lashes. John stared at her high breasts and curved young figure. She was very pretty. The girl with her, in contrast, had brown hair, emerald eyes, and a fuller figure.

"Girls!" the bookseller greeted, and his eyes seemed to warm. "It's a cold night for you to be out."

"May I light the fire, Papa?" the fair-haired girl asked. "We have been walking and looking in windows, and we are chilled."

"Of course," he said, and continued tooling some leather.

John watched the girl strike the flint against steel. A spark flew at the tinder and a red glow spread. She reached for the leather bellows on a peg beside the hearth, and as she worked them the flame hissed against the logs and sticks. Memories stirred within John and he could see Margaret lighting the fire in the cottage at Elstow. The older girls warmed their fingers, and the youngest one pranced about, radiating good spirits.

"My young friend, I want you to meet my wife's stepdaughter, Mary Roberts," the bookseller said. "This is her friend, Jane Lane, who is visiting her." He indicated the other girl.

"And I'm Elizabeth Barnes," the child said, running toward him. "They call me Bitsy. You may call me Bitsy, too."

John smiled. The child didn't look like the sister he had lost.

Her eyes were dark with long lashes, and her hair, which curled about her shoulders, was as black as a black rook's ring. But she had the fire Margaret had had and also the capacity for friendship.

"My name's John, Bitsy. Do you live here?"

She nodded. "My father has a butcher shop near the Swan. Mary Roberts is my cousin and Jane Lane is my friend. Will you be my friend, too?"

He thought he had never seen such an appealing child. "Yes," he said, "I want to be your friend."

When the older girls approached, plying him with questions, a warm glow spread through him, almost as if the fire they had started on the hearth had been transferred to him. How did he like life in the Roundhead Army? Had he ever seen General Cromwell? Their eyes bugged when he told them he had fished with him. What was the General like when you knew him? Have you seen any action? Were the manor houses and the estates of the Royalists around here to be besieged?

His answers grew guarded. Why were these girls so interested? Just what was Mary Roberts' special concern?

"Mary is of the state religion," the bookseller explained, as if he read John's mind. "Her father, my wife's first husband, had a living in Worcester. Her mother died and he married my wife. Mary's father was tortured by some rebels when Sir Lewis Dyve, mistaking his orders, marched out and left his fortress to the Parliamentary troops."

"Papa Matthias, I am trying to remember that General Cromwell is changing the Parliamentary rebels. 'Tis said the New Model Army has no more murderers, torturers, thieves, tapsters, rogues, or monsters. It will soon be an army of religious men. But I still don't believe they can beat the King, Princes Maurice and Rupert, and their well-trained Cavaliers!"

John sensed that she was acting. There was a glint in her blue eyes that belied the smile on her face. She hated Cromwell and all Parliamentary men. He could hardly believe her. What was she up to? And did she hate him, too?

"Nobody should have to suffer in order to worship as he chooses," he said slowly, watching her.

"Are you a dissenter, Mr. Bunyan? Or a papist?"

"Ye hate both?"

She stared back at him as if he had struck her. She was disconcerted and her answer was an evasion. "The Anglican faith is the faith of England."

"No longer, Mary," Mr. Cowley intervened. "Presbyterianism is rapidly becoming the national religion."

"The King is the head of the Church and he is an Anglican."

"I take it you would brook no other faith," John said quietly.

Mr. Cowley came to her rescue. "Young man, indulge our Mary. Permit her to cling to her beliefs. She left all her friends to come and make her home here. She is very young."

His tone dismissed the matter and John said no more, but he was certain that Mary had Royalist sentiments and would bear watching. Her attitude was in keeping with all he had heard about Worcester and its vicinity. It was almost curfew time, so, bowing politely, he said good night.

The following Thursday, when he went back to the shop, he found the white-haired bookseller alone. Once again he greeted John with a friendly smile and pointed him to the shelves where the books were kept.

Within the hour Mary came in alone, wearing an apricot cloak and a black velvet bonnet with a yellow feather. A smile lit her face when she saw him.

"Oh, Mr. Bunyan, I've been thinking how wonderful it must be to be a soldier. I wish I were a man," she gushed.

Before he could reply, she started asking questions again. Were his missions exciting? Had he been on one that week?

"I have been assigned to one in the morning," he told her, thinking there was no harm in that.

"Is the captain a man of honor?"

"You yourself said that General Cromwell was building a great army."

"And so he is," she said meekly. "Don't you agree, Papa Matthias?"

"Indeed I do," the bookseller said, without looking up.

As John walked back to the barracks, he had again the feeling that Mary was a girl to watch. Yet he had to admit that her fresh beauty and feminine appeal tugged at his heart. For an instant, when he thought of her eyes, which were as blue as the sky, and of her disarming smile, he told himself it was ridiculous to suspect she was spying to get information for the King's Army. She certainly didn't look like a spy.

The next morning, as John was dressing to join the detail, Harry came to him and begged to go in his place. "I'll make it all right with Captain Bladwell," he said eagerly. "I am so bored I'll go crazy if I can't get away. Please, John. I'll give you three shillings when we get our back pay."

Three shillings! To John, who was trying to save enough to buy his own tools when he got out of the army, that was a lot of money. He wanted to go on the mission, but he reluctantly agreed to let Harry take his place.

That night when the troop marched into the barracks, John looked for Harry. He wanted to hear about the day's siege. But Harry was not with the others!

"Your friend was hit in the head with a bullet as he stood watch in your place," Captain Bladwell informed him bluntly. "The Lord must have some special work for you to do to spare you. If you had come with us today, you would have been lying in his grave."

"Harry dead!" John exclaimed. "And he was standing guard in my place!"

He couldn't believe it. Not Harry, his playmate on Elstow Green, his companion on many escapades, a schoolmate he had known as well as a brother.

He couldn't sleep that night. His thoughts dwelt on Harry, who had often been selfish. And mean. And immoral. He had blasphemed God and man. Trembling, John reached toward the empty space on the bed he had shared with Harry. Where was he now? Was he standing before God, the terrible judge?

A chill wind seemed to blow on John's spirit as he meditated. Doubt and terror assailed him. Questions tumbled through his brain—questions about eternal punishment, hell, the damned soul, death, heaven, the universe, the purpose of man. Harry's voice echoed in his ears: "What would the Devil do if it were not for such as I?" "Could I be saved if I appeared before the tribunal of a terrible judge?" John asked himself. *"Is Harry damned?"*

For days the garrison buzzed with talk of Harry's death, and John brooded. The shock slowly passed, but not the anguish caused by John's fears. The thing that had happened to Harry might easily have happened to him. His friend, Harry, was gone, and John realized anew that the hereafter was frighteningly mysterious. He began listening to the long sermons and reading the *Soldier's Bible* and *Soldier's Catechism*. His heart wrenched sickly, and black depression settled over him every time he thought of the state of his own soul.

6 ONE DAY, late in May, John entered Cowley's Bookshop and found Colonel Okey standing in one corner in deep conversation with the shop owner. They looked like conspirators, for their voices were low, their manner almost furtive. John found himself wishing he was near enough to overhear what they were saying.

In a few minutes Mary came in, followed by Samuel Butler, the Governor's secretary. Seeing her laughing and talking with a man as clever as Mr. Butler brought John a twinge of jealousy. Mr. Butler, who was in his middle thirties, wrote verse that Mary read and often quoted. She bowed to John and went to the shelves where she began dusting the leather-bound books.

"Is it difficult to write what's deep within you?" John asked the poet.

"If you want others to believe something you cherish, young man, try putting it on parchment. The pen is mightier than General Cromwell's sword!"

"Is it indeed?" John was incredulous.

"Take the poet, John Milton. He has put aside his poetic ambition to champion three kinds of liberty—religious, domestic, and political. He first published *Of Reformation Touching Church Government*, a few months later *Of Prelatical Episcopacy*, and the following year, 1642, *The Reason of Church Government*. His passion for a just victory over tyranny burns in his writings!"

92

"I wish I could read them."

"You may," Mary offered. "Papa Matthias has all of them. He swears by them."

"And you, Mary?"

She avoided his eyes. "He can write. As Mr. Butler says, he burns with his beliefs."

"I wish I were an educated man like John Milton!" John sighed. "There are things within a man that would out."

"A man. You look like a stripling to me," Mr. Butler said in an ironical tone, and his green eyes seemed to smile by themselves.

John's face flooded with color. In that instant he felt very small, and he wished he could dive under Mr. Cowley's table.

But Colonel Okey, having finished his conversation, was thumping past him. He lifted his hazel eyes and stopped walking.

"So you are a soldier! It does my heart good to see Thomas Bunyan's eldest son in the uniform of Cromwell's Army."

"I wasn't conscripted. I joined. I believe in the Parliamentary cause, sir. My grandfather believed in it."

"But your father doesn't. We had to browbeat him to get him to make crude weapons for a company of dragoons I command at Windsor."

"Then ye have seen him of late?"

"A few days ago. Did you know that you have a new brother born in Elstow? Your father had the nerve to have him christened Charles!"

John hadn't heard. He saw no reason to say that his father, as long as he lived, would favor the King. Men were hung for less. While he stared back at Colonel Okey, trying to figure what to say, Mary joined them and sank in a curtsey with a billowing of her blue gown and a swish of petticoats. A smile had replaced the solemn expression on her face.

"We have missed you, Colonel Okey. You must have been very busy of late."

"A command such as I have does keep a man busy."

"And what is taking place at Windsor, Colonel Okey? Are

affairs so complicated that I cannot count on John Bunyan's company for supper next Sunday?" Her voice was so casual that it concealed her probing.

Colonel Okey grinned. "The garrison should be able to manage without John's services on Sunday afternoon."

"Then you will be in Newport on Sunday?"

John hesitated. He had the feeling her questions were not as innocent as they seemed. "I may be ordered to help defend Leicester," he lied, watching her.

"Leicester?" Colonel Okey exploded. "I've heard nothing about a possible attack on Leicester!"

"Details about the war and what is to happen might bore Mary, sir. May I walk outside with you?"

Colonel Okey's eyebrows were raised. "Yes, indeed. Come."

"I need exercise," Mary said quickly. "I've been in all day. May I come for the walk?"

"No. Confidential talk," John said. "Another time."

Her face fell as Colonel Okey reached for the latch.

When the heavy door swung noisily open and the night air enveloped them, he said, "Bunyan, I am glad you came with me. I was followed to the bookshop tonight. Newport is full of the King's spies. I may have need of your brawny arms." Then, after a moment's silence: "What about this defense of Leicester?"

"Y-you see, sir, Mary Roberts has Royalist sympathies. Jane Lane, a daughter of a Royalist officer, Colonel John Lane, has been visiting her. Mary's father was an Anglican clergyman who died at the hands of some of our troops."

"Then you think she is a spy? It could be. Matthias Cowley is our ears in Newport. I have just returned from a secret mission for General Cromwell. I've been in Scotland where I learned that King Charles is vowing to finish us before the end of the summer."

"The Scots will help him?"

"Yes. The Marquis of Montrose has agreed to come to England to help check what he called the 'insurrection' here."

The colonel kept looking back, and John found himself turning, too, to stare at the shadows, as Colonel Okey led the way. There came the sound of thudding footsteps and the colonel paused.

"We'll have to make a stand for it, Bunyan."

Colonel Okey's sword came out, gleaming in the blackness and John reached for his own short blade.

What followed was like a nightmare. A tall, broad-shouldered man and a band of three formed a semicircle, their blades glinting as they converged on Colonel Okey all at once. There was the clink of steel. In the blackness the leader looked like William Vierney. John lifted his blade and hurled it at the nearest assailant.

The man gave a cry of pain and dropped heavily. Colonel Okey pressed himself against the wall and John reached for the fallen man's sword. Lifting it, he attacked one of the remaining men. The leader fled into the Quiet Woman, a neighboring coffeehouse. With Colonel Okey's help, the other two men were soon stretched on the cobbles.

"Footpads?" John asked.

"Not ordinary footpads. They must know I am carrying some papers from General Leslie to General Cromwell.

"For a minute I thought I recognized the big one. He looked like my old schoolmaster, William Vierney, from Bedford, who is said to spy for the King."

"Vierney? Which way did he go?"

"Into the Quiet Woman."

"Come. Let's go after him."

John moved behind the colonel, under the painted sign of a headless woman done in red and black, and through the heavy door. The Quiet Woman, a coffeehouse and infamous sink of iniquity, was frequented by the scum of the army, footpads, and tapsters. The raftered room was thronged and noisy, but conversation died like a blown candle when John and Captain Okey entered. A blue haze of smoke hung over the bar where a servingman was pouring steaming black coffee from a copper kettle and cooling it with raw brandy. A frowzy woman was lolling at the bar, and a dozen or more men sat at the tables before tall tankards. William Vierney was nowhere to be seen. John began to believe that his imagination had played him a trick.

"Did a tall man come in here just now?" Colonel Okey bellowed, his hand on the hilt of his sword.

Nobody answered him. John stared at each man. None of them resembled the hated schoolmaster.

The woman at the bar, unusually tall for a woman, had turned her back and seemed to be trying to hide her face. John walked around her slowly. The dark face froze and glittering black eyes looked into John's. They belonged to William Vierney.

John reached for a tankard on the bar before him, and set it hurtling at Master Vierney's evil face. Several of the other men rose and began converging on them.

Colonel Okey called to John. "Come, Bunyan. Quickly. We can't fight eight."

John slipped around the end of the bar near the door, eluded the men, and joined the Colonel. They began running along the narrow street toward the Saracen's Head. Just before they reached the inn, Colonel Okey paused in a darkened doorway. There was a click of a latch and a door swung open. John stepped quickly through it, following the Colonel, and the bolt slid into place.

The room inside was lighted by a single candle. A man rose from a narrow cot, rubbing his eyes.

"That you, Okey?" a deep voice asked.

John stared, unable to believe his senses. The man was Oliver Cromwell. He stood tall, his large brooding eyes troubled.

"I had the devil of a time reaching you. I was followed and attacked. If it hadn't been for this young man, I fear the papers would have fallen into enemy hands."

Oliver Cromwell raised his thick brows and his mouth fell open.

"You?" he whispered.

Colonel Okey looked surprised. "You know each other?"

96

"Young Bunyan was my fishing teacher," General Cromwell said with a laugh. "Whenever I have to think and rest, I find the best fishing spot around and catch a string of fish with some very special bait, honey balls!"

Two weeks later King Charles rode north, storming Leicester and attacking the eastern counties. The King was resplendent in royal ermine and black breastplate; his Cavaliers wore chain mail, gauntlet gloves, and cuffed leather boots. "The Marquis of Montrose is on his way from Scotland to help us subdue the rebels," the King was reported to have told his nephew, Prince Rupert. "There will soon be an end to the insurrection of England!"

John was one of the foot soldiers called out to march in Cromwell's newly trained brigade, which was to join Lord Fairfax who was coming from a siege of Oxford. On June 14 at Naseby, a small village in the Midlands, the Parliamentary Army met the King's forces.

Wearing steel helmets, the Roundheads went into battle waving Cromwell's flag, the Cross of St. George, and reciting the Forty-first Psalm:

"The Lord will preserve him and keep him alive; and he shall be blessed upon the earth; and thou wilt not deliver him into the hands of his enemies. . . ."

Every soldier there trusted General Cromwell. Many of the men worshiped him. He flung himself into the thickest part of the fighting. His courage, and sincere belief that he was doing God's will made him a natural leader. At his signal the trumpeter sounded the charge. "God is with us!" the General roared, his square jaw set, his armored doublet vivid red in the sunlight. Sitting straight in his leather saddle, he flourished his sword and urged his horse into a canter.

Amid the thunder of hoofs and swirls of dust, men in armored breastplates charged the enemy in their high-plumed hats, fine uniforms, orange sashes, and expensive leather boots.

The confusion was terrible as Prince Rupert of Bavaria rushed up the hill carrying the Stuart banner, cutting through with his sword, attacking the flank of General Ireton's brigade. "For King Charles and Queen Marie!" he shouted, riding recklessly, shouting encouragement to his Bluecoat Cavalry.

In the fierce fighting that followed, John's powder ignited spontaneously, throwing the men about him into a panic. He had some minor burns before the fire was extinguished.

When he faced the enemy once more, he couldn't turn his back because his breastplate covered only the front. There was but one course—to fight in a hand-to-hand engagement. A big Cavalier aimed his blade at John's head. John ducked, but lost his footing on the moor, now slippery with blood of men and horses. John White, seeing his plight, circled the Cavalier and dug his sword into the man's heart. John's knitted and tasseled Monmouth cap was lost in the scuffle. A sword ripped his cotton stocking, tearing the flesh of his leg, from which blood spurted. The brown doublet and breeches, that had cost him seventeen shillings, were torn, too.

A line of Roundheads swarmed like ants over a high hill, and Prince Rupert led his Bluecoats through the right lines. Butchery followed when the King's foot troops attacked the trained New Model men under General Fairfax. The long blades of the pikemen ripped into the flesh of man and beast. Colonel Okey's dragoons charged. The King's reserve marched against the Broad Moor in the center of the battlefield where General Cromwell and his brigade engaged them.

Then suddenly John saw the Royalist lines scatter, and volleying ceased. The enemy was in retreat and General Cromwell's cavalry was riding after them. The King's Guards were retreating, too, protecting him as they went, while the royal infantry was being slaughtered. The Bluecoats, riding after Prince Rupert, formed a man-made wall to aid the King's scarlet-coated men, until the King had escaped toward the northeast and the mountains of Wales.

When John heard the news of the King's escape, somehow he

wasn't sorry. If King Charles could be persuaded that his rule wasn't absolute, he would make a good King. And after all, he was the King.

John could see hundreds of bodies lying in untidy rows with soldiers walking gingerly between them searching for the living.

The morning after the battle when John was with some soldiers around a barrel of cider a citizen of Naseby had sent, General Cromwell appeared out of nowhere!

"Men, you know the rules!" he thundered. "We're not through fighting. You need to keep your bodies fit. Milk will be better." He spoke with such ferocity that the men paled.

Colonel Bladwell came up just then to announce that Sir Samuel had ordered a public thanksgiving. The soldiers attended, but all day and far into the night they celebrated and the little tavern at Naseby rocked with song and laughter. Temporarily Oliver Cromwell and the other officers were so busy reading the King's secret papers, which had been left at his headquarters, that they were too busy to mete out the usual punishments.

That night hundreds of campfires were lighted and ale was brought in. John was sitting against a rock wishing he were back in Newport with Mary when a plump little trollop walked up with a deliberate swinging of her hips.

"Like me?" she asked, seating herself brazenly on his lap.

For an instant her nearness made him giddy. But as she brought her face close to his and he saw the obscene glitter in her eyes, he thought again of Mary. He leaped to his feet with an oath, shoving her to the ground. She landed with a resounding plop, and all the men around howled with laughter.

The following day word spread through the camp that the King's papers had revealed a treaty between the King and the Irish Confederated Catholics in which he agreed to all their demands in return for military assistance. He had agreed to the demands of the Scotch Protestants, too! He would agree to anything to gain a victory.

"We can leave the King and his treachery to God!" General

Cromwell told the assembled troops. "God has shown us that He will by things which are not bring to nought things that are."

It was a week before John saw Mary again. He was about to enter the Quiet Woman when she came down the street in the twilight, eating an apple. How trim her figure was. Even if she had Royalist sympathies, her blue eyes and her corn-colored hair were beautiful.

"Good evening, John Bunyan. How does it feel to be a conqueror?"

"It had to be, Mary. The King was doing everything illegally."

She frowned. "What will happen now to people like Jane Lane, her brother Charles, their father, the colonel, and others who honestly believe the King's rule should be absolute?"

"I don't know. I only know no man should have that much power over the lives and consciences of others."

She moved close, lifting her lips invitingly. He did not intend to take her in his arms and kiss her, but he did. And to his amazement, she did not struggle; she kissed him back. The war's almost over, he thought. She isn't doing this just so I will answer her questions. She likes me!

"Let's take a walk," she suggested. "You will be going home so soon."

"Shall we see each other again?"

"I hope so, John."

He slipped his arm around her tiny waist, and they strolled up High Street and down to the river, on past the church and then back. They talked about themselves, their childhood, their dreams, before she spoke of the garrison.

"Sir Samuel Luke is to return to London to take up his duties there, since the Self-denying Ordinance required that he give up his command."

John was surprised. He hadn't heard. Where did Mary get her information? Sir Samuel had been a severe governor, but he was respected for his fairness. John supposed his Uncle Edward, who was the Governor's personal servant, would go with him. John had purposely avoided his kinsman, for fear his age at mustering in might somehow be revealed if they met.

When General Fairfax marched immediately into Sometshire, routing the King's Army at Langport and again at Kilsyth, John did not accompany the Parliamentary or Roundhead forces. But that fall of 1645 he was sent to the siege of Basing House and took part in the fighting that resulted in the defeat of the Marquis of Winchester.

Captain Bladwell called John to his tent the night the siege ended.

"I have received a request from Colonel Okey to send you to Bristol," he said. "You have made yourself a reputation for being a good scout, even if you are a rogue and a blasphemer. Colonel Okey believes the Prince of Wales is hiding in the West. If he can be found and captured, our negotiations with the King will be easier."

The captain went on to explain that earlier in the year the King had sent his son Charles into the West. He was now the Duke of Cornwall, General of the Western Association, and a general of the King's forces in Wales and England. He had been living in a castle on the Scilly Isles, but he had eluded Edward Hyde and the other Royalist politicians.

"Are they seeking James Stuart, the Duke of York, too?" John asked.

"Lord Fairfax is after him, but it is Charles Stuart's capture that will make the Parliamentary victory complete."

"You want me to capture him?"

"No!" Captain Bladwell said impatiently. "Your job is to scout around, and if you locate him get word to Colonel Okey!"

"What if I am captured?"

"We will give you a Royalist cloak, cap, and shoes. In the baggage you will take there is a wig and the doublet and breeches of a Royalist officer. If you should be accosted by men on our side, you will have to explain. Of course they might not believe you, so the mission is dangerous. But to carry papers proving

101

your identity would be more dangerous. Do you still want to go?"

"Yes."

Two days later at twilight, John was riding cautiously through a thick woods near Windsor when a trumpet sounded and a voice rang out. He dismounted and moved toward the edge of a clearing, from which he could see a large troop of Royalists encamped on the banks of the Severn. Hidden in the thicket, he watched them unlace their armor, back and breastplates. Soon the smell of joints basting filled the countryside and John realized that he was hungry.

He lay on his stomach listening and watching the Royalists until the autumn moon had climbed above the treetops, and multitudes of stars peeped between the branches. He went for his horse, but to his consternation, the animal had wandered off. In his excitement he had forgotten to tether it.

Suddenly he was frightened. All about him were the enemies of freedom. The long black shadows cast by the tall oaks covered him with a protective dark. Closing his eyes he slept, hemmed in by the King's men.

When he awoke, it was still night. Except for three sentries who marched back and forth in the firelight, the Royalists lay in their blanket rolls. John wanted to continue toward the West to seek information as to the whereabouts of the Prince, but without a horse he realized travel would be difficult.

Carefully he circled the camp, keeping out of sight until he reached the edge of a vast clearing. Then he began to run and was halfway across the open space when he heard a sentry bellow, "Man deserting."

A shot rang out, but the sentry was out of range. John ran on, and within a few minutes there came the thud of galloping hoofs. He turned and saw some black shapes on horseback coming after him. He dived into thick shrubbery which scratched his arms and face, but he couldn't penetrate very far because of the long thorns on the bushes. He lay still, hoping his pursuers would pass.

102

As he drew back so that the soldiers would not see him, he touched something warm and his heart seemed to stand still. As torchlights lit the darkness John's eyes almost popped out of their sockets. A leg was sticking out not far from him.

"Creep back, whoever you are. Your leg shows," John whispered.

The leg was withdrawn just before the horsemen galloped past.

"Sit up now," John said, after all was quiet once more.

To John's surprise a youth in a tattered uniform and close-fitting skull helmet of the Parliamentary Army crawled out from the thicket. John stared at him intently. He was nobody John had ever seen before. He was tall with large bright eyes, and had long black hair which looked as if it had been notched by a knife and rounded by shears. In the starlight his complexion appeared swarthy, and his ugly mouth had a thick lower lip. He was clean-shaven and young. And there was an air of dignity about him that appealed to John.

"My name's Will Jones," he said. "I'm a woodman at Woburn Abbey, a new recruit in Colonel Okey's brigade at Windsor. I got separated from a patrol sent out to see what was happening. I wouldn't want the King's men to take me."

Will didn't have the accent of a country fellow, and when John mentioned it, the soldier said he had formerly lived in London and had but recently moved to Woburn.

John explained his own disguise and asked if the patrol had had any news of the Prince of Wales.

"You are looking for Prince Charles? I heard that Lord Wilmot was keeping such a close watch over him that he escaped so that he could have a little peace. Why must you hunt him down as if he were an animal? The Roundheads have victory. Why can't you let the Prince alone?"

"I wouldn't do him any bodily harm for all the gold in England! I honor the Prince as I do his father. But I believe that the King errs in claiming absolute power. He owes freedom to his subjects, and it's your colonel who sent me to find him. If the Prince could be held captive, the negotiations with his father would be simpler."

"I realize how precious freedom can be."

"The King is not God."

The young man sighed. "You would protect the life of that rogue, Charles Stuart, if need be?"

"I would give my own life for him!"

"There is a plot in Parliament to capture, imprison, and kill him. His life hangs by a strand of wool. If anything happened to the King, some would prefer that there should be no son to rally to."

"There are many who fight under Cromwell's flag who would never allow murder. God save the King! As for Prince Charles, one day England may need him!"

"Maybe. I pray so!"

John nodded. "I wonder what he's like."

"I know. He visits the Earl of Bedford at Woburn. The Earl started out on the side of Parliament, but now he serves the King. Young Charles has the looks of his mother, Queen Henrietta Maria. But his disposition is more like his father's. Odd's fish! What a reputation he has with women, even scullery maids."

"I hope Colonel Okey doesn't find him."

The youth's black eyes narrowed. "Odd's fish. I wonder if it was Colonel Okey's own idea to capture him."

John caught his breath. He didn't want to give too much information to anyone, even a fellow Roundhead. "Maybe," he said cautiously.

"Perhaps it would be just as well if he were caught."

"Why do you say that?"

"The Prince is not a very admirable young man."

"Then we should get along fine together." John snickered. "Me, a tinker, and his Highness, the Prince of Wales!"

"Odd's fish. That's not so hard to imagine. I think he would like you. You are of the stuff great Englishmen are made of! But he would soon make a Royalist out of you."

They moved back along the edge of the clearing until they found a place where the shrubbery was not so thick and thorn-laden, and here they stretched out for the rest of the night. . . .

John woke to find his companion sitting beside him holding a sheep's bladder of water. A yellow sun painted the sky over them.

"Why didn't you wake me, Will?" John demanded, sitting up and rubbing his eyes.

"I was sleeping hard myself. I have been awake only long enough to find a stream. King's men are gone." He coughed so hard he wheezed, and John slapped him hard on the back.

Will handed him the bladder, and as John drank thirstily, he noticed that Will's face was livid and he was trembling.

"You have a fever!" he said.

Will smiled feebly. "If we can just get to Windsor, I have friends near there."

"But you are not able to travel!"

"I must."

They started pushing toward Windsor, moving quietly over the pine-needled carpet, trying to stay under cover. Each time they heard hoofbeats they managed to get out of sight. By late afternoon Will's coughing was almost incessant, and John put his arm around him and helped him along. How weary he was himself. His bones ached with fatigue.

"I can't go any farther," Will murmured just before darkness fell.

"We'll camp for the night," John said. "There's a creek over there. I'll try to catch some fish for our supper."

Will lay down on a mossy knoll in a thick part of the forest, and John took off his own cloak and covered him with it. Then he lit a fire, got out a hook, some bread and honey, and went fishing.

Just as he was returning from the creek with two fat fish, he heard voices. It was dark and torches flared in the blackness, circling through the trees. John watched, his heart beating violently.

"What's that?" Will whispered, sitting up.

"The King's men. See the scarlet doublets!"

Will stared. "You're right. The King's own guards in scarlet coats and pantaloons. We'll never escape now."

He managed to scramble to his feet, his black hair hanging over his forehead, and his deep black eyes mysterious pools. He seemed older now, and he had, somehow, the air of being master of the situation.

"Don't panic," he said. "Let me handle this. Get up that tree and stay out of sight. Whatever you hear or see, keep your mouth shut!"

John wondered later why he had obeyed, but he did. Quick as a cockroach, he climbed up the giant elm.

"Give me quarter!" Will called, waving his arms so that the guards could see him. "In the name of the King!"

The soldiers approached swiftly. An order to halt was given, and the men sprang from their saddles.

Then out of the darkness below John heard Will's voice, "Men, I need your assistance. I am the Prince of Wales. I am ill of a fever, and unable to reach Windsor."

Such boldness stunned John. His heart was heavy with misgivings, as the guards surrounded Will, pointing their swords and muskets. Just as John was about to leap down on a big man directly below his hiding place, one of the men let out a roar.

"Your Highness! We have scoured the country for you. Are you well? Unharmed? My Lord Wilmot will be relieved that you have not been captured by those rebels!"

With a mixture of surprise and respect the men-at-arms stared at the young woodman.

"I am well, thanks to one of those rebels. He may have saved my life, for I have an ague. He covered me, built a fire, fed me. He cared for me as tenderly as a mother."

"We will pursue him!" the leader said.

"No, we will not go after him!"

"Whatever you wish, your Highness."

Poor Will's mind is unhinged, John thought, but the fool Cavaliers believe him. Breathlessly he watched as they knelt and kissed the hand Will held out to them. Then Will took off his dark doublet and tight breeches, buff accoutrements, and iron skull cap, and piled them at the foot of the tree.

"I will leave my disguise. I no longer have need of it," he said casually without looking up. "Somebody might need it. Now, some clothes, if you please."

One of the men undid his saddle roll and took out a pair of breeches and a red doublet such as he himself wore.

Will put them on, and a few minutes later he rode off, shepherded by the men in the bright-plumed hats and red uniforms of the King's guards. When the clop-clop of horses' hoofs had died away in the distance, John climbed down from his hiding place and changed his clothes.

Dressed like a Parliamentary soldier again, he began to travel toward Windsor. He was free, but he was worried about Will. What would the Cavaliers do to him when they discovered the trick he had played upon them? John was tempted to try to overtake them to rescue Will. But he was on foot and their horses were swift. He began to pray one of the few prayers he ever made which was not in the Prayer Book: "God, I know you're there. I don't have much in common with you. I'm such a wicked lout. But Will has courage; he's worth six of me. Save him from those cold-hearted Cavaliers! Amen."

Darkness covered Windsor. The big clock struck twelve clanging strokes just as the sentries around Colonel Okey's tent heard the sound of running feet. A bearded youth in a Parliamentary uniform rushed up and demanded to see the colonel. One of the sentries left his post to hasten to their commanding officer. He touched him gently on the shoulder and he woke at once and sat up.

"A young soldier who says his name is Bunyan to see you. He's alone."

"Bring him in."

By the time John Bunyan was shown in, Colonel Okey had lit

a candle and put on his dressing gown and slippers. His young chaplain, George Downing, who shared his tent, hearing him move about, had dressed and joined him.

John's clothes were muddy and in disarray. His eyes were bloodshot and he was limping. For a brief moment Colonel Okey stared.

"There are bands of Cavaliers everywhere," John blurted. "They are searching for his Highness, too. I was trapped in the woods with Will Jones, a woodman serving our Army. We found no trace of the Prince, but I never met anyone so brave as Will. If it hadn't been for him, I would have been captured."

"A-ha!" Chaplain Downing said sarcastically. "It must be wonderful to have such a comrade."

George Downing's head looks like a dirty cheese, John thought. His round pimpled face was caked with dirt. He had little round eyes, sharp canine teeth, ferocious black brows, and a bearded face.

"You say that this woodman's name was Will Jones?" Colonel Okey asked.

"Yes. That was his name. Did you send him, sir?"

The colonel's face turned purple. "No. Failure was not among my orders!" he bellowed. "Has it dawned on that thick skull of yours that Will Jones might be the Prince of Wales?"

"The Prince——" John's mouth dropped open in dismay. He remembered the way Will had talked about the Prince. "If he were not the Prince, how would he know so much about him? But if he were the Prince," John asked himself, "why didn't he have me hung?" He *was* the Prince of Wales. Suddenly John was sure of it. "Yet he helped me escape," he murmured, "and even left me a uniform."

John stared at Colonel Okey, feeling very small indeed. "Odd's fish! I let him go."

"It seems to me he let you go. And where did you pick up that oath, 'Odd's fish'?"

John thought for a moment. "Will—I mean the Prince—used it all the time."

Colonel Okey's big fist came down on the table before him.

108

"Then he surely was the Prince. That's a well-known exclamation of his. I've a mind to have you horsewhipped."

"I was stupid. He was so dusty and I never expected to find a prince in a Parliamentary uniform."

"You're a fool, Bunyan, a bigger fool than your father. Get out of here before I kick your backside. What a chance you had to strike a blow for the Commons! And you muffed it."

"I'm sorry, sir——" John began, and stopped suddenly.

He wasn't sorry at all. There were men who would like to see the Prince dead. John Okey might be one of them. The Prince would probably escape to France where Cardinal Mazarin had offered asylum to all the Stuarts in the name of Louis XIV. The war was almost over, and it would be tragic if anything happened to young Charles.

7 THE TRIUMPH of the Parliamentary forces raised some important questions: What is freedom? What is tolerance?

The Presbyterians in the Commons showed no tolerance for those who did not share their beliefs. The intolerant Archbishop Laud had been executed on Tower Hill in 1645. Oliver Cromwell continued to champion the cause of liberty of conscience and opposed Presbyterian bigotry. "Let each man worship as he please," he said everywhere. "I am a Puritan, and I will worship as I choose. Others should have the same right." Lord Fairfax concurred with him. The Army, which was made up of men who had sacrificed much for liberty, refused to disband until it was a reality. "We fought a King's tyranny. Why should we permit a Parliament to tyrannize?" they asked. "Blood has been spilt for freedom. We will not disband until we have freedom."

But the breech between Presbyterians and Independents widened, as Scotland pressed for the establishment of the Presbyterian faith as a uniform religion. Henry Ireton, aided and abetted by Algernon Sydney, worked for the Independents, although Cromwell remonstrated with Ireton who was now his son-in-law.

The King played one group against the other, making worthless promises to both, but refusing Parliament's demand to establish the Presbyterian Church and abolish the Episcopal or English Church. His Queen begged him to accede to the wishes of Parliament, since conformity couldn't be enforced anyway, as long as Lord Fairfaix and Cromwell stood with the Army in the way of such drastic uniformity. In spite of all opposition, Parliament remained unmoved.

"He who ventures his life for liberty of conscience," Cromwell wrote the Speaker of the House of Commons, "I wish he trust God for the liberty of his conscience. . . . All that believe have the real unity, which is the most glorious, being the inward and spiritual, in the body and in the head. . . . And from brethren, in things of the mind, we look for no compulsion but that of light and reason."

The struggle came to a head when Parliament voted to make Presbyterianism the uniform religion in England. A Presbyterian Synod was organized in London and all men were ordered to swear to a covenant. The Army decided to act.

John Bunyan mustered out of the army July, 1647, and returned to Elstow parish. After his escapade with Charles Stuart, he had been transferred to the command of Colonel Hammond in Captain Charles O'Hara's regiment. He had volunteered to go to Ireland to help subdue the King's supporters there, but the regiment had not been sent.

At home once more, he was overjoyed to learn that the war was over, and happy to hear that the Prince of Wales had boarded a frigate and escaped to France.

"Five hundred Parliamentary troops have seized King Charles," Papa announced one day. "They dare to hold him a prisoner! Cromwell has incited to mutiny. It's a wonder ye weren't among those brave men!"

"All the Army men want to do is to be sure they get what they fought for," John said tiredly.

"To think a son of mine would rebel against his King and country!"

"Since you feel that way, Papa, would you like me to live somewhere else? There's a vacant cottage on the curve of the Elstow Road."

"Now Thomas . . . John," Anne intervened in her loud voice. "We are happy to have ye here, John. This is your home, and ye will soon finish your apprenticeship. In the meantime your father needs ye. He won't admit it, but he's pretty proud of your independence."

"John, sometime I forget your mother raised ye to think for yourself." His father's voice was surprisingly gentle.

"Can't you see, Papa, that the Army is the only guard now against oppression, injustice, and violence?"

"The loyal subjects of the King think otherwise!"

John stayed on at Elstow, helping at the forge. The bitterness and anger at his father's swift marriage were gone; he could accept Anne as the woman who ran the house. He was grateful for her. And he enjoyed being with Willie, who was now twelve and a student at the Grammar School. Little Charles had died, but another half brother, Thomas, was a friendly little person who screwed up his face and smiled to get attention. John liked to hold him on his knee and tell him tales about dragons and witches. John Knox was over ten years old now and he still limped, but he followed John everywhere, happy to have him home again.

Yet John was not completely happy. He joined the other young men of the village in drinking bouts, pouring wine down his thirsty gullet. The people of the village were aghast at his cursing. Sometimes his sprees lasted two days and once again he had the reputation of being the leader of many youthful escapades.

As the weeks passed, John was assailed by a powerful emptiness. There was a great lack in his life, and he wasn't sure what it was. Mary Roberts was constantly in his thoughts, and he wondered what she was doing, and if she ever thought of him. He went regularly to the Elstow Abbey Church because he continued to worry about his soul, especially when he remembered Harry. Christopher Hall, appointed under the late Archbishop Laud, shook his finger when he preached about sin, but said little to help anyone who was a great sinner.

On the national scene, Henry Ireton, believing Cromwell to be losing his power, transferred his loyalty to the Army agitators. He charged Holles, Waller, Massey, Glyn, Stappleton, and six others with being troublemakers and demanded their removal from Parliament. The accusation he made against them was that they were attempting to negotiate a peace with King Charles on his terms, agreeing to take punitive measures against Army rebels.

Lord Fairfax and Oliver Cromwell despaired of reconciling the King, and joined the Army in its efforts to triumph over his tyranny and treachery.

Parliament, encouraged, passed a law which provided that any man who denied the doctrine of the Trinity or of the Divinity of Christ, or that the Bible is inspired, or that there is a resurrection or future judgment, and refused to retract such heresy, would be put to death!

Mary Roberts watched the national events with anxiety. Her beloved King was in danger. For months now he had been a prisoner in Hampton Court and Windsor. Many Englishmen wanted him to be restored to Whitehall, but busy with their own everyday lives they did nothing to bring about his restoration. Mary was concerned over Cromwell's growing power. Too many idolized him, lauding him as the savior of liberty.

She found herself thinking constantly, too, about the Parliamentary soldier from Elstow, John Bunyan. There was a certain crudeness about him, but how pleasing he was. She dreamed of the bright blue eyes in his half-smiling face, the pronounced cleft in his stubborn chin, the way he held his head, his straight shoulders, his ambling gait, his laugh, his eagerness for knowledge, his search for it, his love of books. All these were her fondest memories.

When she consulted Papa Matthias, his dark eyes twinkled behind his narrow spectacles.

"I thought you were brooding over some man," he said with a laugh. "If he's John Bunyan, he's just twelve miles away."

"But I cannot go to him. How could I, Papa Matthias?"

He scratched his bearded chin and thought for a moment. "He asked me to let him read more of John Milton's works. Why not go to visit Jane Lane's cousin William and his wife? He is a tobacco pipemaker who has recently moved to Bedford, near

Cromwell's present headquarters, sent there, I surmise, by those who would restore the King, to report the feeling of the citizens."

"But he turned against the King!"

"Mebbe so. I have always doubted it. Anyway, you could take John my prize copy of Milton's *Areopagitica*, which calls for uncensored publishing and freedom of speech as our most precious rights."

"But what if he doesn't want to see me? What if he's married to some village girl by now? I would be making a fool of myself."

"He hasn't married. Every letter I receive asks how you are, and what you are doing."

Mary waited until a family friend, a rector named John Gibbs, was going to Bedford. When she asked if she could accompany him and deliver a book to a friend, he eyed her with a knowing smile.

"That friend just wouldn't happen to be named John Bunyan?" She nodded.

"He used to ask a lot of questions when he came to church in Newport. He has a remarkable mind for a tinker."

The ride to Bedford was delightful, and Mary's spirits rose as they journeyed. Flocking white clouds moved against the blue of the sky. The willows were silver and green along the roadway. Birds flapped their bright wings and twittered joyously. Violets and daffodils sprayed the countryside. In the meadows cattle and sheep grazed contentedly. The ploughed fields were planted in even rows. And over it all the sun shone golden.

It was late afternoon when Mary and John Gibbs reached the Great Bridge over the River of Ouse. The square in front of the stone Swan Inn was filled with chattering, laughing people.

"What is all the excitement?" the rector asked, drawing the cart to a halt.

"Ironsides! Cromwell himself!" a goat-faced man told them.

The crowd surged and roared as the General approached followed by a troop of horse, young men in breastplate topped with white collars, tight breeches, ridged steel caps; they rode in rare

114

precision, their basket-hilted swords at their sides. The rattle of drums grew in the High Street as the huge man rode on, his big figure tense and his light brown hair cropped around his rugged face.

"There's John Bunyan," the Reverend Mr. Gibbs whispered, and discreetly disappeared.

Mary's pulse quickened. Yes. There he was. Standing up on the railing of the bridge, watching the troops go by and brandishing his powerful arm as he cheered for his hero.

"John!" she called.

He did not hear her, because of the noise and confusion, so she elbowed her way through the jostling crowd until she stood below him. She called his name again. A look of disbelief crossed his square face. The next instant he dropped to the bridge beside her.

"Mary. Mary."

"It's good to see you, John."

"How I have missed you!"

She drew a shivering breath. "And I have missed you."

"Come. We can't talk here with all this noise."

He made a path through the throng and they walked up the riverbank. In a shady place beside a willow that hung over the water, he paused and turned to face her.

"Seeing you is having a dream come true," he said, and his deep voice broke a little. "I couldn't get you out of my mind."

"Then why haven't you come to see me?"

He was silent for a long moment, staring down at her fashionable plum-colored gown. Then his gaze wandered over his brown doublet, short knee breeches, Welsh cotton stockings, and low laced shoes.

"Mary, I didn't think there was any hope. You wouldn't want a country bumpkin courting you. You wouldn't want to be married to a tinker——"

She interrupted him. "Why not?"

"I have nothing; no money, no tinkering tools of my own," he faltered. Then his eyes began to sparkle, and he put his arms around her, drawing her close. "Odd's fish! I'm going to ask you, anyway. Mary, will you marry a poor man that loves you so much that he's fool enough to reach for the sun?"

She lifted her lips and he kissed her. She clung to him as if she would hold him forever.

When he let her go, a frown furrowed his brow. "You know what a rapscallion I am, Mary. But if you'll have me, I'll go to church twice on Sunday. I won't swear or drink too much. I'll work until I have enough to buy my own tools. I'll make our furniture in the evenings while you read to me. And I'll never——"

She placed her finger on his lips. "Don't make too many promises, John. There'll be more to break. What does the past matter? What does it matter that we have not a dish or a spoon between us? We have each other."

"God knows I'm a low creature."

"That's not what Papa Matthias says. You have one great drawback, your admiration for General Cromwell. But I can even forgive that if you let me hold to my beliefs."

"Such as?"

"I want to see King Charles on the throne again. There are men in the House of Commons who would like to murder him. Colonel Ireton, Oliver Cromwell's son-in-law is a scoundrel and a fanatic. Cromwell has grown disgusted with the King's stubborn refusal to agree to peace on his terms. I'm convinced the King's very life is in danger."

"Surely some compromise will be worked out. As for your right to disagree with my beliefs, don't forget I fought for freedom. That means freedom for those who disagree with me, too."

She held out John Milton's book, which she had wrapped in a piece of homespun. "That's what this book says. Papa Matthias thought you would like it."

She watched him unwrap it and smile like a child. There was something impish about his smile.

"I will read this to you while you weave and sew. Tolerance demands an open mind, ye know!"

They laughed together.

116

"There's one condition I had better mention," she said brightly. "The divine who marries us must be an Anglican."

A mischievous light appeared in John's blue eyes. "All I care about is getting the girl I want. Anyway, I was brought up in the Church of England."

"Don't keep me waiting too long, John."

In the months that followed John worked very hard. He made a few trips to Newport, and with Mary dreamed of the day they could be man and wife. He read John Milton's *Areopagitica*. Its strong plea for toleration made him feel the importance of un-censored books in influencing others. He found himself wishing, as he often did, that he were an educated man with the ability to write well. And although he tried not to take God's name in vain, sometimes he forgot and the oaths blurted out.

One cloudy August morning, walking along the High Street in Bedford, he paused to look in a bookshop window. Sometimes Timothy Vane, the shopkeeper, sold worn books for a shilling or two. Behind the small-paned windows John could see a table piled with old volumes. If I stop now, he thought, I won't earn much money this morning. I'll come back this afternoon.

Just as he was about to continue his rounds, he noticed that one of the leather laces that tied his shoes was hanging. When he leaned over to fasten it, the heavy anvil iron, which he and a friend had recently molded, slipped from his back and fell on to his big toe. He yelled in pain, and a volley of oaths spewed out.

"Ye wicked wretch!" a woman's cross voice shouted. "The Devil take your obscenity. Get away from our shop. We don't want a Devil-worshiper like ye near our young uns. Get, or I vow I'll call a constable!"

Theny Talbot Vane stood there, her hands on her fat hips, her moon face contorted with fury. The naïve bookshop keeper had married her, but looking at her John remembered the day he had seen her lying with Master Vierney. He thought of the lewd tales about her. It was said she carried on with peddlers, hangers-on at the inns, even the immoral married men of the town. If ever there was a woman who loved the flesh, it was Theny. Yet now she was blushing with fury at his blasphemy!

Abruptly he left. All morning he limped about on his injured toe. The lowest woman in Bedford had been shocked at his swearing, and had reproved him, declaring him unfit to come near her bastard children!

I'm lost, he thought. God has turned his face. His soul plunged into the pit of despair, and he began to wonder if it had perished with his fleeting goodness and the breaking of vows he had made to Mary. Scenes of his boisterous youth trooped through his mind: his drunken stupors, his obscene cursing, the brawls, the fisticuffs, the mean pranks, and orchard robbing.

That night John slept restlessly, for his toe ached painfully and his conscience ached, too. Once he awakened to see through the small, leaded panes of his dormer window a flash of lightning breaking on the darkened sky, and to hear the far roar of thunder. He got up and limped to close the shutters.

Back in bed his thoughts turned again to his sins . . . and Mary. She knew what he was and yet she wanted to marry him. Like most men he desired to spend his life with a good woman, to have children. This girl he loved was like a lighthouse in a storm. She personified goodness . . . and she loved him. His spirits soared.

Why wait? he thought. He had almost all his tools now: anvil iron, pliers, snippers, smoldering iron, and hammer—he lacked only a roundhead for shaping pot covers.

He fell asleep and dreamed of Mary in a plain gray gown which clung to her curving body. She unbraided her corn-colored hair and it came cascading down around her shoulders. Her eyes were warm and his heart flooded with tenderness as he moved across the intervening space to take her in his arms. But a wall separated them. He could not touch her, and he woke up aching with longing.

The next morning he rented the still-vacant cottage near Elstow Green. It was a small box-shaped dwelling with two dormer windows, a thatched roof, and wooden shutters. A wooden slat fence

118

enclosed the grounds and a neighbor's hens scratched out in front.

Then he borrowed Papa's old horse, and whistling cheerfully, he rode across the meadow and took the winding road to Newport.

Mary and John were married a week later. There was little preparation, but she looked lovely in a tight white gown. Papa Matthias, Dame Cowley, Cousin Bitsy Barnes who was now eleven, and three neighbor women of the parish were the only ones present when they took their vows. John was in a daze. The full realization of the miracle made his heart thump as he slipped the wedding band upon her finger.

Afterwards Bitsy gave Mary a brass kettle. Papa Matthias and Dame Cowley presented them with some bookshelves. And the women's gift was a set of pewter plates and a pewter pitcher.

In the months that followed John was more content than he had been since his mother and Margaret had died. Each afternoon when he came home, Mary waited for him under the door lintel and opened her arms. In the cold weather a fire crackled in the wide hearth. Regardless of the weather outside, the minute he slipped into the low-ceilinged room he forgot the cares of the day.

He often spent the evening making furniture while Mary read to him from two books that had belonged to her father, *The Plain Man's Pathway to Heaven* by Arthur Dent, a parish minister of Shoebury, Essex, and *The Practice of Piety* by Lewis Langley, a Bishop of Bangor.

The former was presented in dialogue. Four characters conferred under an oak tree on heavenly matters: Antilegon, a Cavalier; Theologus, a preacher; Asunetus, an ignorant man; and Philagathias, an honest one. As John read it, or listened, his old fear returned. A great sense of sin settled like a heavy burden on his back, and he felt as if he were staggering under it.

Yet the author had some clever dialogue: "Sweet meat will have sour sauce." "A fool's bolt is soon shot."

But he expressed his dislike of "doubled and redoubled ruffs, those stouting farthingales, long locks, and foretufts."

Theologus objected to a man's swearing "by clock, or pie, or mousefoot. It was never a good world since starching and steeling, buskes, and whalebones, supporters, and rebatoes, full moon and hobby horses" came into use.

"Even plain country folk will flaunt their pride like courtiers," and the old problem is verified: "Every Jack will be a gentleman and Joan as good as a lady."

Antilegon: "It seemeth you are an Anabaptist, you condemn all swearing."

"Drunkenness is the Metropolitan City of all the Province of Vice."

"Many lazy and lusting youths . . . forget we must one day give account."

John kept remembering that he, too, would one day have to give account and restlessness churned in him. And a description of an unsaved man from *The Practice of Piety* terrified him.

To all outward appearances John became a reformed man. He no longer frequented the taverns. He swore less. Every day he read a few passages from the Old Testament. He dressed in his gray homespun each Sunday, and walked with Mary to the Elstow Abbey Church where Christopher Hall preached about the narrow way, the broad road, Hell, and the Celestial City.

One night when he returned home, he found Mary weeping. She was sitting on the joined stool before the blazing fire, her face in her hands, sobbing as if she would never stop.

He ran to her, knelt on the floor beside her. "Dear one! What has happened? Are you in pain?"

She lifted her head, and her eyes were grave. "The Army is going to murder the King!"

He listened, trying to calm his wildly beating heart, but her news almost set his hair on end. Jane Lane's cousin, William, who had just returned from London, said the King was to be tried like a common criminal if a plot to purge the House of Commons of his supporters succeeded. His enemies were claiming that the people, represented by the House of Commons, had the supreme authority, even when the consent of the House of the Lords and the King had not been given.

John let out a string of oaths. "The Army has gone too far. The

120

people have certain rights, the right to worship as they choose, the right to speak their mind, the right to be represented in government. But merciful God! They have no right to execute the King!"

"Could John Okey intervene?"

"He thinks as the Army does, but I doubt he would approve murder!"

"Go to him then!"

John shook his head. "Four companies of his dragoons have been stationed in Bedfordshire. But he's in London in the midst of all the controversy. You know we have no money. I can't go to London. Anyway, Colonel Okey wouldn't listen to me!"

For a few weeks John forgot to worry about his soul, as he listened to the street talk about the happenings in London. Colonel Pride, a powerful army man, forcibly ejected the Royalist members of the House of Commons. The trial of the King took place in the name of the House of Commons and the people. He was accused of treason against the realm for beginning a war to secure his own personal power. The King stood in the great hall of Westminster quietly listening to his accusers, but refusing to answer. On the fifth day sentence was passed upon him as a traitor, murderer, tyrant, and enemy of England. And John Okey sat in judgment on the King, one of eleven who signed the death warrant.

"The execution was a dreadful sight," William Lane said. "I was in London buying material for pipes, and I went to see it. King Charles appeared on the scaffold erected outside the Banqueting House at Whitehall, wearing a black embroidered cloak, a white shirt, fine breeches, and gloves, as if he were going to a party. Two huge executioners with black masks hiding their faces cut off his head with one blow, and held it up for the gasping, sobbing crowd to see."

"If Oliver Cromwell permitted it, he must have believed it was the only way," John said defensively.

"England has come to a sorry state," Mary said furiously, "when she murders her King!"

The King's death failed to bring peace to the realm. A Council of State was created. Statues of King Charles in the Royal Exchange and other parts of the realm were pulled down and smashed. That May, a Commonwealth and Free State was declared, in which there would be no king and no House of Lords. In Scotland the Royalist Argyll and his adherents sent an envoy to young Charles who was at The Hague, urging him to return as King. In Ireland the factions united against the Rump Parliament. Holland responded by recognizing the Prince of Wales as Charles II, refusing to receive representatives of Parliament. France withdrew its ambassador. Eleven English ships, commanded by Prince Rupert, left the Hague and began attacking English trading vessels.

In England the Royalist cause received renewed vigor. Lords Copell and Holland and the Duke of Hamilton, who had been kept in the Tower for their loyalty to the King, were executed. Many citizens who had sided with the Army and the Commons now became antagonistic. A king had been murdered.

But Oliver Cromwell took command, and victory followed victory. John Lilburne, a fanatical soldier, led a mutiny at Burford, but Cromwell soon subdued the rebellious men. Yet these men, called the Fifth Monarchy men, continued to circulate John Lilburne's tracts which declared that the four monarchies of Cryus, Nebuchadnezzar, Alexander, and Caesar had passed away. The Fifth Monarchy of Jesus Christ had come. They had supported Oliver Cromwell at first, but now he wanted to be an earthly ruler; there were to be no earthly rulers. Ireland rebelled and Oliver Cromwell marched to conquer it. Three thousand were put to the sword, and General Cromwell announced that this had been necessary to prevent another Protestant massacre. While this was going on, Prince Rupert anchored near the coast, and Robert Blake drove him off.

That July of 1650 a daughter was born to John and Mary.

"We'll name her after you," John insisted, and laughingly Mary agreed.

As the weeks passed John noticed that the baby's eyes did not focus. One night, when she was two months old, it occurred to him, as he learned over her cradle, that the little one might be blind. Slowly he passed his hands back and forth in front of her eyes. She was as blind as the belfry bats of Elstow Church!

In the chaos of his thoughts he remembered a passage in the Scriptures which said the sins of the fathers would be visited upon the children unto the third and fourth generation. *Is it because of my sins the baby is blind? Has God's terrible vengeance been wrought upon little Mary?*

"No, John," his wife told him. "God bestows his blessings on the just and the unjust alike. Don't torture yourself with blame. Keep asking God's forgiveness as every Christian does."

To add to his worry, Mary had some severe attacks of the ague, which caused her to stay in bed. At these times he waited tenderly on her, making posset and broth. One morning his stepmother came with a wooden box containing a new drink called tea, which was becoming popular throughout England. Mary enjoyed sipping it so much that he worked and scrimped until he had accumulated enough to buy her another box. Proudly he brought it home to her, and his heart swelled as she clapped her hands like a pleased child. It wasn't what he was used to drinking, but to his surprise he enjoyed it, too.

When John attended church, Christopher Hall had one parishioner who listened to every word. If any shifted on one of the hard benches, or went to sleep, John Bunyan rebuked him. Yet there were still the occasional bouts in the taverns, and the ringing of the bells in the church tower. He continued to join in the sports of the village, too—dancing, bowling, wrestling, and games. John enjoyed the Fairs and the holiday celebration and in them he forgot his fears. Yet he was not happy. He felt a lack within him.

One fall day he stood watching some of the youths of Elstow ring the bells as he and Harry had often done. What if those heavy bells should fall and crush me? he thought, as he often had when he was a boy. He imagined the Devil sitting on the huge beam that supported the bells, leering down at him. What if the Devil loosed the beam? What if the vengeful God shook the steeple, so that it fell to mash me like an old turnip? I have worshiped the Devil too long instead of Christ. He turned and fled.

To forget his anxiety John began making a fiddle. He had longed for one for many years. One warm September day John was soldering, and drops of water ran down the red hair on his chest, and soaked the top of his breeches. The dampness made the hair on his head separate in wispy auburn curls. But John worked without even stopping for the midday meal.

Willie came in late that afternoon and exclaimed, "John, you have made a fiddle fit for a king! I wish I could make things with my hands the way you can!"

John looked at his younger brother, who was becoming a good tinker, too. While John was muscular, large of body with a bright, almost roguish face, Willie was solemn and lissom with mild brown eyes. John could sing by ear and liked fast, lilting airs, while Willie sang in a tenor voice like an old-fashioned troubadour. They would have some enjoyable musical evenings as soon as John fastened strings to his fiddle.

The sun was sinking as he put down his tools and looked at the instrument with pride. It was a good fiddle, shaped like a regular violin, well-proportioned, and fashioned of thin iron plates painstakingly soldered on his tinker's anvil. He had spent six days making it. A fiddle like that would play many a tune and last a long time. He had been a good tinker before he was fourteen. He liked his work and he had recently discovered that he liked to preach, but he would always be a tinker. Working with his hands made a man proud.

He placed his fiddle on the shelf, and left the workshop. As he started into the cottage he noticed that the thatch on the roof hung down over the windows; it needed trimming. He must do that soon. But tomorrow would be Sunday and he would go to

124

church. It seemed these days as if the vicar was preaching directly to him.

The following morning as Christopher Hall, dressed in the usual surplice and bands, climbed into the high oak pulpit, John leaned forward eagerly. The Sabbath was to be observed, the vicar said, in prayer and meditation. Thus could a Christian honor God—and not in noisy cavortings on the Green. The vicar was looking right at John; and he moved restlessly on the wooden bench.

After church he walked home thinking about what the preacher had said and a feeling of guilt smothered him.

As he was eating the chicken Mary had cooked, she asked quietly, "John, what is the matter? Something has made you morose. Was it the sermon this morning?"

How good it is, he thought, to have a sympathetic wife to confess my sins to! She listened intently while he told her how troubled he was, that he knew he was a great sinner, and a hypocrite.

She smiled gently. "John, shake the sermon out of your mind and finish your dinner. After all, isn't playing games on Sunday better than drinking strong waters and taking the Lord's name in vain? You have improved a great deal. Think about what the vicar said, but don't let him ruin your appetite."

Wonderful Mary. Understanding Mary. What would he ever do without her? His heart melted like butter over a flame. He spread a warm piece of bread thickly with homemade cherry jam. He forgot all about Christopher Hall and the frightening sermon, and gobbled until he was so full he could hardly breathe. A warm glow spread through him, and when Mary busied herself with the plates and pots, he changed his clothes and started for Elstow Green.

The wind was blowing colder all the time as he walked along the road, the vicar's words still sounding in his ears. If the vicar was right, he would be sinning again that afternoon as he played at bowls and cat. At the Green he found Froggy Foster, Tad Sorrow, and some of his other friends waiting.

John won the first two games. As they were playing a third, he gave his cat, or piece of wood, such a blow with the broad end of his stick that it flew high in the air. As his eyes followed its upward flight, his ears strained for an intelligible sound because he was certain a Presence was there, filling the immensity of sky over him. It was then that he imagined he heard the Voice calling his name. In the blue, cloudless sky a face seemed to appear looking down, mysterious, terrifying.

The Voice came again, clearly now, speaking his name: "John Bunyan, wilt thou leave thy sins and go to the Celestial City where the shining ones dwell, or have thy sins and go to Hell?"

A wave of terror flooded him, drowning his consternation in fear. He dropped his tapered stick, and the cries of his companions echoed around him: "John, what is it?" "Ye look as if ye have seen a witch!" "Are you sick, John?"

How could he tell companions like Froggy Foster and Tad Sorrow that he had seen the face of Jesus Christ and heard His Voice? He stooped, picked up his stick and his cat, and gave it another blow. But that was the last Sunday he went to the Green. . . .

After that day the terror continued to plague him. He increased his attendance at church, going every time there was a service. He shunned the taverns. Even Christopher Hall noticed the change in his life. Some people who had avoided hiring him as a tinker began to seek his services. He traveled about the county mending iron hip bathtubs, roofs, gutters, pots, pans, and other articles.

In December there was a great deal of snow, but when the roads were passable, he went where he was called. One Monday morning he rode slowly along the Potten Road toward Wilmington, which was about three miles from Bedford, thinking about Mary and little Mary. The baby was growing plump and her soft "a-a-a" was music to his ears. He loved to feel the grip of her tiny fingers on his big thumb.

Again the disturbing questions tumbled through his brain. Was her blindness his fault? Would he ever know what it was to be saved? Would the inner unrest never cease?

The wind blew harder and harder, and he pulled his woolen cloak tightly around him. Heavy snow began to fall. When he reached Wilmington, he drew rein in front of the gray church which had a square tower like the one on the Elstow Abbey Church. He dismounted, tied his horse to a post, and went inside to pray.

The coat-of-arms on the tomb of Sir John Gostwyck was designed with horses' heads, which Papa had told John had replaced stars. As Master of Horse to Henry VIII, Sir John had once been an important squire in England. Now, how many had ever heard his name, except in this place where he had lived? Man is nothing, John thought, except as he follows Christ. Everybody, every living thing is dying. What's important is what a man does on his pilgrimage.

Kneeling, John prayed out loud: "Father of our Lord, You know how low I am. I'm not fit to kneel in Your presence. Show me the path Your pilgrims take. Make me a good pilgrim. Amen!"

Half an hour later a steward at the mansion to which he had been called directed John to repair the metalwork on two of the century-old buildings: the pigeon trap built to catch pigeons to insure a fowl supply, and the stable where King Henry VIII had bedded his horse. By the time John had finished the work on the pigeon trap, his fingers were numb with cold and he was shivering. A groom lit the fire on the stable's huge hearth, inviting him to warm himself.

John sat on a stool, staring into the flames, rubbing his icy fingers together. The odors of leather, manure, and oats filled the raftered room. The fire roared while, outside, snow floated down against the small windowpanes. It was a wonderful moment, and John wished he didn't have to get up and return to his work.

After a while he rose and, taking up a tool, carved his name on the old stone slab above the long mantel:

JOHN BUN
YAN

He added the year, 1650.

After I'm gone, he thought, maybe some groom will notice my name, and wonder who I was. *Where will I be then?*

The steward appeared, interrupting his reflections. He held out a little posset jug with a broken metal top, and asked him to mend it. John shook his head, explaining that the pressure required to fasten it on would break an earthenware vessel.

"Then take it along. We have no use for it," the steward said. "Give it to your wife."

John was very grateful. It was a beautiful jug with a crisscross blue pattern. He had little money to buy Mary any gifts. Happily he took it with him.

When he got home that night, he found Mary sitting in the middle of the bed, holding little Mary tightly.

"Oh, John! I thought you would never get home! I saw a mouse."

"Will you sit there a few minutes while I run over to Papa's and borrow a trap?" he asked.

"Yes, but hurry! I'm terrified of mice!"

Anne lent him a trap and he vowed to make one, himself, right away. Mary had not had any supper, and he helped her prepare it, assuring her the mouse would not appear while they were moving about, and that when it did, the trap would take care of it.

After supper he gave her the jug, and watched her clap her small hands like a delighted child.

"Oh, John, it's beautiful. It will look nice sitting on the shelf above the hearth. Can we really keep it?"

She placed it in the center of the shelf, handling it gently, almost as if it were a living thing. And his heart lifted. He had given her so little. It didn't take much to make her happy.

That night they caught the mouse, and he set the trap again.

That summer the Prince of Wales landed in Scotland, and was forced to accept the terms of the Presbyterians. He signed a document admitting that his mother's Catholic religion was idolatrous, and that his father had been a tyrant. Scotland began raising troops. An English Army led by General Cromwell marched north to fight David Leslie and the Scots, attacking at dawn, capturing ten thousand, killing three thousand, and confiscating all weapons and baggage. In the meantime Charles was crowned at Scone, an event which the Commons declared high treason.

Colonel Okey was often in Bedford in these days. He had bought the Honor and Manor of Ampthill, and the Manor of Millbrook. He told John of the unrest in France, too, under the rule of Cardinal Mazarin, who had suspended Queen Henrietta's pension. She was living in poverty!

Toward the end of September, 1651, Bitsy came to visit Mary. The afternoon she arrived John had just returned from Bedford where he had heard that the Prince of Wales had almost been captured, but that Jane Lane had been one of those who helped him escape!

"It's so exciting. Think of Jane having a part in the escape of the heir to the throne of England!" Bitsy said, her dark eyes very bright. "She told me all about it."

"Sit down," Mary said eagerly. "I want to hear it all, everything!"

"He fought in the Battle of Worcester, and fled to the house of a friend of Jane's in Friar's Street. While General Cromwell's brigade rode through the street searching for him, he changed his clothes to some a woodman might wear, and Lord Wilmot took some shears and notched his hair. Then they let him down from a rear window in a blanket. He mounted a horse that was waiting and galloped into Foregate Street by the Townditch while the cries all over the city were: 'God save Charles II!' "

For an instant John closed his eyes and the years rolled back. He was in the forest with Will Jones, the woodman, who was a fine companion.

"I'm glad he escaped," John said. "I hope they never catch him!"

"Do you want to hear the rest?" Bitsy's eyes were wide as she described the march of Charles to Aberdeen before the Battle of Worcester. On Saturday the Sheriff and Mayor had proclaimed him King. After the battle my Lord of Buckingham, the Earl of Derby, and my Lord Wilmot, who accompanied him everywhere, had ridden with him through the Wrottlesley Woods to Brewood Forrest and Whiteladies where they had all slept at Tong-Castle.

There Charles had rubbed some chimney black on his face, and put on green breeches and a doeskin jacket. With a wood bill in one hand he had stood in the rain, hidden in a woods, and watched General Cromwell's men gallop past.

The Roman Catholics his father had persecuted came to his aid, hiding him in priest holes which they had had to provide to save their priests. Without the Catholics of England he would never have escaped, for Cromwell's men were everywhere.

At one town a king-catcher had offered a blacksmith a thousand pounds to tell him where the King was. A change of disguise was necessary, and Charles became a tenant's son named Will Jackson.

Jane Lane lived at King's Bromley near Litchfield where he was. Lord Wilmot had sought her aid. Mounted on a double gelding she had gone riding with Will Jackson as her attendant. None of the group who rode with them had any idea that Will was the heir to the throne.

Knowing he would share the same fate as his father if he stayed in England, Charles decided to find a ship that would take him to France or Spain. A former guard named Peter Pope recognized him, and volunteered to go to Bristol to find him passage, but he discovered that there would be no ship leaving that port for a month.

The party went to Lyne, thinking perhaps a ship might be found there. They met a trooper in Cromwell's Army who bragged that he had killed the Prince of Wales. When the villagers heard the news, they rang bells and made a bonfire, dancing around it in joy while Charles looked on. The captain of the only ship to leave Lyne was locked in his cabin by his wife, because it had been proclaimed that day that any who aided or concealed the King would be executed.

At the Bridgeport Inn, a blacksmith noticed several types of horseshoes on Lord Wilmot's horse, which he had been asked to shoe. He told the hostler that the party had traveled through several counties and that one might be the King. The loyal guard, Peter Pope, overhearing the conversation, announced that he had been a guard in the Prince of Wales's regiment, and that none of the three men was Charles.

While the King waited for a ship at Trent, time and time again he passed boldly through regiments flying Cromwell's Cross of St. George.

One morning Charles boarded a ship, and sailed to his second exile. Nobody rejoiced more than Mary, and despite the loud protestations of those who wanted no more kings, John was happy, too. He had liked "Will Jones" very much.

8 THE SPRING of 1652 came early with frequent rains. The sky was pouring water the April day that John reached the slope which rose from Houghton Conquest to Ampthill Heights. Rivulets ran down the side of the rise like a freshet on a mountain slope. The ascent would have been impossible for a horse, but John had managed it on foot.

He had slipped as he started up toward the ruins of the old castle. Hill Difficulty, he thought, as he slid down to the bottom, his hands covered with slime. I am going up! he thought. He got to his feet and made another attempt, but his progress was slow and exhausting. Only by inching along on his hands and knees was he able to manipulate his body to the summit, where he fell back exhausted on the wet green and lay panting until he had recovered his wind.

Ahead stretched a long avenue of elms, leading to a beautiful rose-colored mansion. There two of Henry VIII's wives had suffered, looked down at the cornfields, elms, oaks, green meadows, and the glorious chalk hills. The regal pinnacles and colonnades made John think of a fairy palace. Even from the tradesman's entrance, to which he went, he could see the gilded corners of its tall towers.

When John had mended the iron hip-tub he had been asked to mend, the steward showed him his master's collection of antiques and books, many of them dating from the time when they were

132

illuminated by hand and carefully copied. The armor, shields, and swords were very old.

Before John left, the steward took him into the top-floor bedroom. From the windows he could see rows of chestnut trees, forests of oak, fir, and beech. Beyond the park, the ploughed fields were black. Horses grazed in the meadow, and hens fed behind the time-worn stables. And miles away rose the blue and white chalk hills, the delectable mountains! He stared in breathless wonder at a cherry tree, white with blossoms, that stood in a corner of the garden. The grassy slopes beyond the ploughed earth were dotted with grazing sheep.

The next morning he could still visualize the beautiful house and the landscape around it, as he wandered through Bedford giving his tinker's cry:

> "Have you any work for John Bunyan?
> Have you any pots to mend?"

Nobody sought his service.

At the Swan Inn, he turned into the weed-grown fields which led to the ruins of an old Norman castle at the summit of Castle Mound. Demolished on the orders of Henry VII, after a mercenary had taken one of his justices prisoner, the ruins were always romantic and mysterious to John. The ancient Priory of the gray monks was gone. Trinity Mill, which had once driven water from the Castle Moat, stood silent and deserted like an old house haunted by the ghosts of centuries past. Down the river he could see another mill, and on the opposite side Duck Mill with the bubbling water of its dam white against the green of the trees.

John paused below the old fortress. For an instant he imagined St. George wielding his magic sword in defense of the invisible castle. John sat down on a fallen tree trunk, ate his meal of bread and cheese, and dreamed of mighty deeds until he realized that the sun was beginning to set. Mary would have supper ready and tonight she had promised eel stew. He leaped up, slung his tinker's pack on his back, crossed the bridge, and took the short cut through some narrow streets toward the Elstow Road.

His mind was still on his dreams. How he wished he could do something for England. But there were great men doing that. Oliver Cromwell continued to be his contemporary hero. Fearless, selfless, John was sure Cromwell always thought first of what God wanted him to do. And there was John Milton, who vowed he would continue to use his pen as a sword to prick the consciences and minds of men.

A voice broke into John's thoughts. "Without God man is nothing," it said. It came from one of four women who sat in front of the cottage he was passing.

"If only all men could know God's promises, the love of Christ, and be born anew into a state of Grace which protects them from Satan's darts!" another agreed.

A third said, "God is a God of Love and never a God of vengeance. We must share Him with others."

John paused on the path as the women continued to discuss their conviction and joy. One, a plump little woman with a cheery voice, apple-pink cheeks, and sparkling blue eyes, was busy with her spinning wheel. Her small feet moved quickly and her hands were agile as she said that every man must have a new birth. The second had an angular face, framed by fluffy white hair which peeped from her white cap. The third, probably in her thirties, wore a blue dress and cap, and spoke quietly but fervently. The fourth was frail and small, but her voice was strong as she spoke of what the Bedford congregation had done for her.

John moved off without speaking to the women, but he was shaken. They seemed to have the peace that he was seeking. He was certain that the outward assent of many who called themselves Christian would never bring salvation, but joy shone forth from the faith of these women, and he found himself envying them.

He thought about them so much that one day he went back and found them in the same place. He drew a long breath, walked directly up to them, and asked them to tell him about the new birth.

The apple-cheeked woman, who introduced herself as Sister Munnes, spoke first: "Everyone must have a new birth. Take the chick. When the egg is laid, it is no chick. It is in a shell that has to be warmed. So men dwell in darkness until Grace quickens them. Then they hatch into life and liberty!"

"I am a village tinker of Elstow, a mean peasant. Can I be quickened?"

"Christ was a workman. The Bible tells us a man is saved by faith," Sister Spencer, the white-haired woman, told him. "If he has no faith he is lost."

"Our minister, Brother Gifford, would be glad to talk with ye," said Sister Munnes. "He used to be a very wicked man. He was born in Kent, and he became a Royalist Major. He was captured during the fierce Battle of Maidstone, and was to be hung with eleven others. The night before he was to die, his sister came to say good-bye. She found the prison guards in a drunken stupor, and unlocked the door."

"That was a narrow escape," John said.

"For three days he lay in a ditch while Cromwell's men beat the woods for him. Then he escaped to London where he disguised himself. He came to Bedford after some weeks and began to practice medicine, since Dr. Francis Bannister was growing old. But the Major drank strong waters, swore, gambled, and lived a debauched life. One night when he lost more than he had —the last of his major's pay—he shook his fist at God, blaming Him."

"Yes. Yes. Go on," John begged.

"Shortly after that his sister gave him a book, *Last and Learned Work of the Last Four Things:* Death, Judgment, Hell, and Heaven, by George Miller. It made him think. He suddenly knew that he loved God and would never lose sight of his face again. His sins were forgiven, because of God's Grace, and he vowed to preach to others. Sister Cooper, formerly a grasping, greedy woman, was converted by his first sermon."

"And your church? The Bedford Meeting?" John pressed.

"It started with twelve Christians, taking the twelve Apostles as the model," Sister Spencer informed him.

Sister Bosworth, the woman in blue, had eyes that seemed to smile by themselves. "Our church was founded on faith in Christ and Holiness in life without respect to outward and circumstantial things," she explained. "We preach and encourage Grace and Faith. Unprofitable arguments are avoided. We try to help each other and those who are not of our faith. We share our happiness."

John asked them who the other members of the Bedford congregation were and learned that John Eston, senior, an elderly widower who was Mayor of Bedford, was one. A former mayor, John Grew and his wife belonged. There were also Anthony Harrington and his wife, Sister Fenne, and a younger woman, Sister Norton.

"Come to our meetings," Sister Munnes invited in her cheery, birdlike voice. "Come and feed your soul, young man."

"We'll put you on our prayer list," Sister Spencer said brightly. "You'll never be able to escape."

As John was walking from Elstow to Bedford not long after that, the thought struck at him: If a man is saved by faith, why not test my faith? If I could work a miracle, then I'd know. . . : Kneeling, he was about to ask God to give him the power to dry the muddy potholes on the road. Then he thought: What if I should fail? I guess I won't try for a miracle today.

In the weeks that followed John turned to the writing of the Ranters. One Ranter claimed that he had attained to such a state of perfection that it was permissible to satisfy his lust and not to sin in doing so.

There was nothing satisfying here, and John began reading the Epistles of Paul, which dealt with salvation by faith. Slowly, carefully, he read all of them.

Then he had a dream in which a high wall separated him from a mountain; above it he could see a glowing sun. He shivered in the icy air. If only he could reach the other side of that barrier! Frantically he began to search for an opening. Suddenly a hole appeared, and through it he could see the four women of the Bedford Meeting dwelling in warmth on the sun-drenched mountain. He desperately wanted to reach them, but he could not penetrate the wall separating him from them. Darkness surrounded him as he shivered in the ice and snow. He longed to reach the sunshine where they were, but the hole was so narrow that he could not squeeze through. He shoved and pushed until he had widened it enough to get his head through. Then, by dropping his pack from his back, he maneuvered his shoulders into the sunshine, and at last his body. He raced toward the shining ones and sat down in their midst, warmed by the light and heat.

When he awoke, his heart was heavy. He believed that God sometimes sent messages, even warnings, in dreams. This dream must mean that he was shut away from the Son of God. The mountain could be a symbol of the Church of the Living God, the sun the Truth of Christ, the wall the world, the gap the Christ who is the way to the Father. None could reach it who refused to drop his pack of sins and leave the world behind.

There were moments after that when he felt confident God loved him, that his sins were all forgiven. Sometimes he talked of this love to the crows that sat on the ploughed land, to the fish in the river, and to the cattle in the green fields. Then his doubts returned. What if I'm not of the elected? How could God love such a low creature? In which church can I find God?

General Cromwell had been made Lord Protector and in that role he recognized no one form of church government. There were no church laws or ordinances enforced and no church courts. But the shameful fact was that the liberty granted according to Articles 36 and 37 did not extend to "Popery or Prelacy." Even in Bedford, Catholics were denied the right to vote.

In the existing situation John was free to worship where he chose. He sought the companionship of the shining ones, and listened to Brother Gifford preach.

The Bedford congregation met in St. John's Church where an ancient hospital had been founded in the twelfth century; the present buildings had been erected in the thirteenth. When the vicar of St. John's, Theodore Crowley, had been sequestered by the Commonwealth, the Bedford corporation had presented Brother Gifford in his place. The Parliamentary and Puritan influence were in the majority on the Bedford Council, and the Puritans were given every consideration.

Sunday after Sunday John walked the two miles from Elstow to attend the services. St. John's stood at the end of a flagged path which led from the street on the south side of the Great Bridge. He liked to walk about in the burying ground, divided from the rectory and old garden by a brick wall. Beyond another side of the wall meadows stretched toward the baptizing place, Duck Mill Pond on the Ouse.

The inside of St. John's had none of the gloom that filled the Elstow Abbey Church. Some gray stone slabs were marked with the names of a dozen rectors, and members proudly pointed to a Communion cup presented to the church, by Queen Elizabeth and inscribed "for the Parish of St. John in Bedford." Rows of high-backed pews lined either side of the single aisle.

When John visited Brother Gifford at the rectory, which had once been the hospital, the portrait of an old rector, Andrew Denys, whom he had seen around Bedford many years before, stared down at him; John felt as if he were seeing a ghost. The rectory was always a pleasant place with its diamond-shaped leaded and latticed windows, oaken beams, and paneled walls. When the weather was good, John sat beside Brother Gifford under a mulberry bush in the garden, discussing salvation, faith, election, forgiveness, and the Cross.

Whenever John left the rectory, he was sure God loved him, but at other times he seemed to himself as loathsome as an adder. And the Tempter came to whisper, "Sell Christ. Sell him. Sell him! Forget that He is. Live and be carefree!"

One morning Brother Gifford preached from a text found in the Song of Songs, "Behold, thou art fair, my love." Christ's love, the minister said convincingly, is not withheld from sinners. Hope started to flood through John, but then the words from another text sounded in his heart: "Simon, Simon, behold Satan hath de-

138

sired to have you!" John listened while Brother Gifford went on to confess that he had committed almost every sin, and had been headed for the City of Destruction. "God has saved me," he concluded. "He can save you."

John, walking alone after that between the villages, often found himself envying the birds and animals which had no souls to be possessed. The conviction grew that he was in chains, bound to the Devil because he had sinned so much that his heart had been hardened. The slimy-eyed face of the Devil seemed to peer at him from every bush. Sometimes he could even feel the Devil's clawlike fingers raking his clothes.

Every time John came to a bookshop, he went in and looked at the books, hoping to find one that would help him. One day he came across an English translation of Martin Luther's *Commentary upon the Epistle of St. Paul to the Galatians*. It had been published at "Blacke Frears by Ludgate" by Thomas Vautroulier in 1595. Martin Luther, John discovered, had first been a friar "in what blindnesse, superstition and darkness, in what dreams and dregges of Monkish idolatrie, he was drowned, his history declareth. . . ."

John bought the book and that night, as soon as supper was over, he read all of the preface which described the darts of conscience that prodded Martin's further seeking until he became God's instrument.

"Mary!" he cried excitedly when he had finished it, "God chose Martin Luther, a peasant's son. He was a sinner such as I. He chose him. *He can choose me!*"

"That's what I've been telling you, John, for nearly five years," she said quietly.

"He struggled, too. His story is as if it had been written out of my heart!"

Night after night John read the reformer's words. Martin Luther had been tempted as he often was. "O Christ, go if You will," John whispered after a long sleepless night.

At dawn, he rose and dressed quickly. He left the cottage taking the path toward the Abbey Church where he threw himself down on the dew-laden grass, he beat upon the earth with clenched fists, and cursed God. Passages from the Scriptures began trooping through his mind: "My Grace is sufficient for Thee." "Him that cometh to me, I will in no wise cast out." But I am Esau, he argued. It's too late. My birthright has been sold for a mess of potage. *Christ has gone!*

All that day John was so miserable that he couldn't work. I wish I were dead, he thought over and over. I'd be better off. I'm lost forever.

That night when he went to bed, he couldn't sleep. Tossing from side to side, he kept Mary awake, and hated himself for that, too.

When dawn came, the room was very cold and a thick coating of frost covered the dormer window. He rubbed a clear spot, and saw a fresh blanket of snow on the road. Moving noiselessly so as not to wake Mary, who had fallen into a sound sleep, he put on his woolen breeches, doublet, cloak, shirt, hose, and heavy shoes, and tiptoed along the hall to the other bedchamber. Little Mary was asleep on her barred wooden bed. The reflection of the rising sun reddened her little face. Poor little blind child to have me for a father, he thought, and tears rose to his eyes.

The yellow sun was high in the blue sky when John reached the rectory. The air had warmed and the snow was beginning to melt. It would soon be spring.

Brother Gifford, himself, opened the door, and led the way up the narrow stairs to a room with a sloping roof and wide hearth. He lit the fire and pointed John to the armchair on one side of it while he sat opposite. John sat down and stretched his legs toward the warming blaze while Brother Gifford leaned against the high-backed oaken chair.

"Are you finding the answers to those questions that torment you?" the minister asked, looking at John contemplatively.

"There have been times when I've thought I have. But God can never forgive such a man as I."

"Don't hold anything back, John. Tell me what's in your heart."

"The Devil sits on my back driving me. I told Christ to go."

Brother Gifford's deep black eyes warmed. "That's nonsense, John, Christ doesn't take orders. He will never go."

"I cannot shake off my despair. Never was a man so miserable!"

Brother Gifford speared a finger toward the Bible on the small table near them. "There you will find the solution to all your problems!"

"I read and read it. Its passages fight with each other in my brain. I feel like a mouse in a maze."

"John, how can I help most? By answering your questions? Praying with you?"

"When I'm under the darkest cloud, as I am at this moment, I know the light is shining in those pages. 'Do you not see yonder shining light?' I ask myself. Your pure faith is always like medicine to me, but how can I escape my doubts?"

"Run from them to hope."

"The burden on my back is too great. I cannot run under it. I'm a guilt-burdened sinner."

"The Scriptures teach us that when we repent, our sins fall away. If you believe that, the next time your doubts trouble you, remember Christ's promises. Faith risks all for eternal life."

"I do not know the meaning of the Cross."

"A Christian forgets self and takes it up. Our Lord told us to lose our lives in the service of others. But love is necessary. Without love, a man who calls himself a Christian is a perfect hypocrite."

"But I'm so pliable. Religion has no real root inside me. It's all on the outside."

"I think your inner soil has been planted."

The next time John returned to the rectory, it was May. Brother Gifford, wearing dark breeches and a loose doublet turned back to display a spotless white shirt, led the way to the garden.

Under a young cedar tree, they sat side by side on a stone bench. The grass beneath their feet was green and clumps of daffy-down-dillies sprayed yellow against its bright grandeur. In a corner of the garden, a honeysuckle bush gave off fragrance that mingled with that of the cherry blossoms nearby. A thrush sang from its perch on the wall near the rectory door. Bees hummed in the soft air, as they winged above the blossoms. And somewhere a dog barked in joyful yelps to welcome the glorious morn.

"I understand now, my dear friend, what you tried to say," John told him. "I was so obsessed with my own problems that I had no love in my heart. Bring on an army of lions. I'm ready for them!"

"Then you have lost that burden?"

"It is lighter than it was. It isn't easy to die to self. But I have two new Christians who want to talk to you, Lettice and William Whitebread. Talking to them helped me."

"It isn't easy to be a Christian."

"You've never misled me about that!"

John Gifford knelt, and John, strangely moved, knelt on the grass beside him. Their prayer asked God to show John the path which leads within high and close fencing walls, the walls of salvation.

John had some work to do that day at Ampthill. It was dark as he returned home, but he felt a strange calm. Even the stars spoke of the divine love that steadied him. He felt like a waterman on the Thames who had almost drowned in a storm but had reached the bank.

Mary stood inside the door waiting. She opened her arms as she always did when he came home.

He hugged her, and then backed off to say, "Mary, I would like to move to Bedford. I need the strength of Brother Gifford and the Meeters there. I am going to be baptized."

"But you've already been baptized, John. Didn't your mother take you to the Abbey Church when you were born?"

"Brother Gifford suggested it as a new beginning!"

"I wouldn't discourage you, John, if the decision makes your eyes shine that way."

142

"Then you will come with me?"

She was quiet for a long moment, her oval face thoughtful. "To Bedford? Yes. But you understand how I feel about the Church of England. There will be one in our parish there."

"As Oliver Cromwell says, 'Let every man worship as he please!' And every woman."

They both laughed.

John's stepmother stayed with the baby and Mary went to Bedford with John the day he was baptized. As they walked along Duck Mill Lane between orchards and vegetable gardens to the tree-shaded inlet, he reflected that he could honestly join the Bedford Meeting now.

Brothers Gifford, Eston, Grew, and Harrington greeted him. At the foot of the moss-covered steps which led to the water's edge, the four shining ones stood smiling.

How deep and dark the inlet looked! John, who couldn't swim, and who had almost drowned twice, paused. Brother Gifford went ahead of him into the river, turned and held out his hand. What if I step in a hole? John thought. He began to tremble, but with resolution he took the minister's hand. It was a strong, firm hand. And in that instant all his fear vanished and great joy seized him. A Divine Presence filled his being. He walked beside the evangelist until the water reached his waist.

"Do not be afraid, John. You need never be afraid again," Brother Gifford said, just before he lowered him under the surface.

And there was no fear in him, only joy and peace. All the pent-up agony of the last five years melted. He knew his life would never be his own again. God had taken charge of it.

The following week the Whitebreads and a trader named Robert Holstock were baptized.

"The faith of the Meeters has a miraculous power," they all said, "when it can change a sinner like John Bunyan."

In April of 1654 another daughter was born to Mary and John. Bitsy came to help Mary until she was strong again, and they named the child after her. The baby was christened in the Elstow Abbey Church, and Bitsy was her godmother.

"Is she blind, too?" John asked that night, as Mary sat nursing Elizabeth.

"It's too soon to tell, but I don't think so."

Two weeks later Mary announced that she was sure this child could see. John passed his hands before her eyes, as he had done with little Mary, and when Elizabeth blinked and followed the motion, he thanked God.

That year of 1654, following Elizabeth's birth, saw many reforms in the realm. Many members of the Rump Parliament had left or been expelled, so that the skeleton membership had threatened the constitutional rights of the nation. The Rump Parliament was succeeded by the Barebones Parliament, so named after one pious member who prayed so much that he was nicknamed "Praise-God" Barebones. Many reforms and some revolutionary ideas filled the Rump Parliament's agenda, and when it had been dissolved in December, the new Parliament had gathered. There were four hundred representatives from England and thirty each from Scotland and Ireland. Royalists and Catholics continued to be excluded from voting in their shires. Yet this Parliament was closer to the ideal of a free one, and it had already legislated many reforms and concluded a Peace with Holland.

"The Lord Protector is showing new favor toward the Jews," John heard Anthony Harrington remark one morning after the church service. " 'Tis only right. He plans to settle some of them in London!"

"What of the Quakers?" John Eston demanded.

"The Protector is clinging to his principle of religious freedom to all except Catholics. He fears Catholics as much as the Malignants or Royalists."

"The Quakers frighten me," John Bunyan said.

Brother Gifford frowned. "The Quakers claim to have an inner light. I know they live like Christians."

"Nowhere do the Scriptures speak of an inner light," John Eston protested.

After that John often thought about the Quakers. He kept reminding himself that every man had the right to worship according to his conscience, but he asked questions to which he found no answers. Wasn't it idolatrous to follow some light other than Christ's?

Moving day was the first Saturday in April, 1655. Early that morning John hitched his father's horse to the cart, and loaded it. He drove the bony animal along the Bedford Road. Beside John sat little Mary, and Mary, holding the baby.

The cart behind them was piled high with their belongings: two joined stools, a board table, two benches, a crude settle, a homemade bed and trundle bed, a cradle, two goose-down mattresses, an armchair, a few pieces of clothing, a spinning wheel, some pewter plates and platters, the prized jug with the zigzag pattern, the kitchen utensils, John's books, tinker's tools, and materials.

In Bedford he guided the horse into a rough, unpaved street leading to St. Cuthbert's Parish Church where a white weathervane sat on the square turret. John drew the cart to a halt before a half-timbered cottage with a thatched roof, two chimneys, a dormer window, and low gables. It had taken time to find a cottage they could afford, which was not too close to the town ditches or "kennels," which served as drains for the borough. This house was far enough from the Saffronditch so that the noxious smells which it exuded would not plague them.

Mary carried the baby, and John led little Mary through the tall grass to wait inside the door while he got her a chair and the baby her cradle. He returned to the cart and began unloading the other furniture.

Mary told him where to put each article. There was a sizable family room on the left and a parlor on the right. The family room had a brick chimney and wide hearth with a long shelf above it. The chimney had a built-in oven and there was a diamond-paned window at rear of the family room which gave plenty of light. Behind the parlor was a small room he was to use as a library. Stairs led from the hall up to a large sleeping chamber where he placed the beds.

A small building in the garden behind the library would serve as his shop and forge. From there the view was beautiful, for green meadows stretched toward Newnham and blue hills rose beyond. This would be a fine, new life.

Soon after moving to Bedford, John met Tad Bradshaw on High Street. His father was having a difficult time, he said, with all of the prejudice against the Anglicans. He, himself, was married, had two sons, and was living in Shoe Lane, London, where he was trying to help the reprobates who filled the city's dirty alleys and lanes.

"Have you heard, John, that our old schoolmaster has been pensioned by the Commonwealth?" Tad asked. "Colonel Okey reported him to the commissioners for the ejection of scandalous ministers and schoolmasters. Lucky children today!"

"That's good news. I'll never forget the hard time he gave you and Mel Mooney. Where is Mel these days? Have you heard?"

"He went into the priesthood. For a time he was in Ireland. I haven't had any news of him in several years."

"If ever you see him again, tell him I asked about him."

One warm August day, as John worked the bellows at his forge, a gentle breeze was blowing through the doorway. Somewhere a bird sang. Two hornets buzzed in and out. In the meadow a black cow grazed. A goose waddled about on the dried mudpath. Happiness welled within John. How could any man ask for more? He felt like Paul who had nothing and yet all things.

The peace was broken by the sound of running feet. John Okey appeared on the path, his graying locks awry, his hazel eyes wide.

"John Bunyan, can you make a drinking vessel like a posset

cup or jug, but with a longer spout? Brother Gifford is seriously ill and cannot raise his head. His wife, Margaret, thinks she might get some nourishment down him with the proper cup."

John's heart sank. "He is critically ill? What's the matter with him?"

"Being a physician, he has diagnosed his own disease. He has consumption."

Above the fast beating of John's heart, his mind said, "Brother Gifford who interpreted the Gospel to me! My friend who taught that no man of his own power can escape the darkness in this world."

He reached for his snippers and a piece of metal, and said, "I'll make one right away."

While he worked, John Okey straddled a bench and talked to him. Brother Gifford's untiring work to carry the Gospel to others had tired him, he said. His wife had pleaded with him not to spend so many long hours in the saddle. The overwork had taken its toll.

"With rest, can't he recover?"

Colonel Okey shook his shaggy head. "He realizes that it is only a matter of time."

After a while John asked the colonel how he was getting along at Ampthill. Colonel Okey said that the Quakers were everywhere. One of them, John Crook who was a member of the Little Parliament and one of the local justices, had turned his estate between Woburn and Ampthill over to them. They were sincere, but they interrupted meetings to denounce force in any form and to proclaim nonviolent resistance."

John snorted. "In this world?"

"These beliefs are not for this world. How could any man sit down and twiddle his thumbs while England was being raped?"

They were both quiet for several moments.

"There's another matter I want to discuss with you," Colonel Okey said slowly. "Now is as good a time as any."

"Yes, sir," John invited.

147

He paused in his soldering and waited. Colonel Okey was frowning and he had a look of pain in his eyes. Town gossip said that the colonel had been unhappy ever since he had been relieved of his command of the regiment of horse a year ago.

"You have wide shoulders, tinker, that hint at unusual strength. If the Lord Protector continues to gain in influence, his power will become absolute. Few men can resist the corrupting influence of power. Some of us are convinced that the liberties we fought for are in danger."

For an instant John was too shaken to speak. When he had recovered from his surprise, he said, "I won't hear of any intrigues against General Cromwell. He's of the same faith as we are and a very moral Puritan. Anyway, never will I have part in treason against a ruler."

"You fought in the first Civil War."

"But I had no part in murdering the King of England!"

Colonel Okey winced. "Since I am one of the regicides, you think me a murderer?" he shouted, his face red, his eyes snapping beneath their bushy brows.

"I am not your judge."

"Don't you realize the fate of England is at stake?"

"The Protector is one of the greatest patriots England has ever known. I will support him until I know he has changed."

Colonel Okey reached for the drinking vessel which John held out to him. He shook his long hair like a dog shaking off fleas. "The day will come, tinker, when you will understand why I had to talk to you this way," he said in a voice that was almost gentle.

But John's ire was aroused. "Colonel Okey, sir, I think you're a traitor!"

The old soldier stamped out, the veins in his neck swelling, his free fist clenched. "Nobody ever called me that before!" he bellowed.

He had appeared to be furious, yet John had the feeling that he was rather pleased about something.

That night Mary, who had been making cherry jam all day,

was so tired that she went to bed right after supper. John joined the members of the Bedford Meeting as they gathered in St. John's. Ten women and three men knelt in a wide circle to pray. When it came to John's turn to speak, he folded his hands tightly and beseeched God to spare Brother Gifford.

"We have no right to demand that God accept our will," Anthony Harrington told him later, as they walked together to the bridge. "Effective prayer is made with the provision, 'Not my will, but thine, O God.' "

Each day John asked for news of Brother Gifford's condition, but Mary, who was expecting their third child, was sick a great deal and in John's preoccupation with home affairs he did not have time to dwell on Brother Gifford's grave illness. When the child, a boy, was born, they took him to St. Cuthbert's where he was christened John.

A few weeks later Brother Gifford died quietly, with Margaret sitting on a stool beside him while some of the members of the Bedford Meeting waited downstairs. As he clung to his wife's hand, all his dissolute life trooped before him. The certainty of death struck him, so that he cried out. But in his last moments his faith returned, and there was something childlike about him as he bade his family good-bye before he closed his eyes, gave one long racking cough and was gone.

The bells of St. John's tolled in long, mournful strokes calling the people to come to pay their last respects to the preacher, who, in recent years, had changed many lives. And the people came in the September sunshine—John Eston, John Grew, Anthony Harrington, John Whitebread, Robert Holstock, John Bunyan, the good sisters of the Meeting, and the newer converts.

Mary stayed in the cottage in St. Cuthbert's Street with the little Bunyans and the two Gifford children.

The sermon was brief and the words of the Scriptures spoke of life and not death, of joy and not sorrow, of what love can do to atone.

As the plain wooden box was lowered into the deep grave, which had been dug in the churchyard under a tall elm on the side away from the river, John could feel tears burning behind his eyes. Margaret Gifford stood weeping at the foot of the coffin. And John wanted to cry out that their good friend and minister wasn't dead at all, but living in that City he had talked about where there was one street which was gold, and surrounded by love, and joy, and peace. John Gifford had finished his pilgrimage.

Who will succeed Brother Gifford? was the question everyone asked. Wishing to be cautious, the congregation took their time and considered three men. John Okey, hearing of their dilemma, volunteered to consult the Protector on their behalf, and in January, the Protector advised the choice of a young man of twenty-three, John Burton.

"If there is anything I can do to help you let me know," John Bunyan told the pale young man. "Brother Gifford helped change my life, and I feel a great responsibility, for I am here while he is gone. I want to spread the truth, too."

There were times after that when John almost regretted his rash offer. Brother Burton sent him into the country to talk to others two or three times a week. John would gather the people about him on the market square, in the Moot Hall, or on the Green, and confess the change that had come over him. He neglected his work and his family.

"Perhaps I should stay at home more with you and the young uns, Mary," he said, "but the Lord, in the form of Brother Burton, is making mighty use of me."

"You must do what you will, John. The children and I are all right." Though she smiled sweetly, he noticed how white she looked.

Some months later a daughter was born to Margaret Gifford, and soon after that John and Mary had another son.

"Let's name him Thomas," Mary suggested. "That was your

grandfather's name, wasn't it? He must have been a great man."

"To me he was," John said. "He always took a stand for what he believed to be right. And my brother Thomas does his name proud."

"Four children," Mary said with a sigh. "Now we have two daughters and two sons."

"If we keep on, we'll people Bedfordshire. Now I must work harder than ever at the forge."

But he didn't. He continued his preaching in the surrounding villages.

Colonel Okey sent for him one cold February day. John found his old friend in a state of fury.

"Freedom of a proper kind is one thing, tinker," he bellowed, "but the country is filling with these Quakers, who have only contempt for the Word of God."

"Do they?" John asked, his mouth opened wide.

"At least the Levellers, or Fifth Monarchists, work to bring in the Kingdom. The Quakers just sit, or go about getting good Baptists mixed up."

"I don't have all the facts, but I could try to get them and warn people as I travel through the villages."

"It's a wonder John Milton does nothing."

"Maybe the Quakers aren't as bad as we think."

Colonel Okey led the way upstairs where he pointed to a hole in the roof, and their conversation ended when John climbed through a window to reach it. But he kept wondering what the Quakers really believed. If they were idolatrous, as some Baptists thought, somebody ought to do something about them.

I'll write a pamphlet, he thought. I'll try to use my pen. He began asking questions, talking to members of the Quaker faith, and had soon completed *Some Gospel Truths Opened*, which protested as dangerous the mystical beliefs of the Quakers, and declared that there is a historical as well as a spiritual Jesus, who had lived as a man and literally died.

To John's surprise Matthias Cowley, to whom he sent the manuscript, decided to publish it. People bought and read it and by spring it had caused so much discussion that Edward Burroughs, a young Quaker, replied with a treatise entitled, *The True Faith of the Gospel of Peace*, "contended for in a spirit of meekness against the opposition of John Bunyan, a professed minister in Bedfordshire."

John outlined a reply, and wrote in a consuming heat. The pen was mightier than the sword!

9   THE LAST Sunday in April of 1657, as John was crossing the flagstone path toward St. John's, he heard someone calling his name. He turned and saw that it was Mayor Grew, a member of his church, who had bad news to impart:

"John Okey, who has helped our church so much, has been arrested on a warrant issued by the Lord Protector and the Council. Sergeant Digby apprehended him, and took him to London. He'll probably end up in the Tower!"

"Is he accused of some conspiracy against the Commonwealth?"

The Mayor nodded. "It is difficult to understand. Maybe Okey has made some mistakes. No man's judgment is always right. But I always thought him a loyal Englishman."

"Perhaps he is confused."

"The Protector is frightened. He fears an insurrection of one of the groups which plague the Commonwealth."

"Can't something be done to save Colonel Okey?" John writhed as he pictured the Colonel's head upon the block on Tower Hill.

"If it were not for a meeting of the Bedford Council over which I must preside, I would go to London and plead his cause before the Protector."

"I'll go," John said impulsively.

"You might just make the proper appeal—if the Protector will see you. From what I hear of your preaching, you can speak passionately. And your attack on the Quakers has stirred discussion. Some copies of your pamphlet may even have reached London."

"I knew the Protector briefly when I was a boy," John said quietly. "We once fished together, and he talked of liberty and what he called the 'verities.' He's a reasonable man."

"Perhaps not now when he's afraid. And yet a tinker like yourself, a man of the people, might do more than some of the rest of us."

"Will you let me try?"

"Yes. Some of us will provide the money for a hired horse and your other expenses. Go, with our blessings."

John spurred the tired horse as he neared the walled city of London. It was late afternoon and he had been warned that after dark the gates would be locked for the night. Too, friends at Bedford had told him about the danger from footpads and rogues in the shadowy streets and alleys.

The lanterns on the postern at the gate were being lighted as John rode up. A sentry with raised rapier barred his way. Another guard in a box questioned him about his identity and business. John explained that he had come from Mayor Grew of Bedford to consult the Lord Protector.

"See one of the secretaries," the man advised. "If your business is really important, he can tell the Protector and advise you concerning it. Dozens come to see his Greatness. Few do. He is too busy."

"He'll see me," John said confidently.

The guard looked John up and down. "Wal, now, ain't that great?" he said, and smirked at his companion. "Maybe we have a Member of Parliament here, or at least a baron or a duke."

They laughed good-naturedly.

John soon forgot their joke at his expense as he rode along the city's streets, passing taverns, ordinaries, shops, houses, churches, and parks. Through some of the latticed windows lights flickered; others were shuttered and dark. Silhouetted against the sky he saw a mass of chimneys. There were church spires, too. He felt a stirring in his heart. *This was London.*

How often had he lain in the grass before his father's thatched cottage near Harrowden and watched the travelers to London galloping by on fine horses, or riding in bright and gilded coaches. Day after day, month after month, and year after year he had dreamed of going to London, too. And here he was!

The wind blew noxious with the odor of slop and human excretions. London had its ditches, and garbage littered the streets. Gasping for breath, he urged the horse into a trot until the air smelled clean again. He noticed an iron fence which enclosed a garden. Beyond a sprawling mass of great buildings was etched against the rising moon.

That must be Whitehall Palace, he thought. The Lord Protector, my old friend, lives inside those walls. Tomorrow I shall see him and ask him to release Colonel Okey.

John turned the horse around and began looking for an inn. When he reached the heart of the city, the houses and shops seemed to jostle each other. The streets were thick with choking dust, as hackney coaches, wagons, sedan chairs with bearers, an occasional glass coach, and men on horses moved along.

Thinking that progress would be less difficult through some of the side streets, John turned his animal into a narrow lane. He was horrified by the filth everywhere. Suddenly he saw a dark shape lying on the cobbles and guided the horse around it. It looked like a body. Forgetting the warning not to dally in dark places, he drew rein and went back.

A man lay sprawled there. John dismounted and stooped over him. He could smell strong water on his breath. He tried to rouse him, but the man was so drunk he didn't even mutter. John dragged him by his feet to a doorway where he propped him up, then he mounted again and continued his search.

Monstrous signs were everywhere, swinging on poles, the particolored boards picturing griffins, hogs in armor, lions, elephants, kings, queens, the Protector, angels, devils, and mermaids.

When John saw one near the strand with a helmeted knight facing a dragon, he drew rein. The St. George and the Dragon would surely be a good inn. The hostler greeted him, asked him to pay in advance, and told a tavern boy to show him to a room.

155

The hostler had a long wide nose, heavy eyelids, and black hair that stuck up in spikes. He must be the dragon, thought John; he looks like one.

The next day, which was Friday, was one of those cloudy, foggy days so frequent in London in April. John went to Whitehall Palace early, and found it heavily guarded. All about the gray stone buildings, sentries in scarlet barred his way. When he stated his business, one guard called the major-domo who told him that the Lord Protector was not at Whitehall. Affairs of state had so wearied him that he had gone away to meditate and relax. As a matter of fact nobody knew where he was, but if John's business was pressing, would he see the Secretary? The Protector would be too tired to see anyone when he returned.

Disappointed, John declined to see the Secretary, went out, and walked along the Thames with its fog and mud-caked, winding banks. He could make out the dim outlines of skiffs and barges on the river. He kept walking until the fog lifted and the sun came out in its warmth and splendor. Then pausing, he looked back. Whitehall, the Palace of former kings, now the residence of Oliver Cromwell, sprawled behind him, and up the river on the opposite bank was another palace. Lambeth! There, clad in pilgrim clothes, lay the body of the pilgrim bishop, near the altar where he had knelt to pray for guidance.

Where was the Protector? John thought for a while. If he planned to be back that night, he must be in the vicinity of London. But where? He noticed a tall, gangling boy fishing from a barge tied up at the bank. And suddenly John knew. The major-domo had said the Protector had gone off to meditate and relax. He was fishing of course! But where?

Water hemlock and birds were everywhere. A waterman called to him, "Oars. Oars. Westward ho! Eastward ho! A ride to London Bridge. See the fine arches and elegant houses. Visit the Tower and Tower Hill. A trip——"

John interrupted him. "I have no time to see London now. I

am looking for a friend. He has probably gone fishing along the river. Where do the fish bite best? That's where he would be."

The waterman scratched his balding head. "Wal, now, that would be down near the Town Ditches under the city walls. There be big bream, pike, and perch. I can row ye there."

"No," John said quickly, thinking that if he was right and the Protector was there, he would not want strangers hanging about. "I need a walk."

"It's a fur piece. Straight ahead past London Bridge."

"I like to walk and it has turned out to be a fine day."

"A waterman has a hard time," the man grumbled. "Now if yer friend fancies eels, 'tis the other direction he would go. Down t' Kew."

John thanked him, and strode off. When he came to the great arches spanning the river between Southwark and the city and saw London Bridge, his steps slowed. Fashionable shops and elegant houses were strung all across it. He wished he had time to explore them, especially the bookshop. But he would be back. He lifted his eyes, and his mouth fell open. In the center of the bridge was a spiked gateway. The hair on the back of his neck prickled as he stared; a paralysis of fear held him rooted in his tracks. A human head topped one of the spikes, and a raven was picking at one glassy eye.

The sight so upset John that he felt no thrill when he saw the Tower across the river. He scarcely heard the sound of music and song that came from a decorated barge filled with well-dressed young ladies. He was wondering what crime the beheaded man had committed. The Protector wouldn't tolerate unnecessary cruelty. Perhaps the man was one of the Fifth Monarchists, John thought. I hope he wasn't a Catholic. He took another look to be sure he wasn't Mel Mooney, who had become a Jesuit priest.

Marshy land lay ahead, but John kept on. This part of the riverbank was lonely, isolated, and his thoughts were morose. Perhaps John Okey had already been executed, but that "thing" back there was not he.

157

Then just ahead, John saw a man sitting on a muddy rock, holding a long fishing pole in one huge hand. His sad-colored suit, looked as if it had been made by a tailor's new apprentice. On his big head was a broad hat with a simple band from which fishing hooks protruded. Although he resembled a farmer, there before John was the Lord Protector of all Great Britain, unguarded and fishing while he read a book. When John paused before him, he noted the book's title, *The Compleat Angler* by Izaak Walton. John waited eagerly, expecting to be recognized. Instead angry eyes stared from the Protector's ruddy face, which looked as if it had been carved from a square of red oak.

"Who the devil are you? What are you doing here?" he said truculently.

John saw how tired he looked, and his love for his idol rose like a great throbbing tide.

"Don't you remember me, sir?" he asked softly. "I am John Bunyan, the tinker's boy from Elstow."

Ashamed of his brusque greeting, the big man shook his graying head, gave him a smile, and a welcoming wave of the hand that held the book.

"Of course I remember you. What are you doing in London?"

John dropped to the rock beside him. "I came to see you. I learned at Whitehall Palace that you had gone for a day of rest. I asked a waterman where the fishing was best, and here I am."

"What can I do for you?"

John took a deep breath. He wasn't going to mince matters. "Release Colonel Okey. He really wants what is best for England. He would never harm you!"

For an instant an odd smile turned up the corners of the Protector's big mouth. It was like a secret smile which was replaced by a scowl.

"Okey will remain in the Tower."

"But he is a man of his word. If he promises loyalty and that he will cut himself off from these Fifth Monarchists and other insurrectionists, will you let him go?"

"You speak boldly, John Bunyan." A hard and glittering expression came into the Protector's deep eyes. His voice was sharp. "There are times when it is dangerous not to act to avoid insurrection. The Commonwealth to survive must move to finish those who would destroy it. The Fifth Monarchy men in the realm even now plot to seize London. One leader, Thomas Venner, has ambitions to wear a crown. We are compiling evidence and when we have enough, they shall hang!"

"Allow me to disagree with you about Colonel Okey, your Excellency. He is at heart a true patriot."

"Colonel Okey will remain in the Tower."

"There is talk, your Excellency, that you wish to wear a crown. Many fear your power. They are honest enough to say so!"

The Protector sighed. "Perhaps they have cause to fear. And stop calling me 'your Excellency'! There are those who wish to make the Protectorate hereditary. Some have approached me about becoming king. They reason that, as king, I might be more effective against the Stuarts and their intrigues!"

"But you said England was done with kings! Your wisdom and honor will keep you to the promises you made to the common people!"

The big man paused before he spoke again, gazing reflectively at the pole in his hand. At length he said, "Don't think I'm not praying that I will know what is right. I've done a lot of things wrong. I vowed as a young man never to take a human life, yet I agreed the King had to die. Since then some executions have been necessary."

"But surely you would not hang Colonel Okey. Let me visit him at the Tower. I have the feeling he is not sure these insurrectionists are right."

"You have great loyalty to your friends, John. Colonel Okey's heart is all right." Again there was that odd smile, almost as if Cromwell were keeping some delightful secret.

"You once likened man to the chalk hills. Sometimes I pretend they are mountains. I call them the Delectable Mountains. Do you remember what you told me the day we fished at the Hillersdon estate?"

The Protector shook his head. "That was a very long time ago, John."

"You said that there were 'verities,' values that are as indestructible as gold. I think I know now what you meant, sire."

"John, you talk like a Christian."

"I think I am one now, sire. I attend the Bunyan Meeting in Bedford. You remember when our minister died how Colonel Okey consulted you as to a wise choice for his successor? Colonel Okey has sponsored our church, contributed money, helped arrange meetings. Sometimes I preach, too, in the villages."

"You cannot get your mind off Okey very long, can you?" the Protector said indulgently. "On Sunday, after church is out, I will see that you are given the password to the Tower. Where are you staying?"

His heart leaping like a fish, John told him. Perhaps Colonel Okey would be safe. Maybe his head would never top one of the spikes on London Bridge.

"Sir, there was a head on a spike on London Bridge. What had that man done?"

Again the deep eyes shot fire. "He was conspiring with a group at the Nonesuch Tavern to bring Charles back. We have ways of ferreting out such traitors. He deserved to die!"

"His head was placed there as a warning to others?"

Oliver Cromwell nodded. "My informers tell me that the sentiment for a king is growing. That is another reason some members of Parliament press me to accept the crown."

"But you won't."

The Protector looked sharply at John. "What makes you so confident?"

"Even your enemies say you are an honest Protector. Sometimes, where Catholics and Malignants are concerned, your policy seems pitiless. But you have united Scotland, Ireland, and England. You have ten divisions of an army throughout the realm that have brought peace. Our navy is the finest in the world. You did all this in the name of freedom. How then could you accept a crown?"

160

The Protector sighed. "God did all those things. I have always believed that I am merely one of His instruments wielding His sword."

"I know little about government, sire. I have been told that our liberties grew up under it. King Charles thought he was not bound by what has gone before. You don't believe that."

"A protector is something new in the realm. My power has never been defined. That worries some politicians. The end of last month at a feast in the Banqueting Hall at Whitehall, I was presented with an invitation to become king."

"You didn't accept?"

"I told the committee that it would receive my consideration, but I will decline it. I have no ambition to wear a crown. You're right about that."

A sudden jerking on his line brought the Protector to his feet. He pulled in a fine perch, took it off the hook, and added it to those on a big forked stick. He squinted up at the sun.

"I had better get back to Whitehall," he said in a flat voice. "Remember me to all my friends in Bedford."

John was about to tell him that the Mayor had sent his greetings when he noticed a sinister-looking man coming along the bank. There were two more men coming from the opposite direction, a pock-marked fellow and a heavy man, big of limbs and head.

"Sire," John whispered, "there are men coming at us from two directions. I'm not sure I like the looks of them."

The Protector lifted his head quickly. "They are not pretty fellows." He dropped his pole and John saw that lines grooved his brow. Backs to the wall, John and the Protector waited.

The three men reached the spot at the same time. They shot furtive glances toward them. The pock-marked fellow held his hand under his cloak and John heard the clicking sound of a pistol being readied. Instinctively he moved in front of the Protector, as the pistol flashed in the sunshine. The other two men flung themselves on John, pinioning his arms.

"Knaves!" John hissed, his body tense. "Let me loose!"

161

But the hands that held him were as tight as iron bands around a barrel as they dragged him away from the Protector.

"If you want to fight, you abominable cutthroats, I'll take you on!" Oliver Cromwell roared.

With a deft movement he grabbed his assailant's arm, and shook it with such violence that the pistol dropped to the mud. The heavy man left John to his companion, and ran at the Protector while the pock-marked one tried to retrieve the weapon. But the Protector shook him off, dived to the ground, picked up the pistol, and hurled it into the river. The brutish man threw his arms around Cromwell, and together they hit the ground, rolling over and over down the bank to the water's edge. John struggled so to free himself that his captor called for help, and the pock-marked man rushed to flank him on his free side. Powerless to go to his hero's aid, John winced when the assailant briefly held the Protector's head under the water. But with a tremendous heave the old soldier propelled his enemy into the air, and the next moment was on top of him. His huge red hands circled the cutthroat's neck and squeezed until the man gave a jerk and lay still.

The Protector seemed to swell even larger and to grow redder as he rose and stumbled purposefully toward John and the other men. He pulled out a long blade, his eyes shooting fire.

"By the breasts of the Virgin!" the pock-marked man cried to his companion. "Come on!"

They let go of John and ran, lumbering across the marshy land.

The Protector shook his head. He was panting heavily and muddy water dripped down his big, red face.

"Let them go!" he said between clenched teeth. "We'll find those foul fiends and mete out punishment. I would know them anywhere. God preserved us. Now, help me throw this carcass into the river!"

John felt sick and he wanted to turn away, but he forced himself to lift the ugly head with its bulging glassy eyes, while the Protector raised the feet.

"Heave!" came the order. And John heaved. The body landed with a splash in the brown water.

162

Calmly the Protector stooped and washed his hands. "That's that," he said. "Now I think you'd better accompany me back to the Palace."

"Did those men know who you are?" John asked as they strode along. "Or were they cutpurses?"

"They knew me," the Protector said sadly. "I try to be careful, but today I felt as if I had to be alone. My staff has been begging me not to play the fool."

As John walked about London the next afternoon, his thoughts raced to and fro. Could John Okey be involved with the attempted assassination of a ruler? He had been one of the regicides. Did he want to take the Protector's life, too?

Bewigged gentlemen in feathered hats, smelling of perfume, wearing silks, velvets, and lace ruffles were strolling about; ladies, powdered, patched, and decorated with gold and precious stones, fine gowns, ermine-trimmed cloaks, and tall velvet hats clung to their arms. There were ragged urchins as well; Puritans with cropped heads and shapeless clothes like his own; bawds, and other evil-looking creatures.

Gilded and painted coaches rolled through the rutted streets, and beautiful horses were everywhere.

At majestic St. Paul's the cries of the merchants in the church-yard reverberated with the bells which struck the hour of four, and with the clatter of hoofbeats and the voices of those who sold and those who bought. John browsed in the bookstalls until he found two books he wanted: a worn copy of Walton's *The Compleat Angler,* which the Protector had been reading, and a pamphlet-type publication, *The Tenure of Kings and Magistrates.* The latter had so stirred the populace in 1649 that Milton, its author, had become famous and was now on the Protector's staff. They cost John a shilling. Holding them under his arm, he walked through the narrow lane behind the cross in the corner of the yard and into the Broad Street of West Cheap.

Footsteps padded after him. He turned and saw a rotund man with a cherubic face dressed in the broad hat and dark coat of an

Anglican rector. Somehow the man looked familiar. He was whistling a tune as he waddled along, looking about him. John smiled to himself. He couldn't know this man; his nerves must be on edge after the events of the day before. Continuing east from St. Michael's Church toward Cheapside Cross, he waited for the Anglican to overtake him.

"Good evening," John greeted. "Will you be good enough to direct me to a tavern where the food is cheap but of good quality? I am a stranger in London."

"Take any of those three paths: Bread Street, Friday Street, or Cheapside. They converge at the Mermaid. The tavern was a favorite haunt of Shakespeare, Donne, and Jonson. But it is noted for many things, including its mutton!"

"Then that is where I will sup."

"It's a respectable place and no stewhouse. I'm on my way there. Follow me."

The churchman waddled ahead of John and paused before a weather-beaten sign which pictured a pink and green mermaid. They walked under it, opened a heavy wooden door, and went inside.

Around the long boards groups of men sat eating, talking, laughing, and drinking: gentlemen, scholars, Puritans, perfumed popinjays, louts, oafs, and ruffianly fellows. The gentlemen wore periwigs, beribboned coats, velvet or brocaded breeches, plumed hats, and huge cravats that hung outside their coats. The Puritans were conspicuous, too, in their sad-colored coats, plain breeches, white shirts, and wide collars.

John looked about the huge raftered room lit by candles which flickered in the wall sconces. In imagination he could see the great who had wielded mighty pens seated where these guests were seated tonight. More than ever he longed to so use his pen as to prick the consciences of men.

The aproned hostler greeted them, and led the way to a table where five other guests sat. John's companion ordered mutton and watercress salad; John duplicated the order. They relaxed in the genial atmosphere, listening to the idle chatter around them.

The smell of fowl roasting on the spit over the snug fire heightened John's appetite. He noticed that the table was spotless and the floor very clean. At last a scrawny boy brought the mutton and watercress, and they began to eat wolfishly.

A musician in a green silk doublet and red breeches fiddled a gay tune. The clergyman tossed him a shilling. John began to feel content. This day had been exciting, and the happenings of the previous one seemed unreal. He grew drowsy.

The sound of voices raised in argument made him sit up. He listened to a beplumed gentleman happily describing the punishments meted out to the Irish Catholics under the direction of Henry Cromwell, the youngest son of the Lord Protector. Then a Puritan said staunchly that tolerance was the product of religious indifference. A Presbyterian took this up, insisting that since John Calvin had spent so much time advising Archbishop Cranmer and others in the establishment and framework of the Church of England, Presbyterianism, which Calvin had codified, was the true religion of England.

John noticed that his Anglican companion was twisting and untwisting his plump white hands, that his brown eyes glinted with anger, and the veins in his neck stood out. Again conviction came to John that he had seen this man before. When a lull came in the conversation the clergyman spoke quietly, though his nervous fingers belied his calm.

"If all men cannot agree on how to worship Almighty God, is it necessary to persecute, torture, and kill? Gentlemen, I was in Ireland when the conquest began under General Ireton and continued after his death under General Ludlow. I know whereof I speak. I saw men, women, and—yes—little children, dying of starvation. I saw many put to the sword. I saw hundreds sent to a slavery worse than death. Thousands enlisted in the service of Spain and France."

There was silence. Every man at the board paused to stare at the speaker. And in that instant, as John looked at him, his heart gave a great leap of recognition. He was no Anglican, unless he had renounced his faith. He was an old friend, a Bedford school-mate, Mel Mooney. *What was he doing in this disguise?*

"You sound like a papist!" a sour-faced gentleman in brown periwig and velvet said truculently. "Take heed! You know what happens to papists!"

"What happens to papists?" John found his voice. "I was in the Parliamentary Army. I thought I fought for freedom of faith. The Divine Will can never be measured by men who try to ob-cure it to fit their selfish interests, or even the best interests of the state!"

"Anyone who tolerates unsound beliefs in others is burying God's Bible," the sanctimonious Puritan said. "He doubts his own beliefs."

"We were speaking of the sufferings in Ireland," Mel said, his chin raised pugnaciously. "Those who had participated in the Protestant massacre years ago—and I grant you that was horrible, too—were put to the sword or banished, excluding only those who had proved their favor to Parliament. Scores of Catholic land-owners forfeited a third of their estates. And how is the standing army supported in England?"

"How is it supported?" one of the men asked indifferently.

"Any man who, under the dictates of his conscience, bore arms for the King, pays a tenth of his income for its support," Mel ex-plained.

John found his voice. "If the Protector be a despot, what a grand despotism! The results can be seen in the peace and pros-perity we know today."

"'Tis true that the Government's policy has achieved its goal," Mel agreed. "Ireland participates in this Government. It has the same number of seats as Scotland—thirty. But the outrages com-mitted by both groups and the hatred can never be obliterated."

"I, for one, believe that the Protector should be vested with more power. He should have the title of 'King,'" the gentleman in the brown periwig remarked.

"God forbid!" Mel said reverently, getting up and starting for the door.

166

John followed. They strode along side by side.

"Do you know who I am, John?" Mel asked.

"I remember you," John confessed. "Where have you been the last eighteen years? You're not an Anglican?"

"No. Five years ago I took my final vows and became a Priest of the Church of Rome. Because I have been active in trying to protect those of my faith, I am a hunted man."

"To help others you risked death to return to London!"

"There are things worse than death."

"Would you like to meet Cromwell and secure his protection?"

Mel stopped walking. "Are you out of your mind, John? In the first place, he would never see me. In the second place, he fears the influence of all priests."

"You're not up to any treason?"

"I am not. Rest assured of that."

"Then I will keep your confidence."

"A Major Wildman has founded a Republican Club at the sign of the Nonesuch in Bow Street. I belong!"

"What is the club's purpose?"

"To work for a more republican government."

"The members think you are an ousted vicar?"

Mel nodded. "From Bedford."

"What if they find out the truth?"

"I may lose my ears."

John walked through the darkness, his thoughts whirling. The country was split into so many factions that it was not difficult to understand why the Protector felt the need of ten sections of an army led by major-generals who watched for insurrectionists. What if Mel was really allied with those who wished the Protector's death? He had to find out.

"Would the Protector's assassination bring justice and true toleration?" he asked slyly.

"I do not hold with murder. Those of the Republican Club want only a government with more real freedom. None would plot treason!"

John sighed with relief. "Then if ever I can help you should you return to Bedford, you can find me in St. Cuthbert's Street."

That night John propped himself up against the pillows and read John Milton's treatise, aghast at its audacity. No wonder it had caused a stir and resulted in the author's appointment as Secretary of Foreign Tongues for the Commonwealth. Milton pointed out that rulers were responsible to the will of the governed, that the people should call selfish rulers to account, and if necessary execute them. Once an ardent Presbyterian, the writer now served the cause of toleration and the Independents. Passion burned in this treatise for a just victory of liberty. What a war a mighty pen can wage, John thought as he snuffed out the candle.

The next morning, when John awoke, the church bells were ringing, reminding him of the sweet sound of the bells of Elstow Abbey Church. He thought about his father, brother Willie, young Thomas, and his stepmother, who saw that the whole family attended church regularly. These days Papa didn't think of trying to go to the tavern or climb trees at church time. But he continued to hate Oliver Cromwell, calling him the "usurper" and talking about the day when Charles II would return.

John dressed slowly, ate a hearty breakfast, and started out to find a place of worship. At first all London seemed to be asleep. Then the traffic began to increase and the sun peeped over the red gables, the rooftops, and the vanes of the churches, bathing them in a golden light.

And suddenly the whole city was alive. The church bells began to peal everywhere, drowning out the roar of traffic. Foot-passengers moved in all directions. When John came to St. Paul's churchyard, a bawd in a crimson velvet cloak and with a bonnet tied over a curled gray wig, passed him going toward the front of the fine, old Gothic church. Behind her, two by two, followed six young women in dark hooded Puritan-style cloaks. John stared. On their feet they wore shining silver slippers! Like a general leading a charge, the bawd marched into the church, the girls following close behind her.

A gentleman, standing at one side of the wide door, caught John's eye and smiled.

"That's a sight, isn't it? That's Mam Bard who used to run the stewhouse known as the Cardinal's Hat. It has been purged by order of his Excellency, the Lord Protector. Nowadays she serves the new China drink, tea, and a brew she calls coffee. The tea is fair, but the coffee is horrible; she keeps it in the pot for weeks. But old Mam makes her girls go to church. Patriotic, she says, and wants to co-operate with the Protector. Some doubt her heart is pure."

The gentleman threw back his head and laughed so heartily that he set his wig askew, just as a lady stepped from a glass coach to join him. He winked at John, straightened his wig, and gave the lady his arm.

John followed them into the big church, because he was afraid that, if he looked for a noncomformist congregation, he might be late for the service. After all, this was God's Church, too.

When John returned to the inn before noon, there were no messages. Nobody had asked for him. Slowly he ate dinner, and had just finished when he heard a woman's voice asking the hostler where she would find "J. Bunyan." It was a girl dressed in a hooded gray cloak. When he was pointed out to her, she came toward him and curtsied.

"Mr. Bunyan, your friend asked me to tell you, Green Ribbon," she whispered. "Five o'clock today."

"Green Ribbon," he repeated in a low voice, thinking the Protector was clever to send a woman; any spies hanging about would be watching men.

He thanked her, walked with her to the open door, and she disappeared into the busy street.

Somewhere a clock was striking the hour of five as John arrived at the arched gate of the Tower of London. A beefeater in crimson and black barred his way with lifted halberd.

"The password?" he demanded.

"Green Ribbon."

The man stepped back, lowered his weapon, and stood at attention as John moved past him into the outer yard. As he neared the Bloody Tower, he saw to his right a high-barred gate; he had heard of Traitor's Gate through which the miscreants of other ages had vanished from life. To his left, a group of time-blackened buildings rose ominously against the clouded sky.

At the Bloody Tower, John went under the raised portcullis where a sentry asked him who he wished to see. While the man went to find out where Colonel Okey was, John gazed up at the gray fortress, thinking, as he had often thought when passing the pitiful prisoners chained to the wall of Bedford Gaol, that it would be better to die than to be so fenced off from life.

The sentry returned and led him inside the gloomy place, up a flight of winding, hollowed stairs to the very top where he inserted a huge iron key in a heavy wooden door, opened it, and bade John enter.

A figure rose from a high-backed chair silhouetted against a barred window. To John's surprise Colonel Okey advanced to meet him, smiling and holding out his hand. The light, streaming through the window struck his square face, giving it an odd radiance, softening it, changing it.

"Come in. I've been expecting you."

The sentry bowed himself out, leaving the door ajar. John stared, unable to believe his own eyes. The prisoner was clean-shaven and wore a fine white shirt, good black breeches, and buckled shoes.

"You—you were expecting me?"

"I had word you had come all the way from London to save my life. Such loyalty, John Bunyan, has touched me. I shall not forget your friendship."

"But how could you know?"

Fear rippled through John's flesh and made the hair on the back of his neck rise. He felt almost as if a streak of fire had seared him. This situation was so uncanny that his heart sounded in his ears like thunder. Colonel Okey, locked in a stronghold like the

170

Tower, knew everything. *Such knowledge was supernatural!*

"Oh, yes," the colonel continued. "I know, too, of the fresh conspiracy against the Protector, how he beat off his assassins, and saved *your* life!"

"But how could you possibly know?"

"Have a seat. It's time we had a talk."

John sat down at the table, looking around in astonishment. The surroundings were nothing like those prisoners were said to have to put up with. No rats squeaked from the corners. There was no dust anywhere. Sunlight was streaming through the window. The stone walls had atmosphere, for they were time-blackened and covered with inscriptions left by the martyrs of the ages. Over in one corner was a bed with a mattress. There was a table, laid with a linen cloth and silver-covered dishes. John could smell browned meat and it made him hungry.

Colonel Okey read his mind. "No, you're not dreaming, John. The Protector has just left and we agreed to take you into our confidence."

Colonel Okey lifted the silver cover from the largest dish, and picked up a knife to separate the beef. After John took a chunk, the colonel passed a round loaf of bread, and a dish of watercress seasoned with herbs.

Wonderingly John asked, "Why are you being treated as few royal prisoners have ever been treated in the Tower? Why is the Protector consorting with a man accused of treason against him?"

"John, actually I am one of the Protector's Chief Informers. One of my duties is to ferret out the dangerous enemies of the Commonwealth. I joined Wildman's Republican Club and met with its members until I was certain most of them are harmless. But they needed a warning, so a number of them were arrested. It seemed a good idea to include me in that number, so that none would suspect."

"Then your connection with the Millenarians, or Fifth Monarchy men, was for the same purpose?"

He nodded, smiling. "Oliver wants public freedom. He believes it well for the people to take a part in their government.

171

He expects some opposition, but he is against treason that threatens the Commonwealth."

"But you must have a large force of men doing this ferreting!"

"Yes. The Secretary of Foreign Tongues is kept informed, and he meets propaganda head on."

"Then your head never was in danger of being severed?"

"No. But if those who conspire to place the crown on Charles succeed, my head will be the first to roll down Tower Hill."

"God forbid!"

"God forbid that Charles be restored, or that my head roll down Tower Hill?"

"You know I liked young Charles. But Oliver Cromwell has a great heart. He is Britain's executive power. My loyalty is to him. But I would not want to see you lose your head! Otherwise, I would not have bothered to come to London."

"We need your help, John. You travel around Bedfordshire preaching, tinkering. Nobody would suspect you of having any contact with the Protector. You could be very useful to the Commonwealth."

"I would never stoop so low as to inform on my friends and neighbors!"

"We are not asking you to do that, John."

"You told me that liberty is in danger."

"That I did. The truth is it is in danger from those who would overthrow the Commonwealth, those who plot the return of the Stuarts, and the more radical Fifth Monarchy men such as one scoundrel named Thomas Venner."

"If you're loyal, why did you talk to me the way you did about the Protector?"

"To test you, John. You yourself told me about Mary Roberts' loyalty to the Stuarts. Matthias knew. I had to find out if you had been influenced by a pretty wife."

"If I had had any traitor's blood, you would have let it!"

"We can take no risks. Now this is what we want you to do: simply tell me how people are thinking and of any rumored plots against the Commonwealth, or the Protector's life."

172

"And you are asking me to report on my own wife?"

"No. We're not worried about Mary. She is too busy raising your family to take much part in any intrigue. But she is to know nothing of this. Nobody must know, Mary least of all."

Licking his fingers over the last morsel of beef, John reflected. William Vierney had managed to have himself reappointed as a part-time teacher in Bedford. Any treasonous movements would probably center around him. There was William Lane, a cousin of the Royalist sympathizers by that name. William had once worked against the Royalists; but he might have changed again. But he was John's friend. Could he inform on a friend? Oliver Cromwell, he decided, was the executive power and his first loyalty would be to him, especially where the great man's life was concerned.

"Tell me in detail," he said in a whisper. "What do you want me to do?"

10 The news soon spread through the shire that the Lord Protector had refused to wear a crown, although the kingship clause in the Act of Government had carried two to one. But by the new Act he was empowered to appoint his successor, and this was alarming to some of Bedford's citizens. Many had signed a petition, opposing as dangerous the contemplated change in government from a commonwealth to a monarchy, "whereby we conceive a foundation is laid for a new, most bloody, and desolating war."

There was further excitement when it was learned that wagonloads of Spanish silver had been sent to London and were being made into English coins. People wondered where the silver came from. Had Admiral Blake removed it before he sank those Spanish ships? Few cared that it was confiscated money; the Treasury of England had been replenished.

The new Act provided that Parliament was again to meet in two houses instead of only one, the House of Commons, and gave the Protector the right to appoint the seventy members "of the other House," the House of Lords. And by it, liberty of worship was granted to all except Socinians, Papists, and those who denied that the Scriptures were inspired. Some grumbled that the Protector chose the members of the House of Lords, some of whom wanted only approved, educated men to preach. But as John traveled about the shire, he failed to learn of any organized plot against the Government.

174

He wrote another book against the Quakers, *A Vindication of Gospel Truths Opened,* which Matthias Cowley published. John accused them of being similar to the Ranters. "The Ranters made them [the doctrines] threadbare at an alehouse," he wrote, "and the Quakers have set a new gloss upon them again by an outward legal holiness."

"John, don't you think you can do more by positive preaching than by tearing down the beliefs of one particular religious group?" Mary asked one night at supper. "I want to die and be buried an Anglican. Is it fair to denounce the Quakers for their preference?"

"When it is idolatrous?"

She shook her head, her eyes searching his face. "Are you their conscience? I think they're good Christians."

He felt the color flood to his cheeks. "I preach positively, Mary," he said defensively. "In the morning I am going to Stevington to preach to the Independents."

But that Sunday as he walked along in the early sunshine, he reflected that perhaps he was unfair to the Quakers. After all, as a group they were willing to suffer for their faith. He didn't write against the Presbyterians, although he loathed the spiritual arrogance of some of them. He didn't attack the Independents. A number of Puritans were going to extremes in declaring joy sinful and innocent pleasures the enticements of Satan. Maybe Mary's right, he thought. I guess I'll just leave the Quakers alone for a while and concentrate on preaching the Gospel and tinkering. After all, who am I to judge?

As he remembered his own sins, he imagined that the heavy load was on his back again, weighing him down. I have been of arrogant spirit, he confessed. And here I am going to preach to others about their sins!

Walking up the steep hill that led into Stevington, John felt more depressed than he had at any time since his conversion. He had come to preach, and he couldn't. Not today! His own sin was smothering him.

The bells pealed out as he passed the old stone church, and the sound cheered him a little. Some ducks rose from the gleaming river below, sailing across the Ouse to the fields green with unpulled corn. His path led down the hill and across Dancing Meadow to the Holmes Wood.

Under the tall trees, beside a shimmering inlet, Stephen Hawthorn, the minister of the Stevington Independent Church, was waiting. The members began to gather, and when it was time to start the service, they seated themselves expectantly on the mossy ground.

Stephen, a man who looked like a kindly bull, took John's arm and led him aside for a moment of prayer. John bowed his head, and the minister's words were like fire in his brain: "Our Father, Guide thy servant this morning. Give his message wings to lift the hearts of Thy children to a new consecration to Thee. In His Blessed Name, Amen."

The service that followed was a nightmare to John. Stephen gave a long introductory talk about what God had done for a tinker. He was a poor speaker and everybody looked bored. When John began to preach, his voice was shaking. One man closed his eyes. A woman nodded sleepily. The memory of his sins lay in his heart like a stone. Nothing he could say this morning would point anyone to God. He tried, but the words would not come from his heart. He had failed God.

As he started home, he felt emptied, drained of his faith. The sense of his failure overwhelmed him: "God, take this burden off my back!" he prayed. "I am so weary of my guilt."

The sun came out just as he reached the top of the hill in Stevington. It painted the village cross in golden light. And in that moment a huge black thing fell from his back and rolled down the hill toward the Holy Well, disappearing into a cave where the pure water washed it away. The rocky cave was like the tomb where Christ stood, risen, holding out his hands. Angels guarded the opening, and one rose into the air, and lighted on John's back in the exact spot where the big black guilt had been. A sense of being cleansed filled John: through the atonement he had been freed. Christ's death had redeemed him.

176

After that day, it was as if the angel sat on his back driving him until he had to tell others about Christ's Grace. Preaching became a passion. He wrote a book about careless men who, like the smith's dog, lay beside the forge while sparks from the flames flew into his face.

At the end of August, 1658, John galloped along the highroad toward Colonel Okey's home at Ridgemont. He had been released from the Tower shortly after John had visited him there. John had some information. Perhaps it wasn't important, but he had heard William Vierney telling people in the market place at Bedford that the Protector's fall was imminent. Vierney said that the Lord Protector had, himself, recently done the very thing he had criticized Charles I for doing: he had dissolved Parliament.

As John galloped up to the hitching rail, Colonel Okey emerged from the big stone house. His face was grave and, without greeting, he announced, "A messenger just brought a letter from London. Oliver is dying! The Royalists will probably seize the opportunity to bring Charles back."

Emotion choked John, so that he could not speak. In memory he could see the rough-hewn face, honest eyes, and determined chin. The Protector had worked so hard at trying to make England what it should be, he had worn himself out. He was really giving his life for the glory of England and the liberty which had never come.

"Is there no hope?" John managed.

"None. He has appointed his eldest son, Dick, to succeed him. Dick's a weakling. There will be chaos. Then Charles will return!"

"If Dick is so ill fitted to govern England, why would Charles' return be so terrible?"

Colonel Okey turned white. "For one thing I'd lose my head."

On September 3, the anniversary of the victories of the Parliamentary forces at Dunbar and Worcester, Oliver Cromwell died. A sense of appalling calamity spread through Bedford. The people came out of their houses and stood in excited groups. The

Lord Protector was dead. The few who hated him—like William Vierney, William Foster, and Froggy Foster—were overjoyed, while those who had loved him trembled and wept.

Of all the mourners walking the streets of Bedford, John Bunyan was the most miserable. Oliver Cromwell had been his friend, the friend of all who truly loved England. How could he be dead when he was so indestructible, so powerful? John remembered the deep rumble of his laugh; the warmth of his manner; his ferocity when angered; his gentleness, too. And now he was gone. What a king had failed to do, he had done. He had subdued Ireland and Scotland and made England a great power. Freedom of thought and religion had come for many, even if he had been hard on the groups he feared. But a central authority was necessary. He had made mistakes, of course. No man was perfect, and John had loved him.

When it grew dark, John crept back to his forge, sat on his work bench, and bowed his head. Grief so terrible gnawed at him that he didn't want to eat, although Mary came out to tell him that his supper was growing cold. Bells rang slowly, mournfully all over Bedford. John sat until the bells of St. Cuthbert's stopped ringing, and then he went into the cottage where Mary tried to comfort him.

Colonel Okey left for London to attend the funeral and brought back a copy of the *Commonwealth Mercury* of the week of September 2–9. It had a deep black border and immediately after the news of Oliver Cromwell's death was the announcement: "There is lately published *A Few Sighs from Hell*, or *The Groans of a Damned Soul* by John Bunyan."

"That's a piece of doubtful wit on the part of some Royalist," Colonel Okey said grimly. "But perhaps it will help sell your book."

One night about a month after the Protector's death, when John came home, he found Mary in bed. She lay on her back looking very white, her yellow curls spread over the pillow.

"John, I'm sick. Please send for Dr. Bannister and Bitsy."

178

As he bent over her, she put her arms around his neck, kissed him with hot, fevered lips. "I hated to worry you, John, but I've been spitting blood for weeks. . . . I kept hoping. . . . I don't want to die and leave you and the children." She broke into tears.

John tried to reassure her before he rushed out to find the doctor and to ask John Grew to send a messenger post haste to Matthias Cowley at Newport.

The doctor came out of the bedchamber shaking his head. "I've let over four cups of blood, but she hasn't rallied. She is sinking fast. I fear she won't last the night."

Not Mary, John thought. Not my Mary. In that instant he wished he could die in her place.

All the next day she lingered, tossing and mumbling. She was still breathing when Bitsy arrived the morning after that. Her lovely black eyes streamed tears as she and John spoke to Mary, but she never knew them.

As the church bells tolled that Sunday morning, Mary died quietly, closing her eyes and simply ceasing to breathe. Gently John folded her white hands across her breast and went downstairs.

When the funeral service had been read by the vicar at St. Cuthbert's Church, the mourners followed the young men of the parish who bore the wooden box to its hole in the autumn sod. Above the grave stood a twisted tree its barren branches speaking of death and life to come.

John spent a sleepless night, remembering Mary as he had first seen her, asking himself how he could care for four children, all under ten.

At cockcrow, when he rose to prepare breakfast for Matthias and Bitsy before they left for Newport, he found Bitsy already up and busy breaking some eggs into a bowl.

"Dame Grew has been here and brought some soup for your dinner. The good dames will not let you and the children starve," she said.

179

"There is nothing better than good thick soup," he answered, realizing how fast Bitsy was growing up.

"Dame Grew said her husband is worried because the duly elected members to Parliament are being kept out."

"On what grounds?"

"Sir Samuel Luke was excluded by the test of 1648, by which Presbyterians were to be kept out."

"Colonel Okey was afraid of chaos."

"Papa Matthias says the Presbyterians are in the majority in Parliament if they will just stand on their rights."

"Richard Cromwell is not the man his father was. But I have problems of my own!"

"I spoke to Uncle Matthias about me staying to help you. He said people would talk."

"Your uncle is right. I'll have to stay at home, and work in the forge."

"What about your preaching?"

"If God wants me to preach, he will provide someone to care for my children," John said, trying to convince himself.

Twice a week women of the church came to help John with the housework and the cooking. Others came, too, bringing bread, cakes, and meats they had prepared. His stepmother, Anne, his father, and brothers walked the two miles from Elstow every Sunday afternoon.

"Anne," John said one day, hanging his head sheepishly, "I know now how my father felt when he was left alone with two boys. I can see why he married so quickly."

Anne placed her hands on her ample hips. "Now, John, it does my heart good to hear ye confess that. Ye've been holding it agin me all these years."

"I've always liked you, Anne, ever since the day you introduced John Knox to me."

"Count on me to do what I can, John. But why don't ye look for another wife?"

"So soon? No!"

180

"Ye have the children to think of, John. Don't shove the possibility aside."

There were lonely moments for John, during which Anne's words returned to him. The cottage was alive with memories. Everywhere he looked he saw Mary—sitting at the wooden table he had made, lying on the bed they had shared. The mice got in that winter and were running all over the cottage before he knew they were there. As he set the traps, he could hear her voice, "John dear, mice may be small, but they're nasty. Make me some traps like your stepmother has with wooden blocks that will drop and kill them. But you will have to set them; I could never touch one!"

Some of the happiest times were when Bitsy and Uncle Matthias came from Newport. Their visits became more frequent as the year passed. When Elizabeth was with the children, they were quiet, content. The baby seldom cried. Little Mary sat for hours while Elizabeth told her stories, and the eagerness with which the blind girl awaited these visits was touching. Bitsy was a fine cook, and she seemed to delight in preparing appetizing dishes that smelled as delicious as they tasted. And how good it was to have Mary's empty chair filled.

One morning, almost a year after Mary's death, as John handed Bitsy a platter, his hand brushed hers and the color flooded to her cheeks. He was disturbed that he had an almost uncontrollable urge to take her in his arms.

Bitsy's too young, he told himself. I'm thirty and she is eighteen. She must never discover the way I feel. Even if she would have me, to marry her would be unfair. But how beautiful she was. Her hair shone like the raven's wing. Her eyes were like strange, bright flowers. Her milk-white skin was soft and smooth.

In spite of John's determination, his heart hammered every time she was near him. And once, when she stood in front of him and lifted her dark lashes, he had to clench his fists to keep from making a fool of himself. Then one evening Matthias hinted that Bitsy wasn't interested only in the children.

"That's ridiculous," John said sharply.

But he could dream. He had always dreamed, and he thought of her as he rode to the villages, as he worked at his forge, or walked the streets.

"Are you made of stone, John?" Matthias asked when he stepped into the workshop one day. "Can't you see that Bitsy is smitten with you?"

John's brows lifted. "With me? What do I have to offer a young girl like that?"

Bitsy, appearing in the open doorway, heard the words. Her voice rang clear when she gave him her answer. "Yourself, John. You're all I want."

She came toward him, her eyes shining. She lifted her lips, her breathing quick. He forgot that Matthias was standing there. He forgot all about his vows not to love her, as he crushed her warm body in his arms, and planted hungry kisses on her mouth, her throat, her smooth brow.

"Bitsy!" he whispered huskily. "I cannot believe it!"

"Nor I, John. Go ahead. Ask me."

"Ask you what, Bitsy?"

"To marry you, of course."

"Now that is what I call an embrace," Matthias said with a chuckle. "When will the wedding be?"

The banns were read the following Sunday in St. Cuthbert's Church, and simple preparations were made for the ceremony.

The afternoon of the wedding the sun was shining and the wind was warm with a suggestion of rain. All Bedford was astir, for a wedding was an event.

Bitsy was a smiling bride, although very different from Mary. She wore a white lace veil hanging around her shoulders. The skirt of her gown was full and the whisk that tied in her tiny waist was of handmade lace, too. A white rose was pinned on her breast, and John thought it was symbolical of the beauty and the purity of her heart. Her eyes upon him were warm, and her fingers

182

trembled. Since the bride was an orphan, Papa Matthias gave her away.

The vicar's surplice was crumpled and he read the service in a singsong voice. He was sloppy, too, about details and their names were not signed on the register. But the bells rang out with joyous peals as they left the church. John was the happiest man in Bedford as he helped Bitsy into the waiting carriage, which John Okey had provided.

John's mind was at rest when he was away from home, for the children loved Bitsy and were safe in her keeping. But, as he went about his preaching, he discovered that some of the Presbyterian ministers disapproved of unordained and uneducated preachers. One of them, the Reverend Thomas Becke, went so far as to have John arrested one February day for preaching without a license. However, he was allowed to go when William Dell, a preacher at Yelden, heard of the persecution and invited him to preach in his pulpit then and again on Christmas Day.

Tumbledown Dick, as Richard Cromwell was called in derision, resigned and retired to the country. The confusion was too much for him. A strong movement was begun to bring the King back. General Monk, who had served under Cromwell in Scotland, volunteered his services and an army to protect Charles.

Everything began to change in the shire. William Vierney applied to the Council and was reinstated as head schoolmaster. Parliament voted to bring the King back, and emissaries were sent to Bruges at the end of April with enough money for a monarch's triumphant return.

What will happen to Colonel Okey? John wondered. Will he really lose his head? John worried so much that one day early in May he rode out to visit the Colonel and found him in a state of terror. He confessed he didn't know what to do; he had remarried and did not wish to leave his wife. The bride came in just then to offer John a glass of cold milk. She was much younger than the colonel, and said she had been the widow of John Blackwell, who had been known to Bunyan as a man of importance and wealth. But he, too, had supported Oliver Cromwell.

"I don't know what Charles Stuart is like now," John said with a frown, "but he once proved to be my friend."

Colonel Okey shook his head. "That was once upon a time. He is said to have little sentiment now. I wager he wouldn't even see you."

"I could try."

"No. I fear I shall have to leave England."

May 29, 1660, was the thirtieth birthday of the returning King. The sunshine cast its warmth over the fields of Islington, Fleet Street, Lincoln's Inn, and the Strand as Charles rode into London. From the city's belfries the sound of bells mingled with the shouts of his joyous subjects. Beautiful maidens strewed flowers before him, his elegantly clad companions, and the escorting soldiers. The people waved and danced their joy. Their elation was a promise of loyalty to their rightful King come to wear his crown. Oliver Cromwell's reign of morality and severity was at an end.

After dark, bonfires were lighted in the streets, even in the squalid quarters near the Thames, Shoe Lane, and Fleet Street. At the stewhouses, such as the Cardinal's Hat, strong waters flowed freely. The brothels were filled that night and the carousing went on into the morning hours.

Within a month, as John Okey had expected, proceedings were started against the regicides. There was a furor among the King's new Council when Chancellor Hyde, who had shared the King's exile, announced that John Okey had disappeared. An order was given to search for him, and a reward was posted.

In Bedford, William Vierney took full possession of the school. Once again his manner was haughty and he defied the town's authorities to interfere with his management or discipline.

Early in July, John Okey, Jr., came to John Bunyan to tell him he had been held for questioning. He had told the authorities he did not know his father's whereabouts, and the King's deputies had vowed that sooner or later they would catch him.

"If he has fled the country, they'll have a hard time finding him," John said reassuringly. "Don't fret, John. Tell your stepmother not to fret. Your father should be safe for the time being."

The young man shook his head. "William Foster told somebody that Sir George Downing is to be sent to the continent to search for him."

"Sir George Downing! Your father gave him his post as a chaplain in his regiment. The ingrate! The scoundrel."

"There is the reward. It is sad what some men will do for money."

As the months passed, travelers from London brought disturbing news. While the King caroused, Chancellor Hyde was allowed to rule in his stead! And to add to the unrest over this situation, it was rumored that William Foster was up to some foul work in the shire, and that William Vierney was conspiring with him.

Anthony Harrington came to warn John that he would probably be arrested for preaching without a license from the Government.

Soon the former Royalists were in power all over the shire. The Episcopal clergymen returned to their livings; Giles Thorne to St. Mary's and Theodore Crowley to St. John's.

The Bedford Meeting was turned out of St. John's, and that September, John Burton, its minister, died, hurried to his grave by worry over what the future held for Dippers or Meeters, as they were now called.

To show the people that the Royalists meant to rule, the bodies of Oliver Cromwell; his son-in-law, Ireton; and an Independent named John Bradshaw were exhumed and hung at Tyburn as a warning to any who might wish to rebel. Later they were re-buried in unmarked graves.

Charles was interested in the arts, and to the delight of the nation, John Milton, now blind, was shown mercy although he had written an attack on the King's father.

Anthony Harrington, who was aging, was one of those in Bedford who dared to raise his voice against all that was going on in London. "The Presbyterians in Parliament were too anxious for the King's restoration," he said everywhere. "No conditions were imposed, and Chancellor Hyde will do just what Charles I tried to do, throttle conscience!"

About a year later, during the Parliamentary recess of September 13 to November 1, the magistrates of the Quarter Sessions in Bedford ordered the use of the Liturgy and the Book of Common Prayer of the Church of England for general use. And the see of Lincoln, vacant sixteen years, was filled by an old man of seventy-three, Robert Sanderson.

One cold evening that November, John Bunyan was seated before the fire with the children at his feet, and Bitsy beside them, spinning.

"Recite us a funny verse, Papa," Mary begged.

"Tell us a 'tory," chanted the round-faced Elizabeth.

The younger children laughed and clapped their hands.

Promptly John recited his favorite couplet, one which he frequently used to keep the children interested and quiet when he preached:

"An egg is not a chicken by falling from the hen,
    Nor is a man a Christian 'till he is born again!"

"Tell us anudder," said Little Tommy, his blue eyes wide.

"All right. Listen to this one:

"Look yonder. Ah! Methinks mine eyes do see
    Clouds edged with silver, as fine as garments be!
    They look as if they saw the golden face
    That makes black clouds more beautiful with grace."

"Do tell us a story, Papa. Just one," Mary said softly. "Tell us one about a great hero."

"A great hero? Now, let me see. . . . I could tell you about Christian."

"Who's he?" they chorused.

"A pilgrim who had to fight his way to the Celestial City. Terrible dangers beset him, but he was very brave, braver than the Golden Knight, braver even than St. George. Would you like to hear one about him?"

"Yes. Tell us about Christian."

"Well, it was this way. There was a man named Christian, who was plagued by a burden on his back. And as he was walking in the fields one day, he cried aloud, 'What shall I do to be saved?' . . . And then he met Evangelist. . . .'"

When John had finished the story, Bitsy told the children it was time for bed.

As she was herding them toward the stairs, a knock sounded on the door and John went to open it. Paul Cobb, the Clerk of the Peace stood there, his face wearing a formidable look, but his brown eyes like a scared rabbit's. There is something so stern about him, John thought, that he would make a good morkin. Trouble must be brewing!

"May I come in, John? There's a matter we ought to discuss."

John invited him in and offered him a chair.

Cobb said abruptly, "Ye had best stick t' soldering pots instead of trying t' save souls in meetin's. Under the new government the laws which forbid unlicensed preachers to preach will be enforced. Ye could get yourself in trouble."

"Did Dr. Foster send you?"

The man shuffled his feet and looked at the embers. "That's my job," he said truculently. "Seeing that th' law's obeyed."

"I will go on mending pots in the daytime weekdays, and work at saving souls Sundays and nights."

Paul frowned. "We don't want any trouble in th' shire. Can't ye pretend t' do what the Government wants and appear at the established church once in a while?"

"I prefer the Bedford Meeting. I like the simple form of worship. Are you a Christian, Paul?"

Paul drew himself up. "I'm in St. Paul's Parish. I go to church every Sunday and on holidays!" In your silver slippers? John thought, remembering the girls from the Cardinal Hat.

Aloud he said, "I have to talk to others about Christ and His salvation. If that is breaking the law, I shall continue to break it."

"There is nothin' I can say t' dissuade ye?" Paul's round eyes narrowed.

"Nothing."

"This is fair warning, John Bunyan. Many Puritan preachers have had to flee their churches. Others have fled from England."

"I am not going to flee."

"I was afraid of that," said Paul, scratching his pointed ear. "That may be a decision ye'll regret."

John sighed. "I know you have your duty. If it comes to the point where you have to arrest me, there will be no hard feeling."

"Don't be a fool, John. Ye know th' way th' Wingates feel about Meeters. Anne Wingate is William Foster's wife. Francis, her brother, is the Justice at Harlington."

"I realize that. The Wingates suffered during the war because of their loyalist sympathies. I have heard there is a Royalist hiding hole under the gables at Harlington House. Maybe I can hide there."

"That's not funny!"

"A sense of humor helps."

"It's dead serious. The tide has turned. Wingate and Foster will ferret out Meeters and Conventicles. The punishment is imprisonment or banishment!"

"God will take care of me when I am doing His will," John said with utter conviction.

But after Paul Cobb had left, John sat staring moodily into the embers. From upstairs Bitsy's rich voice sounded as she led the children in their prayers. I might as well face it, John thought. If I persist in preaching, which the authorities call holding conventicles, I will be arrested. Then what will happen to Bitsy and the children?

188

In the chaos of his thoughts he went again over the months since the Restoration. Freedom had been taken away. Immorality and even lewdness were the fashion at Whitehall, where the ladies acted like bawds and the gentlemen made the most of it. Everyone knew that King Charles had a succession of mistresses and even bastard children. With the gentlemen of the court, he even frequented such notorious stewhouses as the Cardinal's Hat. Everywhere there was assignation, prostitution, adultery, and even the unnatural vices such as the one fostered by James I. Surely God would send a plague or some terrible scourge to bring men to His feet and remind them that he demanded obedience.

In such an hour how could he, John Bunyan, a simple Puritan preacher promise not to spread God's Gospel?

II   The road to Lower Samsell, the Barton Hills, and Harlington curved perilously down the face of a steep hill, and John eased the horse John Grew had lent him carefully down the frozen mud, his hands on the reins ready to pull the animal up if it slipped. Snow flurries blew against his face, blinding him at times, obscuring the road and snow-covered fields stretching like a white sheet on either side of him.

Ever since he had mounted the horse that morning, John had felt a premonition of danger. He longed to wheel the animal and ride at a swift gallop back to Bedford. He wondered if it was known that he was to preach that day at Harlington.

"William Foster is just waiting to seize ye," Paul Cobb had told him.

"Please listen to what the Clerk of the Peace says," Bitsy had pleaded, her black eyes pain filled. "You love the outdoors. You couldn't endure being in jail."

Am I being a fool? he thought as he rode along. Bitsy is carrying our child. Do I have the right to bring disgrace and poverty on her and the children? Can I leave my family to shift for themselves as easily as I would shed my cloak?

For an instant he allowed himself a surge of anger. The old social order was triumphing over the ideals of freedom and conscience. The cruelties and injustices which were being perpetrated were not worthy of the King of England.

190

John reached Westoning and turned left up the steep hill, then right along a potholed road that led to Harlington, the end of the thirteen-mile ride.

As he neared the farmhouse where he was to preach, a wreath of mist rose over the moat like a white ghost. The branches of the leafless trees were feathered with snow. The portcullis was up and the hoofs of his horse resounded with a clatter as he rode over the drawbridge. The snow-draped roof of the old house seemed to melt against the white woodland.

Suddenly a figure leaped out of the woods and blocked John's path. Big hands reached for the reins and pulled him to a halt.

John looked down into Mel Mooney's pleasant face and let out a shout. "Mel! What are *you* doing in Harlington?"

"S-h-h-h!" Mel held a finger to his lips. "I came to warn you that a warrant has been ordered for your arrest."

John felt the blood drain from his face. Then Cobb's warning was true! Weakness and fear spread through him.

"As long as I live," Mel continued, "I will stand against this state-centered despotism! I feared to stay in London. They think here that I'm an Anglican sent by Archbishop Juxon." Mel grinned widely.

"Then the situation is as bad in London as 'tis rumored?"

"Chancellor Hyde is a despot. Juxon acts like a Christian, but even an archbishop is powerless under Hyde's heavy fist. I have been going through the shires warning my people of the persecution that's coming."

"How do you know my arrest is imminent?"

"The magistrate told me when I visited him to inquire about Dissenters in the vicinity." He grinned again. "You are number one on their list."

"I don't know what to do," John said weakly.

"I wouldn't go near the Meeters!"

"I must not forget that the Cross is the standing-way mark by which all who go to glory must pass. I will go on."

"God go with you and the blessed saints preserve you!" Mel

raised his plump hand in blessing, turned, and waddled quickly into the forest where the big trees soon hid him from sight. Only his tracks remained, big footprints in the snow.

John's host, a wrinkled man in his early seventies, met him at the door. "Have ye seen any strangers, John?" he asked anxiously.

"No strangers."

"Magistrate Wingate has issued an order for your arrest. The constable and the magistrate's servant were here early this morning asking about ye. If we do not hold a meeting, they cannot arrest ye."

The cleft in John's chin deepened as he said he would take a walk and decide what to do. The farmer stared after the sturdy, broad-shouldered tinker, and his heart warmed. Brother Bunyan had bright blue eyes set off by reddish hair which curled about his shoulders. There was an impudent lilt to his slightly turned-up nose. It was easy to guess what his decision would be. With the John Bunyans there was usually a wrong decision and a right one.

He was not surprised when the preacher returned, and said, "If we run like mice, how can we witness our beliefs?"

A few minutes later, as Brother Bunyan was reading from the Scriptures, the heavy outer door creaked open. There was the thumping of feet in the hall, and two men appeared, a tall one and a short one, in heavy snow-powdered cloaks. The tall man, moving toward Brother Bunyan, held up a paper.

"If your name's John Bunyan," he said in a voice that didn't have his heart in it, "I have to arrest you for conducting a conventicle."

"It's better to be persecuted than to persecute," Brother Bunyan quietly told the Meeters. "Don't look so downcast. Freedom's not dead in England!"

"Come," the constable interrupted. "Magistrate Wingate is waiting."

"Just a minute!" said a booming voice from the hallway. A big man in the clothes of an Anglican vicar stamped into the

192

room. "Gentlemen, there must be some mistake. I will vouch for Bunyan's loyalty to the King!"

The clergyman stood there, his round face very red from the cold, his vestments and cloak covered with snow. The constable hesitated a moment, almost quailing before the fire in the big man's eyes. But finally he shook his head.

"We have found no weapons, but he is holding a conventicle. You know, your Reverence, that we cannot tolerate Meeters, these days. I have to arrest him." He waved the paper.

"Then I'll just come along," Mel said, "to be sure he gets a fair trial."

John's heart sank. If Froggy Foster should appear at the hearing and recognize Mel, he would be in trouble, too. But there was a determined set to Mel's square chin and John knew that nothing he could say would change the priest's mind.

"How long is it since you saw Froggy?" John whispered, as they rode side by side ahead of the constable and the magistrate's man.

"Twenty years."

The magistrate's man, noticing that they were whispering, rode up and motioned Mel to drop behind with the constable while the magistrate's man rode with John, as if he were a prisoner who might try to escape.

The old Wingate House stood at a corner of the crossroads near a time-worn church. Pillars with big balls on top flanked a wooden gate. The lawn in front of the mansion was covered with snow. Two elegant marble pilasters looked almost as if they were holding up the red-tiled roof, and five dormer windows extended across the upper story.

A servingman led the way to a parlor where a woman, who appeared to be a member of the family, told them that Justice Wingate had been called away and asked them to return next day.

193

"I will be responsible for the prisoner," Mel said in a voice that rang with authority.

"All right," the constable agreed, "I suppose there is no objection to leaving him with a vicar. But guard him well!"

Mel took John's arm and propelled him out to the waiting horses. They galloped together toward the town.

"All right," Mel said in a terse whisper. "Now is your chance! Ride off!"

John slowed his horse. "Me? Run like a criminal?"

"Yes. Stop here. We'll dismount. I'll tell them you struck so suddenly that I was powerless to stop you."

John stared at his old schoolmate. There was a smile on Mel's round face, and in that instant John's heart warmed. Mel was ready to sacrifice his life, if need be, for a friend.

"Do you think I would let you do this?"

"If you're worried about what the authorities will do to me, there is Somebody who will take care of me."

"No. I won't run. I won't let you take the risk. I won't desert Bitsy and the children."

"Then I'll go bond for you."

"An Anglican cleric going bond for a holder of meetings! Mel, that heart of yours will get you into great trouble."

Tears filled Mel's warm brown eyes. "This whole life is trouble. My life has been a struggle ever since I was ten. Ours is an age of trouble."

They took a room in a nearby inn. John had no appetite, but Mel ate a whole leg of mutton. They chatted until midnight, and John told Mel about Bishop Thirleby, how all the Anglicans except Queen Elizabeth had loved him because of his sweet spirit, of his burial in the clothes of a pilgrim.

"This seems to be a time when pilgrims are going out in every direction," Mel said thoughtfully. "There were the pilgrims who set sail for the new land. Many fled from Ireland to find a place to worship God in peace and safety. Many Baptists fled to Holland, and other places on the continent. Some fled from Ireland."

The last thing Mel said before he fell asleep was, "The bishop has the right idea. We are all pilgrims and strangers upon the earth. Heaven is our home."

In an oak-paneled room Justice Wingate was waiting. Dressed in a black judicial robe, he sat at his polished desk shuffling papers. Although he was about John's age, his hair was graying and deep lines etched his aristocratic face. He doesn't want to be unkind, John thought. He has suffered, too.

In a few minutes the justice lifted his eyes, looked searchingly at John, and then addressed the constable: "What evidence did you find at the farmhouse?"

"Your Honor, I am presenting the tinker arrested yesterday on your orders. We found no evidence of treason against the Crown, no weapons, no incriminating papers. The tinker was at Harlington to conduct a service of worship."

The Justice drummed his thin fingers on the wood before him. "The Conventicle Act forbids the gathering of more than five persons, other than a family, at any place other than the parish church."

"This man meant no harm," the constable said firmly.

"He broke the law. The punishment is imprisonment for three months unless he does public penance and promises never to break this law again. If he does break it, he will be hung or banished."

John took a step forward. "I went to the farmhouse to preach Christ's Gospel."

"Why can't you attend to your tinkering, John Bunyan? Why do you have to break the law?"

"God's tinker mends souls."

"I shall break the neck of these meetings!"

"Perhaps," John said quietly.

Justice Wingate pounded the desk. "Since you persist in your stubborn stand, there is only one course we can take—to make an example of you so that other Meeters will take heed!"

"We will make bond for the prisoner," a woman's voice said. A white-haired woman who had been at the meeting the day before came forward. Two other women followed. And in a corner near the door stood Mel.

"Know this," Justice Wingate said sternly. "If the prisoner preaches before he is arraigned at the Quarter Sessions Court next January, your bond will be forfeited."

"Then I will not allow these good women to make a bond for me. I can never promise not to preach!" John thundered.

"Very well. I have only one recourse—to draw up a writ committing you to Bedford jail."

While the writ was being prepared, John waited in the gloomy hall alone. The women had gone; Mel had discreetly disappeared. Thoughts kept whirling through John's mind. If he had to wait for the Quarter Sessions he would be in jail seven or eight weeks. He felt a surge of anger. All he had done was to lead in the worship of God, and he was being sent to jail like a cutthroat or a cutpurse!

In a few minutes the front door opened and a man of arrogant bearing strode in. He paused, staring at John with weasel eyes. John knew him by sight; this was Dr. William Lindall, a curate who was related by marriage to the Wingates. He was one of God's ministers. Surely he would intercede when he heard what had happened.

"What are you doing here?" Dr. Lindall demanded in a clipped voice as John rose to face him.

"I am here because I held a meeting yesterday to pray, read the Scriptures, and preach."

"You had no right to meddle by holding a conventicle!"

Words from Peter flashed into John's mind: " 'As every man hath received the gift,' " he quoted, " 'even so let him minister the same.' "

"There was a coppersmith who annoyed the Apostles. Have you forgotten him?"

John lashed out with words like a whip. "I remember the Pharisees who helped spill our Lord's blood!"

"Aye, and you should know about Pharisees!"

John was silent, staring back at the curate. There were many

Anglican clergymen who acted like Christians! Dr. Lindall was not one of them.

" 'Answer not a fool according to his folly,' " John said quietly.

With a grunt Dr. Lindall brushed past him into the hearing room and slammed the door.

When the constable came out with the writ, John followed him to the gate. Just as they reached it, Anthony Harlington and John Grew from the Bedford Meeting rode up. They told John that a messenger had been sent from the Harlington congregation with word of his plight, and that, as a result, they had come to intercede for him.

John and the constable went back again to the gloomy hall and sat on a wooden bench to wait. It seemed an eternity before the men from the Bedford Meeting came out of the hearing room.

"The Justice says he will release you, if you agree not to do anything to endanger the King's authority," Anthony said with a frown.

"The King's or Chancellor Hyde's?" John demanded.

"If you say certain words, it will be all right," John Grew said solemnly.

"Only if the words are not against my conscience will I say them."

"The Justice wants to see you."

Twilight was settling over Harlington House as John went back to the hearing rooms. Justice Wingate sat at his fine desk, his plump face obscured by the dimness. Two shadowy figures stood behind him—that Judas, Dr. Lindall, and William Foster of Bedford, the Meeters arch-enemy. Foster's face, which was narrow and cunning, was illuminated by a pair of unusually bright eyes. As a servant lit two tall candles that stood on the desk, Foster spoke in his oily voice: "Consider carefully, John. There is no need to be foolish about all this. I'm here to help you."

"What do you want me to do?"

"Dr. Lindall and I have been discussing your case with Justice Wingate. Nobody wants to send you to prison."

John looked into the three pairs of eyes focused upon him, at the worried faces. They don't want to make a martyr out of me, he thought. Too many people are infuriated by their tyranny. *They're afraid!*

"Tell me what I have done that is wrong."

The three exchanged furtive glances.

"How can it possibly be lawful for an ignorant tinker to preach?" William Foster asked in a voice furred with feline softness.

He looked at the obstinate tinker. There was defiance in the way he stood, his sturdy shoulders thrown back, his head held high. With the populace already upset, this bumpkin was dangerous. If only we could persuade him to conform, William thought. But probably nothing could ever force John Bunyan to do anything he believes is wrong. With him the stakes are freedom and independence for his kind. For an instant William felt a glow of admiration; there were too few honest men in the realm. And there was within this tinker that which made him a leader and gave people confidence in what he said.

"I must tell others of the Lord Jesus Christ," he said now in a firm voice. "What is wrong with that?"

"Carry out the writ. Take him to jail to await the verdict at the Quarter Sessions," Francis Wingate said frostily. "That's all we can do with the oaf."

12 JOHN STARED wistfully through the iron bars of the little window. Brilliant stars sparked the dark sky above Jail Lane. John White, his old army companion who was the under-jailer, did not try to keep from him the bad news that filtered through from London. And tonight John felt as if his heart would break. Colonel Okey was being sought on the continent and, if he were found, he would be executed.

And Bitsy and the children had no means of support. Some members of the Bedford Meeting were supplying their food—and his, since each prisoner had to provide his own. Bitsy was learning to make lace. He was allowed to tag leather laces, and on Tuesdays and Saturdays, which were Market Days, sell them to the passers-by.

There was the sound of heavy footsteps coming down the corridor, and Paul Cobb came in, his thin face grave.

"Your wife has been taken very ill. Dr. Bannister is attending her. If you promise not to preach again, or hold conventicles, I will release you to go to her bedside."

John's heart contracted. Bitsy ill? Would she lose the baby they both wanted so much? What of the other children? If she was helpless, who was caring for them? For a moment John was tempted. But then he shook his head.

"Rather than conform, I will lie here until the moss grows over my eyes and my lips, and my flesh falls from my bones! Don't you understand that?"

"These men will not let a tinker stand in their way. John, your very life is in danger."

Paul turned and walked out, shaking his head, his back stiff, his steps heavy.

John sat on his stool staring at the wall, until John White came on his rounds.

"I see Paul Cobb was at ye again," he said with a grin. "The powers that be usually break others down one way or another. I was thinkin' that ye're still as tough as the day ye sassed Captain Bladwell."

"Confidentially, I feel anything but tough. I'm frightened! It isn't easy to oppose their power."

"I have orders to lock ye in one of the dungeons. It's damp and the rats are hungry! I can't see why ye persist in resisting."

"Because many men gave their lives for the very values these men now seek to destroy. Because man's mind has to be free to serve God. Because it is wrong to do anything that conscience tells me is not right!"

"In the eyes of Royalist England ye are committing the unforgivable. Ye are defying the commands of the powerful. Ye not only refuse to worship in the Church of England, but ye dare to preach without their consent. Oh, John Bunyan, ye're a fool, yet somehow I'm glad ye are."

John arched an eyebrow. "I'm a fool, but you're glad I'm a fool! Thank you."

"Surely the King will not permit such tyranny to continue. But some say he doesn't know what's goin' on, that he's too busy beddin' women and carousin' t' know. All the theaters, which Cromwell had closed, have been opened. Rare motions, or shows with puppets, fill the streets. They tell me there's a new one—'Jonah and the Whale'—at Fleet Bridge. The King likes his pleasures and attends all the plays."

"What is playing at the theaters?"

"Froggy Foster has been down to London. He saw a Jonson play, 'The Devil Is an Ass.' The lady and her lover speak from two balconies. Froggy says the style in clothes has changed, so that clothes are of the gayest materials, belaced and furred. Canary wine flows freely, and there is much drunkenness and debauchery."

"Oliver Cromwell would turn over in his grave."

"The whole realm is in upheaval."

Bitsy had lost the baby and had been ill for three days, but she was up and around again. When Christmas Eve came, John sat alone, thinking how much he missed her and the children. John White would have allowed them to come as often as they wished, but he had orders that their visits were to be restricted.

"I wonder if I'll be permitted to see my family at all?" John asked himself, as he sat on the straw that was his bed, while the candle on his table flickered in the blast that blew through the cracks around the barred window.

The chimes of the clock of the neighboring church rang five times. He closed his eyes for a moment and imagined he was sitting before the hearth at the little cottage in St. Cuthbert's Street. He could hear the cheerful crackle of the fire and the chatter of merry voices as the children romped around the room. He heard his daughter Mary's sweet voice asking him to tell a story. He could smell the burning wood, the baking bread. And he could feel Bitsy's arm about his neck, the warm lips of the little ones kissing him good night. He sighed. Christmas Eve in jail was a lonely time.

When the children are allowed to come, he thought, brushing a tear from his cheek, I must have a story ready for them. Christian had grown in stature since his first appearance and they always wanted to hear more about him.

John lay on his back on the straw mattress, gazing up at the beamed ceiling and letting his imagination transport him out of his sorrow, out of his prison.

For the moment he forgot the ache of loneliness, the cold, the drab prison walls. He was in his world of dreams, living in his hero, Christian—a man with red blood flowing through him. The characters and the temptations he met became real. John's friends and enemies sometimes were in the scenes he imagined, but they developed, as Christian had, into flesh and blood creations until he heard them speak and saw them walk. Day by day Christian struggled heroically toward the Celestial City.

The next morning John felt cheerful. John White had told him Bitsy would bring his Christmas dinner and just before noon she appeared, leading little Mary by the hand. Both wore Puritan-gray gowns with snowy white collars, severe white caps, and dark cloaks. And behind them trooped the other three, Elizabeth, Thomas, and John, each with a bundle or a dish. Little Thomas had a brown loaf of bread, and Elizabeth held out the jug he had once brought so happily to her mother, saying, "Homemade soup, Papa!"

"Oranges, Papa," John shouted, holding up a blue bowl of the delicious fruit.

"Hickory nuts!" announced Mary. They all chorused, "Merry Christmas, a very Merry Christmas!"

"I wish I were a bad man like you, Papa!" little Thomas said. "Everybody likes bad men."

Bitsy's face reddened. "Hush, Tom. I told you Papa is in jail because he will not do what wicked men tell him to do."

"Your papa does not like to be away from all of you," John said slowly. "More than anything else he would like to be at home to see that you grow up to be good men and women. But there are some things a man has to do, if he loves God. Mind your mother, and go to church regularly, and listen to the preacher. Don't forget to read your Bibles and pray to God often. Then I'll have nothing to worry about, for you'll be feeding your souls."

"Like Christian?" John demanded.

"Yes, just like Christian. He had a hard time at first, until he was born again. Since then he can do anything that is in God's will for him."

"Tell us another story about Christian!" they all chorused.

"Let your papa eat while the soup's hot," Bitsy said. "Then he'll tell you a story."

The family had had their dinner before they came, and John enjoyed every morsel of his, while they all talked at once. When he had finished everything except three of the oranges, the children gathered about him, and Bitsy with the love shining from her eyes sat on the stool facing him. And since God had given him such a family, surely He would provide their material wants. John determined to sell as many tagged laces as he could, but not to worry any more. God was a friend he could trust. . . .

"Now, I saw in my dream, that just as they [Christian and Pliable] had ended this talk they drew near to a very miry slough that was in the midst of the plain; and they, being heedless, did both fall suddenly into the bog. The name of the slough was Despond. Here, therefore, they wallowed for a time, being grievously bedaubed with the dirt; and Christian, because of the burden that was on his back, began to sink in the mire. . . ."

Paul Cobb came early that January morning when the Quarter Sessions was to convene to conduct John to the Swan Inn where his trial was to take place.

"I hear the Archbishop of Canterbury does not agree with Chancellor Hyde's policies relating to the Church," Paul remarked, as they walked along the street. "Some are saying there would have been no Civil War had Juxon been in Laud's place in 1642."

"People speak well of Archbishop Juxon. He must be a fine Christian."

"Chief Justice Kelynge hates all Roundheads because the Commonwealth imprisoned him because of his Royalist sympathies. And Justice Wingate, Dr. Foster, and William Vierney have been agitating to your detriment. I warned you!"

"I can't understand why they hate me so."

"The recent uprising of the Fifth Monarchists fanned th' flames. They tried t' take London. Thomas Venner, th' leader of th' insurrectionists, is one of those who will be executed next week. Chancellor Hyde is a very influential man an' he wants heads."

John was quiet, remembering the head he had seen on London Bridge, and the tar-blackened corpse swinging on the gibbet at the crossroads. Cold fear gripped him.

As they neared the river, there was a whir of excitement among the loungers along the bank. The Market Square began to swarm with men, women, and children. Everybody talked at once. They viewed John with sympathy or curious interest. Many spoke: "We're sorry, John." "It's an outrage ye've had to be shut up in jail all this time." "You are in our prayers."

Before the inn Bitsy was waiting, beautiful in a green dress a neighbor had given her, her hooded cloak unbuttoned, her eyes clouded. She took her husband's arm, lifted her head high, and walked into the inn with him.

Just inside stood his stepmother, and there were tears on her cheeks. Behind her was his father, his hair gray now, his face lined.

"The good God help ye, son," he said in a choked voice. "Those justices won't."

The Chief Justice of the Quarter Sessions, John Kelynge, sat at a table in the Swan Inn Chamber, reading the warrant which had been issued for the arrest of one John Bunyan, a tinker who thought he could preach. It was nine o'clock by the hourglass on the wide mantel above the hearth when four associates filed in and took their seats beside Justice Kelynge.

For security's sake this tinker would have to be severely dealt with, and forced to conform to the established church. The thought occurred to the Chief Justice that the Lord Chancellor Hyde, now the Earl of Clarendon and the most influential man in the Privy Council, might reward him with a title and an important appointment, if he made an example of this bumpkin.

The regicides who had sat in judgment on Charles I were being executed and banished. Of the thirty members of the Privy Council, perhaps a dozen had been the friends of Oliver

Cromwell, but they were needed now, because they were influential. Feeling was running so high against all enemies, that loyal Englishmen were coming into their own. The remains of Pym and Blake had been removed from Westminster Abbey and reburied nearby in St. Margaret's Churchyard. This tinker's trial should be handled in such a way that it would bring approval from high places in London. If he could make an ignorant and most impudent tinker bow before his authority, he would establish himself as a man of judgment and ability.

"Bring in your tinker," Justice Kelynge ordered, leaning forward in an armchair, his eyes on the wide doorway.

Although the fire in the huge chamber was burning, for an instant, as John faced his judges, he felt chilled and his legs trembled. The man in the middle, whom he knew must be the Chief Justice, scowled darkly as if to ask how this person—this tinker—dared defy the authorities of *the* Church. Justice Kelynge was wearing a black periwig and clothes of black velvet relieved by a white shirt and white lace. Two rings with precious stones sparkled on his fingers and he wore brilliants on his shoes. His long thin face had the gravity of an executioner's. His lips thinned, and behind the gray-green eyes there was hostility, implacable and cold.

The other four justices did not look reassuring. They did not appear to be happy over their responsibility, but sat in scowling silence, staring at John as if he were a wild animal. Two of them had reason to be prejudiced: Sir Henry Chester of Lidington, who was an uncle of Francis Wingate; George Blundell, who had lost everything under the Commonwealth. Sir William Beecher of Howbury and Thomas Snaggy of Millbank appeared to be somewhat less antagonistic.

John realized that a fearful ordeal was facing him, but he had put on his simple Puritan clothes, and hoped the inspiration of the moment would see him through. The stakes were his freedom, the security of Bitsy and the children, and perhaps his life itself.

Every seat was occupied and the paneled walls were lined with standing people. Many were John's friends, and he read compassion in their eyes. But there were hate-filled faces, too. William Foster, John noted, sat with his nephew, Froggy. William Vierney's hard eyes glared, but he gave no sign of greeting and John averted his own eyes.

The Chief Justice cleared his throat and shuffled importantly through the papers in the case. John had studied his copy of the monstrous bill of indictment carefully; the fact that justice was in the power of John Kelynge was a bad omen. Never had a judge's manner been colder or more remote from the mercy of the law.

John's heart raced as the justice began to read the bill's accusations which stated he was indicted for "devilishly and perniciously abstaining from coming to church to hear divine service, and for being a common upholder of several meetings and conventicles to the great disturbance and distraction of the good subjects of this kingdom, contrary to the laws of our soverign lord, the King."

Justice Kelynge paused to let the weight of this document settle on his audience, and his eyes, resting on John, were like two hard stones.

"How do you plead, John Bunyan?" the clerk demanded.

John did not hesitate: "Your Honors, the justices of this trial, I stand before you accused of refusing to come to church and of disturbing the peace by holding unlawful meetings, implying that what I have done is treasonous. I have gone to God's Church and am a member of a Christian body. I only wish to do good."

Chief Justice Kelynge spoke sharply, "But do you come to your parish church for divine service?"

"No."

"Will you acknowledge the King's ecclesiastical supremacy?"

"I am proud to acknowledge him as King of the realm, but not King of my conscience."

John saw the justices go rigid, and fear caught coldly at his throat. A few days before a proclamation had been made prohibiting all "unlawful and seditious meetings and conventicles under the pretence of religion." The Baptists and Quakers had been especially named, but John couldn't acknowledge King Charles, the drunken adulterer, as God of his soul. Am I being a fool? he thought. I am not called upon to renounce God's supremacy. The justices want me to promise not to go about the shire attacking the supremacy of the Church of England in which I grew up.

"Why don't you attend divine service?"

"God doesn't command my attendance."

"Doesn't He command you to pray?"

"Not from a particular prayer book!"

"Then how?"

"The apostle Paul said, 'I will pray with the Spirit with understanding!' "

"Let him speak no more," roared Justice Chester. "He has the brass of a laborer!"

Kelynge ignored his colleague. "The Common Prayer Book has been used since the day of the Apostles!" he exploded.

"Will your Honor be pleased to show me the text from the New Testament that commands me to use it?"

"You need it to pray!"

"I can pray very well without it."

"Then Beelzebub is your God!" Justice Blundell said sharply.

"If so, it is odd that we have the comforting presence of God among us at our meetings. Blessed be His Holy Name!"

"Peddler's French!" the Chief Justice snorted. "Leave off your canting. Tell us, if you can, what makes you, a tinker, think you are God's gift to man!"

" 'As every man hath received the gift, even so let him minister the same unto another, as good stewards of the manifold grace of God.' "

"Then follow your gift of tinkering, and let educated preachers follow their calling!"

Chief Justice Kelynge's face had gone red. His long nose twitched, and the glare that he fastened upon the accused was evidence that John's fears were justified. There could be but one sentence. John knew, however, that he had to make any who doubted know why he was doing what he was doing.

"In my quotation, the Apostle is speaking of preaching God's Truth."

"Then you confess the indictment. According to precedent, if a prisoner substitutes long chatter for a plea, his plea is *nihil dicit*, or guilty by confession."

John lifted his head and threw back his shoulders. "I confess we have had meetings to exhort each other. I do not confess any guilt!"

"Let the accused hear the sentence of this tribunal," the Chief Justice said, and two bailiffs moved forward to stand beside John.

"You are to be held in jail three months longer, and if you continue to refuse to attend your parish church, you will be banished from England. Should you return without the special permission of the King, your neck will stretch for it."

A low murmur ran through the group of spectators, like the murmur of a wave before it hits the shore. Chief Justice Kelynge hammered the table with his gavel in an attempt to still the displeased assembly. But people were surging forward to extend their sympathies to John, to announce their belief in his innocence. He had lost his case, but he had stood on principle, and the losing affected the rights of every Englishman.

As the bailiffs led John out, he had a glimpse of Bitsy's white face, and the torment written there filled him with contrition. He shook off the hands that pinioned his arms, and turned once again toward the justices.

"If I were out of jail today," he shouted, "I would preach the Gospel tomorrow with God's help!"

13 MARCH WINDS blew, and the daffodils painted the greenwood. John yearned to wander through the fields and under the tall trees. It seemed to him that he had been in jail a lifetime, but it had been only a year and a half. Imprisonment was torture to a man who loved to fish, hunt, and rove the countryside. Too, he needed exercise; his muscles were growing soft and flabby. Yet he had much to be grateful for; the people of Bedford, especially his fellow members of the Bedford Meeting, visited him often, bringing food, clothing, and clean straw. Bitsy and the children were not going hungry, for she had learned to make fine lace, which sold readily. He was still permitted to make and sell tagged leather laces. The underjailer, John White, showed him every consideration, allowing him to write, and to preach to the other prisoners in the dayroom. One of the prisoners, John Rush, a Quaker—apprehended two months after John's arrest, because he, too, would not conform to the Church of England—had brought with him some books which he allowed John to read. One of them was George Foxe's *Book of Martyrs*. When John's pastor, Brother Burton, had discovered how inspiring John found it, he had brought him a copy as a gift.

One night, as John sat on his square stool, reading the tale about John Huss telling his persecutors that he willingly received the chains for Christ's sake, he reflected that persecution now all over England was as bad as it had been in Huss's day. Freedom was being impaired in France, too; since the death of Cardinal

209

Jules Mazarin, the twenty-three-year-old Louis XIV had been showing great cruelty toward the Protestants.

John's thoughts were interrupted by the sound of footsteps and the bolt thudding back. The heavy oak door to his cell swung open, and John White admitted Bitsy. John leaped to his feet, and she held out her arms, a great tenderness on her lovely face. He clung to her as if he would never let her go.

"You can apply for a pardon, John!" she said exultingly. "The King's Coronation is to take place, and to celebrate it prisoners will be freed!"

"All of them?"

"No, but to be sure you're among them, I am going to London to see Lord Barkwood, our representative."

He shook his head. "My enemies, the enemies of freedom, are powerful."

She smiled deep into his eyes. "I love you so, John. At least we can do everything we know to get you out."

"What if I fail?" Bitsy asked herself as she looked at the man she had married, at the lines that grooved his brow, his pallor, the puffiness that had crept around his eyes. He's wonderful, she thought. While there was something very earthy about him, almost as if he were a part of the land, the valleys, the woods, the hills, and the rivers, there was something spiritual, too. He had a steely quality, so that when he thought he was doing right, nothing could make him do anything else. Ruthlessly, with a single purpose, he turned from all temptations to compromise. "I'll do everything I can," she vowed.

While John waited for news of Bitsy's mission, he wasn't lonely. He had many visitors, and the jail was full of other Dissenters taken at conventicles, among them Samuel and John Fenne, members of his church; William Wheeler, the ejected rector of Cranfield; John Donne, the ousted rector of Pertendall, apprehended while preaching at Keysoe to sixty worshipers.

Time and time again John preached to them, trying to lift their hopes. How peaceful it was to worship together without fear of informers who wanted to collect fines. John White often stood inside the door listening, too. He kept asking questions, and had recently asked to be baptized.

For several hours each day John sat at his table writing. Some of his sermons proved to be the beginnings of books which could find their way in to print through the prison bars.

One afternoon Froggy Foster's flat face with its popping eyes peered through the opening in the door, and the fear was born that Froggy would inform his uncle that John was writing, busily, thus calling attention to what they would consider treasonous pamphlets, and causing his paper and pen to be taken away from him.

"What a fool you are to send yourself to jail," Froggy jeered. "Don't count on a pardon. You're not awaiting trial. My uncle says you're a convicted man."

"I couldn't do anything else, Froggy."

Froggy shook his head. "And all you needed to do was to have the vicar say your prayers, and worship as the King directs."

In that instant John pitied Froggy, his uncle, the schoolmaster —all who believed only what they saw. Things unseen were as real as things seen, but they didn't know it.

In London Bitsy found Lord Barkwood courteous and even sympathetic. He advised her to see Justice Matthew Hale when he came to Bedford. Justice Hale might have been lenient had it not been for one of his colleagues, Sir Thomas Tweeden, who insisted that John was a threat to the Crown. The justices agreed that John had to get a writ of error, stating that his trial had been unjust.

Bitsy consulted Edward Wild, the High Sheriff for the shire, who placed John's name on the list of prisoners to be freed, but the justices removed it, pointing out that, having been convicted, he could be freed only by a writ of error, or a pardon from the King.

Anthony Harrington, a fellow member of the Bedford Meeting, investigated the legality of such a writ, and discovered that if a prisoner applied for one and failed, he could be imprisoned for life! John decided not to make the application, and Bitsy, alone in her bedchamber, wept in shuddering sobs, for she knew now that John would be away from home for a long, long time.

On April 23, the King was crowned with great ceremony. It was reported that the people were wild with joy, and that the revelry went on for days.

The next month Anthony Harrington carried one of John's manuscripts to London, and when he returned, he reported that Sir John Kelynge, who had been elected to the Cavalier Parliament, was in Chancellor Hyde's favor and was more powerful than ever.

For a year the prisoners kept coming. John was moved from a cell to the dayroom where as many as twenty men slept. He preferred it here because there was some daylight, although the crowded conditions made writing very difficult.

One April morning in 1662, the door swung open and there stood Mel in a vicar's garb, looking dusty and weary. He had lost weight, and black circles framed his eyes. Anyone could see that he had suffered.

"The King is marrying Catherine of Braganza, a devout Catholic, next month," he announced. "The situation is desperate now. We are still in as much disrepute as the Puritans. The dungeons and lodging rooms in the London jails are crowded to capacity. I've been on the run ever since we parted."

"What do you mean when you say the situation is desperate?"

"Feeling runs high with some members of Parliament because the King dares to marry a Catholic. They remember that his father did the same thing, and fear the future Queen's influence."

"But why do you have to run?"

"Hadn't you heard? The King has issued an order for the arrest of all Catholic prelates!"

"And we thought freedom would come. We fought for it!"

212

"I bring bad news of another nature. Last week your friend John Okey was executed."

John's heart sank. "Are you sure?"

"Yes. I saw him die."

"Was it . . ." John paused, unable to continue.

"He was a refugee at Hanau for two years. When he visited Delft, he was arrested. Sir George Downing was instrumental in his apprehension. The scaffold was erected on Tower Hill, and before his execution Colonel Okey spoke out, so that everyone could hear him. 'I bear no malice against George Downing,' he said. 'I will meet my Maker without any hatred in my heart.' There was something triumphant about his death, for he died like a Christian."

Mel handed John a pamphlet. "He wrote this while he was waiting to be executed. It expresses his faith in God and His Son, Jesus Christ."

"Colonel Okey did that?"

Mel nodded. "And I have the feeling that a lot of others are going to need all the encouragement they can find!"

"Can't somebody talk to the King? Surely it is not his idea to persecute everybody who strays from the Church of England!"

"No. It is Chancellor Hyde's."

"Mel, promise me you won't do anything foolish. Why don't you go to Ireland for a while?"

Mel's large brown eyes looked steadily at his friend. "John, you're asking me to do something you wouldn't do yourself. I must stay here and minister to others. I will stand against this self-centered tyranny of the politicians as long as I live!"

"Just don't take unnecessary chances!"

"I'll try not to. Sometimes I wish I were the King!"

The royal marriage took place that May with a secret Catholic ceremony followed by one in the Church of England. And the citizens of Bedford expressed the hope that the bride might have enough influence upon the King to get him to do something about the universal intolerance. The day after Christmas he announced a Declaration of Toleration, but Sir John Kelynge and other politicians immediately set about trying to get it revoked. Sir John drew up an Act of Uniformity imposing an oath on teachers and ministers, and compelling the use of the Book of Common Prayer. To the dismay of all Catholics and Nonconformists the act became law. Only ministers ordained by an Anglican Bishop were allowed to preach. But the Baptists, Catholics, and other Nonconformists worshiped in woods, hidden glades, barns, and secret rooms. When John learned that many priests and Jesuits had been arrested, he worried about Mel. Mr. Mooney visited the jail to ask John if he had heard from him; but there was no news of him, he seemed to have disappeared.

Bitsy came to see John one afternoon and, with tears in her eyes, told him she had had to pawn his anvil iron. Mary had been sick and in need of her care and she had been forced to neglect her lace-making. The doctor had to be paid. . . .

His anvil iron! How proud he had been when it had been molded. He remembered how his fingers had trembled as he had inscribed his name and the date. That had been fifteen years ago. He had had a sentimental attachment for the tool, but he managed a smile and told Bitsy not to worry.

Another sorrow struck at him a few weeks later when Mary died. She was buried in the parish cemetery, and John White let her father attend the funeral. That night John walked the floor of his little cell, while a young Quaker, Thomas Green, tried to comfort him.

That same night John Rush, the elderly Quaker, was taken ill, and John gave him his cloak and one of his coverlets, since the jail had no fireplaces and the January wind was blowing through the cracks into the damp room. Rush's wife, Tabitha came in from her cell to care for him, but he died three days later, begging God to forgive those who had persecuted him.

John thought he had never been more depressed than he was after the body of the gentle old man had been removed. He opened his Bible to the Sermon on the Mount, and as he read, the realization swept over him that souls were growing strong by persecution. A shaft of light flooded the dayroom where he sat and there came to him a vision of the Celestial City. He saw the New Jerusalem not as an outward home of God's Church, but as the very symbol of the Church itself. The saints, he thought, are a routed army, but a better day is coming when all the dragons, spiders, and evil spirits of Antichrist will be known, and all the beautiful will sing and blossom. The Scriptures said that God's City has twelve gates, three to each arrow of the compass, to show that God has people in every corner of the globe. The names of the twelve Apostles are written on the foundations of the city, and the Apostles' teaching hold up the walls. And in this City of God there is not to be, as in the world, a Popish doctrine, a Quaker's, a Presbyter's, Independent's or Anabaptist's, thus destroying and confusing souls. The city is of pure gold to show the invincible spirit of His people. Oliver Cromwell had said long ago that not even fire will destroy gold. It can only burn and consume dross, but the gold remains. So it is with God's people; the more they are persecuted, the more they grow. And there is but one street in this city where God's own walk in one light and one way. It is Antichrist who has brought all the odd nooks and by-lanes, but the men who have golden hearts will know the way.

John knelt to thank God for his suffering, and told Him he would preach and write about the Holy City, so that others could know, too. As soon as he rose, he went to his table, sat down, and began. . . .

Despite his vision, the bad news that kept coming to the prison deprived him of his peace. That fall of 1664 the plague struck Holland, and in London the Council met to try to figure out a way to keep it from crossing the channel. But at the end of November two Frenchmen in Drury Lane died of it, and terror began to spread. In February another man in the same parish contracted it; the citizens avoided Drury Lane, or passed through that section holding handkerchiefs to their noses. In the adjoining parishes of St. Andrew and Holburn others died; then the disease moved to St. Bride's and St. James Clerkenwell. In April, when the warm weather set in, there were twenty-five deaths a week.

The weather turned cooler in May, slowing the epidemic, but in June it spread rapidly. Some of the victims concealed their illness to keep from being isolated and to prevent the authorities from closing their houses. The second week in June one hundred and twenty-five people were buried in St. Giles-in-the-fields, the London parish in which the plague had first appeared after crossing the channel. The Lord Mayor was besieged with requests for health certificates and the permissions necessary to leave London. Every day wagons and carts filled with fleeing citizens rolled out of the city into the shires, and even the King and his court left for Oxford.

Fear gripped Bedford the following December when word came that the dreaded pestilence had struck Newport. John sat in his cell one cold evening thinking how terrible it would be if Bitsy or any of the children caught it. He remembered how swiftly it had struck in Elstow when he had been fifteen. There were no candles left and John sat in the twilight wondering if he would ever be freed. A new Conventicle Act had been passed in May of 1664, and in October of this year another cruel law, called the Five-Mile Act.

Depression continued to bite at him. Sir John Kelynge had become Chief Justice of the King's Bench, so that, even if John wanted to risk the consequences of losing a suit for a writ of error, there would be little possibility that he could secure one. The only way he could get out would be to sell his soul, and he would never do that. The King wouldn't pardon him; he would be too afraid of Chancellor Hyde. Yet John's offense was only a statutory misdemeanor.

In a week, he thought sadly, it will be Christmas again. If only I could spend the night at home. But I won't ask John White because if he let me go and anybody found out, he would be punished.

There was no warning sound of footsteps. John hadn't even been aware of a sound in the corridor outside, but suddenly the bolt was moved back and the heavy door creaked open. A shape appeared in the dimness, a big figure in a long cassock.

"John, are you there?"

John's heart leaped. "Mel! What are you doing here?"

He held out a paper bundle. "I came to bring you some candles from Bitsy. And here is your supper." He plunked a tray down on the little table.

"What's the matter with Bitsy?"

"She has been working hard, trying to set aside a little money for gifts and goodies for the children's Christmas. A shopkeeper was coming for some lace, and she hadn't finished it."

John sighed. "Nothing can kill the Spirit of Christmas. Do you remember the year the extreme Puritans outlawed all festivities? There was to be no bell-ringing, no celebration. But the merry-making went on in secret."

Mel helped John light a candle. Thomas Green came in with his own tray of food. Mel sat down on the straw mattress, and chattered while they all ate.

The plague, he said, was abating in London, but there were still a number of cases. Some thought the filth and rats had some-thing to do with the epidemic; the ditches stank, and rats ate the garbage thrown into the streets, and people continued to die.

"What have you been doing?" John asked.

"Ministering to the stricken. Nurses are scarce. You never saw so many miserable, hurting people. Door after door has the warn-ing cross, and the death cart rolls through the lanes, and streets echo with the driver's gruesome call, "Bring out your dead!" He shuddered. "I'll never erase the horrors from my mind. Hell could not be so bad!"

"What a beloved fool you are!" John remarked between mouth-fuls. "It's a wonder you didn't catch it."

"I took every precaution. The doctors know the pus from the boils can infect others. I washed my hands frequently. I burned any rag or clothing that touched the boils. I even aired the sick chambers. It was a great opportunity; 'tis easy to make converts of men about to die!"

"If the plague gets me, you can nurse me," John told him with a wry smile. "But don't expect to hear me ask for your extreme unction!"

"God forbid you catch it. Your years in jail haven't done your health any good!" Mel said fervently, crossing himself.

"Jail doesn't do anybody any good. Pray God you will not be arrested in Bedfordshire. There are informers everywhere."

But Mel was caught. Two days later he returned to the day-room a prisoner! Paul Cobb, now completely under the influence of William Foster, had looked through a window, seen Mel giving the last rites to a dying neighbor of his father's, and realized who he was.

"At least we can sing my favorite Christmas carol, 'O Thou Man,' together," Mel said with a grimace. "I always wanted to sing Christmas carols in the Bedford Gaol."

But John saw that the muscles around Mel's mouth were tight, and that his hands were trembling.

The Mooneys came every day with food for Mel. In a jail all of a prisoner's expenses were charged to him. Sometimes Bitsy, or some of the members of the Bedford Meeting, brought them both a treat. The Fennes, who had both been convicted of attending more than one conventicle and knew what it was to be in jail, furnished roast beef and dumplings on Sunday. Mel was so grateful that he could hardly speak of the kindness shown him without tears coming into his eyes. But he said that, in a way, it was a relief not to have to listen for that knock on the door and the footsteps of a constable coming to lead him to prison.

John determined to do everything possible to help Mel through the trying period of adjustment when a man's body weakened and his soul cried out hour after hour, day after day, and temptations came creeping to make him change his mind.

Three days after Mel's arrest temptation struck in the person of Paul Cobb, who always seemed to come late at night when a man is tired and prone to compromise. The aging Paul was a dour individual with iron-gray hair, stooped shoulders, and a mouth that turned down at the corners. Wrinkles creased his thin cheeks, and anyone could see at a glance that he was not a happy person.

"Mel Mooney," he said in a persuasive voice, "I have come to inform ye that mercy might be shown ye. Now if ye would accept a living in the Church of England, the Committee on Ministers——"

"No! I have taken vows!" Mel said through stiff lips.

"Can't ye take other vows? Or do ye hate the Church of England? Could it be true that ye hate God's people?"

Mel shook his head wearily. "I hate no one. Perhaps my sin has been in underestimating the power of atoning love. But I took solemn vows. I am a priest of the Church of Rome!"

"It would be more profitable to be a rector with a fine living in the Church of England. Your work would be legal."

Mel's mouth was tight with anger. Swifter than a weaver's shuttle, he leaped off his stool and stood facing Paul, his square chin thrust out, his fists clenched.

"I have a mind, and with God's help I will decide where my allegiance will be!"

Paul blinked and backed away, and his eyes looked more like a scared rabbit's than ever. Sickheartedness struck at John because men like Paul allowed power and the safety of the moment to endanger their souls.

"We don't want so much trouble in the shire!" Paul rasped. "Can't ye do what the Government asks and take some more vows with the established church?"

Mel set his jaw again. "No!"

"All right. Be a fool, Priest. Many have lost their lives trying to be heroes."

Mel's bloodshot eyes met John's, and suddenly they brightened with a light John had never seen there before. The sickheartedness left John, and a strange exultation took its place as Mel added, "As my good friend, Bunyan, says, 'the Cross is the standing-way mark by which all who go to glory must pass!'"

And John thought of the many who had suffered for conscience's sake—John Rush, John Okey, Oliver Cromwell, and all the Dissenters who had died bravely, or lived in anguish behind prison bars. Assurance came that freedom would come to England.

The Church of England would be greater because of their stand; it had been the church of John's youth and he would always revere it. It was God's Church, too, and the fact that a few selfish men wanted to make it the only church was no reason to despise it. But men's minds and hearts must be free!

Paul let out an oath. He began shaking his fist and shouting, "One thing I know, Papist, ye'll regret your fool pride. We have two dungeons underground. Bunyan was once in one of them and he can tell ye what they're like. Eleven steps and ye're in total darkness where the hungry rats swarm over ye, an' ye're so cold and damp ye would prefer your Purgatory. I will recommend that ye spend Christmas there to correct your thinking. Then, if ye continue as stubborn a cuss as th' tinker, I hope they lop off yer damned head!"

The furious man banged from the room, slamming the door, and bolting it after him. Mel's big shoulders lifted and he managed a smile, but there was no mirth in it.

He was incredulous. "When the little man gains power, it does strange things to him. He cannot see why anyone should hold to his own beliefs."

"You are carrying your cross, Mel."

"*His* Cross!" Mel said softly. "Not yours or mine, John, but *His*. We only share it."

Within the hour two constables came for Mel. He greeted them in a hearty voice, and his eyes were merry as he asked if he could say a Mass for their souls. He chuckled when they stiffened.

Shuddering with apprehension, John watched them flank the priest and longed to swing his mighty fist at them, but Mel's eyes signaled caution.

Christmas Eve found John alone staring into the darkness. He closed his eyes, trying to imagine he was at home. At times like this he was grateful for his strong imagination: he could picture Bitsy decorating the house with green boughs of holly and making a fine pudding with nuts and raisins in it. John or Thomas would have killed one of the hens, and Elizabeth would be bustling about tying ribbons to the candleholders. The children would be chasing each other around the board table, shouting and laughing noisily.

His thoughts were interrupted by the appearance of his friend, John White.

"Any news from London?" John asked, as he often did.

John White shook his head. "All I hear is that the King is engaged in battling Parliament when they should be uniting against the envious Dutch."

"There is something I want to ask you——"

"Yes, John. Ye can go home. That's what I came to tell ye. But be back before dawn."

For an instant John had a foreboding of evil. He cast it off, for he was going home! Wrapped in an old cloak which Bitsy had patched with care, he bade his friend good night, slipped out into Jail Lane, and sped toward St. Cuthbert's Street.

When he opened the cottage door and stepped in, thirteen-year-old Elizabeth saw him first. She was tying a bow on one of the candles on the shelf above the hearth. Bitsy was stirring a pudding. Young John was hammering on a piece of wood, and Thomas was reaching for a bunch of herbs tied beside the chimney piece.

"Papa!" "Oh, Papa!" "Papa, they let you come home!"

John hugged Elizabeth and tweaked her curls. Her features were like her mother's, but she had dark hair and eyes like Bitsy's.

Bitsy's face was glowing as she ran into his arms.

"Sweetheart," he whispered, with yearning and affection.

"John dear, you're home!"

"Just for tonight," he told her.

While he bathed his face and hands in the blue bowl which Elizabeth placed on the settle in front of the hearth, the family clamored all at once, telling him their Christmas plans. They had killed the fattest hen. Anthony Harrington had brought a whole cheese. Bitsy suggested a little family service of worship that night to thank God for sending him home. There was to be a meeting at Josiah Ruffhead's, but, of course, John couldn't let anyone know he was away from his cell, or John White might be punished.

Bitsy placed before him some thick soup she had warmed, and a round loaf of bread. How good the meat and vegetables tasted. A warm glow spread through John. When he had finished every drop, Bitsy took a bowl of oranges off the shelf, and he ate three of them, licking his lips when he finished.

The churning within him had subsided. All the torment and restlessness were gone. He sank into his armchair beside the hearth, stretching his long legs out toward the blaze. In this dear, familiar place, he was at peace. The harrowing days, the discomforts, the tragedies that had surrounded him for over five years were as unreal as some of his dreams.

When there was a lull in the conversation, the inevitable plea came. "Tell us more about Christian!"

"Well, Christian fell into a swoon, but when he woke up they renewed their discourse about the Giant's counsel. . . ."

It was five o'clock and Bitsy was still sleeping quietly. All night John had lain beside her, feeling her head on his shoulder, her warm breath on his neck, and their common warmth had erased the chill from his bones, the loneliness from his heart. All his impulses urged him to stay here, but reason ruled that he should return to the jail. Quietly he slipped out of bed, took his clothes downstairs where the embers still glowed, dressed quickly, and went out closing the door softly behind him.

All Bedford was asleep. The cottages in St. Cuthbert's Street were dark and he did not meet anyone as he walked along in the starlight, his face bitten by the cold, his mass of reddish hair blown by the winter wind.

He reached the jail, felt his way along the unlit corridor and entered the dayroom. When he lay down, the straw of his bed felt like ice beneath him, but he rolled up in his coverlets and thought of the warmth of Bitsy's body and the flickering flames in the fire at home.

As dawn was peeping through the small, barred window he heard a movement outside in the corridor. Maybe the door to the dungeon had been left open and some of the rats had found their way upstairs. Poor Mel. He would not complain, but it was a pity they could not eat their Christmas dinner together! In a few minutes a head appeared at the opening in the door. Clearly John saw Froggy Foster's ugly face, the protruding eyes. Hands as skinny as a witch's gripped the iron bars. The sight startled John so that he closed his eyes quickly, trying to still his racing heart. After a while there were stealthy receding, footsteps, and he heard the outer door shut.

It wasn't long until there was a heavy tread, and the dayroom door opened. John White stood in the path of daylight that filtered through the window.

"Thank Heaven ye're back. I just met Froggy sneaking out. Ye can come and go as ye please, John. Ye know when ye should return better than I do. Froggy's trying to get work here. If he does, God have pity on all of us!"

"He won't return today?"

John White smiled happily. "William Foster told me yesterday that Froggy was going to accompany him to Harlington House for Christmas dinner. We shall have a very, very merry Christmas!"

"Then you will let the priest come up?"

John White went for Mel. The news of Foster's absence had spread. People came all day with goodies, fruits, pudding, and pies. By the middle of the afternoon the little table was piled high, and John White accepted their invitation to supper.

Mel was in a happy mood, his trials for the moment forgotten.

The days passed. Thomas Green came and went in the dayroom, but there were fewer Nonconformists in jail than there had been in a long time. John had nobody to preach to; because of the extreme punishments the Meeters were becoming more and more clever about their gatherings. John was writing the story of his conversion, which he called *Grace Abounding to the Chief of*

Sinners. But after five or six hours of writing, he always had to get up and walk back and forth.

At such times he longed for his violin, but John White had refused to allow him to keep it there. "One of the authorities would be sure to find out, and there would be retribution. Froggy asked me the other day what ye're writing. Something is boiling in his nasty little mind."

When the parishioners at St. Paul's sang, their voices sounded sweet on John's ears. He sang along with the familiar tunes, but he often wished he had an instrument to play. One morning he sang so loudly, rocking back and forth on his square stool that he fell backwards onto the cold stone floor. As he scrambled to his feet and righted the stool, he had an idea. Four wooden rails held the four legs of the stool together. Why not make a flute from one of the rails? But he would have to have a thin blade to hollow it.

On Sunday night he went quickly through the darkness to his home, and when he left at five the next morning, he took a long, thin knife with him.

The work of shaping the flute began. He carefully hollowed a piece of one of the circular rails, working a little each day. Whenever he heard anyone coming, he hid the blade under his jacket and replaced the rail on the stool, fitting it quickly into the socket. At last the flute was ready to have its fingering holes made. But how? The layer of wood was thin. If he tried to make the holes with the point of the knife, the wood might crack. Was all his work for nothing? He thought about burning the holes with a candle, but the flame was too big. Perhaps if he thinned the wick, he could burn tiny holes!

His hands were steady when he finally held the small light to the hollowed wood. He worked carefully. And when he had finished, he lifted the flute to his lips; it had a wild, sweet sound.

Every night that week John played softly to himself. He played the old tunes, the chants, psalms, and ballads; and he played some new ones, improvising melodies. The days passed pleasantly, but on Sunday, John White came bearing terrible news. Mel had brought the plague to Bedford!

"Is he very sick?"

The jailer nodded. "He's down there sweating and panting. There be big boils under his arms. I'm going to ask the authorities to close the jail, let everyone go free temporarily except the felons; they can be locked in the Town Clink on the Bridge."

"Isn't it in bad repair?"

"That it is. We may even have to take the felons to Harlington House."

"I'm going to the priest. Fetch me a bowl of boiling water and some rags."

"There be no rags," he said, but he brought the hot water quickly.

John took it, lifted the candle in the horn candleholder and started down the steep, winding stairs.

Mel was lying on some moldy, dirty straw, breathing heavily. Rats were swarming around him, young ones and old. He didn't have the strength to chase them off. John rearranged the straw under his head to ease him. The stench in the place was overpowering!

"My old friend," Mel murmured. "My faithful friend."

John saw that his tongue was thick and white. Blood trickled from the corner of his mouth.

"Do not try to talk. I'll take care of you."

"The plague. I'm sure——"

He lifted his arms, and John winced at the sight of the dark buboes which bulged enormously, filled with blood and pus, ruptured and running. There were four under one arm and two under the other!

John took off his own shirt and began to tear it into strips.

"You know what I'm going to do, Mel, put hot cloths to the sores. We must drain that pus."

Mel moved restlessly all the time John was wringing out the strips and placing them on the boils. Once he opened his eyes wide, winced, and screamed. A great shudder passed through his body, and John was convinced that Mel was going to die. If only you could have lived to see a free England, he thought, and the depth of his own agony astonished him. He could find no will to keep the tears from blurring his eyes.

The priest reached out with a hot, trembling hand, and touched John's sleeve.

"I'm glad we didn't conform. I leave you *our* torch. Guard it well!"

Mel fumbled in the pocket of his vicar's robe and found his rosary. His lips moved as he fingered it lovingly. The faltering words were scarcely audible, but John bent close.

"Our Father—who art—in Heaven—hallowed be—thy name. . . . Thy kingdom—come. Thy kingdom come—to England, too. . . . Thy will be done. . . ."

Again a great shudder went through Mel's body as his voice trailed off; the luster drained from his eyes, and John knew that Mel had left him.

Sitting on the cold stones, he remembered the first time he had seen him. Master Vierney had just asked John to state whether or not he had been infected by the views of Oliver Cromwell and others like him. John had felt alone and very frightened until he saw two faces; one of them Mel's with its warm, brown eyes. Their faith had been similar in that it had been in Jesus Christ, though the expression was very different. They fought against the tyrants for the right to disagree.

Wearily John climbed the eleven steps leading up from Bedford Jail's dungeon. The doors to the lodging rooms were all open, and empty. The outside door was flung back as if the inmates had left in fright. He went to the dayroom to pick up his quill and the manuscript he had been working on—his autobiography—and then stepped quickly into the dark streets of the town. He didn't know what time it was until he heard the cry of the night watchman:

"Ten o'clock and all's well.
Don't neglect your cat. Remember that.

226

And look to your lock
For it's ten o'clock!"

The children had gone to bed when he walked into the cottage. Bitsy was combing her long, black hair, started up, and ran toward him. He held up a warning hand.

"Don't come near me. I've just come from Mel who died of the plague! I need some hot water, and plenty of rags."

Bitsy soon had the kettle boiling, and he bathed near the door, using lye soap and then wrapping himself in a clean coverlet, while he went out into the freezing air to hang his clothes on the bushes.

For six months, while the plague continued to rage, John was a free man. William Foster, Paul Cobb, and their constables stayed in their own houses. John spent several hours each day writing and several in his forge. How good it was to work with his hands again.

But he grieved for Mel, whose loss he found overwhelming. Never again would John see his big figure plodding fearlessly about trying to help others, his brown eyes warm, and his round face with its merry smile. Their common destiny had lain in fighting for conscience and England; praying men know that, if they love God, they must sacrifice for His Cause. And theirs was the honor from which England's greatness springs.

During John's months of freedom, grim panic held the borough, as the plague spread from Newport and London. Within three days in July forty people died in Newport and Matthias Cowley was one of them. There were about the same number of deaths in Elstow and Bedford, including Christopher Hall's.

14 At the first flush of dawn that last day of August, 1666, John set out for London, riding a spirited horse that belonged to Anthony Harrington. With the help of the Sisters Fenne, Bitsy had fashioned him some new breeches and a homespun jacket. The new clothes were carefully folded, and packed in his saddle case where the heavy dust could not reach them and he was wearing an old shirt that had belonged to John Fenne, and some ill-fitting gray breeches that had been his father's.

"You must look your best to meet the King!" Bitsy had told him. "Ever since you've been in jail, you've been wearing other men's cast-off clothing. You wouldn't want people to stare."

"Don't make me look like a popinjay," he had protested. "I have no desire to draw attention to myself."

Now as he rode south, he smiled to himself, remembering. There was no finer wife in the shire than Bitsy. He still worried because he knew his growing children needed a man's influence, but Bitsy was doing a fine job of rearing them. It looked as if he would be returned to the jail, but at least he had had these months with his family.

The summer had been warm and without rain, and swirls of dust blew about him as he jogged along. If only the September rains would come now, settling the ground and bringing winds that refreshed.

As he neared London on Monday afternoon, after stopping at

a village the day before to confer with some Anabaptists, his thoughts were active. The Dutch were threatening the country again, as the commercial rivalry between Holland and England continued. The plague was said to have taken over a hundred thousand lives. King Charles had his hands full, but there was no problem greater than the one John wanted to talk to him about, the cruelty and the injustice that prevailed. Both the Conventicle Act of 1664 and the Five-Mile Act of the following year were out of all reason. A conventicle was defined as a gathering of more than five, other than the members of a family. The penalties were outrageous: for the first offense a five-pound fine, or three months in jail; for the second ten pounds or six months, and for the third, after trial and conviction at the Assizes or Quarter Sessions, banishment for seven years or a fine of one hundred pounds. The Five-Mile Act, whose chief promotors had been Chancellor Hyde, Archbishop Shelton, and Dr. Seth Ward, the Bishop of Salisbury, aimed at muzzling Nonconformist ministers and priests. The assembling of any group within five miles of any town or city, corporate or borough, carried the penalties of a fine of forty pounds or banishment.

Too many had recanted at the General Quarter Sessions or gone over to the Church of England and been "profanely bishoped," although their consciences told them to worship as Nonconformists. The remnant that stood against the despotism met, but didn't dare keep a Minute Book, and found the planning of secret meetings very hazardous.

John not only wanted to get the King's help, but he looked forward to visiting his new publisher, George Larkin. Francis Smith, a Puritan, who had published some of his books, had written that he would have to go into hiding until pressures from Roger L'Estrange, the Chief Censor for the Crown, were lifted.

As John rode along, he rehearsed what he would say to the King: "God has shown that he is provoked, your Majesty, at the irreverence and immorality at court, and at the tyranny by the hand of your Chancellor. The plague is waning, but we should take heed. The evil continues. God may send another scourge to make those who sin turn to Him. Witness the threat of the Dutch. . . . How brave the late Protector was, your Majesty. In battle he was always in the thick of the fighting, risking his life for what he believed. You are the King, and you must lead the way to freedom. Why don't you rid England of a Chancellor who will bring only ruin on you and your subjects?"

But what if King Charles refuses to see me? John thought. And a cold wind seemed to blow on his spirit. He is the King, and I am a man under sentence for a misdemeanor, a nobody from a dunghill. But no man's a nobody in God's sight, he argued with himself. Even a tinker from a dunghill is pretty important when he is a child of God. If God chose, he could make me a prince. John sat tall in the saddle, and threw his shoulders back, holding his head high.

It was almost twilight when he reached the open fields outside of the city. Traffic coming and going was very heavy. He noticed a red light glowing in the sky ahead, and saw a black screen of smoke.

Fire! he thought. That could be tragic with the houses of London huddled so close together that the overhanging upper stories almost met.

A rider came galloping from the direction of the city, guiding his horse along the turf at the side of the road. As he flashed by, he yelled in a sepulcral voice. "Turn back. All London is on fire!"

A procession of people followed, some on foot, others on horse, in carts piled with belongings. Jostling each other, they drove John onto the turf, too.

Darkness found him riding slowly along the Thames, staring at the smoldering ruins, spreading over blocks, where houses and other buildings had stood. And to his left blazed London. Even London Bridge was smoldering, the fine houses gone, the shops gutted.

Should I go home? John thought. Even if Whitehall remains, the King will be so busy, he won't see anybody. But when John remembered the weary Christians in Bedford, who were placing their hope in his mission, he knew he could not return until he had talked to the King.

Above and beyond him the flames were racing like fiery serpents leaping and writhing. He could smell the acrid smoke; he could taste it. For an eternity he choked and coughed, until suddenly he felt faint. He fell from his horse in a world of smoke and blackness.

When he opened his eyes, he was lying on the riverbank, his head pillowed comfortably on a soft lap. A gigantic man with a large, long nose like a snout, big protruding ears, and kind, round eyes was leaning over him. John's throat smarted and the smell of burning was everywhere.

"Are you all right?" the man asked in a trumpeting voice.

"Yes, I think so." John groaned and managed to sit up.

Thames Street was in confusion. There were great explosions, men shouting, and frightened horses neighing as people milled about seeking refuge from the fire. John looked for his borrowed animal, and saw that it stood at the water's edge.

"Where are you bound?"

"I have just arrived in London. My name's John Bunyan and I come from Bedford. Thank you for looking after me."

"Not John Bunyan, the *writer?*" The man gave John a mighty clap on his shoulder, which made him wince. "I am Elephant Smith."

It was the first time anybody had ever called John a writer, and he didn't understand how this man would know that.

"Elephant Smith?" he countered, thinking that the name certainly suited him. "Have you read any of my books?"

The man threw his big head back, opened his great cave of a mouth, and laughed heartily. "If I didn't read them, why would I publish them?"

"Then you're Francis Smith?"

"That I am. I hope my reason for sending you to my young friend, George Larkin, is clear to you. Roger L'Estrange, the King's Chief Censor, ordered a raid made on my shop and warehouse. The searchers had a bonfire with a pile of the books. I was fined, as stated, for compiling and printing dangerous books."

"It's a good thing Mr. Larkin had mine."

"Sorry to have to tell you that Larkin's warehouse went up today, too, and I'll wager many copies of your new book with it."

They began to search for an inn. John led the horse, because the streets were filled, and progress was easier on foot. The gutted houses, the smoke-blackened rubble, the gaunt chimneys standing by themselves, the dead animals lying everywhere sent shivers down his spine. The heavy thudding of Elephant's feet on the uneven cobbles reminded John of Mel's walk. He had thought Mel a big man, but Elephant was a giant compared to him.

The city lay as if under a curse. Blocks of ashes stretched endlessly along their path, and on a hill behind them, the fire still burned brightly in the darkness. John's muscles ached long before they paused at a hanging sign bearing the name, The Merry Dolphin.

"The fire is far enough off," Elephant said, "so that I think we'll be safe here until morning."

Thoughts of the misery in Bedfordshire spurred John to action early the next day. After a simple breakfast with Elephant, he went to the Palace of Whitehall, but learned that the King was not there. The Major-domo told him that the King was directing the fire-fighters, and that his brother, the Duke of York, commanded the troops who were trying to prevent looting. John set out to find the King.

When he reached Milford Lane near the Strand, an incongruous sight struck his eyes. Here there was a mill and a ford ran across a little stream and under the Strand to the Thames. A line of men with straining faces were passing buckets which sloshed water, and in the middle, directing the activity, stood a tall man with deep, black eyes set in a swarthy face that had a black thin line of mustache. He was coatless and hatless, and a black curled periwig sat on his head at a rakish angle. His ruffled shirt was dirty and torn, his face blackened with soot and lined with fatigue, but there was no weakness there. "Heave!" he shouted and the men heaved, their sweat rivering clean streaks through the dirt on their cheeks.

John elbowed his way through the line and shoved into the line as close to his Majesty as possible. He saw that what Charles was trying to do was to wet the houses to prevent stray sparks from starting new conflagrations.

"A double line would get it done a lot faster," John bellowed when there was a lull in the commotion.

The King looked directly at him, frowning. Then he commanded, "Form a double line, men. Hurry. There's no time to lose!"

As soon as the line was re-formed, the buckets came so fast that John, joining in, had to move swiftly to catch them. And beyond the Strand men with long-handled hooks pulled down buildings to make gaps the flames could not cross.

London was an inferno of fire and earth-splitting explosions. People shouted and cried out in terror as the crash of falling timbers smote the air.

A slight boy next to John, who didn't look more than fourteen, was breathing heavily. In a little while he buckled and went down in the dust. John shouted to the man behind to fill the gap, and leaping out of line, lifted the youth in his arms, and carried him across the Strand and down to the river.

When the lad regained consciousness, he gave a sheepish grin. "I guess I worked too hard, but ye should have seen the King! He came riding up with a sack of guineas over his shoulder and hired all the laborers he could. 'Save London,' he told us. 'London is the heart of our country.'"

The boy's name was John Strudwick, and he was an orphan apprenticed to a grocer. They chatted about the King for a few minutes, and the boy kept insisting that Charles was the bravest man in England.

John returned to the line, and the hours dragged. His eyes began to burn, his head throbbed, and his legs felt numb. And when he finished passing buckets, the King was gone. . . .

That night St. Paul's Church caught fire and burned, along with the Prison of the Fleet. On Friday the roof of the church caved in.

When the fire ceased, acquaintances met once again on the streets. The *London Gazette*, a paper started by King Charles, began publishing news again, housed in a new building that had not been gutted by fire. It reported that the King was resting after his exertions, and that his physician had announced he would be on his feet again in a few days. Although the finest residential section had been left untouched, all London from the Temple to the Tower had been destroyed, including almost twelve thousand dwellings and ninety churches.

Elephant Smith took John to a meeting the following Sunday, September 9. A group of Baptists had gathered to thank God for sparing the home they assembled in, and for preserving their lives. A young minister, Harry Rupert, preached about repentance, revealing that the grossest sins continued to flourish in the city, despite God's warning. John was scandalized as he listened. The Cardinal's Hat, the most notorious of the cesspools of iniquity, was full night after night, and the sounds of the fiddles and bawdy ballads drifted out into the ghostly city, luring souls to destruction. Everybody knew that the King himself patronized the patched and overpainted young women in their ill-gotten finery. What catastrophe would God's wrath at such behavior bring to London next?

John went up to the young preacher as soon as the service ended, introduced himself, and asked two questions: "What are you doing about the stewhouses? What are the other preachers of the city doing?"

The young man drew himself up. He was an insipid-looking creature with pale watery eyes behind narrow spectacles. "Oh, many preach quarterly about the evil."

"Have you tried to save those girls?"

"*Girls?*" Brother Rupert raised his eyebrows, obviously amused. "How do you propose to do it?"

234

"Preach to them! Make them listen, whether they want to or not!"

Others, waiting in line to speak to Brother Rupert, saw the distress of his face and came forward in a circle to listen.

"Do you suggest that I invade a stewhouse like a general invading a fortress?"

"I will go with you. Let's go tonight. Round up as many Baptists as you can find. It's our responsibility."

"Let the yokel break his heart over the girls in the stewhouses," a well-dressed merchant said with a curl of his lip. "What does one stewhouse matter when the threat of the Dutch hangs like a sword over England? Let the yokel play the fool. Let him be the invasion!"

Somebody snickered, and John, looking at the merchant, a pompous man with a big belly, thought: How can any man who calls himself a Christian turn his head when he passes the Cardinal's Hat? When the "girls" go marching by in their silver slippers? As the man's meaning sank in, John's eyes began to snap, and his nails dug into the palms of his hands.

"The yokel thinks I'm callous," the merchant continued. "He's good and mad. Yokels get madder'n anybody." There was a wicked twinkle in his eyes.

The anger drained from John's heart. This merchant was like a horse in a mill going round and round, his eyes blindfolded so that he never saw where he was going.

"Even if I have to go alone, I am going," John said quietly. "I will be here at eight o'clock tonight to meet those who realize they *are* their brother's keepers."

"You were great. You were magnificent!" Elephant said, as they walked back to the inn. "There will be at least *two* of us."

"There'll be three," a young voice said.

John Strudwick, the grocer's apprentice stood there, his thin, freckled face smiling.

"I didn't know you were a Nonconformist, Strud," John told him.

The boy lived near the Town Ditches, and John walked home with him.

"The smells are horrible," John said in disgust. "I don't see how you stand living so near!"

"Oh, it's not so bad to be here awhile, but to live here always would be to be dead."

"And you have ambition? You want to have your own grocery shop one day?"

The youth nodded, and his brown eyes began to shine. "If ever I get out of here—and I will—I shall prize a better life more than those who have not been here!"

All afternoon, John walked alone through the city, staring at the ruins, wondering what he would say when he went to the Cardinal's Hat, and whether the sights he saw there would make his hair stand on end. He dreaded the passing of the hours. What possessed me to decide to go there? he thought. Does "Christian" have to take the world's sin upon his shoulders?

Elephant was waiting for him at the inn when he returned. During supper the publisher was silent, toying with his bread and cheese. Several times John noticed Elephant regarding him with a troubled stare, and he wished he had not been so hasty.

A little before eight he was trudging toward the house where the meeting had taken place, with Elephant thumping behind him. Nobody will be there, he thought, nobody. To his amazement a group had gathered in front of the lighted house. The young minister was not there, but, including himself and Elephant, there were eight men and over twenty women from various social levels: women with lined faces framed by white hair; young women with pure but earnest faces; the middle-aged, too; and the curious.

"We heard about what you are going to do," one lady told him. "Somebody should have done something besides preach a long time ago!"

"I am here," a gentleman said with a frown, "because my only son spends most of his time at the place."

236

And there stood little Strud. "Don't send me away, sire," he begged. "You said we are our brother's keepers."

A colorful Spanish seaman with brass rings in his ears shoved up, brandishing a dagger. "I heerd ye wuz attackin' the Cardinal's Hat. I'm your man. They took all my money!"

John had to explain that the "attack" was a nonviolent one in which only Christians were to take part. He told the man to put up his weapon.

"I'll even be a Christian for the night," the sailor muttered. "It'd be worth it."

Elephant indicated by nods and meaningful gesture that John could leave the sailor to him.

As the strange procession wound its way through the narrow streets and alleys, a woman's voice lifted in a familiar hymn by William Byrd:

"And rather would I die
And rather would I die of mine accord,
Of mine accord
Ten thousand times, ten thousand times
Than once offend our Lord!"

Other voices blended with hers, and soon the words ran through the city, attracting others who followed, marching and singing, although they did not know where they were going. By the time they reached the Cardinal's Hat, over two hundred people were trailing after them, not knowing why—or caring. Something was happening to break the monotony. That was all that mattered. There had been little joy since the fire.

Standing in front of the stewhouse was a tall man, dressed in the garb of the Pilgrim preachers—a broad black hat with a low crown, a long black coat that came below the knees, baggy knee breeches, high stockings that met the breeches, and plain black shoes with broad toes. He was about six feet in height, broad of shoulder, and his arms were long. Sandy hair hung straight below his ears, and his hazel eyes reminded John of John Okey's. His nose was long and thin like that of an ancient Roman in a painting. When he came forward and smiled, John's heart went out. This man was a Christian.

"I guess you are the Puritan from Bedford who has thrown my congregation into uproar. When I returned from preaching at Soper Lane this morning, my wife told me that a man had come to town. I see you meant what you said. I am Brother John Owen."

John introduced himself, told him of seeing the "girls" from the Cardinal's Hat marching to church in their silver slippers during the Protectorate, how the sight had stayed with him through the years, how some force without himself had made him say he would come here tonight and preach to them. "But I am terrified. All afternoon I've been kicking myself."

"I thought you might need some support. This is something some of us should have done a long time ago."

"Will you preach?"

The minister shook his head. "Somehow I think you can do that tonight better than I could."

Elephant and Brother Owen were right behind John when he pushed open the red-painted door, pausing to stare at what he saw. The scene was like one he had witnessed so often during the war when the soldiers cavorted with the camp followers who moved with the army. Men were lounging around with thinly clad females, embracing in shameless fashion, silver mugs before them. One man was in shirttails.

They all stared at John, and he felt their sneering thoughts on his homespun clothes and plain boots, and their surprise that such a yokel should present himself at a stewhouse frequented by members of the court!

An older woman, who had evidently replaced Mam Bard, scowled darkly. She looked so like a witch, with long hands and a peevish and sour expression, that for the moment, John wished he could take her to Bedford to scare Froggy.

Another gentleman pushed out from behind some curtains of scarlet brocade, and John heard Elephant chuckle.

238

"Sir Roger L'Estrange, the King's Chief Censor," he said in a loud voice, and the look of malice in his round eyes told John he was not innocently embarrassing the gentleman, "What are you doing here? I was of the erroneous opinion that you passed your leisure hours reading elevating literature, the kind you license! You seem to find mine so distasteful. Remember me to your lady, and tell her I'm disappointed in you!"

Sir Roger turned scarlet, grabbed up a miniver cloak and some brocade breeches and disappeared like a rat running into a crack, while Elephant's rafter-shaking laugh boomed out.

"What are you doing here?" the witchlike woman screamed.

John's stomach churned with nervousness, but he threw his shoulders back and looked her right in the eye.

"I have come, not as a customer, but to talk about your souls," he managed in a small voice.

A girl with patches on her painted face and antimony on her eyelids closed one eye with ostentatious ridicule, as another with a wanton look, and a face white with rice powder, paraded past looking John up and down. Her movements were deliberately calculated to be sensuous. The only response she called forth in him was pity. Under that paint and powder she had a young face, and it wasn't depraved. Surely these women must know that they meant nothing to the men who, wanting only the satisfaction of their appetites, chose them as if they were selecting vegetables. Surely these women did not enjoy this. What could anyone say to make an impression on them? What could he tell them?

He wanted to turn and run, but he took a deep breath and began. "Will you force God to call down His wrath from Heaven, or will you hear his Voice? . . ." He told them of his own sins, his agony, his searching, and how God had said that he would not save man, because of what man is, but because of His Grace, which is sufficient for the worst sinner.

And, oddly, his audience was as attentive as the most ardent Meeters. They couldn't believe that this country bumpkin, standing there with his thumbs hooked in his russet breeches, swaying back and forth awkwardly, would have the nerve to do what he was doing. As he continued to talk, he became eloquent, brandishing his arm energetically as he pleaded, argued, and prayed that God would guide each one of them to accept this greatest of gifts, which He was now holding out to them.

When he had finished, John saw that the girl with the rice-powdered cheeks was crying, her tears making a path in the dusty whiteness. Another sniffed audibly, wiping her nose on the sleeve of her satin gown.

Dr. Owen, standing beside John, repeated that Christ was offering them salvation from all the darkness of the earth, and that this was their hour of destiny. As they responded, they would be starting on the narrow road that led to life, or standing in the broad road that led to destruction.

"Whosoever will, come," John said, holding out his arms.

At first nobody moved, and John held his breath. Behind him the "crusaders" who had accompanied him began to sing in low voices:

> "And rather would I die
> And rather would I die of mine accord,
> Of mine accord
> Ten thousand times, ten thousand times
> Than once offend our Lord!"

Then slowly but purposefully the girl with the rice powder, dressed in her expensive gown of crimson brocade, led the way and knelt at John's feet. Two more came to kneel beside her. For a few minutes no one else moved. Then, resolutely, one by one, four more joined them.

After John had prayed, Dr. Owen talked to the girls individually, and they agreed to leave the Cardinal's Hat at once, and come to the fields outside the city the following afternoon to be baptized. To John's amazement the Spanish sailor asked to join them.

"If I can get this salvation," he said, his eyes very bright, "then maybe I can put a curse on my captain. He's meaner'n a African lion with a spear in 'im!"

"Christians don't put a curse on anybody. They follow their conscience. Dr. Owen will talk to you tomorrow with the others."

"Gotta leave port early."

"Then get a copy of the New Testament and read it. When you understand it and really want to become a Christian, come back."

"Too much trouble!" he said with a shrug.

Monday, Tuesday, Wednesday, and Thursday, John went to Whitehall, where the King's red-coated guards told him that the King was still in bed. The *London Gazette* announced that he would be up by Friday, so on Friday John stood around outside the gates, hoping the King would come out. In the middle of the afternoon, one of the new-fangled coaches came banging across the cobbled courtyard. The guards lined up on either side of the wide gates as it rattled through. John ran forward but a mounted guard blocked his way.

"Your Majesty!" John shouted at the top of his voice. "I must talk to you!"

John caught a glimpse of the King as he passed. He was wearing a black velvet suit, white ruffled shirt, and a broad white hat with a black plume curling down the side of it. On his lap was a white-haired spaniel with black spots. Beside him rode a beautiful lady with curly red hair. She wore a silk gown of parakeet green and a tall-crowned hat with golden feathers. The lady leaned out the window, smiled, and tossed John a maundy coin, one of those the King had minted for alms pieces—but the elegant coach rolled on.

Eluding the guard on horseback, John raced after it. He could hear the thudding of a horse's hoofs behind him as the guard came after him, but he ran in zigzag fashion, keeping up with the coach.

"Will Jones! I've got to talk to you!" he yelled as the soldier overtook him, grabbed him roughly by the collar, and held him until the coach was out of sight.

"Be off with ye," the guard muttered, shaking him roughly. "Th' King has no time f'r th' like of ye. Be off!"

"He has to see me!"

"If ye come back, we'll have t' detain ye f'r investigation," the man in the red coat said less gruffly, and John sensed his pity.

The rest of the day John walked about dolefully, looking at the damage the fire had caused. A constable told him that it had started at a baker's in Pudding Lane near London Bridge. The baker told the authorities he had raked out the fire before he had gone to bed that Sunday morning, but the masonry and wood had ignited and set the surrounding timbers sparking. From Pudding Lane the flames had been blown to Fish Street by the high wind, and then Thames Street where combustibles such as brandy, cheese, butter, oil, tar, and wine had been stored.

When John returned to the Merry Dolphin at suppertime, Elephant told him that Dr. Owen wanted to talk to him. John asked Elephant to say that he would visit the minister before he left London.

The next morning John walked toward Whitehall again, in the grip of a suffocating dread that the guards would chase him away. The air was oppressive, and the sky clouded. The weather suited his mood; the money the church had given him for expenses was running out. If he had to return to Bedford without accomplishing what he had come for, the cruelty would go on and on. "O God, he prayed, with You all things are possible. Open the way that I may see the King!"

But again the scarlet-coated men, who tramped back and forth in front of the palace, barred his way.

"You look like a kind man," he told a young guard with buck teeth. "Help me see the King. I have come all the way from Bedford."

The guard paused, holding up his rapier. "Th' plague take ye. If citizens have any complaints, they do not worry the King with them. Would ye like me to arrange for an audience with one of the undersecretaries to the Chancellor?"

"No. It's the Chancellor I want to talk to the King about. In

Bedford they're throwing men and women in jail just for going to church. They take their tools of trade. Surely you're a good Englishman who would not want that! If I could just tell the King——"

"Even if that is true, there's nothing anybody can do. Be off!"

There was nothing to do but leave. Time was melting away like drops of tallow over a hot piece of metal. John had written the people in Bedford that he would not come home until he saw the King, but it looked hopeless. For an instant, as he trudged along, he felt a sudden boiling of his temper within. Wasn't a King's first duty to his subjects?

John turned around and ran back. "I will return tomorrow," he shouted to the guard. "And the day after that, and the day after that until I see him!"

Like a man in a trance, he wandered past a fine house adjoining St. James's Palace. He paused to look through the iron fence at a lady sitting on a bench near a sundial, playing with a small boy. He recognized her as the kind lady who had been in the coach with the King and thrown him the maundy coin. She looks like a princess, he thought. She must be one of the King's sisters. She couldn't be the Queen; he had seen an engraving of her once, and she was tiny like a child.

"Your Highness," he called softly. "Please help me."

She got up and came toward him uncertainly, her white brow puckered a little, her blue eyes questioning. The child toddled after her.

"Haven't I seen ye someplace before?" she asked.

"You tossed me a coin at the gates of Whitehall yesterday, as you rode by with the King. Princess, unless you help me, I'm in trouble. I have come all the way from Bedford to see the King, and they won't let me see him!"

She bit her bow-shaped lip, and the lines in her brow deepened. "I am not a Princess."

"Well, I know you're a lady of quality. Anyone can see, my Lady, that you are good and kind."

The lady dropped her eyes, and he thought her lips quivered a little. Was that a tear glistening in her blue eyes? He couldn't be sure. She was quiet for a long moment.

"Ye are an innocent hulk of a man," she said gently. "What did ye wish to see the King about?"

John told her.

"I'm of the state church, myself," she said. "Charles is up in arms now that the Catholics are being blamed for the great fire! At heart he is one. Don't be too hard on him. The crown's safety lies in his pretense of being nothing but an idler. How could his enemies think there was anything dangerous in such a man? But now might be just the time . . ." She paused. "I know a way for you to see him!"

"How?"

"Be here on Tuesday morning before eleven. The King will be holding a ceremony called 'Touching for the King's Evil.' Ye can go to the Banqueting Hall in Whitehall and I'll have my physician present ye."

"The King's Evil? Your physician? Your Ladyship, I don't understand."

"Stop calling me 'your Ladyship'! Ye'll have to trust me. Just be here!"

She lifted the child in her arms and moved off along the flagged path, a little spaniel squealing and barking after her.

The following Sunday, Dr. Owen invited John to preach in Moorfields. John felt sure that Elephant had surmised he was having financial difficulties, or that Dr. Owen had guessed it, because the preacher not only invited him to his house for dinner but presented him with a small leather purse. When John returned to the inn that night, he undid the draw strings and saw that it contained thirty shillings! He wouldn't have to worry about running short any more.

On Tuesday morning John was in a happy frame of mind, as he dressed in a clean shirt, the fine new coat with buttons all the way down the front, and the new breeches. He put on black stockings, and dusted his shoes. His hair was a trifle too long, so he trimmed it, and carefully clipped his thin mustache.

He went to his appointment early. When the lady appeared at the gate, she wore her red hair in tight little curls about her face. Her blue gown was of a plain heavy silk shirred into a high neckline, and embroidered in gold thread around the neck and wrists. She wore an ornate jeweled necklace, and her white velvet hat was adorned with blue feathers.

She led John around to the front of the fine mansion, where a gilded coach and two spirited black horses waited. A coachman in a yellow brocade suit assisted her inside, and nodded for John to follow.

The carriage rolled through the forbidden gates of Whitehall Palace, and this time the men in scarlet coats did not stop him. They stood at attention as the fine horses trotted past, and the lady fluttered her handkerchief.

"You haven't told me what I must do," John reminded her, as the coach bumped over the cobbles.

"The King will be sitting in state. Get in line with your ticket. Here it is." She handed him a folded parchment. "The chaplains will pray, after which the Court Physician will present the sick. You are supposed to be troubled with a pain in your arm; that is how the ticket reads. When your turn comes, kneel, and His Majesty will touch your arm, and stroke your cheeks with both hands. Beautiful, warm hands, he has!" She sighed. "Later he will place a string of golden angels around your neck. Again the chaplains will pray. After that, come and stand beside me. You will have your audience."

"But my arm doesn't pain. See! There's nothing wrong with it. I cannot come into the King's presence with a lie."

"You *do* want to see the King?"

This lady is going to a lot of trouble to get me into the Banqueting Hall, he thought remorsefully. Without her I couldn't even enter the gates. I ought to be grateful.

"Yes," he told her. "Thank you."

At the great doors to the Banqueting Hall, a lackey in a blue uniform trimmed with gold braid asked to see his ticket. With a wave of her hand, the lady hurried him on and into a line of waiting people.

King Charles sat on a high carved chair at the far end of the long room. The fine chair was placed on a dais upon which was a white rug embroidered with golden threads. John's heart hammered as he looked at his Majesty, who resembled his great-grandmother Mary, Queen of Scots. John had seen etchings and paintings of her. It had been difficult to see who Charles looked like that day at the fire, when his face had been covered with grime and soot. Now he was immaculate in a black satin suit, a white ruffled shirt, a curled black periwig that did not have a hair out of place.

John watched with awe as those ahead of him moved up before King Charles. As they presented their physician's tickets, the King touched some part of their bodies and stroked their cheeks with his bejeweled hands.

When John's turn came, he knelt trembling before his sovereign, the symbol of the greatness that was England! His face began to sweat, his lips felt parched and he moistened them. His Majesty's hand, touching John's shoulder, felt like a flame burning through his coat. The lady had been right; the hands were warm, and how beautiful they were!

When the King placed a blue ribbon with gold angels on it about John's neck, the chaplain nearest him declared, "This is the true Light, Who came into the world." A cold prickling ran down John's back and a violent shudder passed through him. The King was daring to act in Christ's stead. It was blasphemous. John wanted to denounce the act, but his throat was as stiff as marble; he couldn't utter a word. He hurried toward the lady and, as he sat beside her, watching other people kneel, he felt like the deer who has heard the hunter's horn and cannot flee.

Time dragged interminably until everyone in the line had filed out. Then the lady went to his Majesty and whispered in his ear.

246

The King gave an order to clear the chamber. One chaplain, who looked like a snail in a shell, eyed John suspiciously and seemed reluctant to leave. But the King scowled at him so fiercely that he almost danced a Scottish jig toward the door.

"Nelly. Nelly, that heart of yours will get us both into trouble," the King protested, and his mouth pulled down in a half moon.

John thrust himself forward. "I come on behalf of your subjects in Bedfordshire who suffer a yoke of intolerance and beg your help."

The King's eyebrows flew up in surprise. "And what can I do?" he asked haughtily.

John could see that he was very angry. His eyes glittered dangerously and the veins in his temples turned purple.

"Control the bigots who terrorize Nonconformists and Catholics. You are the King!"

"The authorities only enforce the law. We cannot allow the schismatics to defy it!"

"Your Majesty, insist that the consciences of men be respected."

"I suppose you are talking about the Kakers."

John knew he meant Quakers like John Rush, who had died for his faith.

"There are many others, as you know, who wish to worship outside the Church of England."

"Then you dislike the state church?"

"I grew up in it, your Majesty. My wife goes regularly to our parish church and takes the children. But you should understand, your Majesty, that many men and women prefer another faith, as your mother does."

The black eyes narrowed with surprise and speculation. "How does it happen you're not behind bars?"

"I am under conviction, your Majesty, for preaching the Gospel of Christ to some harmless Meeters. For six years I was kept in the Bedford County Jail. Because a Catholic priest, whom I loved like a brother, died there of the plague, the jail was emptied temporarily. I will be locked up again. My crime? No crime!"

John was surprised at the harshness of his own voice.

The King stared back at him in silence, tapping his ringed fingers on the carved arm of his chair.

"Charles, may I speak a word?" the lady interrupted.

He looked at her frowning. "What am I to do, Nelly? I would pardon this yokel to please you. But if I pardon him, I shall have to pardon everybody. There are certain laws on the statute books, and laws are made to be obeyed."

"Couldn't ye declare another indulgence?"

"What right has this fellow to come here to harry me? I've never seen him before in my life!"

"Oh, yes, you have, your Majesty. I owe you my life, Will Jones!"

The King's head jerked around so quickly that his curls bobbed. He pointed a long finger at John. "You! The boy in the tree!"

"When I went to report to Colonel Okey, and spurted out, 'Odd's fish!,' I feared he would horsewhip me. He almost did!"

The King threw his head back and laughed so heartily that tears came to his eyes. Suddenly the laughter died.

"Just because I spared your life twenty years ago, do you expect me to interfere now with the laws of England?"

"But if the laws are contrary to the great Magna Carta and the Petition of Right, are they not unconstitutional?"

The King shook his head. "Tell your friends my advice is to conform. If they do not, they will have to take the consequences."

The lady tried again. "Surely, Charles, you won't refuse an old friend?"

"Friend?" He looked at her sharply. "Nelly, I once met a Roundhead soldier looking for the Prince of Wales, so that his company could capture him to make his father comply with their treasonous demands. It is true he cared for me when I was ill, but I let him escape. I owe him nothing."

"But to please me, Charles?"

The King rose to face her. He moved toward her, and pulled teasingly at the strings of her silk bodice. Then he sighed. "You shall have your way, Nelly. I will look into the matter, and see what I can do. But I cannot promise."

That afternoon John went to report to Dr. Owen what had taken place at the Banqueting Hall.

"I know the Bishop of Lincoln," the minister said," and we are friends. I will write him. In time something might be done. We have been suffering as much here in London. Only the plague and the fire have drawn the attention of the authorities, giving us a little freedom. I fear the persecution will start all over again with renewed vigor!"

"Lady Nelle must be a great lady. Who is she?" John asked. "I am in her debt."

Dr. Owen smiled. "I wish some of the good ladies of our Meeting could hear you say that." His face sobered. "The King says openly that God will not damn him for taking his pleasure, that He hates only cruelty, lies, wickedness, and evil conspiracies! Your 'lady' is little Nelly Gwyn who grew up in the coalyards off Drury Lane, and is now his favorite mistress. She's the best of the lot. The people, who hate the Lady Castlemaine, line up to cheer Nelly as her coach rolls through the streets. They give her homage they do not give the Queen, who is hated by many because she is a Roman Catholic. Nelly never seems to ask anything for herself; it's for the poor she pleads. She is the one who suggests the building of places to care for the sick, the maimed, the orphaned. The Queen herself is said to be very fond of Nell. It is difficult to understand the lack of morality at Court. But don't get any idea of trying to burst into the Palace of Whitehall, to preach to the ladies and gentlemen who need salvation!"

"Why not?"

"Many of them, surprisingly, attend the Church of England. Their vicars have a chance to try to influence them. Don't forget we believe in people going to the church of their choice."

"Well, somebody ought to preach Christ's Gospel to them! You're here in London. The profligates are right under your nose. Why don't you?"

249

15 Sitting on a stone bench in the small courtyard at Bedford Jail one Saturday morning in May, 1670, John was reading an epic poem by his old acquaintance of his army days, Samuel Butler:

> . . . As Montaigne, playing with his cat,
> Complains she thought him but an ass,
> Much more she wou'd Sir Hudibras:
> For that's the name our valiant knight
> To all his challenges did write.
> But they're mistaken very much,
> 'Tis plain enough he was no such:
> We grant, although he had much wit,
> H' was very shy of using it. . . .

John frowned. The words hung irritatingly in his mind. They painted a word picture of a saint who was actually a hypocrite. If it was true, as people said, that Butler was writing a satire on Sir Samuel Luke, the wartime Governor of the Parliamentary garrison at Newport Pagnell, this was unfair. The book, very popular at a court which continued to ridicule decency and morality, had been widely read throughout England. John remembered the garrison rules about church attendance, and the long-faced religion Sir Samuel had tried to pump into the men. While the Presbyterian Sir Samuel was intolerant toward all other In-

250

dependents, he was a just man and a moral one. This was unfair. Yet John had to admit that Butler's imagery was superb as the hero, Hudibras, went looking for adventure. John read on, concentrating on each eight-syllable line.

He always found it helpful to study the language and the imagery of masters of the craft of writing; he found the Bible the most helpful. During his first years in jail, he had produced nine books. Since his return from London after the Great Fire, Elephant had written that Sir Roger L'Estrange had notified him he would not license any more of John's books. Word of John's appeal to the King had reached Sir Roger, and he had never forgiven him for his abrupt appearance at the Cardinal's Hat, or the ensuing loss of girls. Too, since Matthias Cowley had died when the plague had struck Newport, John no longer had his encouragement to write. And the Bunyan children were growing; their needs had increased. After tagging laces all day, and selling them on Market Days, there had been no time for writing, but he had never lost his interest in it.

For months he had waited for the news that the King had acted to end the persecutions. One thing the King had done; when the Conventicle Act had been about to expire, he had adjourned the Parliament before the House of Lords could vote to renew it. For seventeen months there had been freedom. Then the Parliament had met again and passed a new law. Since its recent passage the previous April 11, 1670, the houses of the shire had been subject to repeated invasions by constables who swarmed everywhere, opening doors, peering into chests and cupboards, thumping and hammering the walls.

A citizen never knew when a squad of officers would invade his home or place of business. There were those who backslid and conformed to keep their property. But the majority of the Independents—merchants, weavers, warreners, husbandmen, gardeners, laborers, yeomen farmers—refused to attend the divine services of the Church of England. Even the gentle Anthony Harrington, now a man of sixty, had been forced to run to avoid being taken on a writ *Ex Communicado Capiendo*. And three years before, when Bitsy had been lying in after the birth of their daughter, Paul Cobb had forced his way in, making her answer questions, and searching the house.

"Has the King forgotten his promise?" John asked himself over and over. Or have other affairs of state consumed his time? The June of 1667 following the Great Fire, the Dutch had sailed their ships up the Medway, attached Sheerness, captured the *Royal Charles,* and burned other English vessels. Parliament, forced to make peace, had exchanged Poleroon for the American colonies of New York, New Jersey, and Delaware. All England had been thrown into an uproar at the news. If an enemy can break down the barrier to the Medway, while the King and his debauched Court revel in their lust, the citizens complained, the nation can be overthrown.

And suddenly the late Lord Protector was a national hero. People talked nostalgically of the good old days under the Protectorate when England had been respected and her navy had been the finest on the seas. John wished that Oliver Cromwell could have lived to see his work appreciated.

The King, John conjectured, should have more power to put an end to the terror and injustice, for Lord Clarendon had lost his influence. There were a lot of rumors about that. One was that Charles wanted to divorce the childlike bride who had failed to give him a legitimate heir. Everyone knew he was infatuated with Francis Stuart, a virtuous woman. It was said that he thought the Chancellor and George Villiers, the Duke of Buckingham, a jaded libertine and violent Catholic-hater, had bribed the Duke of Richmond to run off with her and marry her. Clarendon, impeached by a two-thirds vote, had been banished from the realm.

When Queen Henrietta Maria, the King's mother, had died, John had remembered her struggle for freedom of worship, and hoped her loss might influence the King to make a decision as to toleration. But the persecution continued, becoming stronger every day.

John heard someone pattering along the cobbles, and looked

up. Froggy Foster stood there wearing a green coat of the new Persian style, which the King had introduced, and bright yellow breeches. He wore green stockings which made his bowed legs look more like a frog's legs than ever. He had a smirk on his face, and John had an impulse to punch him; he had to steel himself.

"I am your new jailer, Bunyan," he croaked. "Things are going to be different around here. John White is working under me now!"

"Congratulations! I suppose it was very difficult to get the job. You have no influence with anybody of importance in the shire!"

Froggy ignored his sarcasm. "Come, tinker. It's Market Day. Go to your room, get your laces, and we'll chain you outside."

Reluctantly, John rose and put his book down, gathered up his laces, and joined the line of prisoners waiting to go out.

As Froggy was clamping John's iron armband to the big ring in the wall, there was the sound of marching feet. A procession of soldiers and porters led by Thomas Battison, a sour-faced churchwarden of St. Paul's, filed into the center of the Market Square where Paul Cobb waited to aid him in laying the fines.

"I've been pounding on the malthouse door," Cobb bellowed. "Break it down!"

A crowd had gathered, and was talking heatedly, judging from the shaking of heads and angry gestures. A blowsy drab in the front of the crowd raised a shout. "Break it down. Make the dirty Meeter pay his fine. Tear open the malt bins. That'll show 'im!"

John stared in distaste. The slattern was Theny Talbot. She was a tremendous woman now, with a face like a dirty moon, and gray hair hanging in spikes around it. Mrs. Love-the-Flesh, he thought. That's what I'd call her, if I were writing about her.

Paul Cobb stood back, but when some of the soldiers threw their weight against the door, it held. They finally had to get a fallen tree with which to batter it down.

Battison stormed inside, and in a few minutes he stormed out.

"There are only a few quarters of malt left. Somebody must

have given warning that we were coming. Get what's there, and carry it to the room we have at the Swan Inn."

The porters did not budge.

"What are you waiting for?" Battison yelled.

"We'll be hanged, drawn, and quartered like they fixed up Colonel Okey afore we'll see an honest man's living taken!" one of the porters said firmly.

"The Commissary of the Archdeacon's Court shall hear of this. The fines will be levied!"

"Not by us," another of the men said, shaking his head. "Not by us they won't."

The next morning was Sunday, and John was to preach. He held the prison service early, at about seven o'clock, using as his text the Scriptural passage about the straight gate that led to life eternal, and the broad way which led to destruction. The people who were quietly and without violence standing for what they believed, he said, were the ones who saw the world of the senses and the world of the spirit in true perspective.

I must write a book and call it *The Straight Gate*, he thought. It's well to keep Christians thinking.

As he sat with some other prisoners around the table in the dayroom, eating his breakfast of bread and cheese, said John Donne, the preacher from Pertendall, "The more I see of this world, the more I comprehend man's greatest need, salvation."

John Rush, Junior, the son of the old Quaker who had died in the prison years before pointed out that the Quakers, Presbyterians, Baptists, Separatists, Anglicans, and Catholics, while they differed in belief, shared faith in Christ. "Imprisonment and common suffering have brought us all very close together," he said.

"Men don't have to conform to one pattern to be Christian," John Bunyan said with conviction. "One day we shall all walk together in one way in the Golden City on that Golden Street with golden feet!"

"You're getting poetical this morning," a Scottish Presbyterian

254

murmured with a smile. "How is your allegory of salvation progressing? Are you still telling your children of Christian's struggles?"

Before John could reply there was a thumping noise outside and Samuel Fenne leaped to his feet and ran to the window. He let out an exclamation. "The brothers and sisters are entering my brother John's house. With their previous convictions, they are taking a great risk this morning. If they should be caught, the fines will be doubled."

John ran to look over Samuel's shoulder at his brother's house, only thirty yards away. In spite of all the grave consequences, these Christians were quietly and bravely worshiping God as they chose.

In the courtyard below, Froggy, whose given name was James after James I, watched the Meeters going into John Fenne's two-story house. The shutters were open, the curtains were not drawn; there was no effort to conceal the fact that these Dippers or Meeters were defying his uncle's authority. A gloating look spread over Froggy's ugly face; there would be a reward for informing. Informers received one-third of all fines collected. He started memorizing the names of those who were attending.

About the time the Meeters are arrested, I will send some of the prisoners out here to see who is winning this struggle, he thought smugly. John Bunyan will be one of them! John had always made him feel small and unimportant, beating him at games when they were boys, catching the biggest fish, felling the finest deer. Each time John had been sent back to jail, Froggy had been elated and thought: Huh! Now people will see him for the show-off he really is.

Instead John Bunyan's stature had grown; each time he returned a stronger figure, until he was almost legend in Bedfordshire. "It's not my intention, Froggy, to meet violence with violence," John had told him repeatedly. "By quietly resisting, perhaps I can have a small part in changing a bad law." The tinker's books spoke of faith, courage, morality, and salvation.

255

Hero, some of the populace called him, and each attempt to defeat him only added to his fame.

Froggy would always remember one afternoon when a group of boys had been crossing the meadow toward the Elstow Abbey Church. An adder lay on the path. Froggy and the other boys had screamed and backed off, but John had stepped on it, with his foot, and the venom from its fangs had spurted out on his shoe. Then from a safe distance they had watched John kick its head with his other foot, and stoop and pull out its fangs. After that every boy in the village knew that John was their leader, and that none of them could do anything he wouldn't dare.

Now Froggy was having his revenge. He had taken away John's quill, inkpot, and paper, and John liked his writing better than anything else, except preaching and reading his Bible. Uncle William, who was as powerful as the King—almost—agreed that Froggy had shown excellent judgment. There would be an end to the treasonous books; he had personally called on the King's Chief Censor when he was in London.

Thomas Battison, who did everything Froggy's uncle told him to, was asleep when Froggy rapped on the door of his chamber at the Swan Inn. When Tom did not answer, Froggy pushed the door open, crossed to the bed, and shook him. He told him the Meeters were holding a service again.

Froggy hopped happily behind the churchwarden, as he stalked up the street to John Fenne's. When Mr. Battison burst in and ordered them to stop their meeting, John Fenne began to pray for "the little soul of Mr. Battison." The group refused to disband until the service ended, and someone read from the Scriptures: "Blessed are they which are persecuted for righteousness' sake . . ."

As Froggy watched and listened, all the cockiness seemed to go out of him. *Why was it these Meeters always seemed to win, even when they were in the dungeon?* Could some of them be witches? He shuddered at that thought. He had heard witches moaning when the wind blew high, and black cats frightened him, because they might be witches in animal shapes. What if John Bunyan was a witch?

On Monday morning, John noticed that the whole town appeared empty. The shops were shut, the shutters closed. No tradesman moved about the streets or the Corn Market Square.

The morning before he had seen Thomas Battison, followed by Froggy, enter John Fenne's house while the conventicle was in progress. In about an hour, four constables and a company of soldiers marched the Meeters toward the Swan Inn. When Bitsy had come with his supper, she told him that William Foster had held the worshipers at the inn all day, and that he had doubled the allotted fines for those who had a previous conviction.

"The Court acts as if the God of the Church of England thinks the Meeters blaspheme His Name when they meet outside the Parish Church," John told his colleagues.

John Donne's lips thinned, and a wave of pity swept over John. This preacher from Pertendall, evicted from his living because he had refused to conform, had dark circles around his honest brown eyes and his color was pasty. Year after year jail fever had taken men away; he prayed silently that John Donne would be spared.

Suddenly there were the sounds of loud voices, raucous laughter coming from St. Paul's beyond the Corn Market Square. Then out from the vestry came Battison, leaping and running, with a calf tied to his coattails. Men, women, and children bounded gleefully after him, jeering and laughing until the air rocked with the noise. The churchwarden disappeared around John Bartdolf's malthouses, and by the time the constables and the soldiers appeared, nobody was in sight. In a fury they went up and down the street, pounding on doors without response.

For several days after that, Battison went around the town looking like an executioner, his long face set, his brow wrinkled, his black eyes glowering. Everything Mary Tilney, a wealthy widow, possessed, was appropriated, including the sheets on her bed. Thomas Cooper lost three cartloads of wood, which he used to make heels. They took Thomas Arthur's materials for making pipes. Daniel Rich had his best coat confiscated. Every time William Foster and Battison were seen in the streets with the apparitors, soldiers, and constables a warning spread. The shops closed up; the people diasappeared.

That October, St. Cuthbert's vicar read a brief by his Majesty, in which he asked for money "for the poor enslaved English Christians captured in Algiers." When Bitsy told John, he tossed her a sixpence. "Give that to the vicar. Never let it be said that John Bunyan refused to help 'poor enslaved Christians.' "

In January, a letter for John reached the jail by way of his Majesty's mail. Dr. Owen reported that he had talked to the King several times, that his Majesty realized the power of the Puritans and other Christians.

When I spoke to him about releasing you, the King vowed that a Declaration of Indulgence will suspend all penal laws against us. Ashley, the Earl of Shaftsbury, who is the strongest member of his Cabal, or Council, says openly that toleration is the only solution to the unrest, and he has promised to help the King overcome the opposition.

I let him know that it was you who made me feel I should discuss spiritual matters with him. He smiled when I said I preferred your preaching to that of the most educated men. "I found myself liking that tinker," he said, with a shake of his head. "But keep him busy saving souls in Bedford when he's freed, so that he won't storm the Palace for mine. I have a notion he might make a Puritan out of me, and I detest their Godly habits!"

John read the letter to John Donne and Samuel Fenne. "It looks as if we'll be freed soon," Samuel said happily.

"I want to write the book I've outlined in my mind, *The Straight Gate*," John complained. "If I don't finish it before I

258

go home, I won't get it done. I'll forget it. But how can we handle Froggy, so that he'll leave me alone?"

"He's always been superstitious. Make him believe you're a witch," John Donne said brightly.

"But how?"

"It's too bad we can't produce some weird music some dark, windy night," Samuel said, smiling. "Remember how frightened he has always been of thunder and lightning? We used to tell him Old Noll's ghost was after him. He'd run all the way home and lock himself in. He was scared of Cromwell when he was alive, and the mere mention of his spirit sends him into a panic!"

"I have it!" John sat up straight. "I'll play my flute!"

"What flute?" John Donne wanted to know. "Are you out of your mind?"

John took the instrument out of its socket. There had been somebody sick for so long now, that he had not played it for months. He had almost forgotten about it.

John's spirits soared as he planned his attack. What kind of music should he play? Perhaps a dirge or a lament. Why not "Tan Ta Ra Ran Tan Tant" by Thomas Weelkes, a lament on the death of Thomas Morley? The solemn beat made the chills run down John's spine.

Froggy always came sneaking in just before midnight to be sure that nobody was away from his cell. Just before twelve one night, when the wind outside was singing in a minor key, John held the flute ready. Minutes passed before he heard the clang of the door into the corridor. He quickly placed the flute to his lips, and blew gently. The notes were so eerie they made him shudder, himself! John Donne sang in a hollow voice:

> "Tan ta ra ran tan tant, cries Mars on
> Bloody rapier fa la fa la fa la
> Fa la, cries Venus in a chamber.
> Toodle loodle, toodle, loodle loo,
> Cries Pan that cuckoo with bells on his shoe
> And a fiddle, too.

And a fiddle, too. Aye, but I alas lye
Weeping, for death hath slain my sweeting,
Which hath my heart in keeping, which
Hath my heart in keeping. . . ."

John paused, hearing a movement in the corridor outside the door. Quickly he replaced the flute in the socket of the stool, and both he and John Donne threw themselves on the straw, pulling the coverlets up around their necks.

The bolt was drawn back, and Froggy stepped in. "Who—who was playing that flute?" he demanded.

John opened his eyes a slit and peeked.

John Donne sat up, and yawned. "What did you say?" he mumbled. "Flute? What flute?"

"Somebody was playing one!" Froggy screamed, and stamped his foot.

"You might as well know it," Samuel Fenne said in a funereal voice. "We have to tolerate it. John Bunyan's a witch."

"Aw, you're fooling!" Froggy quavered.

"Hadn't you heard?" Samuel's voice trembled, too. "Why did you think John was able to do all those things when he was a boy? He was a witch even then. S-h-h-h. Don't make him mad. He might put a curse on us!"

Froggy made a hasty retreat. John heard him pattering down the corridor, and everybody laughed as the outer door banged.

"I'll get my wife to bring you some paper, ink, and a quill," Samuel said happily. "You won't find Froggy hanging around long enough to locate it. You can finish that book."

To John's delight Samuel's prediction proved true. John White, who had been removed from his post because he refused to pay the tithe to the Parish Church, was brought back as Froggy's assistant, and the first thing Froggy did was to assign him to night duty.

16 The early spring of 1672 found John still in the Bedford Jail, and involved once more in controversy. A rector of Northill, Edward Fowler, had written a book called *The Design of Christianity*. John read it, and thought it was anything but Christian. Within six weeks he had written a reply, the *Doctrine of Justification by Faith*. Fowler had been ejected from his church in Bedfordshire shortly after the Restoration, but he had conformed promptly. In his book, he stated that in matters of worship, Christians should do whatever is commended by custom, or commanded by those over them, or made convenient. John asked what a man would do if he were in Turkey where Mahomet is Lord.

"How any servant of Christ can face two ways like Edward Fowler, I will never understand," John stormed to his cellmates one April day. "I think I'll put him in the story I tell the children and name him Mr. Facing-both-ways, along with William, the Fifth Earl of Bedford, who fought first for Cromwell, and later for the King!"

Before Samuel or John Donne had time to reply, there was the sound of heavy steps treading the stones of the corridor. The bolt was pulled back, and a burly figure stood there—John's father! His beard was white now but still shaggy. John jumped to his feet, and ran to greet him.

"Father! How are you? How is Anne?"

"Fine. But I bring great news, son. A peddler from London is over at the Swan Inn telling everyone that the King has granted a new Declaration of Indulgence which suspends the penal laws against ironheads like ye! Ye will be free, John. Free!"

There were tears in Thomas Bunyan's blue eyes; he sniffled, wiping his red nose on the sleeve of his russet coat.

John's heart was tripping, so that he could hardly speak. Now he could preach and he could tinker. He could sit beside his hearth on the cold winter evenings while Bitsy spun, and the children listened to his tales. He had missed Bitsy in a hundred different ways, and now they would not have to be separated any more.

It was the middle of July before an order to release John Bunyan reached the jail. That summer the country was greener than he had imagined it. The sheen of the Ouse was like that of the floor in the Banqueting Hall at the Palace. As John rode through the shire on a horse the Bedford Meeters had given him, sweet red apples hung on green boughs above him, and overhead was the wide blue sky. The grass was deep, and sometimes when the wind stirred it, he saw a bobtailed hare leaping through it. Redstarts nested in the willows, and there were cuckoos, robins, and wrens, too. The sight of the crows flying over the planted fields made him give thanks that once again he was as free as they.

He forgot his writing until October when Dr. Owen sent him a nasty little book with the title *Dirt Wiped Off*, or a Manifest Discovery of the Gross Ignorance, Erroneousness, and Most Unchristian and wicked spirit of John Bunyan, Lay Preacher in Bedford. It purported to have been published by a friend on Fowler's behalf.

"I believe Fowler wrote it himself!" John told Bitsy hotly. "Perhaps his curate helped him."

"Are you going to answer it?"

"Dr. Owen wants me to."

The very next day he began another book, *Differences in Judgment About Water Baptism no Bar to Communion.* He wrote in his strong sprawling hand: "The saint is a saint before water baptism, and may walk with God, and be faithful with the saints and to his own light also, although he never be baptized."

He remembered as he wrote how his Interpreter, John Gifford, had said that the brethren should stress the great truths of the Christian faith, and prevent separation over baptism and other "externals."

As John met with people throughout the shire, he found himself respected for his courage in refusing to conform, and he was not surprised when the Bedford Meeting called him as a pastor, or elder.

"You have been true to your Christian beliefs," the committee that visited him said. "Your usefulness has grown. As a flock needs a shepherd, the Christians of the Bedford Meeting need you."

"You realize that I must say what I believe is true, and some of you will differ from me at times," he told them frankly. "Nor will I pretend I believe in externals I do not think are essential. I would rather be known as a Christian than anything else. The titles of Anabaptist, Independent, Separatist, Presbyterian, or the like, come neither from Jerusalem nor Antioch but from Hell and Babylon, because they tend to divisions."

"We will try to remember that our beloved John Gifford, in his farewell letter, reminded us that we do not want to quarrel over nonessentials," John Fenne said feelingly.

"Nor must we forget the two requirements for joining the Bedford Meeting—faith in Christ and holiness of life," the Widow Tilney added.

The August day was gloomy and mist lay over the entire town. John's youngest daughter, Sarah, who was five, and three of the neighbor children kept running in and out of the cottage, in the front and out the back, in the back and out the front. He was grateful that the older ones were spending the day at Anne Bunyan's. John liked the sound of children at play, but this afternoon the noise and the thumping of feet interfered with his concentration. He retreated to his workshop behind the house to work on a reply to Danvers and other Nonconformists of London, who had attacked his work concerning Fowler.

How oppressive the air is, he thought absently. No wind came through the open windows and door, and he kept mopping the perspiration from his face. He heard the clock on the nearby steeple strike two.

Suddenly, without any warning, a high-pitched wind began to whine, shaking the branches of the elms, oaks, maples, and willows, sweeping over the cottages and up and down the streets like a tormented spirit. A puppy ran yelping across the grass, and in a few minutes a miserable tomcat flew by as if a tiger were after him. The eerie wail became a fiendish howl and sharp thunderclaps began.

John closed the windows and the door to his shop, and ran through the gathering darkness to help Bitsy shut the cottage windows before the rain came. She was to have another child in about three months, and he was concerned for her safety. He found her coming down the stairs, the house tightly shut, and little Sarah inside.

There was a roar in the distance, sweeping nearer like the thundering of many coaches. A great gust rattled the window; then the rain came.

They went to the casement and watched the raging storm. The sky was the color of the cobbles. Lightning struck nearby and for a moment the whole town seemed to be on fire. The side of a house blew by, barely missing the windowpanes. A large bush rolled down the middle of the street toward St. Cuthbert's Church. After a while a big elm sailed through the air. The house shook and rattled like a ship in a great storm at sea.

"I hope the children aren't out in this," Bitsy said.

"We don't have to worry," John replied. "Anne will see to their safety."

264

In the midst of all the fury, there was a sudden pounding on their door, and somebody shouted, "John, John! Let me in! In God's name, open the door!"

John ran to open it and Froggy darted in, his eyes popping out of his head with fright.

"The curse of Cromwell is upon us for the way the Archdeacon's Court treated the Meeters," he screamed. "I was right out there when Old Noll rode down upon us. I had to find shelter."

His clothes were so wet that a puddle was forming on the floor around him.

Bitsy took his cloak, saying in her gentle voice, "Go into the bedchamber, Mr. Foster, and take off your clothes. John can lend you some of his. They'll be too big, but they'll be dry."

As Froggy started toward the back of the house, John caught Bitsy's eye and arched one eyebrow. Bitsy grinned, lifting her red apron to shoo him after the jailer.

When they returned a few minutes later, she took one look at Froggy and laughed out loud. "There's a bigger difference in your builds than I thought, but at least you're dry, Mr. Foster."

Froggy nodded and went to the window to watch the storm.

"God is awful mad at me," he whined. "I am a mean, grasping toad!"

"Frog," John corrected, laughing. Froggy was so terrified that John pitied him, and added, "But I forgave you a long time ago."

"Then you won't ever witch on me any more?"

"I never 'witched' on you. There are no witches. Most of the poor people they burn as witches are just sick, scared folk."

"There are no witches. My Papa told me that!" little Sarah said emphatically, her dark eyes solemn in her elfin face.

"I've seen them," Froggy protested. "And I heard the flute that wasn't there!"

John explained how he had made the flute, and why. He told Froggy of the plan to scare him away, so John's writing could be done in peace because he was sure God wanted him to write

His Truth in books. But Froggy remained unconvinced; he was sure there were witches.

The storm stopped as suddenly as it had started, and people began crowding into the streets, pointing at the damage. John, Bitsy, Froggy, and Sarah went outside, too, and walked around the town, staring. Women ran about gabbling like geese. Men spoke in hushed whispers of what a bad omen the tempest was. The entire town looked like a battle site with timber trees uprooted and orchards destroyed. One huge elm hung on St. Paul's steeple! St. John's Church was damaged. Roofs were missing from many houses. A coach that had been standing in front of the Swan Inn had been hurled into the air and smashed to pieces. The building in which Mr. Mooney had his butchershop had been leveled.

John heard Olive Foskett, one of the Foskett sisters who were the town's chief gossips, declare happily, "I'm glad God punished that papist! Serves 'im right."

At St. Peter's, John stared in disbelief; one side of the church was missing. At the Widow Crowley's the dovehouse had been shattered, killing all the birds. A boat, lifted from the Ouse, had been deposited in front of John Fenne's. The gates of three inns —the popular Swan, the Rose, and the Maiden Head—had broken to bits. At a fourth inn, the Ram Head, the head hostler and his wife had had to tie themselves to a post to keep from being blown away.

Early in October, John, riding to Leicester, met Froggy on the road. Froggy told him, as he did every time they talked, that the day of the tempest had changed his life, and that he would never forget the kindness he had received at the cottage in St. Cuthbert's Street.

John arrived home the next night just in time to hear his new son's first cry. Widow Crowley was with Bitsy, who had suffered very little. "Oh, John," she whispered. "Isn't our son wonderful!"

He went about his work, thanking God every day for all his

266

blessings, but most of all for his freedom. How joyous it was to travel from village to village, and preach without fear of arrest!

That November at Gamlingay, a village on the border of Cambridgeshire, John took a young woman from Edworth into the Bedford Church. During the service that followed, he had the uneasy feeling that her green eyes were watching him in a way no girl should look at her pastor. Is there an adoring look in Agnes Beaumont's eyes? he asked himself. Or do I imagine it? She makes me uncomfortable. It was a relief when, after the benediction, her brother Sol took her home.

Shortly after that some disturbing rumors began to fly, and John forgot all about the eyes of Agnes Beaumont. The most persistent rumor from London was that there was a secret league between the King, the Catholics, and the dissident Protestants. Starting early in 1673, the Government refused to issue any new licenses to ministers or places of meeting. Parliament forced the King to withdraw his second Declaration of Indulgence in March. On June 14 the Bedford Meeting held a day of prayer and humiliation; the national policy toward religious freedom was again a matter of doubt.

On a clear, cold day in February, John rode from Hitchin through Edworth toward Gamlingay, where he was to preach again. At the house of the Beaumont brothers, he paused to ask for some warm milk. Agnes was there, and her eyes lit up when John walked into the little family room where her sisters-in-law and the children were huddling about a log fire. John had decided that he must have been mistaken about her attitude toward him, but when she jumped up, ran to him, and took his cloak, he had again the strange feeling that she was looking at him as a woman looks at a man she "hankers" for.

After drinking the milk, he rose, put on his cloak, and started for the door.

"Brother Bunyan, let me ride to the meeting behind ye!" Agnes begged, her green eyes pleading.

"Yes," Sol said quickly, "our sister will be disappointed if she cannot attend the meeting. Your preaching gives her great spiritual solace. Our father has recently turned against the church and won't go any more. Take her!"

"I will not carry her."

Agnes began to sob. "You're a preacher and ye can't tell a girl ye won't take her t' meetin'!"

"Since your father feels as he does, he would be angry if I took you."

"I'll risk that."

"There's no reason why she shouldn't go," her brother said. "It be church ye're headin' for, isn't it?"

"Well, I suppose I'll have to take her."

As John galloped along the lonely Gamlingay Road between the uncleared meadows and isolated woods, he had the strong feeling that he should never have agreed to take this girl along. Riding postillion style, she clung to him so tightly that she almost choked him. He wanted to throw her off, and ride on, but he couldn't leave her in that desolate country. He told her roughly to hold arms around his chest not around his neck. He prayed all the way to Gamlingay, sure that he had never endured such a seven-mile ride.

Later, while he was preaching, she gazed at him with such a rapt expression in her queer green eyes that he was reminded of the look in Nelly Gwynn's, as she had gazed at Charles. In all his forty-four years John had never been more disconcerted. He stammered twice, and stuttered once; it was difficult to preach at all.

As soon as the service was over, he found Sister Camlock, who lived within two miles of Mr. Beaumont's farm, asked her to take Agnes as far as she went, and mounted his own horse to ride off toward Bedford.

When he told Bitsy all that had happened, he noticed a mischievous glint in her dark eyes.

"John Bunyan!" she cried. "For twelve years you faced William Foster, all the justices, Paul Cobb, and everyone else who tried to frighten you into conformity, yet this green-eyed farmer's daughter terrifies you. All you have to do is to stay away from her!"

John laughed in relief. "Yes, I shall never go near Edworth if I can help it. If I have to ride from Hitchin to Gamlingay, I will pretend I'm the wind passing through!"

"Then your problem is settled."

But it wasn't. John Wilson was appointed pastor of the Hitchin Church and after a meeting at Bedford, in which he took part, he called John aside. John noticed how serious his expression was, and knew that something was amiss.

"John," the Hitchin pastor began, "are you aware of the gossip going around about you and Agnes Beaumont?"

John felt as if the blood was draining from his body. "Gossip? About me and Agnes?"

"Her father locked her out the day you took her to Gamlingay. He told her he wouldn't let her in, until she promised not to attend the Bedford Meeting any more. She refused, went to her brothers' house, and stayed until the following Sunday. She was forced to agree before her father would let her come home."

"But what does an intolerant father and a wanton daughter have to do with me?"

"The next night John Beaumont died."

"I'm sorry. He was a cussed man."

"I don't know how to tell you this, John——"

"Go on, Wilson. I'm no child."

"A young lawyer named Farrow, who had asked Agnes to marry him and had been turned down, has started the story that you are a widower and had told Agnes to poison her father, so that you could marry her!"

"Surely people don't believe that posh!"

"You never heard such tales as are being spread in the Edworth parish! The funeral has been postponed, the coroner alerted, and a jury picked. If she's found guilty, the penalty for parricide will be burning!"

"Maybe I should go to Edworth and testify. I never heard such nonsense!"

"It's too late. The case is being heard today."

John heaved a big sigh. "I seem to have one problem after another. That's the way in this world."

"There's something else I think you ought to know, John. You're man enough to face it. The Foskett sisters have got hold of the news. No telling what they'll spread!"

John explained what had really happened, thanked him, and went home to Bitsy.

"Darling, don't worry about it," she said. "The truth will come out. Just go on about your work as if nothing had happened."

"But those Foskett horrors! Perhaps nobody will listen to me preach when they get through."

"At least people will notice you when you walk by. And they'll think you qualified to preach about sin!"

John looked at his wife, and she was smiling. There was a twinkle in her dark eyes, and love on her face. And suddenly he knew everything would be all right.

"I guess when a man preaches he can expect things like this," he said. "Satan has seen that his tempting and assaulting could not make me conform, so he's stirring up the minds of the malicious to load me with slanders, trying to ruin my influence for good."

"What are you going to do?"

"Nothing. This may increase my ability to spread the Gospel. I rejoice in reproaches for Christ's sake!"

To Bitsy's delight, as well as John's relief, Agnes was declared innocent. The proof was indisputable; her father was "opened," and three doctors pronounced that he had died from natural causes.

John Wilson, the pastor at Hitchin, preached a strong sermon on a text from the little Book of James, pointing out how malicious tongues had slandered one of God's servants. People who had never gone to Gamlingay or the meetings in neighboring towns, began going in large groups to attend services at which he preached. His name became familiar all over that part of the shire, and his influence continued to grow.

Then suddenly, without warning, His Majesty, compelled by the Bishops, issued another proclamation which ordered the execution of the penal laws again and forbade conventicles.

"Man's conscience is not subject to Acts of Parliament," John preached everywhere in an effort to bolster the Meeters' faith for the days which were to come.

One night, after the children were all in bed, John sat on the little settle beside Bitsy, discussing the alternatives. Bitsy was displaying her usual courage.

"All these years, I've watched you suffer and lift your head. But after twelve years in prison, to face further confinement! William Foster will probably put you in solitary because of your recent activities. And the Meeters need your strength!"

There was the sound of quick footsteps outside, and then three short knocks. John got up and opened the door. A heavily cloaked figure slipped in; he was Froggy Foster. John had been wondering what Froggy thought about the new proclamation, and if he had gone back to his bad habits of informing.

"I meant it, John, when I said I want to be a better man." The glow of the fire lighted his face, and John thought it was not as ugly as usual. "I have come to warn you that thirteen of the county justices are signing a new warrant for your arrest. Same old charge; holding conventicles."

"Why are you doing this?"

There was a bleakness in Froggy's prominent eyes. "I'm frightened. I'm forty-six years old. One day I'll die."

"Does your uncle know you're here?"

Froggy shuddered. "He would kill me, if he did."

"When will they come for me?"

"Tomorrow. But you must hide. Don't let them take you."

"But where?"

"There must be a priest hole on the Mooney farm. We've never been able to find it."

"Do as our friend says, John," Bitsy pressed. "The Bedford Meeters need you. Others need you. The children and I need you, too, but we can manage without you. We're used to it."

For three days after John left, two constables bundled in heavy garments, were stationed at the door of their little cottage waiting for his return. They showed no zeal in pursuing him; perhaps they were not sorry he had eluded them.

But later in the week, William Foster came and questioned Bitsy. She told him truthfully that she did not know where her husband had fled.

"We will get him. Sooner or later we will get him!" the Commissary vowed. "I will never stop searching."

While Foster's men scoured the shire for him, John remained in hiding. Somebody always warned him when the constables were hunting in one place, and he fled to another. His two favorite hiding places were the priest hole in the eaves of the Mooney farmhouse, and the isolated cottage of a friend at Coleman Green, a hamlet where he had often spent the night on his journeys to London. All over Bedfordshire, his friends watched for the searchers, and drew a cross like the Cross of St. George in some public place, so that others, seeing the familiar signal, could pass the warning. It was impossible for the men to serve the writ *Ex communicado Capiendo*, which by law required personal service.

In January of 1676 the constables, sheriffs, and church wardens held a meeting at William Foster's home.

"How can we get John Bunyan in jail when we cannot serve a writ on him?" Foster asked. "He's making a fool out of every one of us. Something has to be done!"

"His disappearance is almost supernatual," Paul Cobb said wearily. "If I believed in witches, I'd declare he was one!"

Someone else said, "Every time a beadle knocks on the door of a place he is supposed to be staying, he has gone, though we confide in no local people."

Froggy, who was shining his sword at his uncle's desk, snickered. "Maybe he is a witch. Or maybe the witches warn him."

"If I could find those witches, I'd slit their gullets and chop up their cats!" Uncle William said in a fury. "He's making the Archdeacon's Court the laughingstock of England!"

"Sooner or later, we'll get him. We can double the number of men, order them to concentrate on taking him," Paul Cobb vowed.

John was in hiding at the Mooney farm on February 6 when Froggy came to tell him that his father had died.

"But you must not go near the Elstow cottage, or the Abbey Church. Uncle William has sent eight men to Elstow because he is certain that you will appear."

After Froggy left, John sat on the only chair in the tiny room trying to decide what to do. In memory he saw his father as he had looked the last time he had seen him. John had stopped at the Swan Inn where his father was having one of his usual arguments, and was about to punch a huge carter. John had stepped between them and diverted them both, avoiding the fisticuff. . . . The day his father had brought the news of the King's Declaration, his face had been shining with joy, not because he wanted tolerance for the Meeters but because he, John, would go free. . . . John had loved him. How could he stay away from his burial?

When he ventured downstairs in the late afternoon, Dame Mooney was bustling around the family room. It was Friday, and she was cooking fish. He could smell it, and the baking bread, and roasting turnips. When he told her the news, she put her big arms around him, and tried to comfort him. When the family sat at supper, he took his seat, too, but he couldn't eat. Memories continued to flood through his mind, and he sat on, until it was time to go to the hidden room under the eaves.

There he lay staring into the darkness, trying to make up his mind what to do. He could attend his father's last rites and be

273

caught, or to stay here and keep his freedom. And the last year and a half had been great sport. There had been some narrow escapes, like the time the constables were coming up the path to Widow Tilney's where he was having a midday meal. Hastily he had donned one of her dresses and a bonnet, and walked right past them. Another time, in the winter, when the Great Bridge had looked as if it were made of silver with long icicles hanging down its span, he had noticed some constables approaching and had run down the bank to join some young people skating on the ice. If he did not attend the funeral, they could not take him. He decided not to go.

For two days the corpse of Thomas Bunyan lay on a bier made of a board laid across two stools. The third day he was put into the plain box the trunkmaker had fashioned, and laid to rest in the frozen earth. Paul Cobb was there in person, scrutinizing every individual who appeared; with his men he followed the widow and sons over the stile and across the wide meadow back to the thatched cottage. They searched the house and the workshop thoroughly before they left, shaking their heads.

A few minutes before midnight, John made his way cautiously across the Village Green toward the Abbey Church. A melancholy moon hung in a starlit sky and a shimmering mist moved up from the marshes and the ponds like a spirit, and drifted over the moss-grown headstones in the old churchyard. The wind moaned like a departed soul seeking rest, and John could feel a chill in his bones.

But when he came to the old postern gate, the wicket-gate of the story about Christian which he had told so often, he saw the shining light hanging beside it, and the chill left him.

He wandered through the cemetery, pausing at the new grave. Beside his father lay Mama's remains and at her head were the graves of Margaret and the infant Charles. In the corner under a barren willow was Grandpa. Pilgrims all, he thought. "Pilgrims and strangers" who sought a "better country," and have found it!

John threw himself to his knees on the cold ground beside

274

his father's grave, and with clasped hands, beseeched God to speak in the stillness and tell him what to do next.

When he rose to his feet, he felt a Presence. God was trying to speak to him there in the graveyard, as he had once spoken on the Village Green. And John seemed to stand outside himself staring at the young John Bunyan, tall and round-faced, but full of bestial strength, tinkering pots and pans, trying to work well, but working as if money were the most important thing, when men needed tinkering more, as they walked the earth confused, unaware that a loving and all-powerful Father was holding out his arms.

In the next instant there came the certain knowledge that God wanted him to finish the story of Christian's progress. Shall I give myself up? he thought. I can't finish a long book on the run, and Froggy will not bother me in jail now.

John looked up at the old, square tower silhouetted against the sky, and a wild longing pulsed in him to hear the sweet bells once more. With a rush of joy, he ran toward the tower, opened the iron-studded door, reached up, and began to pull on the ropes. Up. Down. Up. Down. The sound reverberated over the churchyard, across the Green, above the Village of Elstow, and the surrounding country. And John felt as though his heart would burst with exultation.

The constable at Harrowden would hear the sweet music, and he would come running and take him into custody. In the quiet of a cell, he could finish *The Pilgrim's Progress,* From This World to That Which Is to Come.

17 Day after day John's chamber in the Town Jail was thronged with clear, strange shapes. He set down what he saw—the ramparts of man's soul, as his pilgrim, his feet in darkness, sought for the print of God's shoe guiding him to Beulahland, the river that has no bridge, and the Celestial City beyond.

Sometimes he rose from his visions as the darkness melted into dawn. The mist was lifting from the little island in the river below, and the swans glided on the shining surface. Carts, carriages, riders, and people on foot passed in an endless stream, and soon Bitsy came with his breakfast.

Being in the upper chamber of the North Gate Tower, which housed the Town Jail, was more like being in an inn. The warm sun penetrated in the cold weather, and in the summer the barred windows opened inward, so that there was usually a gentle breeze. Too, the lantern just outside his cell was always lighted, and he could see well at night when he wanted to write.

It was through Froggy's influence that John had been transferred to the Town Jail. Under the warrant for his arrest, the judges had had to imprison him in the County Jail. With the renewed persecution against Nonconformists, it was so crowded that he couldn't write. So he had sent for Froggy one day and told him he must finish a book God had told him to write.

"Will God bless me, if I help?"

"Yes, Froggy, he will bless us both, and with this book, if it is His will, he will bless many souls."

Froggy went to his uncle, told him how John preached night and day, bolstering the prisoners' faith, and that he thought it would be a hardship on them if John were isolated. Then he suggested housing him in the Town Jail. The authorities of the town —remembering how the county authorities had helped them house their prisoners in 1671, when the Town Jail was being repaired, and in 1675 when it was being rebuilt—agreed.

In the new quarters, whenever John had a vision of some scenes of Christian's journey he grabbed his quill, dipped it in the inkpot, and let the words to describe it come pounding from his brain to his fingers. He left the world of his century, and lived with the imaginary people in the places of his dreams.

Then one night Froggy came hurrying in, breathing heavily. "A Censor's Band of Searchers arrives in Bedford tomorrow. They are sure to come here to see if you are writing anything."

The news struck John with terror. He had almost finished *The Pilgrim's Progress*, and if the King's censors confiscated it, he would have to write it again from memory. That would be difficult, and would take months.

"What can I do?" he asked.

Froggy thought for a minute. "Who has the most vicious dog in Bedford?"

"Josiah Ruffhead."

"Put your manuscript under the straw, and come with me."

"What are you going to do?"

"First, I will take you back to the County Jail. If the Band of Searchers find you here, they might think it strange. Then I'll take Josiah's dog into custody as a menace and public nuisance. I will lock him up here."

In spite of his fright, John chuckled. "Froggy, I didn't know you had it in you."

"The day of that tempest, when a big tree almost killed me, I promised God I would change my ways. It was a contract and I keep my bargain."

"I will help you, Froggy. I'll show you the narrow, stony path."

"I don't like stony paths."

"That is figurative, like my allegory of salvation."

"Is that what it is?"

"Yes. God wouldn't want anything to happen to it. Do you understand?

Froggy blinked. "Why do y' think I came here?"

The Censor's Band of Searchers came and went in Bedford-shire. They discovered a copy of Milton's *Areopagitica* at John Fenne's, and burned it, fining Fenne a pound. Other than that, their visit was routine. They threw the books at Vane's Bookshop around in untidy piles, and visited the County Jail, where they found the infamous John Bunyan lying on his straw with his face to the wall, apparently asleep. Although they poked around in the straw, they found no manuscripts, no books. All they could discover at his cottage was a copy of the King James Bible, which had come into general use. At the Town Jail they did not deign to search the felons and the beggars sent there by the Bedell of Beggars. In the upper chamber they found a wolf-hound with dripping fangs and pointed teeth that snapped when they approached. He looked as if he might be mad; they didn't even have that door unlocked!

Toward the end of June of that year of 1677, Dr. Owen pre-vailed upon the newly appointed Bishop of the diocese of Lin-coln, Dr. Thomas Barlow, to approve a cautionary bond for John's release. Two Nonconformists of London, at Dr. Owen's request, signed as sureties. When the order reached the jail, John was happy to pick up his manuscript and go home.

The first day was spent with Bitsy and the children. Elizabeth, who had married Gilbert Ashley the April before, came in early from her home in Goldington. In the afternoon the whole family took a walk through the woods and meadows beyond the town. The wild roses were blooming, and John drank their sweetness into his nostrils. Sarah, who was ten, ran about picking wild flowers until she caught her blue gown in a bramble hedge and tore it. Once, when Elizabeth was walking beside John, she confided that he might become a grandfather. A tide of warmth flooded him, and he remembered his boyhood vow, to be "a grandpa" when he grew up. Young Joseph, who was five, capered about like an untamed heifer. John and Thomas, nineteen and seventeen respectively, fished for bream in the Ouse, and within half an hour caught two that must have weighed about five pounds each. There would be fried fish for supper.

This is what I've been missing all these years, John thought, as they started home. The children are wonderful with none of that gloomy piety. Bitsy slipped her soft hand in his just then, looked at him with adoration, and smiled. Coming home is almost like arriving at the Celestial City, he thought. And one of these days the King and the Earl of Shaftsbury are going to put an end to intolerance. Then everybody can go home.

The next afternoon John invited some of his friends and neighbors to the cottage to hear *The Pilgrim's Progress*. Before he had left the jail, he had read it to some of his fellow prisoners. Thomas Marsom, a young Nonconformist divine, had shaken his head over it at first; a second reading had changed his mind. John Wheeler, another Nonconformist, declared it might make people think. A third, one of the narrow, Puritanical kind, thought it silly. John planned some revisions and he wanted to hear the worst criticism anyone could make.

The Fennes arrived; Anthony Harrington, who had returned from his exile; John Whitebread whose brother, William, was notoriously contentious; Froggy Foster, John White, and the Widow Tilney.

John explained what he wanted, and began to read about the four perils Christian faced, the Slough of Despond, the Fight with Apollyon, The Valley of the Shadow of Death, and Doubting Castle.

And he thought that when he had first started telling the children he had seen himself as Christian. Now Christian had become Everyman. Each character resembled some person or persons John had known; the places were all familiar, and yet a composite of several locales.

His guests were very quiet as he continued the narrative, halting him only occasionally to ask a question.

"Then I saw that there was a way to hell, even from the gates of heaven, as well as the City of Destruction! So I awoke, and behold it was a dream."

John lifted his eyes from the pages, and waited for comments. There was a long silence before Samuel Fenne spoke.

"John, I say it's a work of genius. When you were reading about Faithful, who died 'to bear testimony,' were you depicting our late friend, John Donne? I saw him in every line."

"John Donne, John Okey, John Rush, Mel Mooney, many others."

"I guess I'm Ignorance," Froggy said solemnly. "I recognized myself."

Everybody, except John Whitebread, laughed. He sat scowling, pressing his thin lips together.

"That's the nicest comment you could make, Froggy," John said. "But you are Christian, too. We have a lot to discuss together."

"What about Froggy's uncle, Dr. Foster? Is he Apollyon?" John's son, Thomas, asked.

"Was my uncle that foul fiend, Apollyon?" Froggy demanded.

"Your uncle?" John mused. "You know that gives me an idea. I should add a Mr. Worldly Wiseman to the second edition, if there is one. He would be your uncle's type."

"Enough of this posh! Don't publish that ridiculous romance!" John Whitebread waggled a reproving finger. "It's too frothy. You will lose people's respect. Sometimes your other works have been—shall we say—a bit broad. But they have had dignity. This —this thing has nothing."

"I disagree." Samuel Fenne was insistent. "People will run to the bookshops to buy it."

John looked at the aged Anthony Harrington, who was sitting quietly listening to the others. "And you, Mr. Harrington? What have you to say?"

"Nowhere do you point out that a man has to be immersed to be saved, John," he said, shaking his head. "Yet I like it."

"And you, John White? You haven't told me what you think."

"I saw myself, walking down a wide road to Hell, though God wants me to be His son. I thought: What we do here decides our eternity. Your book's a call to careless fellows like me to come and follow Christ."

"You ought to burn it. It bored me!" John Whitebread sputtered.

John thanked them all for presenting their honest opinions, but John Whitebread was still sputtering, as he went out the door.

"Nobody will buy that book. God has called you to preach. You can't write that kind of thing. Stick to what you know."

"Bitsy, you have heard all of *The Pilgrim's Progress*. Is John Whitebread right?" John asked later that night, as they sat on the front step in the starlight.

She patted his knee. "I've loved your pilgrim for so long now that I would not be a qualified judge. I know I want you to share him with the world."

Again conviction came that God was willing *The Pilgrim's Progress*. It would be fun to watch and see what He would do with it.

On March 25, the first day of the new year, according to the Old Style calendar, John had a letter from Dr. Owen. When Bitsy brought it back to the forge where he was working, he ripped it open eagerly:

Friend John,

Brother Whitebread, who preaches at the home of George Cockayn, a former resident of your shire, is concerned about another new book you have written, *The Pilgrim's Progress*, or some such title. He has told some of us here something about it, and his objections are my reasons for believing we might have a great help here in our common task of reaching the unsaved.

I have taken the liberty of discussing the book with my own stationer, Nathaniel Ponder at the Peacock in the Poultry. He has expressed his interest in the manuscript.

Since my congregation in White's Alley, Moorfields, is always in need of a soul-lifting sermon, I want you to preach the second Sunday in April.

My wife joins me in a cordial invitation to you to be our guest during your stay in the city. . . .

John moved down the road that April day, raising a screen of dust. There was a chill in the air, and he was grateful for the warmth his long cloak gave him. His saddle cases bulged with his best suit, shirt, socks, and precious manuscript. Bitsy had sewed a leather folder to go around it to keep it safe if the rain came. He had only one copy.

"Watch out for highwaymen," she had called, as he turned his horse toward the highroad.

"They had better watch out for me," he replied. "Nobody is going to keep me from traveling like the wind to London."

Now, as he rounded a deep bend in the road, a tall man with wide shoulders stood there, aiming a musket at John's heart. John drew to such a sudden halt that his horse reared, and he almost fell off. He sat there stunned, helpless. He had only the shilling his father had left him, nothing more. But the fear crept through him that the highwayman might take his manuscript, mistaking it for something valuable. The man had oily black hair that hung in long spikes to his shoulders, a nose with wide nostrils set in a grimy face, and the lips were heavy, red.

Slowly John held up his hands. "See. I am unarmed. Here." He reached for the shilling. "This is all I have. It is my inheritance from my father."

The highwayman scowled swiftly. "Ye expect me t' eat that? That be not enough even to post a letter. Takes three of those!"

"But it is all I have."

The bright eyes went over John's horse. They narrowed. "That be a mighty fine animal for a man who only owns one shilling."

"I am a preacher. My people gave him to me to get about the shire."

The highwayman reached out a dirty hand with long, greasy fingernails, and slapped the palm John held out, knocking the shilling to the dust. He spat after it. Then his eyes turned to the saddle cases. He lifted them from their hook, and in that instant John felt as if his blood were spilling out.

"Open them," he begged. "There's nothing there but my clothes and some papers that are of no value to you."

The highwayman burst into hearty laughter, apparently enjoying his victim's distress. "I could use them clothes." He looked down at his own dirty rags. "As for the papers, I'll have th' pleasure o' throwing them in the creek and watching them sink. That is, unless ye can find more shillings."

John vaulted off the horse, and grabbed at the saddlebags. "Take my clothes, but give me my papers." But his opponent held them above his head with one hand and clung to the musket with the other.

The thief, using all his strength, struck John a furious blow with the saddlebags across the face. John got his hands on them, and tugged with all his might. The highwayman reached into his belt, and John saw murder on his face. As they struggled, John could smell the fellow's putrid breath, especially when he swore between his teeth, his face livid with rage. And suddenly a dark narrow stream of blood began to run from his body. He crumpled up, grabbing his belly, and moaning.

John watched him writhe hysterically, give a long shudder, and then lie still. When John turned him over, he saw that in their struggle the highwayman's dagger, which he had been reaching for, had been unsheathed, and had pierced him.

John arrived at Dr. Owen's house in London covered with blood and dust. He had a purple bruise across one eye, and his jaw was swollen. But his manuscript was safe in its case. No wonder the sermon he preached on Sunday about God's care for his servants came from his heart!

On Monday, Dr. Owen took him to the Peacock in the Poultry, which was near Cornhill. He introduced him to Nathaniel Ponder, the stationer, a thin man with quick movements and penetrating brown eyes.

"I will read your book tonight," Mr. Ponder promised. "I'm impatient to know of its possibilities. Come back at ten tomorrow morning."

At ten on Tuesday, when John preceded Dr. Owen into the musty office, the stationer jumped up from his chair and came around to greet him.

"Yes. Yes. Yes, indeed," he prattled pleasantly. "I think we have a book!"

"Then you like it?"

"I tremble at the possibility of what it might do in the way of sales."

"I tried it out on some of my friends. A few of them thought it should not be published."

"If you're talking about John Whitebread, he thinks it's sinful to be happy. Don't worry about friends like that."

"You don't think people will be shocked?"

"It's a departure. That's certain. But let's try it. We can sell it for about one shilling, sixpence."

After the business arrangements had been made, Mr. Ponder relaxed and he and John talked about prison experiences. The stationer had been jailed on a warrant issued in May, 1676, for printing a pamphlet "tending to the sedition and defamation of the Christian religion." But he had been held only sixteen days.

"How did you get out so soon?"

He rolled his brown eyes up piously. "Why I made a humble petition, promising never to offend again. Then I paid the court costs and put up a bond of five hundred pounds!"

"You must make a lot of money out of the books you publish." John was incredulous. "My aim is to spread God's Truth."

Nobody was more astounded than John over the immediate success of *The Pilgrim's Progress*. He had hoped it would sell better than his other books, but had not really expected it to go with such rapidity or in such volume. Licensed February 18, 1678, it was first a small octavo edition, two hundred and thirty-two pages long in addition to his "Apology," the title, and a conclusion, which he added in verse. A few months later there was another edition, which added Mr. Worldly Wiseman, and made the author's spelling more uniform and correct. He had had "pliable" and "plyable," "raiment" and "rayment," "ai" for "aye," "bin" for "been," "thorou" for "thorough."

"Don't feel badly that there are necessary changes," Nathaniel Ponder had written in his pleasant way. "The creative work is what counts. Just leave the mechanics to us. We will concentrate on the tangible and you concentrate on the intangible."

But even before he knew there would be a third edition during the following year of 1679, John began to study word usage and spelling. If I am going to continue to write, he decided, I want to be a good writer. He knew his limitations, but he was certain, too, that God could perform a literary miracle.

He smiled all the time he was inserting some additions about Mr. By-ends to the third edition. There were minor changes, too, such as a description of Christian expressing himself to his family, of another meeting with Evangelist, of leaving the path with Pliable, and an accounting of Christian to Good-will.

Nathaniel Ponder had John White, who had made portraits of almost everybody of importance, do one of Bunyan for a frontispiece. It showed him as a pilgrim, sleeping and dreaming, above a lion in a den. Above this a drawing showed him with burden on his back, his Bible in one hand and a staff in the other, climbing toward a sunlit city on the heights.

After that, edition followed edition. Eight years after Part I of the story had been published Part II followed. Imitators and frauds sprang up everywhere. Within ten years there had been eleven editions of the allegory, and over one hundred thousand books had sold.

John's literary success increased his fame. He often went to London to preach in the meeting houses, and everywhere he spoke huge crowds awaited him. When he was offered the pastorate of one of London's large churches, he declined, declaring he wished to live the rest of his life with his "Bedford folks."

It was August 19, 1688. John was ill in bed at the tall house of his old friend, Strud, near the Church of St. Sepulchre. Strud, now a successful grocer, begged him not to try to go to John Gammon's meeting house in Petticoat Lane. But he had promised to preach, so he dragged himself out of bed, ate a piece of bread and drank some of the China drink, dressed in his plain suit, threw his pulpit gown over his arm, and set out. He wanted to walk, because the meeting place where the service would be held was less than a mile away, and he felt too weak to get into the saddle. Strud accompanied him.

As he moved through the early morning sunshine, his feet felt heavy, his head spun, and his chest began to hurt. But he didn't tell Strud; he feared Strud would make him go back.

On a journey from Reading a few days before he had been caught in a thunder shower and drenched. He had ridden on to London, swooning soon after his arrival, to the great distress of Strud and his pretty young wife.

When he reached the meeting house, he saw that it was filled to the doors, and people were standing on the steps and outside. They made an aisle for him, he put on his gown and walked slowly toward the three steps that led up into the wooden pulpit. The steps were a little difficult, but once John stood looking out at the congregation, he forgot himself, his weakness, his pains.

" 'Which were born, not of blood, nor of the will of the flesh, nor of the will of man, but of God,' " he recited.

Strength flowed through him again, and the time passed quickly, until he concluded: ". . . Consider that God is your Father, and let this oblige you to live like His children, that you may look your Father in the face with comfort another day."

Two days later Strud had to summon a physician, Dr. Brace-girdle, for John was having one chill after another.

"Tell me honestly if I will recover," John told the bearded doctor.

"With proper rest and care, you may. However, you have been overworking. You are in a run-down condition. You must get some sleep."

John took the potion the doctor gave him and closed his eyes, but he couldn't sleep. He felt very cold, and weakness spread through him. He would be sixty years old in November, but he had not considered himself old. The last ten years had been full of plots and counterplots. Now all England was in ferment. Charles I had died in 1685, two years after the death of John's beloved friend, Dr. Owen. James II, the former Duke of York, had shown himself a cruel and devious man. Religious as well as political freedom were again in grave danger. The laws against the Scots had been made too severe. Jeffreys, an infamous judge, condemned many innocent persons, and execution followed execution. When the Duke of Monmouth, the natural son of King Charles, had tried to overthrow his uncle, he had died on the block. In the rebellious counties a Circuit Court had been held, presided over by Chief Justice Jeffreys, who was even more cruel and corrupt than John's Lord Hategood of Vanity Fair. It was evident that King James was scheming to restore Catholicism, although the Pope and his Catholic friends had begged for moderation. "But you will work your will, God," John murmured. "Don't let England be a slave to this monster who is worse than his father, and grandfather!"

"What is troubling you, John?"

John recognized the voice of his friend, George Cockayn. Within the cold shadows of the large chamber he could see others: Strud, Charles Doe, a combmaker from Southwark with whom he had been corresponding.

"You had better send for his wife," he heard Dr. Bracegirdle say. "Tell her there is no time to lose."

After that John's lucidity seemed to come and go. His friends talked in whispers, but he couldn't hear what they said. . . . He was young again at Elstow, romping with Margaret through the green meadows, and fishing for loach in Cardingdon Brook. He could see his sister, her hands full of jelly tarts, sitting at his side giggling or squealing with glee when a fish took his bait. . . . And he was standing on the flag-stoned floor in his father's cottage near Harrowden and there was a burnt-butter odor from the kitchen. Mama was there, and Papa, too. Willie was cramming some cheese into his mouth. Grandpa came in, and took his place at the oblong board, and John was warmed by the glance of the kind old eyes. He was glad, because he was so cold.

There was no such thing as time; time fused with eternity. None of his loved ones was dead. There was no such thing as death; it was an illusion.

But pain was real. His temples throbbed; the pain in his chest came and went. He didn't know when it stopped . . . and the drowsiness began . . . and he dropped into blackness.

"He's sick unto death," Dr. Bracegirdle said. "I don't think he'll know you."

The chamber spun and John spun with it. He heard Bitsy's dear voice in the vast empty vault. He saw her bent head at his bedside; she was weeping. He longed to reach out and stroke her raven-black hair, but his arms were like lead, and he couldn't lift them. He had no voice, and he couldn't tell her that this was not death but life for the pilgrim.

John lay content against the big white pillows, all anxiety ended. The strength he had stored up rose above the weakness of his flesh. Ahead he could see the ramparts of the Holy City and the white flag of the Prince Emanuel fluttering in the breeze. The sweet bells were ringing as he began to move out into boundless space above the river that has no bridge. A mist was gathering all about him like the beautiful mist in the meadow at Harrowden. But it wasn't dark, for the golden doves led the way and "yonder shining light" was beckoning. . . . He gathered his pilgrim's cloak around him and strode home.

288